PAUL METCALF

COLLECTED WORKS, VOLUME TWO, 1976-1986

PAUL METCALF

COLLECTED WORKS, VOLUME TWO, 1976-1986

COFFEE HOUSE PRESS :: MINNEAPOLIS

Dustwrapper photograph by Marilyn Patti. Dustjacket design by Jinger Peissig. Book design by Allan Kornblum. Text scanning and preparation by Becky Weinberg and Kelly Kofron.

I-57 was first published by Longriver Press. *Zip Odes* and *The Island* were first published by Tansy Press. *U.S. Dept. of the Interior* was first published by Gnomen Press. *Willie's Throw* was first published by Five Trees Press, and later reprinted by Mad River Press. *Both* was first published by The Jargon Society. *Waters of Potowmack* was first published by North Point Press. Coffee House salutes the editors of these small independent presses for having presented these visionary works.

This project was made possible by major funding from the Lannan Foundation. Coffee House Press receives general operating support from the Minnesota State Arts Board, through an appropriation by the Minnesota State Legislature and the National Endowment for the Arts, a federal agency; The McKnight Foundation; Target Stores, Dayton's, and Mervyn's by the Dayton Hudson Foundation; General Mills Foundation; St. Paul Companies; the Butler Family Foundation; Honeywell Foundation; Star Tribune/Cowles Media Company; the James R. Thorpe Foundation; Pentair, Inc.; and the Beverly J. and John A. Rollwagen Fund of The Minneapolis Foundation.

Coffee House Press books are available to the trade through our primary distributor, Consortium Book Sales & Distribution, 1045 Westgate Drive, Saint Paul, MN 55114. For personal orders, catalogs, or other information, write to us at: 27 North Fourth Street, Suite 400, Minneapolis, MN 55401.

Library of Congress CIP Data
Metcalf, Paul C.
  [Works. 1997]
  Collected Works, 1976-1986 / Paul Metcalf.
  V. <II> CM.
  Contents: V. II. I-57
  ISBN 1-56689-050-0 (HC: V. I)
  i. Title.
PS3563.E83   1997   97-277
818'.5409—DC20   CIP

10   9   8   7   6   5   4   3   2   1

CONTENTS

I-57
1

Zip Odes
125

U.S. Dept. of the Interior
183

Willie's Throw
245

Both
255

The Island
329

Waters of Potowmack
361

for Anne

I-57

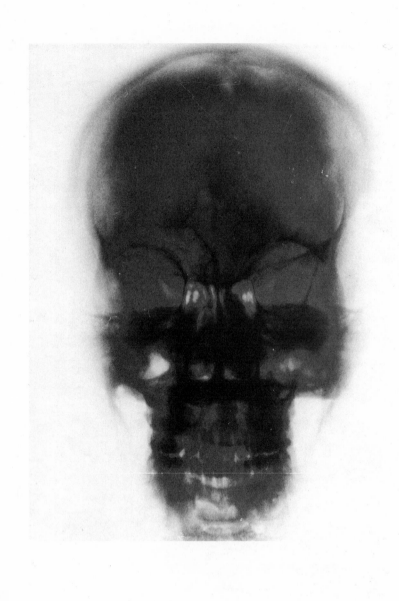

I-57

TEXT AND PHOTOGRAPHS BY PAUL METCALF
PHOTO-IMAGES BY LENI FUHRMAN

Not a poem, not a novel, not a history, not a journal, yet at times some or all of these—*I-57* is an idiosyncratic approach to a place, a region, and to an interior and exterior life . . .

The choice of title is random, dictated by virtue of the book being written during the author's 57th year . . . hence, the title dictates the material: Interstate 57, the state of Illinois, Sikeston, Missouri (just across the river), to Chicago.

The book is a journey, on several levels:
>   From madness to sanity;
>   From inside the skull (a physiological habitation) to outside . . . subjective to objective, interior to exterior . . . from me to you;
>   From then to now, the journeys of history . . . mythological history, locked in the stone, the shapes of the land . . . written history, the history of document;
>   The artifacts of history, objective and evident today . . . and the release of these histories, lodged in the heads of Americans who inhabit and travel the land;
>   finally, the highway itself, I-57, Sikeston to Chicago: the journey and the journal.

There are graphics: photo-images created especially for this text by Leni Fuhrman—subtle abstractions, x-rays of bones, with hints of ferns and rivers—the skull overlying the land, the land within the skull—subjective, interior . . . and, finally, with the journal, Sikeston to Chicago, photographs taken by the author: the land, the place, the people (102-year-old lady, fantastic rock formations, graffiti on the walls, statue of William Jennings Bryan), as they roll up before the advancing driver, presenting themselves.

A poem, a journal, a document—a journal, a record, a release. "One pursues a route, passing from state to state. Taxes are paid, for road use. There is the burden, although it may only in part be chosen. There are signs, to be observed, and choices made. And there are the particulars, the journey itself."

I, 57 . . .

ONE

a.

> the ceiling seemed to be raised,
> the room resonant
> with music!

the floor softens and swirls,
    tipping, sending everything down,
I am fighting my way through deep varnish,
                walking with my feet
turned in, I cannot see to correct my step, I go into tables, knock
against walls,

> walking is just
> losing your balance
> and regaining it

———————

The voices are heard in my head, though often in the air, or in
different parts of the room, each different, speaking or singing in
different tone and measure

There appear to be many, I should say upwards of fourteen, some on
the left temple and forehead, others on the right temple and fore-
head,
    but on each side of the head, as it were over the middle of the
eyebrow, two seem always to sing or speak to a measure more quick,
my thoughts flowing regularly from left to right, guided by these
voices

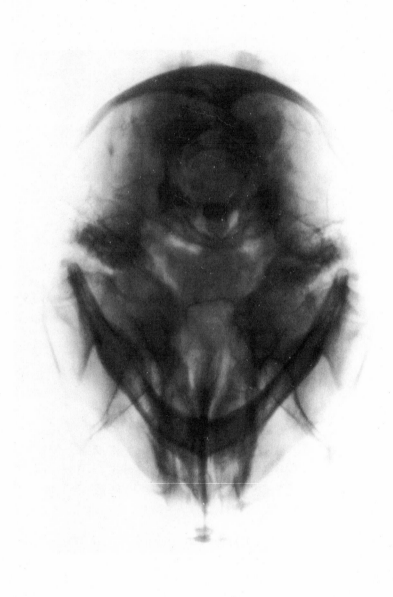

Threads are pulled into my head, carriers of the voices, hearkening
wires and whiz pipes, performing a circular movement, my head as
though hollowed from within

My breathing is clothed with words, I am directed to control my
breath, to breathe gently up one nostril and down another

                                                    I hear
voices in my feet,
                swarming about me like bees,
                                        a roaring train, a
locomotive god,
            pounding,
                    my fingers, my legs, my head, all parts of
me, hearing

                        (the plumbing in the house gone
                        berserk,
                        pipes human,
                        screaming
                        to be let out of the walls)

                        _____

                        there is a timbre to the smell of
                        sweat, blaring music
                        pours into my eyes

                        _____

Something shadows me, I crawl and curl up like a singed bug
                                                    (read
faster! faster! to escape the thing . . .
                        It's here. . . *now!*
                                            a stranger,
sitting in my body
                    a soul, a watery mass covering my eyeballs,
                                                    bulky
ball or bundle, a wadding or cobweb thrown into my belly, escaping
through my mouth,

a soul, sneaking in my ears when I was a foetus,

a

Little Me, in my fingers, or among the convolutions of my brain.

I cross the room, leave myself on one side, re-enter myself on the
other,

like a woman, succumbing
to intercourse

b.

my brain is rubbed raw with sandpaper   a bleeding sponge
my mind is breaking up, crumbling like stale cake   my brains
are chewed chewing gum   they boil and seethe   blood
pours to my brain, my skull too small to contain it, the tissue is
forced through my eyelids, by beating my head on the floor I loosen
the sutures so the brain may expand   I talk with my brains, the
hemispheres go bing

my head cracks, split down the middle   I feel the roots of my
hair drawing together   my nostrils compress above, dilate
below   a sense of revolt crosses my front teeth (my teeth are
in danger)   hot blood pours into my ears, a mad cat gnaws at
my head   my head is clamped, compressed, become pear-shaped
        cords pass through my head, horns ram into my skull
    there are scorpions, aryan and catholic, in my head   crepi-
tations, like sparks, in my right temple   wings beating
        nerves in my neck fill with gas, like a bladder, distending,
dislodging the brain

the skin draws down over my eyes   but there is an electric
motor, pushing behind the eyeballs, and the eyes become fiery,
phosphoric   a   change   in   the   optic   nerve,   a

rotting   and my eyes are drilled out!   they are taken out
of my head, and I see them hanging over me, watching, pursuing
me

a magnetic warp, chilled in its expansion, is diffused from the root
of the nose, under the base of the brain, a veil interposed, so that
the sentiments of the heart may in no way communicate with the
intellect   the fibres at the root of the tongue constrict and
lock   I eat my own pharynx, and hear the swallowing, like
the compression of a new wicker basket   the blood of all my
friends gushes into my throat

my lungs are eaten by lung worms, my diaphragm pushed up to my
throat, my breath comes up fiery

my heart is pulled down in my body, it is a different heart, no longer
my own   my blood is tears that I cannot weep

all the fluids, gases, vapors in my body are ignited and explode!

I have no stomach, someone has stolen it, food pours down my
throat and into my thighs   the whole alimentary system is a
rotten mess, I am full of poisonous shit, I push the shit backward
and forward in my bowel, I can piss and shit only while seated on a
bucket in front of a piano   magnetic fluids, rarified and sub-
limed, are extracted, bubble by bubble, from my anus   if my
stomach were opened, I would stare out at the surgeon

a warm, soft, floppy liver is thrown at my back, and passes into
me   I am waiting for a pig's hide to drop out of my body
the newborn infant will be put back inside me

there have been various changes in my sex organs, small pictures of
my friends may be seen in my loins

a kipper is wedged in my spine, and the spine is bowed, drawn tight,
like a violin string about to snap   my joints are dry, burning,

cracking   the headache descends my spine, vertebra by verte-
bra, as though walking downstairs, and mice run up and down the
column   the spinal cord is finally pumped out and escapes
through my mouth in little clouds

my left foot is about to vomit, my ear is in my thigh, miracles attack
my kneecap, make my feet cold

a pressure of the external atmosphere, a lobster-cracking, attacks
me, stagnates my circulation, impedes my vital motions   I
smell like glue and soot   my nerves enclose me in a stiff, half
burning sort of case or box   the coffin is short and shallow,
my head compressed, my nose flattened

c.

> With lids closed, I stare at the sun,
> and golden yellow bars flash before my
> eyes. Opening, I stare at the sun with-
> out blinking, and it is dazzling, dazz-
> ling! I can gaze right into the sun,
> unperturbed! The filaments aiming at
> my head approach in a circle or para-
> bola. The sun follows my movements,
> fighting its way through the trees,
> seeking the fire within me! I can
> frighten the sun, cause it to pale, by
> speaking in a loud voice, bellowing,
> and threatening it; the sun speaks back
> to me with human words.
>
> All my friends and kindred reside in
> the center of the sun; I am drawn to
> them, drawn to the sun, sucked into it.

I succeed in climbing into the sun—but
things go out of balance, thousands are
destroyed.

The solar system may soon be disconnected.

———————————

Gazing at the sun, absorbing power in the solar plexus, I generate radar, which is a delight to me: I can summon or extinguish it at will, and, moving it into my eyes, I need only stare angrily at an enemy, and he pales, frightens, and departs.

My brain is a magnet, the whole earth pervaded with magnetism from my head.

I receive radio broadcasts with my teeth, the electric refrigerator turning on is a signal to me. The iron in my blood is magnetized, the vibration of vocal cords generates wireless waves. The electric lights glow more deeply, more intensely, more ruddy. Magnetic voices roar along water mains, project along water pipes, emerge from faucets. My breath is fiery, filled with electrical matter; light and sound are projected into my nerves, eyes and ears are not needed.

I am the living, intelligent principle of electricity! I can call into my person all the electrical fluid in the world! All u.s. telegraph wires conduct electric fluid into my body!

Moonshine blessedness flutters toward me.

Every word spoken causes a tearing in my head: the rays attempting to withdraw.

———————————

I control the weather.

Kicking sparks off the stones, I generate thunder and lightning.

As soon as I think nothing, the wind rises.

_____

the stranger turns quickly to his left,
                              rises in his stride with a wave-
like motion,
            and with a second wave-like motion,
                                          rises higher,
                                                    and
disappears entirely,
                  above the tree tops

I am lighter and lighter,
                  I must hold onto you to keep from going up,

only my clothes, bearing heavily on my shoulders, hold me down

watery-looking bodies,
                  transparent and vaporous, float down from
the sky,
            intermingle.

my house is a balloon

_____

my eyes will not move, I must turn my head,
                              but the tail of my eye is
on something else.
                  with each breath I must conquer my lungs anew,
my muscles breathe, I am forced to bellow, to suppress them,
                                                    as I
exhale carefully, my body becomes a beam of light,
                                          a blinding
pinpoint.
            each of us is a corpuscle in the bloodstream, forever
circulating,
            my nose is my penis, my mouth my anus, my ear-lobes

my nipples,
   I am frightened,
      not knowing what goes on,
         inside me.

————————

breathing in,
without opening my mouth,
I extract from the blue and white outline
and the central point

but I must exhale completely,
holding it in space above my head
until all of it hangs there suspended,
a ball of glowing blue light.

re-introduce the blue into my body,
extracting a thread of blue from the ball,
and working it into myself through the top of my head,

force it through myself down to my feet,
bring it back up to the level of my arms
and extend it out,
in the form of a cross,
to the tips of my fingers.

with no breath left,
but without breathing further,
introduce the thread of blue,
like an illuminated electric wire,
into my brain.

a sharp pain,
but continue to force it into me,
the pain spreading along the line,
a giant cold needle forced through my flesh.

the outline above me a square of black
outlined in white light, a white light
in the center, and a cross of blue,
dividing the square in four.

repeat, now, with yellow . . .

I see the rays approaching, the poison of corpses to be unloaded on
my body,
       the rotten cadavers of friends entombed in milk bottles,

departed souls descend on me, little men, living on top of my head,

the folds of the bedclothes are serpents and reptiles,
                       my sister and I
were made by machine, we call ourselves sisters to avoid explana-
tions,
    pissing in a rainstorm, I am not sure but what it is my own
urine bedewing the world,
                   I run and crumble in the ground, run up
the walls of my room,
              everything from which I withdraw my atten-
tion ceases to exist,
       I become commotional

Quiet! Quiet! Can't we have some quiet around here?

I eat the head of the cat, or of the fox, gnawing at my vitals

I am big with young pigs

fast flying, low flying birds, singing birds, swallows and sparrows, all
speak to me

cattle lowing in the pasture convey articulate sentences

my mouth is full of birds which I crunch between my teeth, their feathers, their blood, their broken bones, choking me

———————

ah! the sweet relaxation of madness!

to laugh and cry, chatter and shriek,

whistle, sing, flute, fife, fiddle, run,

dance and wrestle

I cannot remain in bed for bellowing,
                              hurl myself to the floor,

                                                    down
the steep slopes

a wooden peg in my mouth they are crouched behind a sheet held up like a shield force-feeding me with each mouthful I spit howl and curse in one breath spit-howl-curse o god o god o god o god my face a rash of rage my neck stiff with blood ropes spithowlcurse o god o god o god o god a gulp of milk splashed my nose pinched but I will not swallow strangling speech curdling the milk o god o god o god gurgling flying in a mist of milk o god o god soaked with milk dribbling spittle o god

———————

              my pelvic bones a canyon rim
              around my abdomen
              the flesh a mass of shriveled
              welts and ridges, red and raw

              I am clawbelly,
                         raw naked!
              dancing!

              singing!

d.

split in two, I walk in two directions
                              leg, thigh, stomach, and chest,
pulled and tugged, tearing
                    body divided in four, legs cut off, head
and breast severed
                teeth, nose, cheeks, eyes, all separate
                                                    I am
knocked in so many pieces!

---

            the great male and female organs
            hung in midair,
            far away, and infinitely near,
            pulsing in a circular motion,
            to a human pulse, a
            heartbeat

there is no longer reticence, I don't care, I can go as far as I like, I
have so much sex to throw away!

(a man lies on his side, a woman on her back)

            my left side is male,
            my right female,
            power transfers
            from left to right
            hands and arms encircle,
            legs and thighs entwine

if only I could always be the woman, self-embracing!

for the renewal of mankind, I *must* transform into woman!

(when a girl
doesn't want to walk,
it's because
she doesn't want to realize
that there is
nothing
swinging between her legs)

I lie naked, uncovered, voluptuous,

my soul given away, my body

handed over,
I allow myself to be fucked

I am man and woman, selffucking!

(electrical fluid is drawn from me in fellatio, as a turgid organ draws
blood from the brain)

you theenk your roosevelt a man?
ha!
you know staleen?
I seen it,
sixteen eenches cock,
beeger than roosevelt!

e.

I have never stopped writing this, and it has not yet begun

what the hell are you doing? what am I doing, you ask? I am
shakespeare, that's what I'm doing! shakespeare reincarnate! go to it,
shakespeare!

won't you sit here, please, and help me hang onto this pencil?

write, damnit—write something—write anything—write faster, faster!

I write in columns on the wall, three feet wide, on huge sheets of wrapping paper, pasted together, running down the corridor, twelve feet an hour!

I am myself plus

TWO

obtained by necropsy
fresh-dead tissues from the brain
were stained

samples from the septal and ventral
portions of the head
of the caudate nucleus;

and the neural cell nuclei
in the tissues
of the fresh-dead psychotics

fluoresced!

_____

the pineal gland contained a large quantity of gritty matter
                                                    the bones
of the cranium were unusually thin
                                the membranes of the brain and
its convolutions were of a brownish straw color
                                                    the medullary
substance was full of bloody points
                                the consistence of the brain I
cannot describe better than by saying it was doughy
                                                    blood could be
pressed from it as from a sponge
                                the lateral ventricles contained two
ounces of pellucid water
                                on opening the right lateral ventricle
which was much distended, it was found filled with dark and gru-
mous blood
                    the convolutions were so strongly and distinctly marked
that they resembled the intestines of a child

- swollen nuclei and shrunken neurons -
- proliferative fibrous bliosis -
- pigmentary changes -
- sclerosis of the ganglion cells -

- lipid degeneration -

The case that is being made, therefore, is for two basically distinct types of brain pathology in schizophrenia: In the chronic, nuclear cases . . . diffuse frontal lobe damage including destruction of tissue in ventral and orbital frontal areas and associated subcortical structures such as medalis dorsalis of the thalamus and the head of the caudate nucleus . . . In the episodic, paranoidal group, on the other hand, the damage may preferentially be found in the septal, hippocampal, and temporal lobe areas, although frontal damage may occur as well

———————

the cell membrane may be more permeable, permitting the passage, the transport of substances—amino acids, serum globulin— through the neural tissue

antigens,
antibrain
antibodies

in the serum
of the schiz,

promoting malfunction of neuronal systems,

in the hypothalamus
and limbic area,

in the rostral forebrain,

sites of
abundant
abnormal

physiologic
activity

───────────────

spikes and slow-waves from the septal region,

sharp spiking in the anterior septal leads,
less often from the centromedian nucleus of the thalamus,
postero ventro lateral nucleus of the thalamus,
cerebellar nuclei, and hippocampi,
occasionally over the frontal cortex

a greater amount of slow delta, and very fast activity!

dysrhythmia, dysphoria

occipito-frontal asynchrony

less slow wave spindle sleep

> a burst of spikes,
> a burst of slow waves,
> fast spike and wave bursts
>
> bilateral and
> temporal lobe spikes
>
> paroxysmal patterns!

the true frontal spike-and-slow wave complex

THREE

a.

"The upper surface of the base of the skull or floor of the cranial cavity presents three fossae, called the anterior, middle, and posterior cranial fossae."

> *"The middle Mississippi Valley had been rocked by an earthquake but a short time before. John Audubon . . . related that 'the ground rose and fell in successive furrows, like the ruffled waters of a lake.' Great vents opened in the earth, columns of subterranean muck spouted in the air, and the Mississippi, dammed by a downstream upheaval, is reported to have reversed its course for several hours."*

> *"That part of the alluvial country which is contiguous to the point of junction of the two rivers . . . seems to have been the center of the convulsion. There, during the years 1811 and 1812, the earth broke into innumerable fissures, the churchyard, with its dead, was torn from the bank, and engulphed in the turbid stream . . . Along the banks of the river, thousands of acres with their gigantic growth of forest and cane were swallowed up, and lakes and ponds innumerable were formed. The earth, in many parts was observed to burst, suddenly open, and jets of sand, mud, and water, to shoot up into the air. The beds of these giant streams seemed totally overturned; islands disappeared, and in many parts the course of the river was completely changed. Great inundations were the consequence. In many places the gaping earth unfolded its secrets, and the bones of the gigantic Mastodon and Ichthyosaurus, hidden within its bosom for ages, were brought to the surface. Boats and arks without number were swallowed up; some buried by the falling in of the banks, others dragged down with the islands to which they were anchored. And finally, you may still meet and*

converse with those, who were in the mighty river of the West when the whole stream ran towards its sources for an entire hour, and then resuming its ordinary course, hurried them helpless on its whirling surface with accelerated motion towards the Gulf."

The Anterior Fossa:

"At the junction of the two rivers, on ground so flat and low and marshy, that at certain seasons of the year it is inundated to the housetops, lies a breeding-place of fever, ague, and death; vaunted in England as a mine of Golden Hope, and speculated in, on the faith of monstrous representations, to many people's ruin. A dismal swamp, on which the half-built houses rot away: cleared here and there for the space of a few yards; and teeming, then, with rank, unwholesome vegetation, in whose baleful shade the wretched wanderers who are tempted hither droop, and die, and lay their bones; the hateful Mississippi circling and eddying before it, and turning off upon its southern course, a slimy monster hideous to behold; a hotbed of disease, an ugly sepulchre, a grave uncheered by any gleam of promise: a place without one single quality, in earth or air or water, to commend it: such is this dismal Cairo."

". . . a quagmire inhabited by a web-foot people . . ."

"A flat morass, bestrewn with fallen timber; a marsh on which the good growth of the earth seemed to have been wrecked and cast away, that from its decomposing ashes vile and ugly things might rise; where the very trees took the aspect of huge weeds, begotten of the slime from which they sprung, by the hot sun that burnt them up; where fatal maladies, seeking whom they might infect, came forth at night, in misty shapes, and creeping out upon the water, hunted them like specters until day; where even the blessed sun, shining down on festering elements of corruption and disease, became a horror . . ."

"A fetid vapour, hot and sickening as the breath of an oven, rose up from the earth, and hung on everything around."

"The trees had grown so thick and close that they shouldered one another out of their places, and the weakest, forced into shapes of strange distortion, languished like cripples. The best were stunted, from the pressure and the want of room; and high above the stems of all, grew long rank grass, dank weeds, and frowzy underwood: not divisible into their separate kinds, but tangled all together in a heap; a jungle deep and dark, with neither earth nor water at its roots, but putrid matter, formed of the pulpy offal of the two . . .

". . . the stagnant morning mist, and red sun, dimly seen beyond; the vapour rising from land and river; the quick stream making the loathsome banks it washed, more flat and dull . . ."

"But what words shall describe the Mississippi, great father of rivers, who (praise be to Heaven!) has no young children like him? An enormous ditch . . .

. . . fossa, foramen . . .

. . . sometimes two or three miles wide, running liquid mud, six miles an hour: its strong and frothy current choked and obstructed everywhere by huge logs and whole forest trees: now twining themselves together in great rafts, from the interstices of which a sedgy, lazy foam works up, to float upon the water's top: now rolling past like monstrous bodies, their tangled roots showing like matted hair: now glancing singly by like giant leeches; and now writhing round and round in the vortex of some small whirlpool like wounded snakes. The banks low, the trees dwarfish, the marshes swarming with frogs, the wretched cabins few and far apart, the inmates hollow-checked and pale, the weather very hot, mosquitos penetrating into every crack and crevice of the boat, mud and slime on everything: nothing

pleasant in its aspect but the harmless lightning which flickers every night upon the dark horizon."

"The floor of the anterior fossa is formed by the orbital plates of the frontal, the cribriform plate of the ethmoid, and the small wings and front part of the body of the sphenoid . . ."

> *. . . small wings of the sphenoid: Illinois an inverted arrowhead, the Cairo penisula projecting wedge-like into the deep South.*

> *"June 30. We departed about 5 o'clock in the morning. The weather was fair and very hot. About breakfast time we saw a buffalo crossing. We overtook it in the middle of the river and hitched our boat to it for more than a quarter of a league, after which we killed it. We took only the tongue."*

> *"The gentle Ohio is pushed back by the impetuous Stream of the Mississippi, whose muddy white water is to be seen about 200 Yards up the former. We examined the ground for several Miles within the Fork, it is an Aggregation of Mud and Dirt, interspersed with Marsh, and some Ponds of Water . . ."*

. . . cribriform, ethmoid, sieve-like . . .

> *"The high water mark of the tide of humanity that swept out to the Illinois prairies was reached on the eve of the Civil War . . . from the slaveholding states there now poured a fresh stream of immigrants for whom the atmosphere of human slavery became as suffocatingly intolerable as any economic and political oppression in the old world.*
> *. . . Many belonged to the uneducated, non-slaveholding poor white class . . .*
> *Cairo was the Ellis Island for this immigration. Steamer after steamer arrived with cargoes of human freight and the nearby towns of Anna and Jonesboro received refugees until the people protested their inability to provide for more.*

> *Accommodations at Cairo were extremely inadequate . . .*
> *Families were sometimes left a good part of the night on the*
> *cold and muddy levee without shelter or even blankets . . . The*
> *Illinois Central placed them in hog cars which had not been*
> *cleaned since used."*

". . . it is limited behind by the posterior borders of the small wings of the sphenoid . . ."

> *. . . gingko and magnolia, in southern Cairo . . .*

". . . and by the anterior margin of the chiasmatic groove"—the intersection, the point of convergence, of the optic nerves.

> *Horseshoe Lake, a riverbend cut off from the river, at the junc-*
> *tion, the point of convergence, of branches on the Mississippi*
> *flyway:*
>
> *Canada geese, all manner of duck, the American egret, the*
> *great blue Heron . . .*

. . . frontoethmoidal, sphenoethmoidal, and sphenofrontal . . .

> *Va Bache*
> *Va Bache   Va Bache   Va Bache*
> *Near Grand Chain, a fort (1702), French and Indians, under*
> *M. Charles Juchereau de St. Denys . . . at Va Bache,*
> *Juchereau*
> *Va Bache   Va Bache   Va Bache*
> *a fort, a tannery, buffalo skins shipped downstream for*
> *tanning . . . a fort, a tannery, at*
> *Va Bache   Va Bache   Va Bache*

"Its lateral portions . . . are convex and marked by depressions for the brain convolutions . . ."

> *Ullin, Uilebhinn, Fingal's bard, all-melodious*

"... and grooves for branches of the meningeal vessels."

1839, ferried into Illinois at Golconda, thirteen thousand Cherokee: wagons, carriages, horsemen, tramping Indians ... the settlers prevented the pitching of tents, the cutting of fire-wood ...

Came to a halt, thirteen thousand, on the ridge above the flood plain, unable to cross, the Mississippi choked with ice floes ...

Halted, starved, froze, two weeks, for the river to flow smoothly ...

Ice floes, the tears, the river ...

... later, at Wetaug, the spring went dry.

"The Central portion ... is markedly depressed on either side of the crista galli."

A huge tract, a virgin tract, cypress growing in swamp, the lumbermen entered in boats ...

... cribriform, ethmoid, sieve-like ...

"A weary wayfarer was floundering through the mire ... sometimes wading to the saddle girth in water; sometimes clambering over logs; and occasionally plunged in quagmire. While carefully picking his way by a spot more miry than the rest he espied a man's hat, lying with the crown upwards in the mud, and as he approached was not a little startled to see it move. This happened in a dismal swamp where the cypress waved its melancholy branches over the dark soil, and our traveler's flesh began to creep . . . the solitary rider checked his nag and, extending his long whip, fairly upset the hat—when, lo! beneath it appeared a man's head, a living, laughing head ... [the traveler] promptly apologized for the indecorum of which

he had been guilty, and tendered his services to the gentleman in the mud puddle. 'I will alight,' said he, 'and endeavor to draw you forth.' 'Oh, never mind,' said the other, 'I'm in rather a bad fix it is true, but I have an excellent horse under me who has carried me through many a worse place than this—we shall get along."

". . . the commencement of the frontal crest . . ."

"JONESBORO, ILL., September 15, 1858
The third field-day between Lincoln and Douglas has just closed at this town. It is an ancient village in the heart of Egypt, among hills and ravines, and invested with forest as the soil itself. It is thirty miles from Cairo and three hundred miles from Chicago. Illinois is no longer the 'Prairie state.' We have come to it through rocky depths and cliff cuttings; through forests primeval; through sharp and broken bluffs . . .
". . . the time-honored darkness of Egypt . . ."

Rock shelters at Ferne Clyffe, and east of Cobden . . .

1778, George Rogers Clark, Massac to Kaskaskia, marching under the rattlesnake flag of Virginia . . .

. . . chiasmatic . . .

Giant City, acres of hills, forests, fantastic rocks, site of secret meetings, with signs and passwords, of the Knights of the Golden Circle; Confederate spys, draft resisters, perpetrators of treason in the Union ranks . . .

. . . talk of Egyptian secession . . .

Below the American Bottoms, Egypt: the settlers clustering along the rivers, low land periodically flooded, with Thebes, Karnak and Cairo, at the tip of the inverted arrowhead . . .

And inland, the Illinois Ozarks: hills, rocks, forests . . .

"The honey locust is found in all the swails, bottoms and rich hills . . . grows to the height of 40 or 60 feet, dividing into many branches, which together with the trunk, are armed with long, sharp, pithy spines of the size of goose quills, from five to ten inches in length, and frequently so thick as to prevent the ascent of a squirrel. The branches are garnished with winged leaves, composed of ten or more pair of small lobes sitting close to the midrib, of a lucid green color . . . The pods, from the sweetness of their pulp, are used to brew beer . . ."

"The black walnut is found on the bottoms and rich hills—it often rises to the height of 70 feet; large trunk, dark, furrowed bark; winged leaves, which emit an aromatic flavor when bruised; fruit round and nearly as large as a peach."

The Falx Cerebri: sickle-shaped folds of dura matter that separate parts of the brain.

Early trade moved north and south, Chicago to Cairo and down the Mississippi . . . but the Civil War dammed the route, gunboats closed the river, and corn and pork turned north, to Chicago, and east . . .

. . . Cairo died . . .

Earlier, Indians: mounds and mounds along the river routes, the trade routes: obsidian from Yellowstone, Catlinite from Minnesota, Michigan copper and Allegheny mica, shells from the Gulf . . .

Mined flint in the Illinois Ozarks: Archaic, Woodland and Hopewellian peoples found round, ball-like nodules, the covering buff-colored, scattered in the creek beds or buried in the high ridges . . . broken open, the nodules showed the rings of blue-black hornestone flint, for spearheads, knives and scrapers . . .

*Erected great walls of stone at Draper's Bluff and Stonefort:
pounds, traps and slaughter pens for bison, deer and elk.*

. . the crista galli . . .

*Eastward, the saltworks, the Saline River, the United States
Saline: a rock fault, through which springs bring salt, from
deposits deep in the strata. Pungent, sulphurous, the brine
oozes to the surface in a slimy pool, at Nigger Spring, where
slaves replaced Indian pottery with iron kettles, to evaporate
the brine.*

. . . Nigger Spring is on the road to Equality . . .

*On a hilltop, back from the highway, hidden in trees, the Old
Slave House, where Crenshaw captured runaways, chained,
tortured and re-sold them, south . . .*

". . . under cover of the projecting lamina . . ."

. . . the Golconda–Kaskaskia road . . .

*. . . the old Massac trail, Tecumseh walking south, to recruit the
Creek, the Choctow, the Chickasaw*

". . the nerve runs in a groove along the lateral edge of the cribriform
plate to the slit-like opening . . ."

. . . at Elkville, herds of Elk, for the salt lick . . .

b.

"The middle fossa, deeper than the preceding, is narrow in the middle, and wide at the sides of the skull."

French traders in Illinois, as early as 1675. And the area was placed under the government of Quebec, "with the avowed purpose of excluding all further settlement therein . . . The question of preserving the fur trade was becoming more and more vital."

But the English threatened: "Expediency of securing our American colonies by settling the country adjoining the Mississippi, and the country upon the Ohio, considered"—a province, to be called Charlotina, stretching from the two rivers to the lakes . . .

"George, Samual, and John Washington; the Lees—William, Thomas, Francis Lightfoot, Richard Henry, and Arthur: Henry and William Fitzhugh, Presly Thornton, and Benedict Calvert."—June 3, 1763, formed the Mississippi Land Company, "to obtain from the crown two million five hundred thousand acres of land on the Mississippi River, beginning one hundred twenty miles above the Ohio, thence to the Wabash, up the Tennessee one hundred fifty miles above the juncture with the Ohio, thence to the Mississippi; within these boundaries each of the fifty adventurers was to have fifty thousand acres for his own."

Another plan promised to "Settle thereon at least One White Protestant Person for every Hundred Acres . . ."

A letter from Kaskaskia to the Governor of Virginia, August 18, 1779: "As to Indian grants it may be necessary immediately to inform you, that they are almost numberless, only four of them are very considerable, the smallest of which will be near a 1,000,000 acres, and the whole between 7 & 8 millions of

Acres. The grantees all reside in Philadelphia, London, Penn-sylvania, & Virginia and are between 40 & 50, Merchants chiefly. How far it may be proper to make such contracts bind-ing upon the Indians I cannot say."

But the crown would not grant the lands—choosing to protect the value of land speculations east of Appalachia.

1784—after the Revolution—Thomas Jefferson, a plan to divide the Illinois country: "Of the territory under the 43^d & 42^d degrees, that to the Westward thro' which the Assenisipi or Rock river runs shall be called ASSENISIPIA . . . Of the territory which lies under the 41st & 40th degrees the Western, thro which the river Illinois runs, shall be called ILLINOIA . . . Of the territory which lies under the 39th & 38th degrees to which shall be added so much of the point of land within the fork of the Ohio & Missisipi as lies under the 37th degree, that to the Westward within & adjacent to which are the confluence of the rivers Wabash, Shawanee, Tanisse, Ohio, Illinois, Missisipi & Missouri, shall be called POLYPOTAMIA . . .

After 1812, when peace returned to the frontier, the immigrants poured in: a quarter million acres sold, 1817 . . . clustering first along the bottoms, the Mississippi, the Ohio, the Wabash, and up the Saline . . . out of Pennsylvania and down the Ohio, up the Mohawk and along the lake shores, but mostly out of the south, the hill people, Pennsylvania to Georgia: "When you hear the sound of a neighbor's gun, it is time to move away."

. . . good land dog-cheap . . .

(General Gage, 1770: "Let the savages enjoy their desarts in quiet; little bickerings that will unavoidably sometimes happen, may soon be accomodated. And I am of opinion independent of the motives of common justice and humanity, that the principles of interest and policy should induce us rather to protect, than molest them. Were they drove from their

forrests, the peltry trade would decrease, and not impossible that worse savages would take refuge in them; for they might then become the azylum of fugitive negroes, and idle vagabonds, escaped from justice, who in time might become fomidable, and subsist by rapine, and plundering . . .")

(The Prophet, Tecumseh's brother, on the whites: "They grew from the scum of the great water where it was troubled by the evil spirit, and the froth was driven into the woods by a strong east wind.")

(. . . the French named the Shit Islands in the Mississippi . . . and called Peoria Piss Village. . .)

small wings, great wings of sphenoid . . . pterygoid, wing-like . . .

Through Pennsylvania, Ohio, Indiana, pursuing a narrow band of land between snow and ice to the north, slavery to the south, came Birkbeck and Flower, the Englishmen: arrived at Bon Pas Creek and the Little Wabash River in Illinois, took up 16,000 acres, settled the village they called Albion.

"A few steps more and a beautiful prairie suddenly opened to our view. At first we only received the impressions of its general beauty. With longer gaze . . .

. . . the oculomotor nerves, controlling the eyes . . .

. . . all its distinctive features were revealed, lying in profound repose under the warm light of an afternoon's summer sun. Its indented and irregular outline of wood, its varied surface interspersed with clumps of oaks of centuries' growth, its tall grass, with seed stalks from six to ten feet high, like tall and slender weeds waving in a gentle breeze, the whole presenting a magnificence of park-scenery, complete from the hand of Nature . . . From beneath the broken shade of the wood, with our arms raised above our brows, we gazed long and steadily,

drinking in the beauties of the scene which had been so long the object of our search."

. . . here they will find the wide domain, the natural park, whose hills and boundaries are capped with woods . . . parks already stocked with deer . . ."

—*God being indeed an English landscape gardener.*

". . . lawns of unchanging verdure, spreading over hills and dales, scattered with islands of luxuriant trees, dropped by the hand of nature, with a taste that art could not rival—all this spread beneath a sky of glowing and unspotted sapphires."

"A plentiful supply of plumb pudding, roast beef and mince piese were at table . . .

. . . lingula, the process shaped like a tongue . . .

. . . and turkeys in plenty, having purchase four for a dollar the preceding week . . .

. . . the maxillary and mandibular nerves . . .

We found among the party good musicians, good singers; the young people danced nine couple, and the whole party were innocently cheerful and happy during the evening. The company were pleased to say I had transferred Old England and its comforts to the Illinois."

"Not far from Mr. Woods live a Mr. Bentley and lady, late of London, who, here, with a little property, have turned farmers, doing all the labour in the field and loghouse themselves, and, it is said, seem very cheerful, happy, and healthy. In London he had the gout, and she the delicate blue devils; but here milking, fetching water, and all kinds of drudgery, indoors and out, have cured her, and ploughing him. He never, he says, loved her, or she him, half so much as in Illinois."

"Mr. and Mrs. Doctor Pubsley, late of London, live in the only house, which, if it had a servant, would boast of English comforts, politeness and hospitality. She sighs to revisit England, where she might see her friends and rest her delicate hands, now destined to all kinds of drudgery."

"I supped and went to bed in a hog sty of a room, containing four filthy beds . . .

. . . crinoid processes, arranged like posts of a bedstead on the inner side of the sphenoid bone . . .

. . . and eight mean persons, the sheets stinking and dirty. Scarcity of water is, I suppose, the cause. The beds lie on boards, not cords, and are so hard . . .

. . . petrous, squamous . . .

. . . that I could not sleep. Three in one bed, all filth, no comfort, and yet this is an English tavern—no whiskey, no milk, and vile tea, in this land of prairies."

". . . the carotid groove, which is broad, shallow, and curved some-what like the italic letter *f*."

. . . at Mount Carmel, mussels taken from the Wabash, with pearls . . .

John Flack built Boucoup Bridge, at Beaucoup, across the Little Muddy, on the Kaskaskia road.

. . . a notch for the abducent nerve . . .

1779, George Rogers Clark, Kaskaskia to Vincennes: ". . . the weather wet and great part of the plains under water for several Inches . . . Marched across bad plain saw and killed

numbers of Buffaloe, the roads very bad . . . Rainy and drisly
weather . . . The roads very bad with Mud and Water . . .
Marched early thro' the Water which we now began to meet in
those large and level plains where (from the Flatness of the
country the Water rests a considerable time before it drains
off . . . the whole under water Genly About three feet Deep never
under two and frequently waided further in Water, but perhaps
seldom above half Leg deep . . .

. . . the crura, the leg-like parts: peduncles . . .

. . . the Drownded Lands . . . we were now convinced that the
whole of the Low Countrey on the waubach was drownded
. . . geting about the Middle of the plain the water about need
deep I found myself sensibly failing as their was hear no Trees
or Bushes for the men to support them selves by I doubted that
many of the most weak would drownd . . . we found the Water
fallen from a small spot of Ground . . .

. . . tuburculum, a rough, rounded prominence . . .

. . . staid there the remainder of the Night drisly and dark
Weather . . . At Break of day began to ferry our Men over in
our two Canoes to a Small little hill called the lower Mamell
(or Bubbie) . . ."

—a saving mound on the flat-chested land—

The prairie, and the woodland-prairie border:

". . . the beautiful woodland points and promontories shooting
forth into the mimic sea: the far-retreating shadowy coves,
going back in long vistas into the green wood . . ."

In the memory of Appalachian, woodland man, the blue-
stem prairie as the shimmering blue sea, as seen from the
western shores of England, Land's End: fearful, and without
resolution . . .

. . . the broken shores of forest and prairie, land and sea, capes and inlets, promontories and harbors, estuaries and bays . . . westward, the terrifying horizon . . .

Domestic Appalachian man, woodland man, found the forests warming, a natural world . . . the prairie a treeless barren "you can look farther and see less than anywhere else in the world." Woodland Fenimore Cooper's Leatherstocking hero dies, finally, in The Prairie: *". . . the sound of the axes has driven him from his beloved forest to . . . the treeless plains . . ."*

Trees the keys to fertility: a land that would not grow trees would grow nothing: "A great part of the territory is miserably poor, especially that near Lakes Michigan and Erie & that upon the Mississippi & the Illinois consists of extensive plains w^h have not from appearance & will not have a single bush on them, for ages."

No wood, for building or for fire . . .

. . . but only grass, fired by the Indians: "We see whole prairies, containing thousands of acres, like a sea or lake of fire ascending: columns of smoke so affect the air, that it is a complete fog . . . It was the most glorious and most awful sight I ever beheld. A thousand acres of prairie were in flames at once—the sun was obscured, and the day was dark before the night came. The moon rose and looked dim and red through the smoke, and the stars were hidden entirely. Yet it was still light upon the earth, which appeared covered with fire . . . They produce a beautiful effect during the night, the clouds immediately over them reflecting the light and appearing almost on fire themselves . . ."

(Only the English at Albion were unafraid of the prairies— emigrating from English park land, and down the American rivers, without Appalachian cover, to park land in Illinois:

*"I shrank from the idea of settling in the midst of a wood of
heavy timber, to hack and hew my way to a little farm, ever-
bounded by a wall of gloomy forest . . .")*

*Finally, driven from behind by poverty, nerved by necessity,
the American pioneer pushed outward, away from the wooded
bottoms, the timbery borders, outward on the bluestem prairie
. . . to break the tough sod, hitched six to ten yoke of oxen to a
plow, the plow attached to a heavy plow beam, framed into an
axle and supported by wheels cut from oak logs . . . fed his stock
on wild prairie grasses, and raised a first crop of sod corn.*

*Later, tried to raise flax, mustard seed, cotton and tobacco; hemp,
the castor bean, and the mulberry tree with silkworms . . .*

*1872, Montgomery Ward and Company was formed, "to meet
the wants of the patrons of husbandry."*

Causes for early aging in frontier Illinois:
   Heavy drinking.
   Physical discomfort.
   *Stimulation and excitement of the frontier
     situation.*
   Violent religious enthusiasms.
   Early marriage.

. . . the cavernous sinus and the internal carotid . . .

c.

The Posterior Fossa:

*1860, King Edward VII, then Prince of Wales, hunting two
days near Breese, became lost in the Santa Fe Bottoms . . .*

The St. Louis Trace, the Vincennes Trail, and to the north, Indian massacres: Kickapoo, Potawatomi, Ottawa, Chippewa, Sauk, Fox and Winnebago...

"The tenderest infant, yet imbibing nutrition from the mamilla of maternal love, and the agonized mother herself, alike await the stroke of the relentless tomahawk."

... the Shelbyville Moraine, an irregular, tree-topped ridge, a terminal moraine...

... clivus of the sphenoid: slope, rise, gradient ...

Abe Lincoln, age 21, on Goose Nest Prairie: pitchfork and mattock, an ax for zigzag fencing...

Later, 1858: "This morning the procession formed at Mattoon for the purpose of escorting Lincoln to the county seat. It was led by a band of music from Indiana. Following the carriage of Mr. Lincoln was a wagon filled with young ladies, thirty-two in number, each representing a state ... Arriving at Charleston, a vast throng was found waiting the procession ... Oh! how fearfully dusty candidates and cavalcades were when they arrived in front of the hotels."

... Tuscola: flat plain ...

1861, Lincoln, at Tolono station (earlier, back in Springfield, he had roped his trunks himself, and had written, 'A. Lincoln, The White House, Washington, D.C." on cards he fastened on the trunks). "I am leaving you on an errand of national importance, attended, as you are aware, with considerable difficulties. Let us believe, as some poet has expressed it, 'Behind the cloud the sun is still shining.' I bid you an affectionate farewell." And there were voices, "Goodby, Abe."

... on the banks of the Vermilion River, a fine red earth with which the Indians paint themselves ...

. . . the meatus, a natural passage or duct for the facial and acoustic nerves . . .

(The Indians found by the early French were decadent remnants, a hybrid of the earlier great civilizations, the high cultures having been ravaged by small pox, introduced by Spain into Mexico, and raging northward, up the Mississippi Valley . . .

"In its center is the foramen magnum . . ." for the medulla oblongata, the pons . . .

. . . Loda, or Cath-Loda, a mountain dwelling Gallic god . . . or Lotha, a great river in North Scotland . . .

. . Onarga, place of rocky hills . . .

. . . Ashkum, more and more . . .

. . . Chebanse, little duck . . .

. . . Kankakee, Theakiki, Kyankeakee, beautiful land . . .

"There is said to be a petrified hickory tree in the bed of the river Kankakee, near its junction with the Illinois . . . It is entire, and partly embedded in the calcareous rock . . ."

"The jugular foramen is situated between the lateral part of the occipital and the petrous part of the temporal."

. . . the Valparaiso Moraine, low hills and marshy depressions, one of the largest terminal moraines in the world . . .

. . . the internal occipital crest . . .

. . . Mount Joliet, an Indian mound . . .

. . . Blue Island, a glacial ridge, a blue haze in its dense woods . . .

... endolymphatic ...

*". . . there being but very little game in that place, we had
nothing but our meal or Indian wheat to feed on; yet we
discovered a kind of manna, which was a great help to us. It
was a sort of trees, resembling our maple, in which we made
incisions, whence flowed a sweet liquor, and in it we boiled
our Indian wheat, which made it delicious, sweet and of a
very agreeable relish."*

... endolymph, the fluid in the membranous labyrinth ...

She-gang, *skunk, and* shih-gau-ga-winzhe, *onion, or skunk
weed, Chicago: onion, garlic, leek or skunk. Or* Tuck Choe-ca-
go, Mit-Tuck Ka-ka-go, *no tree, not a tree, a waste prairie.*

*"They soon reached a spot where the oozy, saturated soil quaked
beneath their tread. All around were clumps of elder-bushes,
tufts of rank grass, and pools of glistening water. In the midst
a dark and lazy current, which a tall man might bestride, crept
twisting like a snake among the weeds and rushes ...*

... the vagus nerve, wandering ...

*"They set their canoes on the thread of water, embarked their
baggage and themselves, and pushed down the sluggish
streamlet, looking, at a little distance, like men who sailed on
land. Fed by an unceasing tribute of the spongy soil, it quickly
widened to a river; and they floated on their way through a
voiceless, lifeless solitude of dreary oak barrens, or boundless
marshes overgrown with reeds ..."*

*"It was the worst of all seasons for such a journey. The nights
were cold, but the sun was warm at noon, and the half-thawed
prairie was one vast tract of mud, water, and discolored, half-
liquid snow. On the twenty-second they crossed marshes and
inundated meadows, wading to the knee, till at noon they were*

stopped by a river . . . On the next day they could see Lake
Michigan dimly glimmering beyond the waste of woods . . ."

"The next remarkable River is Chycacoo . . . Here the Country
Begins Again to Be very Pleasant, good soil, and Hunting very
Plenty: Such as Buffaloes, Deer, Bear . . . 9 miles up this River,
the Chykoco, the frensh used to make a Carrying Place into an
other River for about 3 miles which falls into the river Illinois
and is deep Enough for Battoes to goe up or down."

". . . but when the water was high . . . when the intervening
lands were drowned . . . no portage obstructed their passage, for
then the waters of the lakes and of the Mississippi basin were
intermingled . . ."

. . . in the medulla, the vital nerve centers for the control of breathing,
circulation . . .

—the waters so nearly even that a change of breeze would float
an object to lake or to river.

"From the lake one passes by a channel formed by the junction
of several small streams or gullies, and navigable about two
leagues to the edge of the prairie. Beyond this at a distance of a
quarter of a league to the westward is a little lake a league and
a half in length, divided into two parts by a beaver dam . . ."

Mud Lake, with enough water to float a boat only in the wet
season. At other times, boats were pushed on rollers, or dragged
by men wading in the lake, up to their waists in mud . . . cling-
ing to the boats to avoid going under . . . their limbs covered
with bloodsuckers . . . 'til they reached the Des Plaines, the river
"equally divided between ripples and still waters."

As early as 1675, French traders below Chicago . . . and later, John
Crafts, on the south branch of the Chicago River . . . firewater,
diluted with fresh lake water, @ 50 cents a quart . . . Francis

*Bourbonnae Dr. to 1 negro wench sold him by Indenture £160."
. . . eight gross of Jews'-harps, to be traded for furs.*

*1783, Baptiste Point du Sable, a "naigre Libre," native of San
Domingo, wandered up the Mississippi built a cabin of
squared logs, and outbuildings, where the Indians passed into
the Onion River from the lake . . . kept a few traps and
blankets, and a mighty stock of rum . . . "drank pretty freely,"
danced and caroused with the Indians, and "drank badly" . . .
1800, suddenly vanished.*

*1793, Capt. John Whistler, progenitor of the painter, arrived
with a company of infantry: built log blockhouses, barracks,
and stores, enclosed with a strong stockade.*

*Indian attacks (1812) forced abandonment . . . Black Partridge,
Pottawatomie chief, came to the fort, warned that "linden
birds had been singing in his ears, and they ought to be careful
on the march they were about to make" . . . officers and men,
slaves, wives and children evacuated the fort, proceded south
along the sandy lake shore, marching on a summer morning
between the water's edge, and a ridge of sand hills, into a half
moon of Indians:*

*. . . heads popped up from the dunes, the Indians fired mercilessly
on the ambushed evacuees: the Fort Dearborn Massacre . . .*

*Blackbird and the Mad Sturgeon . . . "women and children
lying naked with principally all their heads off" . . . "He was
tomahawked and scalped, his face was mutilated, his throat cut
from ear to ear" . . . "The most horrible object I every beheld in
my life" . . . "the bloodied sand-blown corpses left to buzzards
and wolves."*

*"The country around Chicago is the most fertile and beautiful
that can be imagined. It consists of an intermixture of woods and
prairies, deversified with gentle slopes, sometimes attaining the*

elevation of hills, and irrigated with a number of clear streams and rivers, which throw their waters partly into Lake Michigan, and partly into the Mississippi river. As a farming country, it unites the fertile soil, of the finest lowland prairies, with an elevation, which exempts it from the influence of stagnant waters, and a summer climate of delightful serenity; while its natural meadows present all the advantages for raising stock, of the most favoured part of the valley of the Mississippi. It is already the seat of several flourishing plantations, and only requires the extinguishment of the Indian title to the lands, to become one of the attractive fields for the emigrant."

Chicago, September 1833: "a mush-room village," where "thousands of savages congregated to barter away their birthright"... "emigrants and land speculators numerous as the sand, horse dealers and horse stealers—rogues of every description, white, black, brown and red—half-breeds, quarter-breeds, and men of no breed at all; dealers in pigs, poultry, and potatoes; men pursuing Indian claims, some for tracts of land, others for pigs which the wolves had eaten;—creditors of the tribes, or of particular Indians, who know they have no chance of getting their money if they do not get it from the government agents; sharpers of every degree: peddlers, grogsellers; Indian agents and Indian traders of every description, and Contractors to supply the Pottawatomies with food."

"The little village was in an uproar from morning to night and from night to morning."

. . . the mid-brain . . .

FOUR

a.

the epidermis, or scarf skin,
consisting of stratified epithelium,
is accurately molded on the papillary layer,

hard and horny
in the palms of the hands,
soles of the feet . . .

the free surface of the epidermis
marked by a network of furrows,
lozenge-shaped, with

ridges on hands and feet,
at right angles to the forces
of slippage and prehension.

the undersurface of the epidermis
presents pits and depressions,
corresponding to the papillae . . .

cells of the deepest layer of epithelium
are columnar in shape, placed perpendicular to
the basement membrane,
attached by toothed extremities.

(there are prickle cells,
interconnected by bridges)

horny cells at the surface
may contain something like beeswax . . .

among blacks, and, to some extent, all swarthies,
the epidermis contains melanin,

> *also to be found*
> *in the pigmentary layer*
> *of the retina*
>
> *in the eye*
>
> *of all peoples.*

the corium, or true skin,
beneath the epidermis,
consisting of felted connective tissue,
is tough, flexible, and elastic:
thick in the palms and on the soles,
thin and delicate
in scrotum, penis and eyelid.

within the skin,
deep in the reticular layer,
tension or cleavage lines
—Langer's lines—
corresponding closely with the crease lines
on the surface . . .

in the deepest layer, the subcutaneous tissue,
arteries and lymphatic passages,
capillary loops, convoluted vessels,
superficial and deep networks,
feeding and draining the skin

and

the Illinois plain: bottom of a large shallow basin,
the neighboring states the rim

—warped by pressure from beneath,
eroded by wind and water from above

Illinois a shallow spoon,
a series of spoons placed one upon another,
stratified layers of rock,
sedimentary particles converted to rock:
deeply buried at the center,
with pre-Pennsylvanian beds of limestone,
Pennsylvanian coal and clay
exposed at the rim.

decaying vegetation lays down a surface of black soil—
the mantle, the skin of the earth—
over a layer of windblown and waterborne loess;
under this, deposits of glacial boulder clay,
deepest repository of plant food . . .
and beneath this,
at levels beyond reach,
the igneous rock,
fire-formed mother-rock of all formations . . .

the land near flat,
and low,
the drainage shallow:
nitrogen and other nutrients will not leach out . . .

the prairie, the arable surface,
drained by a shallow grid of ditch and tile,

fed by nutrients from inexhaustible subsoil

and

the man blinded will see with his skin,
the myriad of pores above, below, and around the ears.
searching obstacles:

facial vision:
perceptio facialis, telesthesia, paroptic vision,
the sense of presence:

"the effect . . . so pronounced
as to cause me to stagger as though struck"

(motor memory,
temperature sense, the labyrinthine or vestibular sense,
kinesthesis)

the face nerves sensitive,
sounds and echoes,
compression of atmosphere,

tympanic membrane in the ear,
sound waves on the skin,
magnetics, electrics, electromagnetics

vestigial organs in the skin

trigeminal nerves,
hot breath reflected,
the rising pitch of footsteps,
the source a mystery to its possessor:

"a cloud on my face"
"pressure on my cheekbones"
"a shadow on my forehead"

cheeks and forehead as feelers

    (the nape of the neck,
    the top of the head,
    are insensitive)

a creative effort:
be alone, without fatigue and undistracted,

relaxed and without force
without fear,
let the skin see naturally

   (beware the door ajar,
   the air conditioned
   or turmoiled by wind,

   you will hear clearly in sunlight,
   poorly in fog,
   sounds distorted in rain

   it is quieter in winter
   than in summer)

rather than remember directions,
it is better to feel the sun on the cheekbone,

and move by the compass
over the skin of the earth

b.

   sea waters penetrated,
   entering the great valley from the north,
   or from the south, warm waters of the gulf,

   the land split,
   Illinois an ocean sea,
   between the islands of cincinnatia and ozarkia,

   sea surface, sea bed
   oscillating,
   deepening,

marshes to deeper waters,
and these to open sea,

the waters clearing,
silt and sediments settling
to a gentle slope,
too slight to be seen by the eye,
an imperceptible southward dip,
sea bed beyond reach of wave drag and agitation.

the land sinking,
and then upwarping,

finally upraised,
shallow sea waters draining,
the sea bed become a tropic swamp:

coral at Chicago,
palms, club mosses, gigantic horse tails,
the prairie a heaving sea of herbs and plants

and

the man blinded will distinguish colors with his skin
(dermaloptics) and
with the fingers: aphotic digital color sensing.

ocelli, microscopic eyes, nerve endings,
grouped in umbels
and embedded in the epidermis,

"A coarse oval cell
. . . finely granular . . .
with a voluminous nucleus
of remarkable refractive powers"

parallel to, and just beneath,
the surface of the skin.

photo receptors in the cells of the whorls of the fingertips
discriminating the temperature of the waves of light
that penetrate the filamentous structure
of the rods and cones of the skin.

skinembedded retinal photosensitive substances,
electromagnetically translating
tactile into visual,

or the hand held above the colors,
the fingers in motion,
entering an electric color field,
the electromagnetic radiation of the visible spectrum.

(according to Romains, the nostrils are the most sensitive
of surfaces, to colors: the nasal mucosa)

(the right hand, for the right-handed,
the left hand, for left-handed,
will distinguish form)

(the Russians claimed a man
who could see with his forehead or his chest,
a woman who could taste with her forearms,
another who read with her elbow)

> *(Rosa Kuleshova*
> *had a record of epilepsy,*
> *her brain waves fluctuant)*

finger sight, paroptic vision:
an evolutionary vestige
remnant of aquatic ancestry

(like the blind fish
of Mammoth Cave)

the skin a rudimentary retina,
responding to light flashes
with electrical signals

not unlike those observed
in the eye,
from the cell layers
containing melanin

c.

from Labrador, the center of accumulation,
the Illinoisan glacier pushed sixteen hundred miles

to near the crest of the Ozark Uplift,
the beginning of Egypt:

the deepest southern penetration
of North American ice . . .

came to rest on the range's northern flank:
hills to the south,
the beginning of melt to the north.

to the north,
Lake Chicago,
ancestor to Lake Michigan,
grew from waters
impounded between the receding edge of ice
and the Valparaiso moraine,

sedimentary deposition, the Chicago plain,
lying deep beneath the water's surface,

only Blue Island,
a glacial ridge, emergent.

on the land's surface, till:
buff-drab, pinkish, blue,
the texture gritty,
with water-worn cherts,

rock debris, rock flour, boulder trains,
granite till, from the older drift,
to be crumbled in the hand,

gabbro, gneiss, and schist,
ganister, tripoli, fuller's earth.

emerging as glacial melt,
silt-laden waters
receded in mud flats,

dried in the prairie winds,
and swept across the land's surface,
as loess.

became, with weathering and vegetation,
peaty loam, muck, clay,
clay loams, loams, sandy loams,
fine sandy loams, sands, gravelly loams,
gravels, stony loams,

deep peat.

the surface, the skin of the land,
undulatory, slightly billowy,
with numberless gentle swells and shallow sags,

drift billows, crest lines,
scattered knolls and knobs

(Iroquois County
is almost without relief)

in the rocks, caves:
coon den, cave spring, toothless, and unnamed,

fossils,
to be found in road cuts and river banks,
in strip mines and rip rap

and

among the navaho, southwestward, witches emerge at night,
roam about at great speed in wolf skins

ye • na • ldl • si:
one who trots along here and there on all fours
with it!

go to the new grave,
dig up the fresh dead,
cut off bits of meat, here and there,
wherever there is a spiral,
the thumb and finger ends,

spirals and whorls:
minute conical eminences
rising from the skin,
closely aggregated,
arranged in curving parallels

photo receptors
in the whorls
of the fingertips

the medicine man of the connibos
felt that george catlin,

in painting his portrait,
was employing an ingenious mode
of stealing his skin

assume the skin of another,
you will become that other

d.

the man blinded loses light,

loses light, loses love:

(those two little nuts,
two in the head,
that make the world)

> (the terror of losing footing,
> where the earth drops off,
> and does not echo)

but the world is reconstructed:
seated precisely behind home plate,
infield and outfield geometrically imagined,
fast ball or curve, by the sound in the mitt,
the ball well or poorly hit, by the crack,
the grounder skimming the grass,
spikes clawing dirt,

runner out or safe,
by ball in mitt or toe on base, first.

your voice tells your health and age,
your smell your character and virtue,

my tongue has the finest sense of touch

and the man blinded, without confusion of sight,
swings the hammer, strikes the nail clean!

behind the sightless balls (the two little nuts),
a gray pastel
—or luminous globes of light in a foggy night—

fireworks!
the orchestra begins,
the music a riot of colors

the middle register dull red,
ascending to pink, light yellow,
up to white,
in the eighth octave,

descending to magenta,
deep blue,
into black

the touch of plush velour
tastes bitter

taste the colors!

(the brain a hand,
reaching,
touching substances)

blue is smooth,
yellow slippery
red sticky, catching, attracting,

green not rough,
indigo the stickiest,
orange rough and hard,
violet even rougher . . .

hide matches,
build a backyard fire,
see the flames with fingertips!

>   the man blinded is deaf,
>   he is not there,

>   not all there,
>   feeble-minded,

>   dead to the world,
>   eyes closed, asleep,

>   but he does not need sleep,
>   his eyes are always closed,

>   since he is blind,
>   no one can see him,

>   unable to see,
>   he cannot know when he's awake . . .

but in sleep,
the man blinded dreams,

sees stream, valley, mountains
(but stand still,
the footing at the cliff's edge!)

>   south is a cloud of yellow light,
>   straw color,
>   friends are fawn and blue,

>   a woman is bright and silvery,
>   the fish leaps from the stream,
>   speaks in yellow

when he wakes,
one world disappears

e.

the skin piliferous:
save only for palms and soles,
the backs of fingers and toes,
the glans penis
and inner surfaces of prepuce and labia—
save only these,
the skin forested with hair

oaks, hickories, ash, and maples
the winged elm to the north,
cork elm south,
bald cypress in the bottoms of the cache,

swamp cottonwood south,
and the aspens—large and trembling—north,

walnut and butternut,
hornbeam, mulberry, blue beech,
sassafras, sycamore, and sweet gum,
crab, thorn, and buckeye,
basswood, haw,
linden, black gum, catawlpa and tupelo,
sumac, witch hazel, pawpaw and wahoo,
hackberry, sweet birch, black locust,
viburnum

the man blinded will perceive objects
without touching,

to graze lightly
with the tiny hairs,

each a lever,
distributing sensation,

facial vision an animal fear:
goose flesh and hair bristling!

on face, temples, and forehead,
a light brushing,

a cold current
down the limbs,

the contraction of small muscles

FIVE

Sikeston, Missouri—6:00 A.M.—Drury Inn, Open All Year, 68 units— 2 miles and 10 minutes from downtown Sikeston, inception of I-57, bound north and by east

have you got your house in order?

Sikeston: breakfast at Sambo's, fluffy decor from that classic, tiger butter on the hot cakes

On to 57, and the Missouri delta land, river-bordering, Mississippi County . . . shops for souvenirs, trashed figurines; jockeys pickaninny hitching posts, nuns

The bridge, the river, the junction of the rivers,
       the flood plain drownded,
       land drownded,
       the road to Cairo Point,
       the tip of the wedge,

> acerb point of the inverted arrowhead,
> most south,
> most deeply southern Illinois,
> drownded
> trees viable,
> thick

. . . as Dickens says, "where the very trees took the aspect of huge weeds"

but Dickens, who visited here April 9, 1842, invested in a land development scheme—the Cairo Company—saw the company go broke, went out of his way, in *American Notes* and *Martin Chuzzlewit,* to vent his spleen:

"the hateful Mississippi circling and eddying before it, and turning off upon its southern course, a slimy monster hideous to behold"

"a quagmire inhabited by a web-foot people"

. . . Pulaski County . . .

> Cairo a dependent member,
> in darkest Egypt,
> in the groin,
> the joining of the rivers,
> in Dickens' shrubbery
> conjoining of
> all the watery snows,
> Shoshone's to
> Conewango's!

Cairo an inland island, with the two rivers, and to the north, the Cache

> magnolias and gins
> canebrakes, mimosa

south of Richmond
and Louisville,

and of Tunis, in
Africa

. . . today, the sleepiest of southern towns, almost abandoned, on a
business day the streets, black & white, empty

how many years the National guard here, to control the riots?

the first of so many abandoned commercial blocks, the storefronts,
block after block, Ohio Riverfronts, brick and vacant

ghettos and mansions, together, ghostly

northward from Cairo: Thebes, Karnak, Egypt

> (from a highway historical marker: "In the early days of
> statehood, crop failures threatened the existence of the
> isolated settlements in northern and central Illinois and
> trips were made into the more populated southern
> section of the state to obtain grain. Settlers called such
> expeditions 'Going to Egypt' . . ."

the Knights of the Golden Circle, meeting and hiding among
fantastic limestones at Giant City, plotted Egyptian rebellion and
secession, joining the Confederacy . . .

. . . the dreamers of the South from Jefferson forward, dreaming of
a great Rural Slave Empire, spreading from the coastal countries of
South America, through Central America and the Indies, all the
way to the Great Lakes, the very Atlantic and Pacific become Lakes
of the Confederacy, the key to the northern apex of this empire to
be Cairo, the entrance, at the river groin, through the Egyptian
hills, to the northern prairies and the lakeshore

but Illinois went north, dragging Egypt with it. Egypt reversed, inverted, a river-edged wedge, riving apart the Confederacy

A baseball game played at Cairo, October 23, 1866: The Egyptians 59, Magenta 6

Just north of Cairo, in a run-down commerical and third-rate road-house area: FUTURE CITY

Left on Route 3, passed the abandoned gins, under unfinished 57, the road bending toward Horseshoe Lake, water on both sides, highway and railroad embanked out of floodplain and jungle . . . low country Georgia, Everglades, Southern Illinois, Okefenokee . . .

> Horseshoe:
> the sky overcast,
> waters flooding gray,
> whirlpool at the
> culvert,
> a few blacks
> casting at the bridge

moving inland, Cache to Mounds, and the land rises, rolls, becomes hilly . . . fruit land, earth and crop sweet with the molding . . . foothills of the Illinois Ozarks

I-57, Mounds to Ullin, unspecific rolling farmland . . .

. . . looks like hills up ahead . . .

tooling along in our Catalina!

Very strange, quick transition, from deep swamp at Horseshoe, to hillbilly upcountry, to the middle land
Ullin on the Cache: "Do you know that where you are now standing was once the bed of the Ohio River?"

Ullin, Fingal's bard, Stormy Son of War, one of the eight heroes of
Ossian, in those legendary Gaelic romances

breakfast at Sambo's, lunch at Porky's . . . no blacks in either

but where Sambo's was slick and mod, Ullin's Porky's is old country:
you ask for pickles with your sandwich and they bring you a damn
bowl of 'em!

at each step, listen to the voices, the new ear open to the accent . . .
here all deep deep south, with maybe a hint of west
the girl at Hertz Rent-A-Car in Cape Girardeau directing me to
turn *that-a way* (but that was west of the Mississippi . . .

at Porky's, the serving counter, formerly a bar, is 178 years old, of
solid walnut with wooden pegs, built originally by a brewer in
Evansville, Indiana . . . saw service in an inn in Grand Chain . . . has
survived three deaths, in one case the murder of a deputy sheriff . . .
has also survived three fires, and the great Ohio flood of 1937 . . .
until recently there were dents in the surface, marks of the heels of
19th century bar-top dancers, but as Porky's serving counter it
sports new formica

Businesses in Ullin:
          First State Bank
          Goins Star Cleaners & Coin Laundry
          Associated Lumber
          Rives Drug Store
          Kerr's Radio & TV
          Corvine Brothers TV
          Stoner Funeral Home
          Columbia Quarry
          Heilig Brothers Farm & Home Center
          Tamms State Bank
          Howell's Music & Western Wear
          Jordan Truck Service

these country waitresses love to wear 18" beehives, makes 'em look
Egyptian

also, gold ballet slippers

conversation at the counter:
    "What's the difference between a village clerk and a
        town clerk?"
    "One's black and one's white."

no booze at the bar, now, no bar-top dancers . . . formica

Wetaug: the Cherokee chief who died on the Trail . . . and an earth-
quake dried up the spring

. . . entering Union County . . .

Dongola: a mudiria of the Anglo-Egyptian Sudan, lying wholly
within the region of Nubia, extending along both banks of the Nile
. . . habitat of the addax, rarest of Sudanese antelopes . . . durra,

barley, and date palms . . . the Dongolese are Nubas, with a mixture of Arab and Turk: farmers, traders and slave-dealers . . . on both sides of the Nile, castles, now in ruins . . .

Cypress (Johnson County), not a sign of cypress, one hundred thousand acres, bald and virgin: trees cut, stumps hauled, land drained, tilled

doubling back, Cypress to Dongola, on second passing, behind a screen of massive hemlocks: an abandoned farmhouse, windows blasted, forsythia flooding in the kitchen . . . a true New England saltbox, built by some Yankee eccentric, one corner slightly higher than the rest, the fault or quirk beautifully incorporated or masked

old steam tractor, Double E Ranch, Dongola: boiler inspected and approved, State of Illinois, 1974

Southern Illinois Hospital for the Insane, established in Anna, 1869

poverty in Egypt: battered mobile homes, trashed yards, junk cars . . . how can the land be so rich and the people so poor?

West of Ware: driving along the flood plain, flanking the inland Ozarks—like the Blue Ridge as seen from the Piedmont, only here the flat is absolute

Site of the Lincoln-Douglas debate in Jonesboro, "an ancient village in the heart of Egypt, among hills and ravines": now a pretty little park The Four Seasons Restaurant and Lounge in Anna, Illinois, is not the Four Seasons New York City . . . eat your heart out, fourseasonsnyc!

a waitress whose voice would drown Bryan's, with a heart of plutonium, real hard-assed, pert-titted working-man's middle american fast-tongued sweet-legged chick . . .

Frog's legs!

voices from the bar still southern—or just country? radio? TV? stereo? country western? aw, shucks . . .

the chef came out to ask if we had enjoyed the frog's legs—looked like Charles Olson, talked like Burl Ives—the legs looked like neither

From the wine list:

> *Singa Pore Sling*
> stupids, it shld be
> *Sing A*, etc.

Sambo's
Porky's   the day's dining
The Four Seasons

re the waitress: these middlewesterners share an inheritance from The Boy Orator of the Prairie: say it, say it often, say it loud. This is known as being hearty and friendly

Lincoln Motel, Anna: art deco furniture, worn wooden toilet seat a dead airwick: our stinks not absorbed, floating in the atmosphere aux arcs, egyptian

lady at motel: "the traffic in Anna is worse than Chicago!"

———————

Log for Friday, April 11:

> Breakfast at Sambo's, Sikeston, Mo.
> South on I-55 to I-57,
> East on I-57 to juct. U.S. 60
> U.S. 60 to Cairo
> U.S. 51, Ill. 3 and unnumbered roads to Horseshoe Lake and
>   Miller City (Miller City is the counterpart to Flamingo as
>   it used to be, before the tourists, a little fishing village, on

the edge of the gulf of Mexico and the Everglades: Miller
City, bordering the Horseshoe and the Mississippi)

Unnumbered road, Ill. 3 and unnumbered road to Mounds

I-57 to Ullin (near accident here: I'm so fucking tall, almost
beyond range of the full-sweep rear-view mirror in our
Catalina (Owner: Hertz; Registration: Missouri EK4-
081)—as I pulled out of Shell station I couldn't see guy
pulling in—rueful look on his face as we screeched,
swerved, shot gravel)

U.S. 51 to Dongola

Unnumbered road to Ill. 37, and Cypress, then back, same
route, to Dongola

U.S. 51 to Anna

Ill. 146 to Ware

Unnumbered roads to Miss. River levee, then back, same
route, to Anna

SATURDAY, APRIL 12, 1975

Started the day off great: locked ourselves out of the motel—now we'll find out how nice the good friendly lady is, when we wake her up

Breakfast at the Manor House—like all the others, a misnomer of course, but in a different way: clean, simple, unpretentious—home-made biscuits, good sausage

ah, the Motel Lady, up and dressed, and oh so friendly, so kindly, even early in the morning

Thinking about places to be visited and photographed, vis-a-vis places, perhaps more distant, more removed from 57, to command only allusion:

first, there is time, only so much time, for so much to happen—and time is a discipline of formation, as in physiology and human growth pre- and post-natal, physical and cultural:—a phase of growth must occur, and complete itself; at a specific time, in the overall pattern, or it will never happen at all (or grows as a malignancy, a gross, unending compensation)

second, in establishing the interstate as a central discipline, I have created a spine, all of whose vertebrae and ribs must observe formal proportion: which places formal limits to visits and photography, whereas literary reference, as an extension or projection of life itself may occur—but only up to a limit, there are rules here, too, beyond the first limits. Hence, the failure to pursue the Mississippi northwest, and scenic areas on the Big Muddy, etc., is not a loss, but a structural necessity as the river veers northwest, 57 slices northeast—and 57 is my spine, Sikeston to Chicago

> ("I mean something I believe we possess crucially. I think our body is our soul. And if you don't have your body as a factor of creation, you don't have a soul." —Charles Olson)

North of Anna, apples, peaches, blueberries . . . sign in Cobden: "Drive slowly, this is an appleknocker town."

. . . entering Jackson County . . .

> the cusp of the seasons:
> frost in the shadows,
> the trees budding

. . . sharp hills, approaching Makanda . . .

Makanda: chief of the last tribe of Indians to inhabit this area

Makanda isolated, backwater, weird hybrid of southern hillbilly and western ghost, West Virginia and Nevada, a town at once made and destroyed by the railroad, Illinois Central, mainline of mid-America . . . the trashed buildings, the R.R. station converted to town offices, the Long Branch Billiard Hall . . . and Boomer

(just north of here: Bosky Dell, so named by a local preacher with a flair for the flowery)

> entering Giant City,
> massive sandstone cliffs,
> the barriers against which
>
> Labrador ice flowed.
> slowed,
> came to a halt . . .
>
> surfaces carved
> by the eddying
> icemelt

climbing to the top of a cliff, a narrow neck, across which the remains of a stone wall: a pound or trap, used by the Indians, as at Draper's Bluff and Stonefort, to snare buffalo

further, more bluffs, sheer and flat, and Devil's Stand Table:
". . . formed by differential erosion—the top layer is more resistant
than the layers below . . ." —the deep eroded, surfaces hard, intact

graffiti, scrawled on the rock: FREE LOVE (25¢ handling charge)

eastward, now, out of giant city—re-entering Union County—and
"leading upward to the crest of the big ridge that runs for more than
100 miles in Southern Illinois." . . . farms and orchards, rolling hills,
glorious spring sunshine . . . at the top of the ridge, a halt, get out of
the catalina:

> a bobwhite, a
> sarvis tree
> in full bloom

the illinois ozarks a relict area, surviving southern waters, ice from
the north

"GREEN WORLD SLOWLY DYING

by JOHN BARBOUR
AP Newsfeatures Writer

Now, man's shadow falls upon the wild flower.

In the 50 states, nearly 3,200 kinds of native higher
plants are endangered, threatened or recently extinct,
over 14 per cent of the nation's floral heritage.

. . . small inland islands of the continental United States,
locked in by quirks of nature, while man's heavy feet and his
penchant for precious blooms are not locked out.

One such island is Southern Illinois, short of where the
glaciers that wiped out thousands of plants stopped their
southern invasion. They call it 'the other Illinois' . . .

There is a flower that grows in Southern Illinois,
called French's shooting star. It is a small plant, nestling
under sandstone ledges, pretty little pink flowers looping

out of the green heart, accustomed over the centuries to the shadows of crack and crevice. Its existence is threatened.

The common shooting star, a larger cousin, grows nearby, in the sunlight, sometimes only feet away from its fragile relative. It grows in many places and in proliferation.

Yet the delicate flowers of French's are seen only in the cave-like recesses . . . It even has a different number of chromosomes . . ."

. . . limestone springs, with waters said to induce longevity . . .

"Turn right at lodge hall and Presbyterian Church. Turn left at stop sign. Cross I-57 and straight ahead through the village of Lick Creek. Keep straight ahead on gravel road."

. . . entering Jackson County . . .

"As the road curves left across a narrow bridge, Draper's Bluff looms up ahead. The Gulf of Mexico once washed up against this cliff and covered the ground you are traveling on."

"When you come to two trailers on the left look carefully for a standing rock on the face of the bluff. There is a hole about the size of your steering wheel on top of this rock out of which buzzards drink. You can see the white droppings on the rock from the road."

. . . a big depression, a buffalo wallow . . .

"Turn left at Cedar Grove Church sign a quarter of a mile on. Straight ahead another section is called Cedar Bluff. Turn right at little church. Watch on right for cemetery. Stop here and go inside. Note the little concrete markers that lie in a row down through the center marked 'in God i Trust.' This was an Indian cemetery before the coming of the white man. When pioneers began using this cemetery, descendants of the Indians thought there should be something to show that their relatives were buried here, so they made these concrete markers which you will notice is spelled with a small 'i' and placed in this row."

the high land, the bluff land east of Draper's Bluff, sparsely settled, miles and miles . . . as the little booklet says, "each family has to have their own tomcat!"

. . . topography and emanations, southern appalachians . . .

"NOTE: If you turn left at stop sign and go into village of Goreville, we recommend eating at the Dinner Bell Restaurant on the main street—very good food and not expensive. No restrooms here but Shell Station adjacent to this restaurant will be happy to let you use theirs."

so, while our catalina gorges ten bucks' worth of shell, we eschew the restrooms and enter the Dinner Bell

11:30 A.M., the place full saturday midday dinner, the country folk, very ozark, they all real southn . . . the food more like I expect on the road in the south, i.e., lousy

in re, every day is a progression: you begin with the land, rough & raw (the ozarks), then you tame it, make it produce (the prairies), then you make things (industrial north), and finally enjoy (chicago)

the progress of any day, from dawn to sunset, is a progression from the country to the city, from the frontier to the settlements, from the prairie, via the woods, to the cities. Daily, we reverse history

> "In seed time learn, in harvest teach,
> in Winter Enjoy"—Guy Davenport

the Dinner Bell offers Black Cow—35¢

Fern Clyffe State Park seems mostly a tourist, camping facility, little of natural glory, of which we already saw so much at Giant

City (the bluffs, the caves, the stone enclosures, stone formations), and just driving across the country, back and front . . . Draper's Bluff . . . the Indian cemetery

U.S. 45, between Tunnel Hill and Ozark, historical marker: the Ft. Massac-Kaskaskia Trail

. . . entering Williamson County . . .

"GOING STRONG AT 102

CREAL SPRINGS, Ill. (UPI)—'It makes me nervous when I'm not doing anything,' says Mrs. Anna G. Powell. So Mrs. Powell, who is observing her 102nd birthday today, turns out crocheted rugs and makes quilt tops by the dozen. She sells some of them and gives some away to family and friends. She's a veteran of 88 years at making quilt tops.

Mrs. Powell still lives in the same farm home with a son and daughter-in-law where she and her husband set-tled 73 years ago. He died in 1929. The home has no elec-tricity, is heated by a large coal stove in the living room, has no indoor plumbing and the refrigerator operates on kerosene."

Anna G. Powell, born March 29, 1873, birth year of Willa Cather . . . when Theodore Dreiser and Orville Wright were two, Edgar Lee Masters five, that other Wright, Frank Lloyd, a lad of six, Henry Ford ten, and the Boy Orator of the Prairies a schoolboy of thirteen . . . Emily Dickenson was forty-three, Herman Melville was fifty-four . . . as yet unborn: Gertrude Stein and Charles Ives (a year), Sherwood Anderson (three years), Carl Sandburg (five), Vachel Lindsay (six) . . . Thorsten Veblen was sixteen years old, Louis Sullivan seventeen . . . form follows function . . .

Creal Springs a particularly desolate village, the main street, a warm spring Saturday, nearly abandoned, block after block of brick and

glass and worn-wood storefronts, vacant . . . later I learn that this had been a booming resort, the days of the spas, late last century, people came from miles around for the healing springs . . the old brick hotel, pride of the village, gone . . .

park the catalina . . . nearby, a trashed garage, the young hoods creal springs hell's angels, tinkering with their hogs, the least likely leads to a centenarian . . . walk the empty blocks, all there is, nothing, nothing. . . edge of town, an open grocery, through the window a country woman, spinster-type, behind the counter, emily dickinson among the onions, this looks good

camera slung around my neck, news clipping in hand, I figure I'll be taken for a member of the fourth estate, and march in

one customer in the store, a lady, smartly dressed, pants suit, makeup, etc.—creal springs chic . . . I wait. . . then

"Can I he'p you?"

"Yes, I'm just passing through town, I have this clipping about this 102-year-old lady, Mrs. Anna Powell, I wonder if you know her, know where she lives . . . and do you think she'd like to receive callers?"

Conversation ensues, Spinster and Chic . . . both know about her, know where she lives, although Chic doesn't know her personally—which figures. Spinster avers she's friendly, would like to have callers.

Chic (she speaks very fast, though very southern—speed is sophistication): "If you want to wait just a few minutes, I'm driving right by there, I'll be glad to show you the way."

I, gratefully, patiently, "Thank you" . . . I step back, and wait . . . the slab of bacon is sliced.

Chic (nearly ready) "Where you from?"

I: "Massachusetts."

Chic: "You drive all the way out here just to see *her?*"

I: "Oh, no, I'm just passing through."

Chic (bacon and pocketbook in hand): "I was gonna say, you must be mighty hard up for news!"

keeping up with chic is no mean feat, she barrels down the highway at 70 M.P.H., catalina swerving in her slipstream

off the main highway, down a side road, and then to a sudden halt opposite a dirt road . . . chic and I both emerge
  "It's down there, you just keep going, you'll get to it."
  "Thank you! thank you very much!"
  Funny look on her face, she doesn't quite know how to deal with my gratitude: she knows she's done a Christian thing, to help me, but doesn't quite know why she did it, or why I'm doing what I'm doing . . . backs into car and barrels off

dirt road runs flat, disappears over ridge, and, as we cross, veers to the left . . . and there it is—of course—the one lone house, end of the road: . . . a gray box, unpainted, straight up and down

CAST OFF CHARACTERS

  Mrs. Anna G. Powell, age 102
  Floyd Powell, her son, age 71
  The daughter-in-law, Floyd's wife
  Mrs. Anna Powell's adopted daughter, contemporary of Floyd
  Leather-jacket Baptist, son of the adopted daughter

we drive up, step from car, wait for two men strolling toward us, up the path: Floyd and Leather-jacket, as it turns out, walking off their midday dinner, in the quiet midday sun, forsythia . . . we introduce ourselves (writer, photographer, clipping, etc., passing through), they take me for a reporter, but I get no sense that this either helps or hinders: we are, without pretension, welcome . . . Floyd is our host, and we are friends, family, folks . . . all so quickly and gently done

into the small living room, a dark box, the giant coal stove over-heating, for the spring weather

      (heat is a blessing!
      (cherish it!
      (lavish it!

after a little, from the kitchen, comes Mrs. Anna Powell, hobbling
with a cane, followed by Adopted Daughter, and Daughter-in-law

Floyd Powell: a tall, gentle, slender man, wears bib overalls, a large
birthmark on his handsome face, pale blue eyes, both distant and
warm.
Leather-jacket Baptist: pressed slacks, polished shoes, s/m jacket,
the modern generation, going a little to pot and jowl, friendly, but
not open like the others, he comes the closest to treating me like a
reporter . . . a stink about him of small town middle-American
YMCA . . . he is careful to let us know he's Baptist.
Mrs Anna G. Powell: sweetness and strength, both evident, and
almost isolate from one another . . . the will, the act of will, to live
beyond a hundred . . . wears a very good brown crepe dress, with a
pin at the neck: cotton stockings; dressy metal combs in her hair . . .
her skin is almost translucent, as though one looks through it, at the
skull . . .
Adopted Daughter: a plump, well-dressed, self-assured woman, a
little loud . . . might become patronizing or condescending, but
doesn't quite . . . nevertheless clearly of a different world . . . she's
from the city (Marion, Illinois).
Daughter-in-law: must be near seventy; but she has the figure of a
young girl . . . soft, heel-less slippers, soft cotton voile dress, belted
at the waistline . . . she is dainty, and throughout the visit holds her-
self in the shadows.

Mrs. Powell makes much of hobbling to her chair, easing into it,
I standing beside her, cramped in the little room, embarrassed,
camera at neck, in my odd role . . . conversation begins, moves easily

. . . the old lady's quilt tops and seat pads, little circles, her bag of
strips and cotton goods by her chair . . .

. . . the light all wrong for pictures, no place to move, and I haven't
the nerve to ask her to move . . . she tries to pose, a simpering little
smile, all wrong . . . later, I slither to the sofa, slump low, she forgets
me, and I catch her

twice—once by Floyd and once by his mother—we are told the story of the Adopted Daughter: she was born at the same time as Floyd, and her mother died in delivering her, so Mrs. Powell took her in

> Floyd: "She stole my titty, that's why I'm so puny and she is so healthy"—and in his soft Ozark intonations, 'healthy' could easily be 'hefty,' and may well have been, I'll never know.

> Mrs. Powell: "I held one to one titty, one to the other"— she tells this with gestures, lifting what there is.

she was born in ozark, moved in early life to creal springs, into a log cabin, remnants of which remain in the yard . . . "it was a big house, a big room, eighteen feet, with a little room attached" . . . later moved into the present home, which is 73 years old

age 97, broke her hip, developed pneumonia . . . the doctor said, well, this is it . . . recovered from pneumonia, the doctor adjusted, said, well, she'll never walk again . . . marched out of the hospital with a walker, got tired of that, threw it away, now gets around with a cane

sits and sews, to calm her nerves

and delicate dainty daughter-in-law does the hard work, cooking, canning, cleaning, hoeing (floyd, puny, uses the roto-tiller)

more talk about quilts, adopted daughter and daughter-in-law take nancy into the bedroom, to show off more of her work . . . crippled, hobbled anna can't stand it, springs from her chair, swinging her cane, it seems, like james cagney playing george m. cohan, beelines for the bedroom, opens boxes to show nancy her birthday gifts

leather jacket answers questions about her longevity . . . no, there is no record of it in the family, no others lived that long . . . perhaps it is her self-discipline, the way she organizes her life, she eats practically nothing, never has, even when she was younger

(daughter-in-law takes nancy into the kitchen, to show off the grand kerosene fridge . . . it cools things, and makes ice cubes . . . remains of large midday meal on the table, vegetable dishes, iced tea, cake, etc . . . must have been adopted and leather who did all the eating)

. . . time for departure . . .

(another couple arrives, friends, obnoxious, he's a part-time antique dealer, clearly trying to ingratiate himself; hoping for the acquisition of goodies, should 102 years seem to be enough)

I: "If one of these pictures turns out, I'll send you one, when I get home. Okay?"

. . . and here the sweetness comes out, the smile genuine, not simpering, as though she were tasting and enjoying a newly invented word:

"okay"

we are friends

outside, on the porch, floyd apologizes for the appearance of the house, the way it has "gone down"—120 acres, corn, and soybeans, not much of a living . . . more money, now, in strip mining

but inside, all neat, all organized . . . the work is daughter-in-law's, but the will is anna's

scene of parting, on the porch, floyd, leather jacket beside him, telling nancy, come back, any time, whenever you're by, you're always welcome . . . and in the doorway, behind the screen, in the shadows, daughter in-law

we drive off

it is the will of anna, ubiquitous and omniscient in that household, that has carried her into her second century, and has done a strange violence to her "children": she is a mixed virtue in their lives, her survival keeping them young, but unsettling them . . . in their seventies, they are still waiting, the arc of mortality, the luxury of aging, in limbo

puny floyd would like nothing better than to take a nice long nap in the shade of the apple tree . . . dainty, laboring daughter-in-law is forever in her twenties, in the shadows, patient, to be admitted to the family

when anna lets go . . . what happens?

back through creal springs, up to the main highway, illinois 13, four-lane, and into the modern little city of marion

>(east of here, on Hickory Hill, Gallatin County, the Old Slave House, built by John Crenshaw, 1834 . . . 12 X 12 sills, 4 X 12 floor joists)

>(Crenshaw captured runaways, chained, tortured, resold them, south . . . imported a buck nigger, Bob, known as a breeder, installed him in Uncle Bob's room, the breeding room, to engender blacks, for market at weaning)

>(Bob was born in Africa . . . entered Elgin State Hospital, 1940, age 105 . . . died 1949, 114 . . . was said to have fathered, at a rough guess, 300)

"RIDE THE STEAM TRAIN

ENJOY A FOURTEEN
MILE TRIP ON A
REAL OPERATING
ROARING 20S ERA
STEAM RAILROAD

CRAB ORCHARD & EGYPTIAN
RAILROAD

Depot located at
514 N. Market St., Marion Ill. 62959
Just off I-57 and Ill. Rts. 13 and 37
Plenty of Free Parking

GIFT SHOP   ICE CREAM PARLOR"

"WITH A PIERCING WHISTLE Old No. 5 comes steaming into the station at Marion, Illinois, with the engineer, Hugh Crane, at the throttle. A broad smile crosses his countenance as he completes his daily run. Marion, Illinois, has become the steam train attraction for tourists far and wide and is now completing its second year in operation."

"IN THE FALL OF 1972, the first item purchased was a 1911 vintage caboose. It was purchased from Elgin, Joliet and Eastern Railroad . . . Shortly after the locomotive was purchased from the Mid-Continent Railroad Museum in Wisconsin . . . It is a 50 ton Columbia type 2-4-2 and is the only one of that type in service today.

". . . successful in purchasing 5 Illinios Central Commuter cars constructed in the 1920s."

"May 28, 1973 was the inaugural run for the C.O. & Egyptian over a scenic 14-mile trip."

(on crab orchard creek,
a site,
for early
woodland indians)

"Pedestrians and motorists traveling through the area received a
great shock to see the train with steam billowing from the cylinders,
smoke from the stack and the whistle emitting a shrill shriek of days
gone by. Passengers on the train waved back. The feeling was great
and the trainmen were elated."

. . . chugging, jolting, rumbling, out through the ranch-type back
yards, into the country

    uncoupling,
        a triangle switchback,
        recoupling,
    chugging, jolting, rumbling, back into Marion

"AS ONE ENTERS THE OLD DEPOT many memories flood back
into the mind: Days of traveling across country in steam trains or
hearing the whistle toot and the conductor loudly shout 'All
Aboard'; going by the ticket office where countless thousands
of tickets have in all probability been sold, and entering into the
waiting room so common to all railroad depots; the old wooden
benches and pot-bellied stove in the center of the waiting room. All
is present and a wave of nostalgia creeps into one's thoughts as you
go through the room . . ."

"A gift shop has been set up in the depot. It is unique in that if offers
items that are all hand made by members of the Southern Illinois
Arts and Crafts Association . . . Current plans are under way at
present for the transforming of the front area at Market Street into
an old time soda fountain shop. It will be unique in that straw-back
train seats will form the booths as well as the waiting area, along
with old fashioned wire chairs and circular tables. Various flavors of
ice cream will be served along with soft drinks that will be drawn

from old fashioned barrel type containers. A player piano has been purchased and installed in one end of the area and many old-time piano tunes have been purchased on piano rolls."

sattidy nite at tony's steak house in marion. obviously the place where the local monied gentry dines . . . the accents, still southern, but all the talk is money, politics, money, business, money, florida, money . . . our slim, efficient waitress comes from a place called oneida, new york, misses it . . . at a side table, a gay couple—the marion kind?—elegant

the double bed at the marion courts motel has one of those magic fingers massaging assemblies, you put a quarter in the slot for a quarter hour . . . should the contraption ever require service, one should contact:

MAGIC FINGERS OF ILLINOIS

Log for Saturday, April 12:

Breakfast at The Manor House, Anna, Ill.
North on unnumbered road, and U.S. 51, and unnumbered road, to
   Makanda, and Giant City State Park
Unnumbered roads to Lick Creek (got lost, got good directions from a kid on a riding mower)
Unnumbered roads to Draper's Bluff, the old cemetery, and along the Ozark Ridge to Goreville
Ill. 37 to Ferne Clyffe State Park
Unnumbered road to Tunnel Hill
U.S. 45 to New Burnside
Ill. 166 to Creal Springs
Unnumbered (back!) roads to Powell residence, and back
Ill. 166 and 13 to Marion
Tracks of the Crab Orchard & Egyptian R.R. to unspecified destination,
   and back to Marion

SUNDAY, APRIL 13, 1975

breakfast at american farmer's table restaurant, next door to marion truck plaza and skelly's truck stop . . . a short stack, with blueberry syrup . . . gypsy fiddles on the ozark muzak, six ayem, the sabbath

back on 57, northbound, the catalina humming comfortably, mainlining it, on her familiar four-laner

just west of here: energy!

beginning to slip out of the egyptian hills, the land broadening, flattening

8:20 A.M.—Franklin County

sign: Chicago 314 miles

tooling along, musing, I recall Floyd Powell repeating the familiar Illinois story, from the pioneer days, when Shawneetown, on the Ohio, was the largest settlement, and a group of merchants and traders came down from the north, wanted to borrow money from the Shawneetown bankers to start a settlement at what is now Chicago—and the bankers turned them down, said that they didn't think a settlement in that remote place would ever amount to anything . . . and the sad ironic pleasure, the wistfulness in Floyd's eyes, as he told the story . . . the fear, distrust, and haughty envy of the great metropolis, in the shallows near the surfaces, of the downstater

the land still undulating gently, not yet the final flat

8:40 A.M.—Jefferson County (big egg producer, more than 250,000 laying hens, 1973)

holiday inn advertises viking restaurant . . . whatever happened to billy budd?

. . . sea gulls on rand lake . . .

junction with Ill. 15 and U.S. 460, and we're turning west—but east
of here:

1) pearls in the mussels at Mt. Carmel

2) albion, a perfect english settlement, a prairie parkland,
the little wabash and bon pas creek, "already stocked with
deer" . . . "its indented and irregular outline of wood, its
varied surface interspersed with clumps of oaks of
centuries' growth, its tall grass, with seed stalks from six
to ten feet high, like tall and slender weeds waving in a
gentle breeze, the whole presenting a magnificence of
park-scenery, complete from the hand of Nature . . ."

and

3) "In the uncompromising bake of the southern Illinois
sun, the cannabis resin is rising in Kenneth M. Kays'
marijuana patch a few miles from Fairfield. But Kenny
Kays no longer limps through the field, cutting the
plants with a scythe, leaning for support at every swipe
on his good leg, the one he didn't lose in Vietnam.

Kays, Fairfield's most decorated war hero, who glared
hatred at Richard M. Nixon last October as the President
slipped the Medal of Honor over Kays' long hair and
around his neck, has been sent to a state mental hospital.

Neither his father, who operated a greenhouse in this
prosperous farming community of about 6,000 nor any-
body else here seemed to know quite what to do about
Kenny Kays. Three and one-half years ago he came back
from Vietnam, moved into a trailer in his father's back-
yard and began playing havoc with Fairfield's insular
mores. He let his dark blond hair and beard grow full,
smoked marijuana openly and, one local official told me,
'was hanging around with 14-year-old girls.'

For the longest time people just looked the other way, figuring 'the boy would get over it.' After all, nobody else in the history of Fairfield had ever had his leg blown off above the knee in combat and then proceeded to wrap a tourniquet around his thigh and continue to crawl through heavy fire, dragging wounded soldiers back to safety, shielding them with his body.

But, in early April of this year, Sheriff Thomas Cannon Jr. moved in and arrested Kays in his father's greenhouse, where Kenny was growing marijuana. When the sheriff walked in, Kays lit a joint.

'I was just growing it for my own use,' Kays told the sheriff. 'What business is it of anybody else?'

When he spoke, which was seldom, Kays would say that he was a student of Taoism and that marijuana was part of his search for inner truth and peace. There was a trial, and Kays told the judge that he was going to keep on growing pot, keep on fighting for his freedom. He was put on probation.

Kays was true to his word, and a few weeks later he was picked up again in the greenhouse with a couple of dozen plants that were coming along nicely. So he moved the operation to a field his father owned.

On Memorial Day, still out on bond for the second marijuana charge, Kays borrowed his father's car and screamed through town at 60 miles an hour, blowing his horn and running red lights and stop signs. He drove right by the Wayne County Courthouse, where the usual veterans' hoopla was going on. When he was picked up later by the sheriff, he said, 'I wanted to wake the dead.'

'He was very conscious of his body, of staying in shape,' said a man who had know him in high school. 'I figure the loss of a leg was more than he could bear.'"

(from "Bringing it all back Home" by Harper Barnes, NEW TIMES, August 9, 1979)

4) Feb. 19, 1888, a tornado touched down, Mt. Vernon . . .
18 dead, 54 injured

15 and 460 to ashley (8 miles short of beaucoup, where john flack
built boucoup bridge), then north on 51 to richview, and driving all
around this procumbent community, striving to find "the elevated
site of what is now called Old Town, or Old Richview, about half
a mile from the station, and the very beautiful view of the
surrounding country in all directions."

(george rogers clark marched, february, 1779, kaskaskia to vincennes,
the prairies covered with icy waters . . . the land without relief)

(northern boundary of the mississippi company, 1763, festus to
vincennes)

odin, for the norse god, and irvington, for washington irving . . . if
these places were settled today, what names, what burrs, would
attach to them?

. . . entering marion county . . .

driving into centralia: "Well-advertised as the 'Gateway to Egypt,'
Centralia pushes the claim by embellishing the facades of several of
its business houses with a variety of Egyptian motifs." (this from
the state guide, published 1939) . . . so we drive all around this
uncentered settlement, pursuing egyptian facades, and find nothing
. . . downtown quiet, the sabbath, the good burghers spiffed
for church . . . try around the railroad station, a good bet for relict
architecture . . . nothing . . . once more through the business blocks,
and nancy says, "try that one": a left turn and there it is, the news-
paper building, the Centralia Sentinel (est. 1863): doorways and
friezes, cleopatras and pharaohs

fun prairie: between sandoval and odin, the b.a.c. hollywood drive
in: hillbilly hooker & wicked wicked

(west, at breese, the santa fe bottoms, the prince of wales lost, 1860)

driving east on u.s. 50, paralleling the b & o rr, and the old vincennes trace

    (the limits of civilization:

    (north of here, kickapoo, potawatomi,
    (ottawa, chippewa,
    (sauk, fox & winnebago

    (massacres!

        (the stroke
        (of the relentless
        (tomahawk

robbins restaurant, salem, home of the great commoner—the food couldn't be plainer—and that great gumbo of ozark inflection has flattened out, the accents now unspecific

the sunday faces in public places . . . my god, we can't be as awful as we look!

as the land flattens, the restaurants are increasingly difficult to write about: no color, no flavor, they can't even be bad . . . just sufficient

the lady at the bryan museum, filling in for the man who usually takes care of the place . . . a widow lady: "it's sad to live alone" . . . let's us go upstairs (against regulations) to see the bare room where he was born . . . we look into the back rooms, kitchens, etc . . . "don't go to chicago," she says; "don't go to chicago!"

in the museum, the table on which bryan stood as a young boy, delivering declamation to his playmates

a bimetallist and populist . . . along with 'sockless' jerry simpson, 'bloody bridles' waite, 'pitchfork teen' tillman, mary elizabeth 'raise less corn and more hell' lease, 'cyclone' davis, and charles s. hampton from petoskey, 'the foghorn of the skillajalee'

bryan: 'an irresponsible, unregulated, ignorant, prejudiced, pathetically honest and enthusiastic crank'—the new york times

> (as an old man, with diabetes, he went on a water diet, requiring frequent trips to the lavatory—'his habit of leaving the door open was not appreciated by fastidious reporters')

'Mary, I have had a strange experience. Last night I found that I had power over the audience. I could move them as I chose. I have more than usual power as a speaker. I know it, God grant I may use it wisely.'

> (late in life his voice was recorded at the rca laboratories in hollywood, and the engineer exclaimed, 'Look at that meter! Look at that voice! Why, it has absolutely no bass tones. We have recorded thousands of voices, but never a voice like this.'

once, out in the sticks to give a stump speech, he could find no platform or stump to mount, so he mounted a manure spreader: 'this is the first time I've spoken from a republican platform.'

'we simply say to the east, take your hands out of our pockets and keep them out'

'living near him,' observed willa cather, 'is like living near niagara. the almighty, every-renewed force of the man drives one to distraction'

BRYAN'S SONG

'Temperance! The infirm & aged with tottering steps and locks whitened by the snows of many winters, the man, the woman, the youth, the maiden and the children, whose happy faces and joyous smiles make earth a heaven,—all know the meaning of this word and acknowledge its importance.

The saloon is open all the time: from early morn till late at night words of welcome are written above its doors. The evil ones never rest, wickedness never tires: vice never sleeps.

Strong drink weakens the body & poisons the blood.

... his eyes will become blood-shot ... a beautiful red blossom will adorn his nose ... He reels, staggers, falls ... the serpent that was in the cup sends forth its blood

They throng around him, they creep along his limbs, hide in the covers of the bed and from the very posts and chandeliers hang & hiss & thrust forth their forked tongues.

Poe . . . whose heart gathered its inspiration from sighing winds . . . died in a drunken debauch.

What so near approaches heaven as a happy home? . . . How different is the family upon which the blighting hand of intemperance has been laid?

. . . to break the heart is as heinous an offense as to bruise the body or crush the skull.

Intemperance! when I think how it . . . fills with sadness faces once wreathed in smiles, how it takes from the families food & clothes and fire and builds with the results of honest toil, breweries and saloons . . .

. . . caresses harden into blows and words of love change to curses upon his lips.

. . . an atmosphere of filth & vice that would contaminate an angel . . .

I saw the effects of liquor in my native town . . . I saw the effects of it in Chicago . . . that great city where are gathered the representatives of every nation, in that city of marvelous growth & gigantic enterprises where industry & genius combine to excite the wonder of the world, in that city where population surges to & fro like the waves of a mighty sea lashed to a fury by the winds of avarice & ambition, there I saw the effects of intemperance. Within a stone's throw of its marble palaces are haunts of infamy and vice . . .

> . . . but this is not a contest between persons.
> The humblest citizen in all the land
> when clad in the armor of a righteous cause,
> is stronger than all the hosts of error.

> we do not come as agressors.
> . . . we are fighting in the defense of our homes,
> our families, and posterity.
> We have petitioned,

and our petitions have been scorned;
we have entreated,
and our entreaties have been disregarded;
we have begged,
and they have evaded us when our calamity came.
We beg no longer;
we entreat no longer;
we petition no more.

We defy them!

We go forth confident that we shall win.

there is not a spot of ground
upon which the enemy will dare to challenge . . .

. . . the great cities
rest upon our broad and fertile prairies.
Burn down your cities and leave our farms,
and your cities will spring up again
as if by magic;
but destroy our farms
and the grass will grow in the streets
of every city in the country.
YOU SHALL NOT PRESS DOWN
UPON THE BROW OF LABOR
THE CROWN OF THORNS,
YOU SHALL NOT CRUCIFY MANKIND
UPON A CROSS OF GOLD!

in bryan memorial park, the gutzon borglum statue . . . as I take a
picture a little boy, 4th-grader, rides his bike up to nancy, in the car:
"once someone climbed all the way to the top of the statue, and it
has a hole in the top of its head"

near salem is mauvais terre creek, pronounced movie star

north from salem, the land is prairie, the end of the ozarks

from here to chicago, 57 parallels precisely the main line of the i.c.

but before 57, before the i.c., early settlement hugged the rivers and
the lake . . . it was not until construction of the i.c.—a shaft pene-
trating the heart of the arrowhead—that these most fertile prairie
lands were released

a federal land grant, for construction of the rr: 2,595,000 acres . . . "to
build a railroad equal in all respects to the railroad running between
Boston and Albany"

the main line . . . and later, the connectors (vertebrae);

> The St. Louis, Vandalia, and Terre Haute
> The Springfield and Illinois Southern
> The Belleville and Southern Illinois
> The Toledo, Wabash, and Western
> The Indianapolis, Bloomington, and Western
> The Toledo, Peoria, and Warsaw
> Toledo, Peoria, and Western
> The Gilman, Clinton, and Springfield
> The Ohio and Mississippi
> The Indianapolis and St. Louis
> The Cairo and Vincennes
> The Cairo and St. Louis
> The Chicago, Pekin, and Southwestern
> The Bloomington and Ohio
> The Decatur, Sullivan, and Mattoon

in the winter wheat lands: farina

laclede: for pierre liqueste laclede, early french merchant and trader
. . . the town was originally called *dismal*

. . . entering effingham county—heavy in cattle, and the heaviest in
hogs, on all 57 . . .

edgewood: ah yes, at the edge of the wood!

(u.s. 40, following the old national road, all the way out from
potomac country, to terminate, 1850, at vandalia on the kaskaskia)

beginning at effingham, a sense of heavier population centers . . .
effingham the first small city, as opposed to big towns

. . . slipping briefly through a corner of cumberland county . . .

neoga: in iroquois, the place of the diety

2:40 P.M.—coles county

at mattoon, the first shit black gold black rich black earth! . . . the
weather good, the farmers out, even on sunday, preparing

mattoon to kankakee: the great cash grain region, one of the
richest, most completely cultivated farming areas of the world

it was after the civil war that the flat, water-bearing prairie, the
stagnant waters in the hollows, the joint-grass tangled in the
sloughs, were drained . . . mile upon mile of tile installed, bearing
the waters secretly, beneath the feet of the corn, barely subsurface
. . . the bluestem was gone, the land fenced with sod, thorn hedge,
osage orange, and, finally, down from de kalb, bob wire

ten thousand mile of ditch, one hundred fifty thousand mile of tile

> float an issue
> to float a dredge boat
> to dredge a ditch,

> lift the land above the water . . .

> float an issue
> to build the road,

move the grain

to bonded tie and rail

flax, mustard seed, cotton, and tobacco . . . hemp, the castor bean,
silkworms, and the mulberry tree . . . broom corn, corn, and, finally,
the hybrids:
>   will grow off vigorously when planted early
>   stoutly rooted, will resist both summer drought and
>   summer storms
>   neither rotten corn nor chaffy ears
>   (inbred cold-resistant pure-line strains)
>   a deep root system, a stiff stalk
>   seed of a high luster, naturally burnished

"an endless corn field which gave up its last bit of natural nutrition
in 1947 and has since been chemically reconstituted"

>   out here, everything is horizontal, running flat with earth
>   and horizon, never vertical, downward or upward—
>   the only exception being the grain elevators, lifting,
>   elevating the produce of the soil, to the hands of god. But
>   other than this, nothing reaches upward, or goes down
>   into the earth, deeper than the level-moving blade of
>   the plow.

>   so powerful is this discipline of the flat, the level, that
>   graves—downward excavations—may not be dug, and
>   there are no cemeteries, the bodies of the dead, lightened
>   by the release from the burdens of life, are cast into the
>   constantly sweeping winds and blown into obscurity,
>   beyond the eastern horizon . . .

>   but occasionally they circumnavigate the earth and come
>   sweeping in again from the west, to the point of origin:

a young man, standing alone in the open prairie, was recently decapitated by the body of his father, the body blown in from the edge of land and sky, the crotch of the corpse neatly clipping, between shoulder and chin, the head of the young aspirant . . .

lincoln log cabin state park: something all wrong about this, a kind of image of history, a staging of it, a presentation—no doubt what the tourists want . . . the cabin itself is a fake, the original having been somehow lost after shipment to chicago (1892) . . . present structure and furnishings (1929) are reconstituted

very little of lincoln here, goose nest prairie . . . abe has been tiled and drained

charleston: eastern illinois university, a sunny sunday, high-rise dorms on the prairie, bare-chested guys, sharp-breasted chicks, high-rise (you could cut yourself on 'em), frisbees, softball, energy! vitality!

yesterday, from ozark, mrs. anna g. powell, 102, and her young (71) son floyd . . . today: how fast can you go, from what to where may 26, 1917, a tornado touched down . . . 101 dead, 638 injured

on the tv at the holiday inn: mayor daley of chicago is scheduled to appear tomorrow as a witness before a congressional committee on gun control: he wants to outlaw saturday night specials

the neon lavender chairs, on blinding chrome frames and rollers, in the holiday inn dining room, attain an exponential increase of ugliness beyond possibility of camp parody

but the folks in the dining room—god damn, they're folks again— the university people go elsewhere, the *folks* go to the holiday inn

the chic soft gray patina, still gracing my chippewa brogans, is illinois gumbo from the marion truck plaza we're in civilized country: motelevision offers net

from "holiday inn companion, your inroom magazine, april-may 1975/one dollar":

> "it is well known that when you do anything, unless you understand its actual circumstances, its nature and its relations to other things, you will not know the laws governing it, or know how to do it, or be able to do it well"

> —mao tse-tung

Log for Sunday, April 13:

Breakfast at American Farmer's Table, Marion
North on I-57 to Mt. Vernon
West on Ill. 15 to U.S. 51
North on U.S. 51 to Centralia and Sandoval
East on U.S. 50 to Salem
North on Ill. 37 to Edgewood
North on I-57 to Effingham
North on U.S. 45 to Neoga
North on I-57 to Mattoon
East on Ill. 16 to unnumbered road
Around corners on unnumbered roads to Lincoln Log Cabin
    State Park
North on unnumbered road to Charleston
West on Ill. 16 to (bless us!) Holiday Inn

MONDAY, APRIL 14, 1975

R A I N

before breakfast the thought of plunging my rump into that
dayglow magenta at six ayem, and swiveling . . .

well, the chairs are chrome and blue, but a different dining
room . . . "british isle" breakfast . . . and no muzak, I feel
deprived, an emptiness . . .

seem to be a little weary today, maybe it was the coupling at
three ayem

rain makes the brown earth, newly plowed and disked
absolutely black

7:55 A.M.—douglas county

this massive agribusiness of mid-illinois bears no relation
whatever to ozark home-industry farming

arcola: from the italian village of arcole, where napoleon once
gained a victory

arcola is the first little town we have visited in this farm-rich
central area that doesn't seem to have the depressing poverty,
the shattered but still standing architecture of the little towns
of the south

there's a town near here, too small to show on the map, called
gallon . . . used to be bourbon switch

according to the a.a.a. tour book, the place to see is rockhome
gardens, "5 miles west following signs . . . an interesting array of
rockwork and flower gardens . . . authentic amish house and school"
. . . bloody camera is nonfunctional here, but it's just as well . . .
rockhome is campy amish

approaching arthur, a trading center for the amish (original colony settled 1864): the land is lush, houses and farm building immaculate, as though painted this morning . . . a rainy day, no work in the fields, many of the families riding to arthur, the austere black buggies sporting chrome-and-glass rearview mirrors, and orange reflectors

names on the mailboxes: yoder, schrock, kaufman, hilgenberg

tuscola: an appalachian word for—ah, yes!—flat plain

(brief stop here, to replenish supplies of bottled goods)

graffiti in the men's room of the rest area on the south side of u.s. 36, east of camargo: "if you want to stick your cock up my ass, come out and wave at the guy in the torino"

no torino in sight

. . . entering edger county . . .

approaching metcalf, illinois, sign on the highway:

METCALF CENTENNIAL
1874-1974

god damn
drive around the town a little, a stop in at the post office . . . beautiful old interior, too dark to photograph . . . approach the lady behind the grill work (I later find out this is emileen grafton, became acting postmaster june 1, 1944, was appointed postmaster following the retirement of pearl malone) . . . identify myself, say I'm just passing through, I'd like to know how the town got its name, is there anyone around who knows town history, etc. . . . emileen gets a sly look in her country eye, says, "well, I don't know about that, but I'll sell you a copy of our centennial book for a dollar" . . . and she's quickly embarrassed, doesn't want me to think she'd hassle me, almost refuses to take my dollar

later, outside, as I'm focusing on the building, she hangs
back from the doorway, doesn't want to spoil the picture

metcalf, illinois:

Mr. John A. Melcalfe, spelled
Metcalfe, was born in Shelby Co.,
Kentucky, on July 23, 1811, and came
with his parents to this state on
October 16, 1828

Mr. Metcalfe was the
president of the village,
postmaster, deputy sheriff
and constable of the village.

The Metcalfe farm consisted of
three hundred and twenty acres. No
one seems to know when the spell-
ing of Metcalfe was changed to
Metcalf.

Metcalf was incor-
porated in 1885.

Metcalf owes its existence to the railroad passing through the township in 1872.

The Ocean to Ocean Pikes Peak Highway came to the north edge of Metcalf about 1912. This highway extended from New York to San Francisco.

Around 1917, a concrete elevator was built by the farmers and known as the Farmers Elevator Company, about the time World War I broke out and men were called to duty in the Armed Forces and the women were hired to finish the 100 foot high elevator, at 75 cents an hour.

Mrs. Ella Hackett operated a beauty shop at her home in the north part of Metcalf in about 1930. She started hairdressing, with no running water . . .

Sam Miller and wife, Mollie, had a music career. Sam played the violin and was an accomplished violinist, and Molly accompanied him on the piano (chorded). In 1906, they joined the Mainard and Newport moving picture show and traveled through the south furnishing the music.

In the early 1900s E. E. Lewis aided Dr. McCloud of Ridgefarm in research for the curing of cancer. Mr. Lewis moved to Ridgefarm in Jaunary 1904 to devote his entire time to the curing of cancers. He will be associated with Dr. McCloud, under the name of Illinois Cancer Cure Co.

There were two depots at first in the early 1880s made from boxcars, but in January, 1904, the village council compelled the Clover Leaf and CH&D to erect new depots here, as these were almost indecent.

Mr. Roy White, born in Metcalf, Illinois, in the late 1890s was under the direction of Mr. George Boswell, as a telegraph operatior in the 1900s. He was made president of the Baltimore and Ohio Railroad and is now listed in the "Who's Who of America" in Washington, D.C.

John Hanley, owner, and Pete Leath, Keeper, of Segram and Dock, Percheron stallions, place of breeding in 1906 was at the barn in Metcalf, Illinois. Terms: $12.50

On February 3, 1910, the first moving picture show was given in the hall over Mark Hildreth's store, which had been braced and strengthened for this purpose by Al Douglas, who is owner of this great enterprise.

In 1913 B. F. Daugherty was in the poultry business. He raised Rose Combed Rhode Island Reds . . .

Frank Barth—hardware store & a funeral director . . .

In 1912 a Mr. Hickman, a photographer who had been in Metcalf a number of times, purchased the old photographer car, which stood on the south side of the square in Chrisman for a number of years. He had it moved to the vacant lot south of the bank where it was fixed for a gallery.

Buck was never known to carry a gun. His "billy club" was sufficient to persuade the rowdy, or disturber of the peace that he meant business. His calm persuasions were usually sufficient to get the "gun toter" to "turn in" his gun while in town.

Lodges
K and P—1900
Yeoman—1910
Modern Woodman
Royal Neighbors
Pythian Sisters
Odd Fellows

In 1913 the Smith Sisters had a millinery shop.

Servicemen, Jerry Turner and Bruce Jones write thank-you letters to Mrs. J. W. Whitehead at Metcalf thanking the Red Cross members for the sweaters knitted. Bruce Jones wrote "I enlisted in the Aviation Corps last August . . . It is a branch of the service. They are thinking that this branch of service is going to be a success and they are depending on us to win the war. I think we will do our share. It sure is wonderful what they can do with air planes."

The Metcalf Red Cross has been busy and on the job all the time since the last week in August and in that time they have knitted 100 pairs of socks besides sweaters, wristlets and helmets. Mrs. S. H. Honn is considered the champion knitter of them all, for she has knitted 21 pairs of socks all by herself.

Metcalf is always willing to do its share.

September 6, 1918: Pat Breen, a merchant of Metcalf, was the guest of honor at a banquet given in Terre Haute Tuesday evening by the International Harvester Company. Mr. Breen has sold more of the company's implements than any other salesman in Illinois, Indiana or Ohio.

Dr. Hall of Charleston and a traveling dentist also made frequent visits to the village. The latter advertised his presence and profession by wearing a jacket with teeth sewed in polkadot arrangements all over it.

1917—"Jeff Nichols from near Mulberry Grove was trading with our merchants Tuesday and related a peculiar circumstance which happened at his home. He was plowing in the low lands on his place and turned up a petrified fish of the perch species about 30 inches long. When it came in contact with the air the fish crumbled very easily. While digging a well on his place he also dug up a huge log at a depth of twenty feet."

From 1949-1968 the school in Metcalf was a consolidated district and the high school was named Young America.

At the present time we support a missionary in Africa and help the Christian hour on radio Sunday mornings at 12:30.

Dorothy Southard does home mission work in Beauty, Kentucky . . .

Lottie Tresner Norton started submitting her writing for publication in 1955. Her first acceptance was on February 8, 1956. It was a story called "Peter's Answered Prayer," published in a Sunday School paper called—Stories for Children, Anderson, Indiana. She has had 65 items accepted for publication, including 43 stories, 5 articles, 5 plays and 12 poems . . . Her book, *The Big Insect Mystery* was published in 1958 by the Greenwich Book Publications of New York.

Ralph Gaines, who resided north of town, invented and patented a "Baby Jumper," which promised to revolutionize the raising of babies . . .

Frantz L. Kelley invented a rafter cutting jig, for which he filed for a patent in December 1958 and received the patent in August 1961.

TIDBITS

Robert Smith shipped the first new wheat in 1881.

In October 1889 hog cholera was raging in the vicinity of Metcalf.

A fish peddler in Metcalf almost got arrested until he produced a county license in 1908.

In 1908 the Metcalf ball team played 14 games and won all but three.

VILLAGE ORDINANCES

PUBLIC FUNERALS. It shall be unlawful to hold a public funeral for any person who has died of cholera, small pox, diptheria or scarlet fever.

DISORDERLY HOUSE. Whoever shall keep a common, ill-governed and disorderly house, to the encouragement of idleness, gaming, drinking, fornication or other misbehavior, shall be fined not exceeding two hundred dollars.

Ed Hildreth, lately re-christened as the isralite merchant of Metcalf, has ventured forth with a $2200 eight cylinder Chrysler—a real foxy boat . . .

A big corn show, a hog waddle, and a turkey trot.

driving again, back toward 57 . . . metcalf was the tip of a long rib

. . . entering champaign county, second only to iroquois in corn and soybeans . . .
broadlands and longview: what inspirational names!

pesotum: an indian who took part in the chicago massacre, august 15, 1812

. . . 40° parallel, north latitude . . .

tolono: last stop in illinois for abe, on his way to washington

a herd of deer at maroa, 1851

savoy from the french, *la savoie,* in compliment to the princess clothilde, wife to prince napoleon

lunch at ho-jo's in champaign: frozen flounder with a slab of velveeta on a pudgy bun

1:55 P.M.: entering ford county, and, soon after, iroquois coun-
ty, the greatest agricultural county of them all: 263 thousand
acres in corn, 238 thousand in soy beans, 41 thousand head of
cattle, 53 thousand hogs, and 440 thousand laying hens (1973
figures)

illinois:
    state flower: butterfly violet
    state bird: cardinal
    state tree: bur oak

loda: from lotha, a river in the north of scotland . . . or a gallic
god, equivalent to scandinavian odin

drive to cissna park, looking for more amish, or, more properly,
new amish, and find not a trace

onarga: iroquois, "place of rocky hills" . . . huh?????

gilman, birthplace of james robert mann (1856-1922), author of
the mann act: transporting state lines across immoral women,
for purposes
ashkum: iroquois, "more and more" (!)

I think we will avoid driving out to cullom and a visit to hahn
industries, "one of the Nation's largest manufacturers of
ornamental concrete figurines . . . Tours may be arranged"

l'erable: the maple

  . . . entering kankakee county . . .

chebanse "little duck," a pottawatoni chief

just south of kankakee, a gentle oh so gentle rise of land,
thrusting suddenly out of the prairie . . . the valparaiso
moraine?

kankakee, theakiki, kyankeakee, and the holiday inn: I am semi-reclined in my barca lounger, jim beam at hand, head back, feet up notebook propped in what's left of my lap . . . a-h-h-h-h!

this close to chicago, the quality of the clientele in the dining room is impossible to define: business men, fat local ladies, a priest, hippies, a couple of aging good ole boys

decor here is fake antique, fake some sort of classic style, easier to take than the pustulous moderne of holiday inn, charleston

the motels at kankakee (holiday inn, ramada) are in the middle of the industrial-commercial neighborhood, no attempt to create a sympathetic environment . . . I think the customers like this

past out, finally, on the barca lounger, after a steam bath, beam at hand, watching the tube, cubs 4, pirates 2, fifth inning . . . zonk

---

Log for Monday, April 14:

    Breakfast at Holiday Inn, Charleston
    West on Ill. 16 to I-57
    North on I-57 to Arcola
    West on unnumbered roads to Arthur
    North on unnumbered road to U.S. 36
    East on U.S. 36 to Metcalf
    West on U.S. 36 to Ill. 49
    North on Ill. 49 to Allerton
    West on unnumbered roads to Pesotum
    North on U.S. 45 to unnumbered road to I-57
    North on I-57 to Ill. 10
    East on Ill. 10 to Champaign
    West on Ill. 10 to I-57

North on I-57 to Ill. 9
East on Ill. 9 to Paxton
North on U.S. 45 to Loda
East on unnumbered road to Ill. 49
North on Ill. 49 to Cissna Park
West on unnumbered road to Buckley
North on U.S. 45 to Ashkum
West on Ill. 116 to I-57
North on I-57 to Kankakee

TUESDAY, APRIL 15, 1975

yep, we're in the no'th again, breakfast waitresses are friendly but, as
with the outdoor air, the softness is gone . . . depending on whether
you like it or not—atmosphere and accent—it's crisp or harsh

chased around a good bit this morning, through bourbonnais and
back, then out again, looking for kankakee river state park (its
misplaced on the a.a.a. map, they have it east of the deselm road,
and we found it west)

the park open, but almost abandoned, a gray weekday morning,
early spring, the ranger surprised to see us

the kankakee river, an impressive flow at this time of year, cutting
through the morainal lands bordering the prairie, with rock creek
cutting into it from the north, through a little canyon, (like that
other rock creek, flowing into the potomac) . . . I stood on a head-
land, facing upstream, awaiting a flotilla of canoes . . .

> "The party, now numbering thirty-three, embarked in
> eight canoes on December 1 and ascended the river in
> search of a portage to the kankakee. When reached, this
> river was hardly differentiated from the mainland, but
> soon the scene changed, the explorers were floating
> between banks lined with trees which obscured the view
> of the broad prairies beyond. Even in midwinter, Illinois
> seemed to La Salle, as it had to Joliet, a land of great
> promise . . ."

. . . but the canoes never appeared . . .

. . . they must have passed . . .

manteno: a corruption of manitou, great spirit

. . . entering will county: heavy in oats—and 538 thousand laying
hens . . . jesus!

peotone: pottawatomie, "bring" or "come here"

monee: originally *mary,* for the wife of an indian trader the french pronounced this *mah-ree,* and the pottawatomies, having no r sound in their dialect, made it *mau-nee* or *mo-nee*

manteno, peotone, monee, although still little towns, are getting grubby . . . not so much poverty, even less than down state, but without flavor

back on 57, now, in full flood toward the city

. . . entering cook county: 26 thousand acres in soybeans, 6 thousand hogs, 126 thousand laying hens

off to the west somewhere, a 60 foot rise, an indian mound, mount joliet

can't even turn my head to look for blue island . . .

> ("of german and italian extraction
> ("a glacial ridge
> ("rising like an island from the marshland
> ("the blue haze that cloaked its dense woods

. . . the traffic too heavy, jesus, keep your eyes on the road!

approaching the city, the highway infested with cops, everybody suddenly legal, me included

chicago:

> 1849, a few streets paved with planking laid on marshy ground, a few feet above river level, the planks rotting snapping under the weight of horses or even pedestrians, the ends flying up to slap you in the face . . . sand and cobblestones followed, and vanished in the mud . . . finally, 1855, sand was dredged from the river, to raise the streets, and the raw acreage between them, 12

feet ... the streets became huge ramps, running to second-story windows, sidewalks climbed and dipped like roller coasters

First spring sighting of birds in Lincoln Park:

Sparrow Hawk: March 24, 1901
 (Gunner McPadden
Nighthawk: May 10, 1888
 (Big Six Smith
Ruby-throated Hummingbird: May 10, 1898
 (Dingbat Oberta
Wood Pewee: April 27, 1897
 (Yankee Schwartz
Least Flycatcher: April 30, 1898
 (Mike de Pike Heitler (ran a whorehouse in Blue Island)
Bronzed Grackle: March 29, 1897
 (Limpy Cleaver
Lincoln Sparrow: May 10, 1900
 (Blind John Condon
Swamp Sparrow: March 11, 1902 (unusually early)
 (Bathhouse John Coughlin
Dickcissel: May 16, 1901
 (Jew kid Grabiner
Scarlet Tanager: May 14, 1898
 (Schemer Drucci
Purple Martin: April 29, 1901
 (Mitters Foley
Cedar Waxwing: March 27, 1899 (unusually early)
 (Potatoes Kaufman
Loggerhead Shrike: March 14, 1898
 (Hinky Dink Kenna
Blue-headed Vireo: May 17, 1900
 (KIondike Myles
 Northern Parula Warbler: May 11, 1898
 (Hot Stove Jimmy Quinn
 Golden-crowned Kinglet: March 14, 1898
 (Hymie and Izzy

chicago

as illinois goes in threes—south, central, and north—ozarks,
bread basket, industry—so chicago at least as seen from 57:
1) the grubby nothing little outskirt towns
2) the endless prairie-spread, residential and industrial
3) downtown, intensity, rush

ahead of us, in the smoggy haze, the lakeshore skyline . . . and
beyond (it's there, I know it's there, as the rivers have been at our
backs all these days) ahead of us, now: the lake

suddenly a flood of traffic, median and shoulder concrete walls,
combustion compressed: approaching the world's busiest express-
way: the dan ryan

10:45 A.M., sign on right:

```
┌─────────────────────────────┐
│                             │
│      INTERSTATE             │
│                             │
│      ILLINOIS               │
│                             │
│        57                   │
│                             │
│      ENDS HERE              │
│                             │
└─────────────────────────────┘
```

Log for Tuesday, April 15:

Breakfast at Holiday Inn, Kankakee (poached eggs on toasted
    English muffins, very good)
West on Ill. 102, hunting for Kankakee River State Park,
    back to Bourbonnais, then out again, finally finding it
North on unnumbered road to Deselm
East on unnumbered road to Manteno
North on Ill. 50 to Monee
West on connector to I-57

North on I-57 to junction U.S. 30
East on U.S. 30 to McDonalds, for coffee!
West on U.S. 30 to junction I-57
North on I-57 to terminus, junction I-94
North on I-94 to junction Ill. 194
West on Ill. 194 to junction Ill. 594
West on Ill. 594 to O'Hare

Bibliography

ONE

Anonymous. "Insanity: My Own Case." *American Journal of Insanity*, 13:25-36.

Anonymous. (E. Thelmar). *The Maniac*. London, 1932.

Bateson, Gregory, editor. *Perceval's Narrative*. Stanford, Calif., 1961.

Beers, Clifford. *A Mind that Found Itself*. New York, N.Y. 1948.

Benzinger, Barbara F. *The Prison of My Mind*. New York, N.Y., 1969.

Boisen, Anton. *Out of the Depths*. New York, N.Y., 1960.

Bryan, E. "A Study of Forty Cases Exhibiting Neologisms." *American Journal of Psychiatry*, 13: 579-95.

Collins, William J. *Out of the Depths*. New York, N.Y., 1971.

Davidson, D. *Remembrances of a Religio-Maniac*. Stratford-on-Avon, England, 1912.

Graves, Alonzo. *The Eclipse of a Mind*. New York, N.Y., 1942.

Hackett, Paul. *The Cardboard Giants*. New York, N.Y. 1952.

Haslam, John. *Observations on Madness and Melancholy*. London, 1809.

Haslam, John. *Illustrations of Madness*. London, 1810.

Hillyer, Jane. *Reluctantly Told*. New York, N.Y., 1926.

Jayson, L.M. *Mania*. New York, N.Y. 1937.

Kaplan, Bert, editor. *The Inner World of Mental Illness*. New York, N.Y., 1972.

Karinthy, F. *A Journey Round My Skull*. London, 1939.

Landis, Carney. *Varieties of Psychopathological Experience*. New York, N.Y., 1972.

Leonard, W.E. *The Locomotive God*. New York, N.Y., 1939.

Schreber, Daniel P. *Memoirs of My Nervous Illness*. London, 1955.

Sechehaye, Marguerite. *Autobiography of a Schizophrenic Girl*. New York, N.Y., 1951.

Stewart, W.S. *The Divided Self*. New York, N.Y., 1964.

TWO

Cancro, Robert, editor. *The Schizophrenic Syndrome*. New York, N.Y., 1971.

Cancro, Robert, editor. *Annual Review of the Schizophrenic Syndrome*, Vols. 2 & 3. New York, N.Y., 1972 & 1973.

Dastur, D.K. "The Pathology of Schizophrenia." *A. M. A. Areh. Neurol. Psychiat.*, 81: 601-14. 1959.

Davis, P.A. & Davis, H. "The Electrograms of Psychotic Patients." *American Journal of Psychiatry*, 95: 1007. 1939.

Gibbs, F.A. & Gibbs, E.L. "The mitten pattern. An electroencephalographic abnormality correlating with psychosis." *J. Neuropsychiat.*, 5:6-13. 1963.

Haslam, John. *Observations on Madness and Melancholy*. London, 1809.

Heath, R.G. "Schizophrenia: Biochemical and Physiologic Aberrations." *International Journal of Neuropsychiatry*, 2:597-610, 1966.

Heath, R.G. & Krupp, I. M. "Schizophrenia as an immunologic disorder." *Arch. Gen. Psychiat.*, 16:1.

Mirsky, A. "Neurophysiological Bases of Schizophrenia." *Annual Review of Psychology*, Vol. 20, Palo Alto, Cal. 1969.

Rupp, C., editor. *Mind as a Tissue*. New York, N.Y., 1968.

THREE

Ackerman, W.K. *Early Illinois Railroads*. Chicago, Ill., 1884.

Alvord, C.W., editor. *The Centennial History of Illinois*. Springfield, Ill., 1920.

Alvord, C.W. *The Mississippi Valley in British Politics*. 2 Vols. Cleveland, Oh., 1917.

Boewe, Charles. *Prairie Albion*. Southern Illinois Univ. Press, Carbondale, Ill., 1962.

Brown, Samuel R. "The Western Gazetteer or Emigrant's Directory." *Transactions*, Illinois State Historical Society, 1908. Springfield, Ill., 1909.

Brownson, Howard G. *History of the Illinois Central Railroad to 1870*. Univ. of Illinois Studies in the Social Sciences, Vol., IV, Urbana, Ill., 1915.

Buck, Solon J. "Travel and Description, 1765-1865." *Collections*. Illinois State Historical Library Vol. 9. Springfield, Ill., 1914.

Carter, Clarence Edwin. *Great Britain and the Illinois Country, 1763-1774*. Washington, D.C., 1910.

Clerk, Archibald, editor. *The Poems of Ossian*. Edinburgh & London, 1970.

Collot, Victor. A Jouney in North America. *Transactions*, Illinois State Historical Society, 1908. Springfield, Ill., 1909.

Cox, Isaac Joslin, editor. *The Jouneys of Rene Robert Cavelier, sieur de la Salle*. 2 Vols., New York, N.Y., 1905.

Dickens, Charles. *American Notes*. London & New York, N.Y., 1957.

Dickens, Charles. *Martin Chuzzlewit*. New York, N.Y.

Ford, Paul L., editor. *Writings of Thomas Jefferson*. New York, N.Y., 1892-1899.

Gray, Henry. *Anatomy of the Human Body*. Philadelphia, Pa., 1953.

Havighurst, Walter. *The Heartland*. New York, N.Y., 1962.

James, James A., editor. "Geogre Rogers Clark Papers, 1771-1781." *Collections*, Illinois State Historical Library, Vol.8. Springfield, Ill., 1912.

Latrobe, Charles J. *The Rambler in North America, 1832-1833*. 2 Vols., London, 1835.

Mereness, Newton D., editor. *Travels in the American Colonies*. New York, N.Y., 1916.

Parkman, Francis. *La Salle and the Discovery of the New West*. Boston, Mass., 1910.

Peithmann, Irvin M. *Indians of Southern Illinios*. Springfield, Ill., 1964.

Quiafe, Milo M. *Chicago and the Old Northwest, 1673-1835*. Chicago, Ill., 1913.

Sandburg, Carl. *Abraham Lincoln, The Prairie Years*. New York, N.Y., 1926.

Sauer, Carl O. *Pioneer Life in the Upper Illinois Valley—in Land and Life*. Berkeley, Cal., 1963.

Schoolcraft, Henry R. *Narrative Journal of Travels from Detroit Northwest*. Albany, N.Y., 1821.

Schoolcraft Henry R. *Travels in the Central Portion of the Mississippi Valley*. New York, N.Y., 1825.

Sparks, Edwin E., editor. *The Lincoln Douglas Debates of 1858*. Collections, Illinois State Historical Library, Vol. 3. Springfield, Ill., 1908.

Thwaites, Reuben Gold, editor. *Early Western Travels, 1748-1846*. 32 Vols., Cleveland, Oh., 1904.

Writers' Program. *Cairo, Illinois*. Federal Writers' Project, Napanee, Ind., 1938.

Writers' Program. *Illinois, a Descriptive and Historical Guide*. Federal Writers' Project, Chicago, Ill. 1939.

FOUR

Alvord, Clarence W., editor. *The Centennial History of Illinois*. Springfield, Ill., 1920.

Becker, Heywood E. & Cone, Richard A. "Light-stimulated electrical responses from skin." *Science*, Vol. 154, no. 3752, November 25, 1966.

Bretz, J. Harlen & Harris, S.E., Jr. "Caves of Illinois." *RI 215, Reports of Investigations*. Illinois State Geological Survey, Urbana, Ill., 1966.

Buckhout, Robert. "The blind fingers." *Perceptual and Motor Skills*. Vol. 20, No. 1, February, 1965.

Carroll, Thomas J. *Blindness*. Boston, Mass., 1961.

Catlin, George. *Rambles among the Indians of the Rocky Mountains and the Andes*. London, 1877.

Chevigny, Hector & Braverman, Sudell. *The Adjustment of the Blind.* New Haven, Conn., 1950.

Collinson, Charles W. *Guide for Beginning Fossil Hunters.* Illinois State Geological Survey, Educational Series/4, Urbana, Ill., 1966.

Cutsforth, Thomas D. *The Blind in School and Society.* New York, N.Y., 1951.

Fox, Monroe I. *Blind Adventure.* New York, N.Y., 1946.

Goldberg, I.M. "On the question about practice of tactual sensitivity." *Psychological Abstracts,* Vol. 39, No. 1, February, 1965.

Gray, Henry. *Anatomy of the Human Body.* Philadelphia, Pa., 1953.

Guide to Rocks and Minerals of Illinois—Illinois State Geological Survey, Educational Series/5, Urbana, Ill., 1959.

Guide to the Geologic Map of Illinois—Illinois State Geological Survey, Educational Series/7, Urbana, Ill., 1961.

Hawkes, Clarence. *Hitting the dark trail.* New York, N.Y., 1915.

Hawkes, Clarence. *My Country.* Boston, Mass., 1940.

Hayes, S.P. *Contributions to A Psychology of Blindness.* 1941.

Hayes, S.P. *Facial Vision.* Watertown, Mass., 1935.

Hopkins, Cyril G. & Pettit, James H. *The Fertility in Illinois Soils.* University of Illinois. Bulletins of the Agricultural Experiment Station, Vol. 8, Urbana, Ill., 1909.

Ivanov, Alexander. "Soviet Experiments in 'Eye-less Vision'." *Psychological Abstracts* Vol. 39, No 1, February, 1965.

Keitlen, Tomi. *Farewell to Fear.* New York, N.Y., 1960.

Kline, O.A. "The Blind Shall 'See'." *Tomorrow,* Vol 1. No 3, 1941.

Kluckhohn, Clyde. *Navaho Witchcraft.* Boston, Mass., 1944.

Krents, Harold. *To Race the Wind.* New York, N.Y., 1972.

Mehta, Ved Parkash. *Face to Face.* Boston, Mass., 1957.

Morgan, W. *Human-Wolves Among the Navaho.* Yale University Publications in Anthropology, No. 11, New Haven, Conn., 1936.

Newberg, N.D. "Vision in the fingers: a rare phenomenon; phenomenon of Rosa Kuleshov." *Monthly Popular Magazine of the Academy of Science* (USSR), No. 5, 1963.

Novomeyskiy, A.S. "The nature of the dermo-optical sense in man." *Voprosy Psikhologii,* Vol. 9, No. 5, September-October, 1963, as translated and reprinted by the U.S. Joint Publications Research Service, Washington, February, 4, 1964.

Ohnstad, Karsten. *The World at My Fingertips.* New York, N.Y., 1942.

Poggi, Edith M. "The Prairie Province of Illinois." *Illinois University Studies in the Social Sciences,* Vol. XIX, No. 3, Urbana, Ill., 1934.

Putnam, Peter. *Cast off the Darkness.* New York, N.Y., 1957.

Ridgeley, Douglas C. *The Geography of Illinois.* Chicago, Ill., 1921.

Romains, Jules, translated by C.K. Ogden. *Eyeless Sight.* New York, N.Y., 1924.

Rosenfeld, Albert. "Seeing Color with the Fingers." *Life Magazine,* June 12, 1964.

Sauer, Carl O. "Geography of the Upper Illinois Valley." Illinois Geological Survey, *Bulletin 27.*

"Seeing finger-tips." *Time,* Vol. 81, No. 4, January 25, 1963.

Smithdas, Robert J. *Life at My Fingertips.* 1958.

Steinberg, Danny D. "Light sensed through receptors in the skin." *American Journal of Psychology,* Vol. 79, No. 2, June, 1966.

Supa, M., Cotzin, M. & Dallenbach, K.M. "Facial Vision: The Perception of Obstacles by the Blind." *American Journal of Psychology,* LVII.

Villey, P. *The World of the Blind; a Psychological Study.* New York, N.Y., 1930.

Weller, Stuart. *The Story of the Geological Making of Southern Illinois.* Illinois State Geological Survey, Educational Series, Urbana, Ill., 1927.

Wheeler, R. H. "Visual Phenomena in the dreams of a blind subject." *Psychological Review* 27, 1920.

Writers' Program, Federal Writer's Project. *Illinois, A Descriptive and Historcal Guide.* Chicago, Ill., 1939.

Zavala, Albert; Van Cott, Harold P.; Orr, David G. and Small, Victor H. "Human Dermo-Optical Perception: Colors of Objects and of Projected Light Differentiated with Fingers." *Perceptual and Motor Skills,* Vol. 25, No. 2, October, 1967.

FIVE

Ackerman, Wm. K. *Early Illinois Railroads.* Chicago, Ill., 1884.

Alvord, Clarence W., editor. *The Centennial History of Illinois.* Springfield, Ill., 1920.

Alvord, Clarence W. *The Mississippi in British Politics.* 2 Vols. Cleveland, Oh., 1917.

American Automobile Association—*Great Lakes Tour Book, 1974-1975.*

Baldwin, Eugene F. "The Dream of the South—Story of Illinois during the Civil War." *Transactions,* 1911. Illinois State Historical Society, Springfield, Ill., 1913.

Barbour, John (AP Newsfeatures Writer). "Green World Slowly Dying." *Springfield, Mass., Republican,* date not recorded.

Barnes, Harper. "Bringing it all Back Home." *New Times,* August 9, 1972.

Bronson, Howard G. "Early Illinois Railroads." *Transactions,* Illinois State Historical Society, 1908. Springfield, Ill., 1909.

Bryan, William Jennings. "Temperance Speech." (Probably delivered in Jacksonville, Illinois, circa 1887.) Bryan Papers, Manuscript Division, Library of Congress.

Buck, Solon J. "Travel and Description 1765-1865." *Collections,* Illinois State Historical Library, Vol. 9, Springfield, 1914.

Byrd, Donald. Personal correspondence.

Cates, Sidney. "The Day of Super Corn Crops." *Country Gentleman,* March, 1929.

Clerk, Archibald, editor. *The Poems of Ossian.* Edinburgh & London, 1970.

Davenport, Guy. *Flowers & Leaves.* Highlands, N.C., 1966.

Lincoln Log Cabin State Park. Department of Conservation, Divison of Parks and Memorials, State of Illinois.

Dickens, Charles. *Martin Chuzzlewit.* New York, N.Y. No date.

Dickens, Charles. *American Notes.* London & New York, 1957.

Encyclopedia Britannica, 11th Edition. Cambridge, England & New York, 1910.

Havighurst, Walter. *The Heartland.* New York, 1962.

Illinois Agricultural Statistics. *Annual Summary, 1973.* Illinois Cooperative Crop Reporting Service, Illinois Department of Agriculture, U.S. Department of Agriculture, Bulletin 73-1.

James, James A., editor. *George Rogers Clark Papers, 1771-1781.* Collections, Illinois State Historical Library, Vol. 8. Springfield, 1912.

Koenig, Louis W. *Bryan.* New York, 1971.

Landesco, John. *Organized Crime in Chicago.* Chicago & London, 1968.

Menu. Porky's Restaurant, Ullin, Illinois.

Metcalf, Illinois. Compiled by the Metcalf Centennial History Committee, 1874-1974.

Olson, Charles. "I know men for whom everything matters." *Olson: The Journal of the Charles Olson Archives.* Storrs, Conn., Spring, 1974.

Piethmann, Irvin M. *Indians of Southern Illinois.* Springfield, 1964.

Presley Tours, Inc. *A Self-Guide to Scenic and Interesting Places in the Lower Tip of Illinois.* Makanda, Ill., no date.

Quaife, Milo M. *Chicago and the Old Northwest, 1673-1835.* Chicago 1913.

Sandburg, Carl. *Abraham Lincoln, the Prairie Years.* New York, 1926.

Sparks, Edwin E., editor. *The Lincoln-Douglas Debates of 1858.* Collections Illinois State Historical Library, Vol. 3, Springfield, 1908.

Thwaites, Reuben Gold, editor. *Early Western Travels, 1748-1846.* 32 Vols., Cleveland, 1904.

Tse-Tung, Mao. "Quotation." *Holiday Inn Companion, Your Inroom Magazine.* April-May, 1975.

Anonymous. *Crab Orchard and Egyptian Railroad.* No place or date.

Anonymous. *The Old Slave House.* No place or date.

UPI. "Going Strong at 102." *Springfield, Mass., Republican,* March 23, 1975.

U.S. Department of Commerce, Weather Bureau. "Some outstanding Tornadoes, Dates, Number Deaths, Number injured and Estimated Property Damage, 1875-1947." No place or date.

Walter, Herbert E. & Alice H. *Wild Birds in City Parks.* New York, 1926.

Wilson Charles Morrow. *The Commoner, William Jennings Bryan.* Garden City, 1970.

Writers' Program, Federal Writers Project. *Illinois, Descriptive and Historical Guide.* Chicago, 1939.

ZIP ODES

The 51 poems in this collection—one for each state, and the District of Columbia—are arranged alphabetically. They are composed entirely of place names, as they appear, state by state, in the u.s. Postal Service Zip Code Directory (1968 Edition). I have allowed myself liberty in punctuation, in placing the words on the page, in combining one or more names, and occasionally repeating a name, within a poem. However, nothing has been added—there are no "filler" words, or "combining" words.

These are our places . . . as they were somehow named . . . and as the Great Dispenser of Zips has preserved them.

—Paul (Alabama) Metcalf (Illinois)

Alabama

Bon Secour! Brilliant, Coy, Powderly Black!

(Equality)

Madrid, Detroit, Geneva, Havana, Manila
Uptown, Downtown, East Side, West Side

(Kansas, Cuba)

Opp   Loop   Pope
                      Trinity
                   Holy Trinity
                   (Three Notch)

Alpine Arab, Shorter Cherokee,
Eight Mile Chickasaw, Normal Choctaw

Goodwater, Goodway,
Allgood!

SUNNY SOUTH

Alaska

False Pass
Flat Hope

Ruby Nightmute
Clear Sleetmute

Arizona

Surprise!

Blue Bumble Bee,
Happy Jack,
Many Farms,
Mammoth Snowflake

Wide Ruins
Carefree Inspiration . . .

Why?

Arkansas

Marked Tree: Nail Old Joe!

(Cash Reader, Ink Dollarway:
Strong Success Story)

Hasty, Rushing Romance . . . Coy, Prim . . .
Fiftysix Chimes, Forty Four Stamps!

(Okay, Umpire)

Ash Flat, Low Gap, Lead Hill,
Tomato, Strawberry, Wild Cherry,
Evening Shade　:　Sweet Home

California

George Washington
John Adams
Andrew Jackson
Lincoln
William H. Taft
Santa Claus

Tweedy Raisin, Likely Loop,
Big Creek, Dinkey Creek:
Standard Landscape

Fig Garden Village, Fallen Leaf,
Ball Road, Nut Tree,
Monolith, Fort Dick . . . Holy City

Halcyon Happy Camp,
Boys Republic, Childrens Fairyland,
Angels Camp,
Harmony!
Tranquility!
Paradise!

Mad River Subway,
Rough and Ready Rescue!

Terminal Island

Smartville

Colorado

Chimney Rock   Slick Rock   Castle Rock
Boulder   Granite   Bedrock
       Greystone   Silt
                    Snowmass

Joes Downtown Empire
Fair Fountain!
Peoples Model Dinosaur

Paradox   Severance

Two Buttes!
Lay!
CLIMAX!
(Hasty Hygiene)

Connecticut

Short Beach,
Deep River,
Noble Hillside:

Bantam Garden

Delaware

Federal Ogletown
Crossroads Bear
Marydel Manor
Camden Wyoming Winterthur

District of Columbia

Cardinal, Eagle,
Central Friendship

Smokey The Bear Treasury

Northeast,
Northwest,
Southeast,
Southwest—

Seat Pleasant

Florida

Bright Day,
Bright Christmas Holiday,
Bright Century!

Trailer Estates,
Trailer Haven,
Mobile Manor,
Motel Row:
Niceville!

Leisure City

Kissimmee, Venus!
Kissimmee, Mims!
Kissimmee, Lulu!

Siesta Balm,
Open Air Seabreeze,
Surfside Sunshine,
Panacea!

(Mossy Head, Doctor's Inlet)

Georgia

Fry Ty Ty

Box Springs

Dewy Rose, Flowery Branch, Rising Fawn . . .

Hawaii

Captain Cook

Volcano

Airport

Idaho

Spirit Lake   Warm Lake   Sugar City

(b r i d g e)

Ovid   Shelley   Ruebens

h e a d q u a r t e r s

Sweet Dixie Felt Wilder

a t o m i c   c i t y

BIG   BAR

(culdesac)

n a f   o l a

Illinois

Assumption:

> Industry, Fidelity, Liberty, Justice

> Apple River, Leaf River

Preemption:

> Fancy Prairie, Garden Prairie,
> Golf, Goodwine

> Bourbon Joy

> > Muddy Stock Yards,
> > Mid-West Foolsland

> > > (Normal Metcalf)

Indiana

Twelve Points:

English Pence, French Lick

Speedway Battle Ground:
Scircleville! Scircleville!

Soldiers Home: Advance Siberia

Speed, Young America!

Honey Creek:
Broad Ripple, White Swan, Rising Sun

Oölitic Farmland

Downtown Chili Bath!

Gas City

Rainbow Magnet:
Santa Claus Windfall

Friends Harmony

Burr Oak

Twelve Mile, Onward!

Iowa

High Hills, Climbing Hill,
Low Moor,
Lone Rock, Lone Tree,
Morning Sun

Swan, Early Curlew

Anita Bryant: Fruitland (Percival Quimby)

Fertile Cylinder,
Manly Defiance!

Diagonal Gravity?
(Correctionville)

Lost Nation

Kansas

Pretty Prairie, Bird City
Sunflower Bloom

Rice, Maize,
Liberal Gas

Larned University:
Stark Hope, Soldier

Kentucky

Ready ?

EIGHTY EIGHT CRUMMIES STAB BROAD BOTTOM
    HOOKER
ROWDY CRANKS DECOY, TOMAHAWK LONE GYPSY
MAJESTIC DWARF SLAUGHTERS BREEDING BEAUTY

Goody!

Lynch Old Allen!

* * *

Falls of Rough, Head of Grassy,
Wolf, Wild Cat, Ever-Subtle Viper,
Brightshade Cerulean Butterfly

Chevrolet, Ford

* * *

Peoples Quality Narrows:
Public Dice, Flat Julip

Bluehole, Clayhole,
Thousandsticks Marrowbone

Smile, Stay Halfway Happy

Busy Day, Miracle Ages

Louisiana

Supreme Welcome!
Manifest Creole Paradis!

Pioneer French Settlement: Eros Echo

Jigger-Chase-Mix, Jigger-Chase-Mix, Jigger-
Chase-Mix:
Belcher, Grosse Tete

Waterproof Bywaters

Many Weeks, Many New Roads

Maine

Five Islands:

Detroit, China
Dresden, Denmark
Lisbon, Mexico
Naples, Norway
Paris, Peru

Great Works!

Maryland

Maryland Line:

Dames Quarter, Ladiesburg, Loveville:
Druid Accident,
Eden Detour

Bivalve Chance, Bivalve Price:
Commerce

Big Pool, Still Pond, Tall Timbers

Massachusetts

Onset:

Still River, Swift River,
Plum Island, Feeding Hills

Terminal Beach,
Terminal Heath

Nonquitt!

Michigan

Three Oaks, Three Rivers,
Six Lakes, Seven Oaks

Good Hart, Free Soil, New Era!

*   *   *

Downtown Empire,
Alabaster Castle,
Mass Pigeon Peck

Honor Commerce

*   *   *

White Cloud, White Pigeon

Temperance Waters

Twining Waters, Village Garden

Base Line, Sunfield, Blissfield!

*   *   *

Pontiac, Cadillac
        (Shopping Center Romeo)

Cement City,

Bad Axe,

Hell

Minnesota

Welcome, Fertile Mabel,
Welcome, Young America!
     (Motley Apache Outing)

Blue Earth, White Earth,
Sleepy Eye Ball Club
     (... Mound, Loop ...)

Boy River Climax:
     Swift Traffic,
     Twig Pillage,
     Good Thunder!

Mississippi

Alligator Petal
Midnight Bourbon Battlefield

      (Bobo Soso Tippo Tchula)
      (Scooba Toomsuba)

Learned   Kreole
Darling   Chunky Choctaw

      (Itta Bena Eastabuchie Nitta Yuma Noxapater)

  Denmark Egypt

      (Bogue Chitto D'lo)

Money!   Rich! Value!

         (Panther Burn . . .)

Onward!

Missouri

Ilmo   Inza   Iantha   Ionia

Koshkonong   Chula   Cabool

Braggadocio, Bragg City!

Blue Eye Belle / Clever Cadet
Neck City, Quick City
Peculiar Half Way   Advance
          (Devil's Elbow)
Baring, Licking, Loose Creek
Couch Conception / Rocky Comfort

          Black Arab: Fairdealing Competition
          Amity, Fair Play

Golden Grassy Bonne Terre

Montana

Hungry Horse, Lame Deer,
Emigrant Pioneer

Pray . . . Locate . . . Roundup . . .

Sweetgrass Power

Nebraska

Arapahoe Surprise:
Broken Bow, Weeping Water

Rising City,
Republican City,
Sterling Prairie Home

Ong   Ord   Strang

Nevada

Contact Bonanza Annex:

Gold Point
Black Springs
Blue Diamond

Steamboat Searchlight:

Nixon Jackpot
Mesquite
Jackass Flats

D E E T H !

New Hampshire

Berlin

Dublin

Milan

Epping

Gonic

New Jersey

Fair Lawn, Short Hills,
Far Hills, Basking Ridge:
Suburban Ritz,
Ironbound Circle

High Academy: Brainy Boro

Five Corners, Three Bridges,
Dividing Creek

Ship Bottom, Outwater, Sea Bright

Netcong Ho Ho Kus,
Weequahic Lopatcong,
Watchung Rancocas,
Moonachie Wickatunk

Middlebush Willingboro: Alloway!

New Mexico

Dusty Crossroads, Humble City

Waterflow, Little Water

Mountainair,
Ambrosia Lake:
Loving Organ!

New York

Wall Street Speculator
(Shady Whiteface, Alcove Patroon):

"Fine Market,
Rush Purchase,
Great Kills—
Fablus!"
      (Deposit Little Neck Armor)

* * *

Adirondack: Apalachian Andes
Catskill: Grossinger Andes

* * *

"Surprise!
Fine Old Village,
New Lots, New City (Paradox),
Model City, Divine Corners, Village Bliss!"

* * *

Sparrow Bush, Shrub Oak,
Fresh Meadows
Ruby Rosebloom,
Botanical Eden,
Utopia!

* * *

"Academy: Bullville"

(Hermon Melville)

* * *

Ten Mile River, Three Mile Bay,
Sunset, Sundown

* * *

SLINGERLANDS

North Carolina

Star Spray,
Sealevel Sunrise

Gumberry Stem

Pink Hill, Merry Hill,
Lowland Love Valley

Half Moon Horse Shoe

Crisp Chinquapin,
Evergreen Ether

Ash Bath,
Bee Log

Friendly Grace,
Farmer Comfort

Welcome!

North Dakota

Alfred : Alice
Ambrose : Beulah
Arthur : Cathey
Barney : Christine
Barton : Flora
Burt : Hannah
Clifford : Hope
Douglas : Kathryn
Dwight : Loraine
Elliott : Norma

Pisek   South Heart
   (Flasher)   Grassy Butte
Dickey   Golva
   (Cannon Ball)   Velva

Z A P !

Ohio

Athens, New Athens
Albany, New Albany
Bremen, New Bremen
Carlisle, New Carlisle
Holland, New Holland
Lebanon, New Lebanon
Lexington, New Lexington
London, New London
Madison, New Madison
Middletown, New Middletown
Paris, New Paris
Plymouth, New Plymouth
Richmond, New Richmond
Springfield, New Springfield
Vienna, New Vienna
Waterford, New Waterford
Weston, New Weston

Wonderland!

Oklahoma

Apache   Arapaho   Cherokee   Cheyenne
Chickasha   Choctaw   Comanche   Muskogee
Okmulgee   Osage   Pawnee   Seminole   Shawnee

Geronimo!

Disney   Guthrie   Will Rogers   Gene Autrey

Indiahoma Centrahoma

Battiest Mutual Council Hill

Oregon

Clackamas, Clatskanie,
Pistol River

Remote Zigzag Trail,
—Tenmile, Twelve Mile—
Burnt Woods,
Woodburn, Deadwood
. . . Timber Echo . . .

Aloha, Allegany!

Blue River Spray,
Harbor Mist

Fossil Fox

Plush Paisley Bridal Veil,
—Sisters, Brothers, Friend—
—Brooks Brothers Diamond—
Sweet Home . . . Sublimity!

Pennsylvania

English Center, Fox Chase

Eighty Four Continental Drums:
Freedom!   Independence!   Republic!

Brave Village, Burnt Cabins
(Scalp Level, Level Green)

* * *

Spraggs: Roscoe Aitch, Mary D

"Darling . . . !"
Bareville, Pillow, Intercourse, Paradise
(Normalville)

        (Bird in Hand
        (Strong Effort
        (Dry Run
                (Blue Ball

* * *

Listie! Distant Beaver Barking . . .

Three Springs Arnot Twin Rocks

Sinking Spring,
Terminal Waterfall,
Needmore Wawa

* * *

Drifting Gipsy, Palm Reading

* * *

Yellow House, Puritan Home, Suburbia:
Railroad Roulette

Rhode Island

Pilgrim,
Hope, Hope Valley,
Prudence Island,
Peace Dale:

Harmony

    (Friar Buttonwoods)

North,

Westerly,

Carolina,

Wyoming

South Carolina

Cross South,
South of The Border:

Blackstock / Whipper Barony

Round O

Due West:
Six Mile, Ninety Six:

Denmark, Norway, Switzerland, Sardinia:

Silverstreet,
Southern Shops,
Society Hill:

Prosperity!

South Dakota

Interior Broadland Ideal:
Mud Butte,
Big Stone City

Scenic Winner: Lead Igloo

Bonesteel, Firesteel

Blunt Bullhead Carpenter

Red Owl, White Owl, Glad Valley . . .

Tennessee

Only Baptist Bells, Baptist Halls,
Only Baptist Trade

> (Daisy Counce Wilder Guys)

Sweetwater Soddy,
Lone Mountain Sugar Tree

Alcoa Bon Aqua

Texas

Best Art Best Dawn Best Earth Best Energy Best
White Settlement Best Industry Best Plains Best
Boys Ranch Best Sand Best Sunrise Best Sunset

Splendora! Six Flags Over Texas!

Call Barnum, Bailey, Call Tarzan
Telegraph Tennyson, Cee Vee, Sam Houston
Telephone Ben Franklin, Robert Lee
Dial (Dime Box) Seven Sisters:

    Katy, Winnie, Loving Louise,
    Lovelady Pearl, Peggy, Joy,

        Lolita!

* * *

Bigfoot Bend,
Sandy Flat,
Evergreen Thicket:
Dripping Springs,
Agua Dulce

Bronco Blanket,
Muleshoe, Spur

Cross Cut,
Circle Back:

North Zulch

* * *

Coy City:
Welfare Dinero,
Satin Comfort

    (Sunny Side Spade,
    Happy, Smiley)

  Blessing   Goodnight

Utah

Castle Gate,
Sugar House,
Ruby's Inn,
Dutch John

Tropic Vernal Oasis

Bountiful Virgin,
Mammoth Virgin,
Virgin Hurricane,
Virgin Gusher,
Bluff Virgin

Pioneer Eden,
Saltair Paradise

Vermont

Adamant Mary Meyer

North Hero,
South Hero,
Mount Snow:

Wilder Whiting

Virgina

Rural Retreat, Head Waters, Moon Alps,
Ivy, Hyacinth, Orchid, Clover . . .
Radiant Prospect!

> Horsey Community,
> Ebony Driver

Court House Shadow,
Republican Grove,
Upright Council

> Goldvein, Cash Chance
> (Mineral Breaks)

Stuarts Draft,
Brandy Station
    (Check Supply)

> Theological Seminary,
> Temple Trailer

Tiptop Alps: Bon Air,
Bee Colony, Birchleaf, Acorn,
Cardinal Birdsnest,
Healing Springs,
Lightfoot Lively Maidens

> Witch Duck Painter,
> Snowflake Valentines

King And Queen:
Modern Crouch,
Cluster Springs,
Assawoman, Ballsville,
Fancy Gap, Free Union

           Drill Hurt,
           Upperville,
           Natural Bridge

Meadows Of Dan:
Oyster Fries
(Wake Wise)

           Achilles, Dante:
           Dixie Disputanta

Washington

Ocean Shores Opportunity:
Startup Country Homes, Orchards

      (Klickitat, La Push, Lilliwaup, Satsop)
      (Skykomish, Snoqualmie, Snohomish)

Ritzville, Moxee City, Electric City,
Oso International!

       * * *

Hay Farmer Humptulips

Selah!

West Virginia

Borderland Cabins:
Friendly Hometown Comfort Given,
Coalwood Heaters,
Buffalo Shanks,
Pigeon Pie

Blue Jay, Bob White,
Cucumber Flower

Dink Jenkinjones: Odd Man

Colliers Job: Mud, Rock, Sod Levels—Rough Run

Bimm   Bolt   Droop   Duck

Industrial Prosperity!

Jonben, Chloe: Quick Romance

Corn Stalk Shock

L   e   t   t   e   r   G   a   p

Tornado, Cyclone, Hurricane!

Widen Fraziers Bottom!

                    — Jane Lew Jenkinjones

Wisconsin

Plain Dane: Loyal Endeavor, Superior Luck

Butternut, Maple, Poplar, Arbor Vitae,
Brown Deer, Swan, Plover,
Blue Mounds, Black Earth,
Phlox, Lily, Wild Rose:
Bloom City! Dairyland Cornucopia!

Polar Winter

Jump River,
Honey Creek,
Jim Falls Cataract

Butte Des Morts

Wyoming

Frontier Airport Lander,
Devil's Tower, Gas Hills

Little America : Hells Half Acre

* * *

Bill, Frannie, Jay Em, Kaycee—
Canyon Chugwater,
Saddlestring Tie Siding,
Ten Sleep Encampment

(Old Faithful Moose, Recluse)

U.S. DEPT. OF THE INTERIOR

Line drawings in text by Jane McGriff

OSSA

The flesh is burned out,
burned in,
by the creature's bones

muscles tense and full,
motion swift,
skin taut,

bones within

"This drawing is from an ivory carving found in an Ipiutak burial
site at Point Hope, Alaska. It shows the skeletal motif widely used
by the Eskimo artists during pre-white contact days. The Ipiutak
culture is believed to have existed until about 200 B.C. The motif
greatly resembles the decorations of carved objects done in the
Scytho-Siberian style of the region between the Black Sea and the
Ordos area of Northern China (900 to 200 B.C.)."

—Joe Senungetuk.

musculature and rib cage,
hams and flanks,
shanks and shoulders,
junctures of tension

Transcaspia to China, to Han and Chou,

and later, across the ice

the fluted spinal lines,
twisted nostril scroll,
radial strokes on rump and jowl

the body peering through its numerous eyes, ovals at the points of
pressure, the pressure holding points

"If one takes into consideration also the other artistic regions of
Asia, it appears that only in the extreme northeast of the continent,
on the shores of the Bering Strait, are animals conceived in a man-
ner comparable to the animal style of the steppe lands."

"And it is precisely the settled groups of hunters along the coast—
the Chukchi, Koryaks and Eskimo—that have given richest
evidence of their artistic talents."

". . . the almost sexual tension found between the lonely hunter
and his prey."

(Jettmar)

ribs, bones, and musculature emergent,
flesh impressed from within,

apertures at the points of acupressure,
the body's eyes,
where muscle springs from bone

". . . the entire animal style of the steppe lands might have been derived from Shang art, and have then slowly trickled westwards, reaching the Black Sea area some hundred years later."

west   and *east*, to Bering,
from An-yang, center of Shang

flameshape lines

short

hatched

strokes

ANCHORAGE

ALASKA IS STRUCK
BY SEVERE QUAKE;
60 FEARED DEAD

STATE'S CABINET MEETS

Seward Called 'Half Gone
and on Fire'—Evacuation
of Kodiak Base Begun

By The Associated Press

FAIRBANKS, Alaska, March 27—A severe earthquake struck a broad area of Alaska today and leveled the main street of Anchorage, this state's largest city.

[The Alaska Communication System reported that as many as 60 to 100 persons may have been killed in Anchorage, according to United Press International.]

The earthquake was reported on the University of California seismograph at 8 to 8.5 magnitude on the Richter scale . . .

A state trooper in Kenai said he had radio contact with Anchorage. He reported to civil defense officials here that things were "pretty tragic up there."

Most communications with the city . . . were cut off. All airports were unusable . . .

QUAKE RECORDED

AS ONE OF THE WORST

The magnitude of the earthquake that shook parts of Alaska last night was one of the strongest ever recorded on a seismograph.

SCORES PERISH IN ALASKA QUAKE

AND TIDAL WAVES ON WEST COAST;

ANCHORAGE SUFFERS WORST LOSS

WHITE HOUSE ACTS

Emergency Is Declared
—Alaskans Starting
to Clear Rubble

By The Associated Press

ANCHORAGE, Alaska, March 28—One of history's mightiest earthquakes spread devastation in Alaska . . .

. . . the still quivering, snowy ruins . . .

Anchorage, Alaska's largest city . . . suffered spectacular damage from the shock.

Giant, seismatic sea waves generated by the quake smashed a half dozen smaller towns rimming the Gulf of Alaska . . .

GUARD PATROLLING ANCHORAGE;

CITY LACKS WATER AND POWER

ANCHORAGE, Alaska, March 28—Anchorage began today to dig out of the shambles of last night's earthquake.

There are buildings that look a little like ships hauled out of the water, for their foundations have sunk 20 feet below the level of the street.

Bright, glass-walled and attractive new buildings have slashes down their sides.

. . . homes that dropped into chasms that appeared as the heavy quake swept along fault lines in town.

One of the most spectacular sites was the wreckage of the almost finished luxury apartment house The Four Seasons. This building was shaken like a ship in a storm . . .

About 75 of Anchorage's finest homes . . . tumbled down the face of a bluff overlooking Turnagain arm of Cook Inlet.

. . . the slicing line of the earth's slippage . . .

ANCHORAGE, March 29— . . .

. . . It was cracking in big blocks and turning and pulling apart in big cracks where you would be standing . . .

. . . the streets were rippling, the ground pitching . . .

". . . the earth started to roll. It rolled for five minutes. It slammed parked cars together. People were clinging to each other, to lamp-posts, to buildings."

At a wrecked warehouse . . . lift trucks drove through pools of a mixture of liquor, beer and melted snow . . .

Friday night's Alaskan shock was so powerful that it sent seismographs off scale all over the world.

It is believed that an earthquake near or below the ocean, such as near the coast of Alaska last night, produces an undersea landslide, or a sudden dropping or lifting of a segment of the ocean bottom. This leads to the displacement of large amounts of water.

In the case of a drop in the ocean bottom, the surface waters are sucked into the hole, the water flowing from either side and crashing violently together . . .

. . . most of the city was built on a glacial-outwash plain, which rides on thick beds of slippery clay. When earthquake waves raced

through Anchorage . . . their worst effect was to crack the underly-
ing clay and start the whole place sliding toward the sea.

If the continents are moving away from each other across the Atlantic,
they must be moving toward each other across the Pacific . . .
     Alaska is a churning focus of just such action . . .
     The Fairweather Fault and the Aleutian Arc intersect near
Anchorage . . .

Since the earth acts like a solid object, it can be made to vibrate all
over if it is hit hard enough . . .

* * *

HOUSTON IS LIFTED
BY A SURFACE WAVE

HOUSTON, March 28 (AP)—Houston was lifted four inches late
yesterday as a gigantic surface wave from the Alaskan earthquake
passed through the city . . .

. . . the city rose at about 11:08 P.M., shortly after the wave originated
in Alaska, more than 3,300 miles away.

The city fell back gently to its usual altitude 15 seconds later as the
wave passed into the Gulf of Mexico, where it caused a small tidal
wave . . .

Witnesses described it as "weird, spooky . . ."

MEGRIM

"changes of season, atmospheric state, the great aspects of the sun and moon, violent passions and errors of diet"

    hemicrania, cephalalgia, aphasia
    vertigo, ataxia, diplopia

    an obtenebration

stagnation of the exudated blood serum in one half of the head . . . animal spirits . . . cephalic hysteria . . . neuritis of the seventh nerve . . . cerebral neuralgia . . . an ascending neuralgia . . . hemorrhoids and gravel . . . the stealing of blood by the development of shunts . . . worms in the brain

the megrims: hysteric, purulent, insectal, hemorrhoidal, lunatic

    nerve-storms, brain-fag, sun-pain

    tumultuary disorder

*   *   *

"It is well known how for some time a woman calling herself Jeanne the Maid, *putting off the habit and dress of the female sex (which is contrary to divine law, abominable to God, condemned and prohibited by every law), has dressed and armed herself in the state and habit of man . . ."*

". . . she answered that she had taken it of her own will, under no compulsion, as she preferred man's to woman's dress."

a glaring light, as sun on snow, or light with a high rate of flicker, as sun off uneasy waters, will induce migraine

"The times of transition from sleep to wakefulness, or vice versa, are times of peculiar liability to attacks."

allergies, glare, noise, infection, motion, the menses, drugs, booze, hunger, exertion, stress, let-down, psychological predisposition, sexual passion,

>or The Evil Winds:

>the Santa Ana of Southern California
>the Argentine Zonda
>the Mediterranean Sirocco and Tramontana
>the Meltemia of Greece
>the Swiss and Austrian Fohn
>the Autun of France
>the Khamsin of Egypt
>the Thar winds of India
>Canadian Chinook
>Ghonding or Koebang of Java
>Boroh of Sumatra

>the Maltesian Xlokk

* * *

deeply depressed   —   or euphoric

". . . she began to see, in the air, tiny dot and tail phantoms like germs or tadpoles, constantly dropping down out of the range of her vision and soaring up into it again . . ."

the skin of her temples wrinkling and stretching, like the folds of an accordion

the aura, or prodromata

*   *   *

Scintillating scotomata:

> a blind spot partially surrounded by a strange
> figure composed of one or more brilliantly white,
> actively moving (scintillating) lines

> boiling or writhing

> the zigzag arrangement of a rail fence

> luminous angles like those of fortifications

> a singular glimmering

> the fortification lines wiggle their way to the edge
> of the visual field and disappear without a trace

> small, white, distorted stars moving slowly from
> left to right

> multicolored circles

> a bright red, central flickering spot composed of
> many smaller multidots . . . concentric circles of colored spots

> the fortification spectrum, with prominent and re-
> entrant angles

> luminous particles in rapid irregular movement

> a sensation as of moving water before the eyes

> an edging of light of a zigzag shape and coruscating
> at right angles to its length

stars, circles, squares, or squiggles, throbbing, spinning, flickering, and spinning bubbles and balloons

in a visual storm, a brilliant sand dune, the brains shimmering

a road cracking up with a severe earthquake

                              *   *   *

a woman in her mid-twenties whose jet-black hair developed a startling streak of white on the headache side

drooping eyelid or double vision

flee the light; the darkness soothes their disease; nor can they bear readily to look upon or hear anything agreeable; their sense of smell is vitiated, neither does anything agreeable to smell delight them, and they have also an aversion to fetid things

weary of life and wish to die

music could flood his mind like wine, keeping him sleepless and intoxicated throughout the night . . . snatches of melody would ring in his mind for days . . . musical fever

the ears ring as from the sounds of rivers rolling along with great noise or like the wind when it roars among sails

the noise seems to come from the center of the head rather than from the ears themselves

the snowball grew huge and turned blue

snakes, dogs, mice appear

a milky cascade before the eyes

a vast cloud with clashing of fire . . . in the fire was the semblance of four living creatures . . . each had four faces and four wings . . . and their wings touched one another . . . I saw wheels on the ground, like a wheel within a wheel . . . when the living creatures moved, the wheels moved beside them . . . I heard, too, the noise of their wings . . . when they moved it was like the noise of a great torrent or of a cloudburst, like the noise of a crowd or an armed camp . . . I saw what looked like fire with encircling radiance

little people, three or four inches high, making a curious buzzing noise

a distant point of light, approaching, growing, exploding in pain . . . a tiny dwarf, approaching, growing, becomes a giant with a club, beating the patient's head

a sensation of ants creeping up one's arm

my head had grown to tremendous proportions and was so light that it floated up to the ceiling . . . I get all tired out from pulling my head down, I've been pulling it down all night long

I am short and wide, and walk close to the ground

my head fell into a deep hole under the head of the bed

a bright gold-tinted cloud, and with it an appearance of parti-colored rain

a trellis of silver covered with vines and flowers

*   *   *

today my body is as if someone had drawn a vertical line separating the two halves . . . the right half seems to be twice the size of the left half . . . after a few minutes, the right half seems to shrink until it is smaller than the left

sometimes her left arm and breast would suddenly lose their personal significance, they no longer seemed to belong to her

the queer sensation of being two persons

a patient may feel he has two bodies . . . the second body, a few feet away, takes over mental activity while the first suffers migraine . . . the separation is quick and painless . . . although the second body may feel chilly

I am on an inclined plane, a few feet above, looking down at me . . . vibrating from myself, like a speeded pendulum . . . I linger behind, while I go ahead . . . shuddering, I rejoin, stuff my feelings back in

*   *   *

". . . she declared that at the age of thirteen she had a voice from God to help her and guide her. And the first time she was much afraid. And this voice came towards noon, in summer. in her father's garden: and the said Jeanne had [not] fasted on the preceding day. She heard the voice on her right, in the direction of the church: and she seldom heard it without a light. This light comes from the same side as the voice, and generally there was a great light."

"She said that if she was in a wood she easily heard the voices come to her."

"Asked if she saw St. Michael and these angels corporeally and in reality, she answered: 'I saw them with my bodily eyes . . .'"

". . . their voices beautiful, sweet and gentle . . ."

"Everything I have done I have done at the instruction of my voices."

(". . . suspected of many spells, incantations, invocations and conversations with evil spirits . . .")

*   *   *

vasoconstriction of the artery in the brain stem, at the menstrual onset

"A rare form of pain preceded the monthly flow, and was ushered in by a ruddy, indistinct spot, like mist, through which, as it grew, she still saw the dim outlines of objects . . . the red blur took suddenly the form of a near relative, who appeared to her covered with blood . . ."

". . . multiple red circles intertwined and in rapid rotation . . ."

". . . a red eye, approaching . . ."

". . . a huge red spider, melting into revolving red rectangles . . ."

". . . an agonizing desire to kill the person whose image she had seen."

> *Jean d'Aulon reported that she [Joan] had never menstruated.*

*   *   *

in migraine the pain is primarily vascular in origin, and due to dilation and pulsation of some arteries

the ensuing extra degree of pulsation of the big arteries like the temporal

symptoms arise from the constriction of the intracranial arteries and the pain from dilation of the extracranial or scalp arteries

an initial vasoconstriction, followed by vasodilation

biochemicals are released into the scalp tissues

and the pattern changes: after years of striking on just one side it may suddenly switch to the opposite side—or it may change sides frequently

*   *   *

Albucasis (A.D. 936-1013) advised an incision over the temple, the excavation of a cavity of considerable size under the skin and the introduction into the hole of a piece of garlic cleaned and pointed at both ends

Clutterbuck, 1826: Blood letting is no doubt in general proper

> Take the hair of a virgin kid,
> Bind therewith the head of the sick man,
> Bind therewith the neck of the sick man,
> Bind therewith his life,
> That the headache may ascend to heaven

cut a hole in the skull, apply coca

tie a hangman's noose around the head

scrape the plant growth off the head of a statue, hang from the sick man's head by a red string

place a wreath of fleabane on the head

touch the carpet over the resting place of St. Julian

dig plantain before the rising of the sun, bind the root about the head with boneset or mugwort

the brains of a vulture, mixed with the best of oil and inserted in the nostrils, will expel all ailments of the head

boil swallows' nests, and apply to the forehead

mix the juice of elderseed, cow's brain, and goat's dung dissolved in vinegar—drink it down

beat a goat senseless—the pain will move to him

rub the forehead with dill blossoms

take the moss from a skull, dip it as snuff

. . . roses and sugar, nutmeg and poppy seed . . .

 gaze through mugwort at the midsummer bonfire

. . . testes of beaver, bottled in spirits . . .

. . . cupping, blisters, needles, and emetics . . .

stroke the forehead with a live toad

ALASKA IN TRANSITION

April 2, 1978

Up at 5:30 A. M. (EST), having spent the night on an air mattress on the floor of Don Byrd's study. Time to shave and dress, and Marge trundles me to the Albany airport, for the 7 A.M. flight to Chicago, a bright Sunday morning.

Re-constituted eggs at some 30,000 feet—the day begins to come together.

Arrive O'Hare 8:16 A.M. (CST), and effect rendezvous with Jack O'Brien, who is parked just outside the baggage area, as planned. Since I have a 3½ hour layover in Chicago, Jack takes me to his house, for coffee and good talk, in his subterranean Elmwood Park study. I let Jeanne press a second breakfast on me.

Back to O'Hare, raining now, for the 11:50 A.M. Northwest 747, non-stop, Chicago to Anchorage.

But no plane. Seems there was an ice storm in Minneapolis, where Northwest planes are stored, out in the open, and everything froze up. They're taking turns now, wheeling them into hangers, thawing controls. Prelude to Alaska.

Passengers, game and/or disgruntled, increasingly the latter, mill about, and wait. I mill, and wait. Finally go to the bar, for a drink with fellow-passenger, a West Virginia redneck, heavy hillbilly accent, a man who commutes from his home near Morgantown, to his construction job in Kenai—a man right out of the pages of

McPhee, so that I get a sense of *déjà vu* . . . sort of like, "I'll wait 'til they make the movie," only in this case, reality is the movie, less real than the book, of which it seems an imitation.

Boarded at last—4:15 P.M. (CST) the great jet takes off, to pilot's profuse intercom apologies, and we are airborne. Having attained assigned altitude, the plane barely hums with only an occasional jiggle to indicate motion—as though this were a hotel ballroom or convention center, the building suffering the barely perceptible effects of a distant, minor earthquake.

We are served lunch—it must be around 5 now (CST)—and I begin to wonder about my co-lecturers for the conference, whom I do not know, but who are supposed to be on this plane. No way to search them out, in this strange, anonymous space. As de Tocqueville pointed out, we are isolated from one another.

Later, we are asked to pull down our little window shades to darken the room—and we are shown a movie. Something called "Outlaw Blues"—cops and robbers stuff in which the Bad Guys (crooks) are Good, and the Good Guys (cops) are not really Bad, just Dumb. Some very funny chase scenes, in which I become thoroughly engrossed . . . then that sudden, slight awareness—a jiggle of plane, the drone of the jets—and the reminder that all is happening at 30,000 feet, and 6 or 700 M.P.H. So that I have *three* realities to adjust: the movie, the interior space of the plane, and the spaces in which we are all moving.

As the movie ends we lift our window shades just in time to see spectacular mountain views, sunlit Chugach peaks, as we approach Anchorage. A vista I have not had since the Andes.

De-plane at Anchorage, nearly 7 P.M. local time (but nearly midnight in Albany, where the day started—we have passed through Central, Mountain, Pacific, Yukon, and into Alaska-Hawaii). Saradell Frederick, our hostess and conference organizer, had promised to meet the plane—but that was $4^{1}/_{2}$ hours ago. There is no one, and I still haven't found my co-lecturers. I gravitate to the baggage area, claim my imitation Samsonite, and zero in on another lone man, who turns out to be Michael Straight, author, former deputy director of the National Endowment, former editor and publisher of The New Republic, and now a co-lecturer. We exchange formalities, commiserate, and then notice another lone man, about to be greeted by what Michael calls "an academic type." These turn out to be Frank Broderick, history professor, former chancellor of UMass Boston, and co-lecturer; being greeted by Bob Frederick, Saradell's husband, and head of the Alaska Historical Commission. We collect ourselves, pile people and luggage into Bob's Scout or Bronco or whatever (an Alaskan Cadillac), and head for the Fredericks' home, where we are told there's a party in full swing.

Frederick seems an ebullient, enthusiastic man, tells me how *glad* he is to have me in Alaska, how *much* he enjoyed reading *Apalache* (in two nights, in a hotel room in Juneau), what great plans he has for the Historical Commission, how he's gotten money from the legislature, etc., etc.

Driving the outskirts of Anchorage, I'm trying to get an impression of the place—very difficult to do in the gathering darkness. What was it McPhee called it? Oklahoma City with ice? Nothing to dissuade me of this, so far. Except the surrounding snow-covered mountains, the lights of the ski tow twinkling on.

The Fredericks live in what I take to be one of the better new suburban areas, expensive-looking houses, in the higher foothills, overlooking Anchorage—and we reach it over as rough a road, all raw and new, as you would find in Appalachia.

Inside, we are greeted by Saradell, who seems similarly enthusiastic, moves well in spite of a limp. The house, built on the hillside, is different levels, circular iron staircase, etc. New, and white. Ascending, around the rising iron pole, I reach the party, Bob Frederick provides me with a drink, and I am introduced pell mell, one after another, to what I take to be the cream of petro-corporate-academic Anchorage. Names, names, and I find myself cornered with my scotch, some incredibly tasty smoked Alaska salmon, and a verbose character whose name, face, and function have vanished.

Bob eventually rescues me with another drink, and takes me out on the sun deck, if that's what you call it, and the full panorama: the lights of Anchorage, spreading beyond our feet, and, beyond, Knik Arm of Cook Inlet—the flare of an ARCO installation—and, beyond all, the mountains of the Alaska Range. My eye follows the peaks, in the fading light, as they rise, northward, to the farthest accessible point, the last glaring rays of sunset on the tip of Denali: Mt. McKinley.

Into the house again, buffet supper, fine French wines: no place to sit, except on the floor. This kind of discomfort is highly prized— the necessary habits of an impoverished subculture filtering up to the middle class.

I find myself opposite one Dr. Ezra Solomon, economist, professor of economics at Stanford, former member of Nixon's Council of Economic Advisors—and a co-lecturer. Joining us, in what becomes what might be called a conversation, is an ARCO representative, as smooth as the crude he produces. To stir the pot, I begin to lay out some of the ideas I had picked up from Hanrahan and Gruenstein ("Lost Frontier: The Marketing of Alaska"): 1) The existing pipeline, operating at capacity, will produce at least as much oil as West coast refineries can handle; 2) there is a federal law that prohibits the sale of Alaskan (or any domestic) oil to foreign countries; 3) the oil companies are pressing for further exploration, oil leases, etc., not only on the North Slope but on the outer continental shelf, the Gulf of Alaska; 4) there can be no place in the world more dangerous for oil drilling than these Alaskan waters, subject as they are not only to turbulent winter storms but to more or less constant seismic activity; 5) near Alaska—much nearer than much of the Lower 48—lies Japan, a highly industrialized nation that produces virtually none of its own energy, and that looks with a greedy and grasping eye on

Alaska's many resources; 6) one would conclude that there must be at least an assumption, if not actual collusion, shared by the oil companies and Japanese business, that the federal law could be altered or perhaps circumvented, so that surplus Alaskan oil could be sold to Japan; and 7) putting all this together, wouldn't it be wiser just to leave the bloody oil in the ground, until underwater drilling technology in this difficult area achieves greater efficiency, and such oil can be economically delivered and refined in the Lower 48?

The reactions of my new-found friends are extreme. The ARCO man is on more or less permanent assignment in Anchorage, and although he is engaged in Operations, he is clearly well-trained in P.R. He assures me, in a manner not the least crude but very refined, that there is not a whisper of assumption or collusion between the oil companies and Japan. All very polite, and avoiding altogether the unanswered questions. Solomon, on the other hand, who has no stake in Alaska, who is here to deliver his lecture, collect his fee, and get out (the one time I see him at the conference is for his own lecture)—Solomon becomes very angry. I suppose, in his eye, I am the long-haired radical, or at least a conservationist—almost as bad. He rails bitterly against the federal law prohibiting foreign sales, says that Alaska should yield all the oil available and sell the surplus to Japan, thereby releasing more OPEC oil for delivery to the Lower 48. It becomes clear that, in his mind, barrels of oil, like dollars, are a matter of international statistics, to be juggled—that Alaska, as a place, has no reality for him. This, in a few hours here, is my first indication of what later becomes clear as a syndrome: that Alaska, as a land, as a people, has been xeroxed, that it exists only on paper and in computers, so that even the bureaucrats may soon lose control.

Following the party—it is now 2:15 A.M., Albany time—we dignitaries are delivered to the Captain Cook hotel, a posh high-rise in the middle of downtown Anchorage. Restless, still, I step out to a bar next door, for a nightcap. One customer, complaining, and the bartender, commiserating, sympathetic. The problem: this young guy has worked hard all his life, has now acquired his own plane, just when the native land settlements have been effected—he can no longer fly at will about the state, land wherever he sees a clearing: the damn land *belongs* to somebody. Without, surely, being aware of it, he is an analog to the Eskimo who can no longer pursue the caribou, wherever they wander.

Aloha, and good night.

April 3, 1978

The night before, I had the prescience to draw the heavy window drapes, being apprised of the early Anchorage dawn. Waking, and rising, in my 11th-floor corner cocoon, I pull the two cords, and stand there, in my jockey shorts, facing another stupendous view: the city once more at my feet, Knik Arm and Cook Inlet, and two separate groups of snow-covered sun-struck mountains—producing the dual effect of walling us in, isolating Anchorage from the vast lands beyond, yet providing a slight but clear indication and invitation.

After breakfast, I step outside—the first daylight look at downtown Anchorage. Not much less than half the population of the whole state—175,000—lives in Anchorage . . . and it is a city absolutely without tradition, having started from nothing, in 1915 (two years before I was born). Shiny high-rise hotels, apartments, and office buildings, steel, glass, and concrete, erupt among the quaint frame-and-clapboard cottages, the well-built log cabins, of the original village, all in the same blocks.

The conference is to be held at the university, on the outskirts of town, and some of the younger faculty—those without tenure, I presume—are assigned chauffeur duty for us dignitaries. Steve Langdon, a burly, friendly anthropologist, is my man. He arrives in his father's snappy, modern station wagon (everything automatic), which he has borrowed for the occasion. We hit it off at once.

Steve, and Will Jacobs, one of the other "chauffeurs," and, later on, Dick and Nora Dauenhauer—all people in their thirties, I would guess—these are the sources of genuine information—as opposed to the officialdom in and about the conference.

Driving to the campus, the anomalous "charm" of downtown Anchorage vanishes, and we are engulfed by Shakey's, Golden Arches, The Colonel, Home of the Whopper, etc. But always, at every turn, them goddam mountains.

The campus buildings are new—with lavender wall-to-wall carpeting laid against concrete blocks. Academia nineteen-seventies.

For all the effort and money put into this conference, there don't seem to be many people here—and this remains true throughout the three days.

After opening remarks of welcome, by Dean Loftin, I am introduced by Steve Langdon—he has read me well, and has a sense of something he thinks I might offer Alaska.

"Major Speech: ALASKA'S MULTIPLE CULTURES: QUESTIONS AND POSSIBILITIES. Paul Metcalf, Writer and College Professor."

> (But what can I say, what can I offer, what can I do to negate the anomaly of my even being here, under these circumstances? These questions return, as I stride to the lectern— questions that have flickered in and out during the weeks that I have prepared for this moment.

> (Why did I accept? Flattery? The money? A chance to see this place, that had held excitement for me, from a distance? Some of all three, but mostly the latter. And let *them* pay for it. *Them* being who? ARCO? Eskimo? Taxpayer?

> (Still, it takes gall [a quality that Straight and Solomon, I think, have in greater abundance than I]—to appear here as an "expert" from the Lower 48. It is an issue about which Alaskans are schizoid, to the extreme: they can be proud,

arrogant, independent—and in the next breath, covertly or otherwise begging for advice. It is in response to the latter impulse, I suppose, that funds for just such a conference as this are provided.

(Later on, to balance the scales with myself, I pick up and bring home a typical bumper sticker: WE DON'T GIVE A DAMN HOW THEY DO IT OUTSIDE.)

The speech:

1) To deal with Anchorage, with Alaska, as a place—the sense, the dynamics, of re-locating myself, *putting* myself, here.

2) The history of dealing with ethnicity in the USA: ethnic stress, ethnic identification (late 19th to early 20th centuries); followed by the Melting Pot, or the Blender (nineteen twenties to fifties); followed by reassertion, led by the Blacks, of ethnic identities.

3) Quotes from Carl Jung, via Richard Grossinger: "Certain Australian primitives assert that one cannot conquer foreign soil, because in it there dwell ancestor spirits who reincarnate themselves in the newborn"; and—picked up from watching a baseball game—"The American presents a strange picture: a European with Negro behavior and an Indian soul."

4) Quote from Ben Franklin: rum will clear out the Indians, for the whites. The monotony of a monoculture.

5) Extensive quotes from Toni Cade Bambara, *On the Issue of Black English*, on the question of teaching ghetto kids: persistent grammatical errors, in English, which are nevertheless true to African linguistic roots. This offered as an analog to Alaska, the split cultural problems of the Eskimo, Indian, and Aleut.

6) Proposal: a series of regional research and cultural projects—attack each region—using students, locals, natives, whatever—from every angle, every scholarly discipline, every mode of expression. In the end for each region, produce a book, and an arts festival.

7) Alaska is not the last frontier, but the first: first hemi-spheric settlement came across the Bering Strait, into what is now Alaska. Quotes from *Apalache.*

All this received—I guess, somewhat between politely and well. There is no provision for questions and answers—although this is done for the later speakers. Like so much else, this conference is cobbled together as it goes along. Later, Steve Langdon tells me that those quotes from Jung really hit him: seems he is an anthro-pologist, concerned with natives; his wife is Black; and he once played professional baseball, was drafted by the Yankees, in an exhibition game hit a home run off Bill Lee.

I take Steve to lunch, but first we trade cars: he decides he is com-fortable enough with me that he need no longer front with Papa's snappy station wagon, so we go to Pop's clinic (Pop's a psychiatrist, a kindly man) and trade for Steve's beat-up VW van.

We dine at the one hippie-health-food place in Anchorage, good homemade soups and breads, guys in beards, gals in peasant skirts and jeans—a link with the New England college towns with which I feel comfortable. Steve tells me that it was he and Bob Frederick who leaned on Saradell, to get me invited as a speaker. So the impe-tus came from those two, not Saradell . . . Yet I noticed Saradell taking copious notes, as I talked.

Back to the conference, and a panel discussion: "Is There An 'Alaskan' Culture?" On the panel is Willie Hensley, President, Nana Development Corporation, who asks himself the question, "What is an Alaskan?" and answers "An Alaskan is someone with jet lag." Ah, yes, Willie Hensley—one of the Brooks Brothers natives, just back from a trip to Washington.

Willie Hensley grew up near Kotzebue, wintering in a sod house, "across an arm of Kotzebue Sound of the Chukchi Sea of the Arctic Ocean." Trapped whitefish in the late fall, netted fish under the ice in winter, in summer hunted ducks and muskrats, gathered berries by the barrel. A Baptist missionary in Kotzebue took an interest in Willie, and, at age 14 (1956), Willie found himself, fresh from the Eskimo bush, deep in the preachin' country of Yoknapatawpha County: Myrtle, Mississippi. (Brother Ray toured around in a Cadillac, in his bib overalls, preached fundamentalism—and the Blacks worked in the fields for $3 a day).

There followed an educational hegira: a Baptist academy in the Great Smokies, University of Alaska (Fairbanks), George Washington University (D.C.). Today, Willie is a pragmatist. As quoted in *Lost Frontier:* "'Anything that came along that helped us survive, we took ahold of it.' The corporation, he told us, is just another of the white man's tools which the Natives can use to survive, 'To me, this kind of extension of the corporate tool is not much different than trying to pick up an outboard motor, or a steel-tipped spear, or a gun to survive.'" And: "'Now that we have some land, we're not going to let them tax us to death. If we have some resources, we're not going to let them take it. That's the American system—to please the stockholders.'"

Yes.

When the discussion is opened to the audience, the unruffled facade presented by the panel is pierced by an angry young Eskimo student. He is perhaps too angry to make sense.

I meet and talk briefly with Joe Senungetuk's wife. She and Joe—the Eskimo artist and chronicler—attend every session of the conference, their faces serious, grimly absorbed. On behalf of Saradell, myself, and all the rest of us involved in the conference, the Senungetuk attention—both hungry and judging—embarrasses me.

At a break, I have a brief but intense conversation with a middle-aged German lady. She is apparently a woman of culture—she speaks competent English, though with a thick accent—who has lived all her life in Germany, and has only recently come to Alaska —coming directly, with no stops between. She is obsessed with the question: is Alaska the United States? Is she seeing the United States here in Anchorage? She seems convinced that this is a question I can answer.

To judge the USA, from Anchorage!

Following the discussion, films are shown. An intimate look at that peculiar and somehow durable hybridized primitive/modern life of the bush native.

I am alone for dinner tonight, so I try The Crow's Nest, top floor of the Captain Cook. View no better than from my bedroom. Seated with a young oil man, British Petroleum, just up from L.A. He eats ravenously, says he's suffering from jet lag (two-hour time difference). He likes it here, looking forward to the work . . . but his wife doesn't want to leave L.A.

Back to the conference, and an evening talk by Frank Broderick. He is a straight academic, but a rather pleasant man—and more committed, I think, to what is going on here, than any of the others. (He and I agree, the conference seems so poorly attended, that we *must* attend every session—more than anything else they need live bodies.)

Indicating directions in which a college curriculum might go, he suggests that the humanities may be revived by a strictly regional approach—instead of dealing with the "arts" as an abstraction, pin them down, or rather, become aware of how they spring up, in *time* and *place*. Dr. Williams, and Mr. Olson . . . the sense of place finally become useful.

For the conference, though, it is an important coincidence, one of the few harmonizing ideas: that Broderick and I, separately, hit on the regional approach. Next day, Bob Frederick is quick to pick up on it.

April 4, 1978

After breakfast, and before Steve comes for me, I take a walk, down the hill, toward the waterfront—Knik Arm. Elderberry Park, Hostettler Park, the tracks of the Alaska Railroad, dirty chunks of drift ice going out on the tide, people hustling up the hill, in the brisk air, to jobs. At the top, at the bend of the road, the statue of Captain Cook.

Panel discussion: "The interface between Alaska and National Culture." A hot topic—but 'round and 'round the discussion goes, and never seems to get down to business. The question is:

What is an Alaskan? So many peoples, so many races, so many reasons, so many motives, all in conflict, for being here. So much land, so many resources, so much happening, so much moving, all so fast, everyone driven by forces that no one controls, is it even possible to pause long enough to ask the question, what is an Alaskan?

I recall that, during the weeks before coming here, I had spent hours listening to the music of Sibelius, a "northern" composer who had used the general European orchestra, and I raise the question, whether Alaska, as a northern land, might have more affinities with other circum-polar nations, simply using the Lower 48 as a general orchestra—but the panel seems not to want to deal with this. Although later I learn that Hensley has visited villages in Siberia, in search of just this, the northern affinities—and there has been a Conference of Circum-Polar Nations—that seems not to come up for discussion.

I learn that Anchorage is swarming with lawyers—the state, the various federal bureaus, the corporations, petro, and native, all "represented," all litigious. (There is a sign on a little lunch counter downtown: "Legal Pizza.")

Throughout the conference, the panel discussions, a sense of steam-
ing conflicts that never break the surface. Everyone has to live with
one another, everyone is polite.

The natives, the state, everyone schizoid, split. And extreme. There
is little or no middle ground.

(Lael Morgan, in *And the Land Provides*, reports from Bethel
[Bethel, in Hebrew, is House of God, but in Alaska it is Louse-
town, or The Armpit of Alaska]: the volunteer counselors at the
sleep-off center, dealing with drunk natives in from the bush, make
snap decisions: advise them to stay, adapt, learn to handle booze—
or send 'em back to the bush, the tundra, live in the old way, off
the land.)

(But in one of the panels, a sociologist reports that in the mixed
native communities, subsistence and modern mixed, it is those
groups that retain the strongest subsistence base that yield the least
alcoholism, tuberculosis, crime, unwanted kids.)

Lunch today with Dick and Nora Dauenhauer—a warm and
humanizing interlude. They take me to an English-coach-house-
type place, rich furnishings, a fire in the fireplace, intimate tables,
a bit of old Albion in the grub of peripheral Anchorage. Dick is
a young poet, teacher, German-American, and Nora is Tlinget
Indian, a craftsperson, from southeastern Alaska, Sitka area, rain
forest. Together they offer the first of a kind of middle ground, a
love and gentleness—the first that I have seen in this forbidding
and energetic place.

Sitting in the car, briefly, staring at some browned-out weeds at the
edge of the lot, Nora is reminded of some things that *grow*, in her
native coastal rain forest . . . and I am struck with how different that
land is, southeastern Alaska, that tail, dropping toward Washington
and Oregon, having more in common with them, perhaps, than
with Anchorage and the body of land northward. Nora speaks of a
summer she spent once in Fairbanks, how she couldn't stand the

heat. (The temperature there ranges, winter and summer, 160°—whereas Sitka remains, year-around, in the middle ranges.)

Clearly, Nora is not happy here in Anchorage. She misses her homeland—as though it were thousands of miles and an ocean away.

Dick inscribes two books for me, some excellent translations and a long poem of his own, the history of the rape of this land and its peoples. The energy of that rape is something outside him.

Back to the conference, and an afternoon of moom pitchas: some excellent shots of contemporary Eskimo whaling, all the blood and guts . . . the Aleutian Islands, looking like Scottish highlands . . . and an oh-so-lovely promo piece on the pipeline, produced by ARCO.

At the hotel, up to my room . . . oh, them god damn mountains!

Straight, Broderick and I decide to shop around for dinner, we find a restaurant in a quaint little frame house, near the hotel, with a plaque on the front: The Oldest House in Anchorage—1915. I can't quite pinpoint the architecture: Russian-Orthodox-New England-Saltbox.

Michael is very sophisticated, consulting about the wines, etc.—calls us "barbarians" when we stick to our martinis. He's a very cynical man, an old New Deal Liberal, for whom everything since Roosevelt's death has been downhill. He regales us with tales of Teddy's drinking, Rocky's women, etc.

After dinner, us three Humanists get our revenge on Dr. Solomon, the Economist: we file into the auditorium, take our seats together near the front, clearly in his line of vision—and, as he drones on, one by one we nod off.

April 5, 1978

Another morning of panel discussions—"Alaska in Transition"—
now become unspeakably boring. Not a single idea that I couldn't
have or haven't already extracted from the books, more clearly. The
only person who appears to be happy is the one who, at any given
moment, is speaking.

At noon we meet Gordon Smith, Director of the Visual Arts Cen-
ter. He is young, informed, and candid—unlike the smoothie who
runs the Historical and Fine Arts Museum.

The Visual Arts Center is the workshop and gallery for native
artists and artisans—located across the road from the airline termi-
nal. Michael, Frank, and I climb into Smith's car, to go out for a
look.

This is the drive, between downtown and airport, that darkness
had hidden when we arrived: the most unspeakable urban sprawl to
be found on the face of the earth. Beyond Shakey's, beyond the
Golden Arches, beyond the Whopper and the Colonel, beyond
all these lie block after block of rusted Quonset huts, dilapidated
shacks, still functional, hamburgers, used cars, tacos and massages
—and mile upon mile of airplane graveyards, old World War II
hulks and later, rusting in the fields . . . all against the backdrop, the
implacable snow-capped Chugach.

Slogging through the mud, into the Arts Center—not much going
on, but a good place, a sense of *work*. A few pieces hanging in the
gallery, what seems a viable hybrid of ancient design and modern
influx. Fred Anderson, the native sculptor, whose name I had been
given, is not here today.

Lunch, on the way back, at a Mexican joint, tacos and enchiladas, in
the sprawl.

The afternoon, another dull panel—with a single idea emerging: Alaska viewed as a colony of the Lower 48:

I realize that in this city of 175,000 I have seen not a single factory or industry. Alaska is a resource—the oil and other minerals, the timber, the fish—to be extracted, for the benefit of the other states—their own needs returned to them, manufactured, at a middleman's price. Much of the state could be opened to cool-weather agriculture, but little of this is done—the milk I drink in the hotel flies in via 747 freighter from Seattle. The state is treated, in fact, just as Great Britain treated the original 13 colonies: extract the resources, ship them out, manufacture them, and ship them back, on the importer's terms.

In this way, perhaps, the diverse peoples that make up Alaska—Eskimo, Aleut, Indian, redneck, bureaucrat, attorney, and bush pilot—may be united, in their psychology: a pride derived of terrestrial and marine wealth—and the shame of dependent, colonial status. Always, the split.

Following the panel, Saradell drives us into town, for a champagne reception at the Historical and Fine Arts Museum. She apologizes for the candy wrappers in the car, so busy she had no time for dinner the other night, just a candy bar. The woman's energy is almost frightening.

At the edge of the original village of Anchorage is the remains of a greenbelt, now cut up with roads, playgrounds, etc. This was put in, in the early days, as a barrier, separating the habitation from the encroaching forest. But they had to cut it up, at least partially, to discourage ad hoc landings by bush pilots.

I mention that I was unable to find the native sculptor Fred Anderson, whom I wanted to meet, and Saradell says that perhaps it's just as well, he has been aloof and moody lately. She talks about how many generations it's going to take to overcome what "we" (the whites) did to "them" (the natives), how much she has done for Fred and the others, through the Visual Arts Center, how difficult it can be at times, etc., etc.—and the tone is that of a complaining mother: "I've done so much for you, and you don't appreciate me!"

How far apart she and Fred must be! As I ride in the back of Saradell's car, among the candy wrappers—detritus of Saradell's energies—my respect for Fred is suddenly established.

Alaska is a series of veneers, loosely shuffled together, with air spaces instead of glue.

Anchorage Historical and Fine Arts Museum: very posh, very neat, very elegant. I'm told they have a good native collection, but what seems to be more in evidence is traveling shows, of a European flavor. Saradell talks about how she has fought very hard for these, the alternative apparently being romantic Alaskan landscapes, executed by etiolated descendants of sourdoughs.

Long tables set up, with white tablecloths, a fine spread of champagne and hors d'oeuvres, all provided by—who else?—ARCO. Their unhappy-looking P.R. man is there, with his ill-fit three-piece suit and his faceless one-piece wife. But, poor Saradell—there don't seem to be many guests. Much of the wine and goodies go unconsumed.

Earlier in the day, Steve Langdon had been mumbling something about "we're gonna meet the Governor tonight," and I would say, "oh, sure, Steve, sure." So now he blows in, with his gorgeous tall bride, Gladys, and he says, "Come on, let's go meet the Governor." I turn to Gladys: "Is he for real?"—and she just laughs.

I get the impression that Steve and Saradell are not much more than tolerant of each other. In any case, I am kidnapped—Steve, Gladys, and I drive off.

A neat, modern ranch-type house, in what I would call suburbia, except that it's all Anchorage—the home of a clean-cut young lawyer, and his effusively social wife. A relaxed and informal party—wines and ginger ales—in full swing: this is the rising younger white-collar middle-class set. Seems that Governor Jay Hammond is up for election this year, and this is the nucleus of his Anchorage campaign team, putting on a reception in his honor. In due course, the Guv'nah arrives.

A heavy-set, handsome man, warm, bearded, imposing. A Vermonter, a Green Mountain boy, who moved to Alaska many years ago, worked as a bush pilot before getting into politics. A liberal Republican, who comes down on the side of the conservationists in opposition to the exploiters, and he shares the Alaskan's mistrust of all the massive powers, Good Guys and Bad Guys alike, from the Lower 48: Washington, the Sierra Club, etc.

We troop downstairs to the Family Room, to serve ourselves to the roast beef buffet, then troop back up to the living room, careful not to spill—and, wise by now, I capture one of the few chairs. The Governor sits on the floor. (There is a more powerful force at work here, this business of sitting on the floor, than earlier, at the Fredericks: whereas that was liberal chic, this is populist politics. I balance my plate comfortably in my lap, unembarrassed in old-fashioned respect for my back.)

Steve, Hammond, and I talk oil, economics, fisheries, conservation, the press, politics, etc. Hammond talks about the pressures he is under to sell more oil leases, produce instant cash for the state. He points out that OPEC is a cartel; that historically cartels never survive, the members start squabbling with one another; that should this happen in OPEC, with one or more of the members cutting prices, Alaska can jolly well forget about its oil: the entire Alaskan operation is predicated on current OPEC prices. It is a rear-guard action he is fighting, attempting to stem the old boom psychology.

When I leave, I thank the Governor for his attention, and promise to vote for him.

Steve whisks me back to the conference, where Michael Straight is in the middle of his presentation, a combination talk and slide show, with pretty pictures of places like Reston, Virginia, and Columbia, Maryland, those new communities created from scratch —the ideal American life, out of Better Homes and Gardens, TV commercials, etc. Behind all this lie references to a proposed new state capitol, to be built from scratch in the Matanuska Valley: Straight showing the locals how it might be done . . . and also, implicit digs at what has already been done, the ugliness of extended Anchorage. All in all, it seems a rather lofty and condescending performance . . . Mr. Straight takes himself seriously as an Expert from the Lower 48.

In re TV: I recall that the first live television to reach Alaska was the Dallas Cowboys football games. Like everyone else, the oil people bring their own culture.

The conference is over, the corridors are filled with effusive goodbyes, etc. We go back to the hotel, time for a quick drink, then Steve takes Frank and me to the airport, for our post-midnight departure. We check in at the counter, and head for the departure lounge. It is time to say good-bye to Steve . . .

April 6, 1978

. . . I try to give him a bear hug, but he draws back . . . I am embarrassed.

Am I reading too much into this—that Alaskan coolness, the inaccessibilities? I am reminded again of the absence of manufactures in Alaska, that that is what is missing: the 19th century. It was in the 19th century that manufacturing—making by hand—proliferated in the Lower 48; and even though everything was eventually made by machine, it is that first step, making by hand, that is essential to human intimacy. Without it, everything is energetic and stark. Hard porn. Topless and bottomless. The Stone Age, with 18th-century colonialism—and 20th-century technology.

Our flight takes us to Chicago via Seattle and Portland. Frank and I get a little sleep on the first leg.

Seattle is fogged in, but between there and Portland there are occasional spectacular views of the Northwest, a land distinct from the Alaska of Anchorage.

The airport at Portland is green, the grass and growth rain forest lush. I am reminded, for a moment, of Nora Dauenhauer.

Frank deplanes here, and I fly on alone.

At O'Hare, as I wait for the last leg to Albany, who comes striding down the corridor, but Muhammed Ali!

NEW MAD'-rid

January 3, 1789, Col. George Morgan, veteran of the American Revolution, departed Ft. Pitt, to establish a colony in the Spanish territory on the west bank of the Mississippi, where he would be subject to His Catholic Majesty the King of Spain. Col. Morgan founded NEW MAD'-rid.

He was a man out of step with his time: he liked trees, Indians, wild animals.

* * *

John James Audubon: "I was jogging on one afternoon, when I remarked a sudden and strange darkness rising from the western horizon. Accustomed to our heavy storms of thunder and rain I took no more notice of it, as I thought the speed of my horse might enable me to get under shelter of the roof of an acquaintance, who lived not far distant . . . I had proceeded about a mile, when I heard what I imagined to be the distant rumbling of a violent tornado, on which I spurred my steed, with a wish to gallop as fast as possible to a place of shelter; but it would not do, the animal knew better than I what was forthcoming, and instead of going faster, so nearly stopped that I remarked he placed one foot after another on the ground, with as much precaution as if walking on a smooth sheet of ice. I thought he had suddenly foundered, and, speaking to him, was on the point of dismounting and leading him, when he all of a sudden fell a-groaning piteously, hung his head, spread out his four legs, as if to save himself from falling, and stood stock still, continuing to groan. I thought my horse was about to die, and would have sprung from his back had a minute more elapsed, but at that instant all the shrubs and trees began to move from their very roots, the ground rose and fell in successive furrows, like the ruffled waters of a lake, and I became bewildered in my ideas . . .

. . . I found myself rocking as it were on my horse, and with him moved to and fro like a child in a cradle . . ."

*   *   *

"Before any of the whites present perceived it, Black Feather, swinging himself from side to side, observed that the *earth tottered.*'"

*   *   *

About midnight, while the French population were engaged in dancing, the first shock came . . .

A little after two o'clock on the morning of December 16, the inhabitants of the region were suddenly wakened by the groaning, creaking, cracking of the timbers of the houses or cabins in which they were sleeping . . .

. . . the house danced about and seemed as if it would fall on our heads.

a low rumbling, like the sound of carriages over cobbles . . .

the sky dark, the air saturate with sulphurous vapor . . .

. . . a nauseating sickness at the stomach and a trembling of the knees

the ground rose and fell as earthwaves, like the long, low swell of the sea, passed across its surface

. . . the undulation of the earth as resembling waves . . .

as if the surface of the earth was afloat and in motion

a smart motion

the agitated surfaces quivering like the flesh of a beef just killed

a sudden cross shove, all order is destroyed, and a boiling action is produced

. . . blowing up the earth with loud explosions. It rushed out in all quarters, bringing with it an enormous quantity of carbonized wood, reduced mostly into dust, which was ejected to the height of from ten to fifteen feet, and fell in a black shower, mixed with the sand which its rapid motion had forced along . . .

water spouted to great heights, as if it were pressed out of the pores of the earth

the water which was spurted from the bowels of the earth . . .

the surface was sinking and a black liquid was rising to the belly of my horse

landslides at Push and Grace

rocks split asunder

. . . chasms, which remained fearfully deep, although in a very tender alluvial soil . . .

faults and sand-blows, domes and fissures, caving, chasms, crevices, slumps, sloughs, sand-scatters

blasts of air and gas, the earth rolling, fissuring, farting

the trees blown, cracking and splitting, their branches interlocked

trees split in the midst, lashed one with another . . .

forests were overthrown

the noise produced by the agitation of the trees resembled that of a shower of small hail in the forest . . .

people scrambled onto the fallen trees, to escape engulfment

the skull of a musk ox hurled from the earth, coffins extruded from the river banks

clocks stopped, dogs barked, well water roiled

the cattle crowded about the assemblage, the birds themselves lost all power and disposition to fly, and retreated to the bosoms of men, landed on heads and shoulders, crowded about the fires of those who had left their dwellings

bear, panther, deer, wolf, and fox came into the garden

the water thrown up was warm, the ground, underfoot, warm . . .

the water that flowed over the earth, over blood heat

west of the river, the land dropped, to become the sunk country

the country here was formerly perfectly level, now it is covered with slaches, sand hills, mounticules

*　*　*

"It may be necessary to remark in this place, that the navigation of the Mississippi is attended with considerable danger, and in particular to boats loaded with lead. These, by reason of the small space occupied by the cargo, in case of striking against a *planter* or a *sawyer,* sink instantly. That these terms may be understood, it must be observed that the alluvion of the Mississippi is almost in every part covered with timber close to the edge of the river,

and that in some part or other encroachments are contin-
ually made, and in particular during the time of the floods, when
it often happens that tracts of some acres in extent are carried
away in a few days. As in most instances a large body of earth is
attached to the roots of the trees, it sinks that part to the bottom
of the river, whilst the upper part, more buoyant, rises to the
surface in an inclined posture, generally with the head of the
tree pointing down the river. Some of these are firmly fixed
and immoveable, and are therefore *planters*. Others, although
they do not remove from where they are placed, are constantly
in motion, the whole tree is sometimes entirely submerged by
the pressure of the stream, and carried to a greater depth by
its momentum than the stream can maintain. On rising, its
momentum in the other direction causes many of its huge limbs
to be lifted above the surface of the river. The period of this
oscillatory motion is sometimes of several minutes duration.
These are the *sawyers,* and are much more dangerous than the
planters, as no care or caution can guard sufficiently against
them. The steersman this instant sees all the surface of the
river smooth and tranquil, and the next he is struck with horror
on seeing just before him the *sawyer* raising his terrific arms,
and so near that neither strength nor skill can save him from
destruction."

* * *

. . . the perpendicular banks began to fall into the river in such vast
masses . . .

the river was covered with foam and drift timber . . .

the trees on both sides of the river were most violently agitated, and
the banks fell in, in several places, within our view, carrying with
them innumerable trees, the crash of which falling into the river,
mixed with the terrible sound attending the shock, and the
screaming of the geese, and other wild-fowl, produced an idea that
all nature was in a state of dissolution.

. . . during the shock a chasm had opened on the sand bar opposite the bluffs below, and on closing again, had thrown the water to the height of a tall tree.

the trees rushed from the forests, precipitating themselves into the water

in many places the banks of the river sunk hundreds of acres together, leaving the tops of the trees to be seen above the water

the river changed to a reddish hue and became thick with mud thrown from the bottom, while the surface, lashed violently by the agitation of the earth beneath, was covered with foam, which gathered in masses the size of a barrel

a chasm opened in the river, swallowing the waters . . . and then closed, hurling back waves

faulting crossed the river, causing waterfalls

the riverbottom, heaving and doming, arrested the mighty stream in its course

a bursting of the earth just below the village of New Madrid, arrested this mighty stream in its course, and caused a reflux of its waves . . .

. . . the Mississippi roared, the current for a few minutes was retrograde

. . . the Mississippi seemed to recede from its banks, its waters gathered up like mountains . . .

craters in the riverbed, earth openings, creating whirlpools, or sucks . . . spoutings of mud and sticks, blown from the riverbed

The current of the Mississippi . . . was driven back upon its source with the greatest velocity . . . But this noble river was not thus to be

stayed in its course. Its accumulated waters came booming on, and
. . . carried everything before them with resistless power. Boats . . .
shot down the declivity like an arrow from a bow . . .

. . . we were so far in the suck that it was impossible now to land . . .

A man who was on the river in a boat at the time of one of the
shocks, declares he saw the mighty Mississippi cut in twain, while
the waters poured down a vast chasm into the bowels of the earth

*   *   *

the Mississippi:

continental
fluid,
watering,
enriching,
dividing
the hemispheres,

heaving

with respiration

CELTS

the Irish found their way to Iceland by following the seasonal flight of swans

driven from Iceland by Vikings, they sailed their skin craft west to Greenland,

and the Vikings, driving west, discovered in Greenland the remains of abandoned Irish settlement . . .

pursuing still west, to the continental coast, to Vinland, the Vikings found there a settlement they called Ireland the Great, "where men went about in white dress, shouted loudly, and carried poles with banners."

?

three thousand years ago

bands of roving Celtic mariners crossed the North Atlantic

to discover, and then to colonize

from Spain and Portugal, by way of the Canary Islands . . .

following the Celts came Phoenicians from Cadiz, who spoke the Punic tongue

Libyans and Egyptians entered the Mississippi from the Gulf

penetrated to Iowa, the Dakotas

and westward along the Arkansas and Cimarron Rivers, the Oklahoma-Colorado border . . .

Celts in the rivermouths of New England, North Africans in the heartland of the continent, centuries before Christ

Celts ascending the
Connecticut, to
Queechee

Norse and Basque
on the St. Lawrence

Phoenician Iberian
Sunsigns in
New England

Basque Inscriptions,
Susquehanna
graves

Iberian Punic Sungod,
Baal,
at Mystery Hill

South Royalton,
Vermont:
Phoenicians

Ships of Tarshish
to Massachusetts

Phoenicians
at Monhegan

a Celtiberian dolmen,
New York

outdoor altars,
Celtic Vermont

Celtics on
the Cimarron

Phoenician phalli,
South Woodstock

Celtics in
Owasco and Amoskeag

rings of stone,
Burnt Mountain

Tartessian inscriptions,
Moundsville

Oklahoma
Punic

Iberians in Iowa

Susquehanna Basque

Coptic and Nubian
among the Zuni

Libyans in
Mojave

?

Gwynn, an early Celtic explorer of Oklahoma, cut his autograph in
two languages on a rock face on Turkey Mountain, near Tulsa

?

*Early Celtic writing used only
consonants, the vowels were
inferred. Consonants are the
bones of language, of which
vowels grow the flesh.*

Consonants are skeletal, prime.

*(When a man goes deaf, he
gradually loses consonants in
his speech, retains only vow–
els)*

*(Early Celtic writing evolved
from a finger alphabet:*
                              sign

language)

Elephant Valley,
Vermont:
Druidic cupules

Quartz Celtic
Testicle Stones:
South Woodstock

Phalloi,
South Pomfret

Libyans among
the Micmacs

Egyptian calendar
In Iowa

New England
Druids

Osiris
in Iowa?

Tennessee
Phoenicians . . .

NORTH BOLIVIA

"In the setting sun, a man is
sharply outlined from his
immediate surroundings."

—Joe Senungetuk, Eskimo
American, at Kingetkin, far-
thest westernmost extension
of mainland Alaska, at the
tip of the Cape, on Bering
Strait . . .

"The undisturbed snow
crystals around him became
millions of reflectors."

. . . at the end and beginning, ter-
minus and entrance, step-
ping off and landing point,
for all Alaska . . .

and earlier, for all
America—the Americas—
the hemisphere: northern tip
of the Backbone of the
Earth.

* * *

A Man in the Andes (1959):

". . . Here every fragment of the landscape constantly impels, you're like under a pressure, but distant, again that funny combination of exhilaration and relaxation . . ."

> . . . at Anchorage: shut off
> and invited, by the Chugach . . .

". . . all ports of llegada and salida are sink traps, serve to deceive as the nature of what they serve."

> . . . Anchorage.

*　*　*

In the Andes:

". . . nowhere as in s.a. is individual character impressed against its background, framed, clarified—personality emerges with a sharpness as terrifying as the geography."

" . . . every place I visit produces an indigenous personality type by way of companion, even those who travel seem to present themselves to me in the place that naturally, incisively frames them—it is this, the place-sense, the background at all times pushing, projecting, that gives to human personality here an at times well nigh insane clarity, precision."

*　*　*

Alaska: North Bolivia

at the head of the Backbone, the Spine of the slipped and shaken
Earth, north and south . . .

North Bolivia: where character is simplified, clarified, the man, the
woman, determined, produced by the landscape . . .

A Frontier: bones and soul of character projecting, every man, every
woman, a strong station

himself, herself, alone

the clear air admitting no else

Bibliography

OSSA

Borovka, Gregory. *Scythian Art,* trans. by V. G. Childe. New York, N.Y., 1960.

Jettmar, Karl. *Art of the Steppes.* New York, N.Y., 1967.

Senungetuk, J.E. *Give or Take a Century.* San Francisco, Cal. 1971.

ANCHORAGE

The New York Times, March 27, 28, & 29, 1964.

Time, April 3 & 10, 1964.

MEGRIM

Alvarez, W.C. 'The migrainous scotoma as studied in 618 persons." *American Journal of Ophthalmology,* 49:489-504, 1960.

Barrett, W.P., editor. *The Trial of Jeanne d'Arc.* New York, N.Y., 1932.

Diamond, Seymour. *More than Two Aspirin.* Chicago, Ill. 1976.

Freese, Arthur S. *Headaches, the Kinds and the Cures.* New York, N.Y., 1973.

Friedman, A.P. "The headache in history, literature and legend." *Bulletin of the New York Academy of Medicine,* 48:661-680-. 1972.

Friedman, D. "Migraine: With special reference to scintillating scotomata." *Eye Ear Nose Throat Monthly,* 50: 28-35. 1971.

Gould, G.M. "The history and etiology of 'migraine.'" *Journal of the American Medical Association.* 42: 168- 172 and 239-244. 1904.

Graham, John. "Prodromes of Migraine." *Hemicrania,* 3/1:3-5. 1971.

Hachinski, V.C.; J. Porchawka; and J.C. Steele. "Visual symptoms in the migraine syndrome." *Neurology,* 23:570-578. 1973.

Hay, K.M. *Do Something about that Migraine.* New York, N.Y., 1968.

Kayan, A. "Migraine and related disorders of hearing and balance." *Hemicrania,* 4/4:3-4. 1973.

Lennox, William Gordon. *Science and seizures .* New York, N.Y., 1941.

Lippman, C.A. "Certain hallucinations peculiar to migraine," *Journal of Nervous and Mental Disease,* 116:346-351. 1952.

—"Hallucinations of physical duality in migraine," *Journal of Nervous and Mental Disease,* 117:345-350. 1953.

Mitchell, J.K. "Headache with visual hallucinations," *Journal of Nervous and Mental Disease,* 24:620-625. 1897.

Mitchell, S.W. "Neuralgic headaches with apparitions of unusual character," *American Journal of Medical Sciences,* 94:415-419. 1887.

Scott, W.S., editor. *The Trial of Joan of Arc.* Folio Society, 1956.

Smith, John Holland. *Joan of Arc.* New York, 1973.

Speer, Frederic. *Migraine.* Chicago, Ill., 1977.

Sulman, F.G. "Climatic factors in the incidence of attacks of migraine," *Hemicrania,* 6/1:2-5. 1974.

"ALASKA IN TRANSITION"

Hanrahan, John & Peter Gruenstein. *Lost Frontier: The Marketing of Alaska.* New York, N.Y., 1977.

McPhee, John. *Coming into the Country.* New York, N.Y., 1977.

Morgan, Lael. *And the Land Provides.* Garden City, 1974.

NEW MAD'- *rid*

Adams, Alexander B. *John James Audubon.* New York, N.Y., 1966.

Audubon, Maria R. *Audubon and his Journals.* New York, N.Y., 1897.

Bradbury, John. *Travels in the Interior of America in the years 1809, 1810 and 1811.* Liverpool, 1817.

Bringier, L. "Notices of the geology . . ." *American Journal of Science,* 1st Series, Vol. 3. 1821.

Broadhead, G.C. "The New Madrid Earthquake," *American Geologist,* Vol. 30. 1902.

Flint, Timothy. *Recollections of the last ten years . . .* Boston. 1826.

Fuller, Myron L. "The New Madrid Earthquake," *U.S. Geological Survey Bulletin* 494. Washington, 1912.

Haywood, John. *The Natural and Aboriginal History of Tennessee.* Nashville, Tenn., 1823.

Latrobe, Charles J. *The Rambler in North America; 1832-1833,* 2 Vol. London, 1835.

McMurtrie, Henry. *Sketches of Louisville and its Environs.* Louisville, KY, 1969.

Penick, James L. *The New Madrid Earthquakes.* Columbia, MO, 1976.

Shepard, E.M. "The New Madrid Earthquake," *Journal of Geology,* Vol. 13. 1905.

CELTS

Fell, Barry. *America B.C.* New York, N.Y., 1976.

Sauer, Carl O. Northern Mists. San Francisco, Cal., 1968.

NORTH BOLIVIA

Metcalf, Paul. *Patagoni.* Highlands, N.C., 1971.

Senungetuk, J.E. *Give or Take a Century.* San Francisco, Cal., 1971.

WILLIE'S
THROW

I am a lifelong baseball fan, brought up with, and still pledging allegiance to, the Boston Red Sox. I therefore need no lessons in suffering. Despite being relentlessly partisan, though, I believe that I recognize Quality, wherever it appears. It was not difficult for me to be attracted, early on, to Mr. Willie Howard Mays. The attention and affection I have directed toward him, over the years, was perhaps eased by the fact that he played in the "other league." (Had he been a dreaded Yankee, this poem no doubt would not have been written.)

In my casual baseball reading, I stumbled on a paperback called *My Greatest Day in Baseball,* in which several well-known players chose a particular day or play to celebrate—and for Willie, it was this unearthly throw. What caught my eye, in the description, was this phrase: "So that he threw like a discus thrower."

Baseball is drama. It is also comedy (grown men playing a kid's game, for high pay)—but it is comic in the highest sense of that term. It occurred to me that good comedy is produced when the artist takes an absurd idea and pursues it literally and seriously, to its conclusion. Why not take Willie's throw and treat it as Willie's throw *back*—back to the infield, the catcher—and back in history, to the Greek Olympiad—Willie as the young Greek, hurling the discus?

From there on, it was just a question of mining the sources, and letting the pieces fall together: Willie the young Greek, hurling the discus in the Polo Grounds, August 15, 1951.

The throw went *back*. May it, with this small celebration, hurtle forward, from Greece, to New York, to wherever the games may be played. Cheers!

— Paul Metcalf

WILLIE'S THROW

I REMEMBER

what I think nobody else remembers . . .
the way the clouds were against the sky . . .
they were no longer white
but ribbed with gray too,
and you had the feeling that
if you could reach high enough
you could

> *get the gray out of there.*

Still, for the greatest day ever for Willie Howard Mays, you have to go all the way back to his rookie season in 1951. That was the year the Giants made their miraculous comeback in the last six weeks of the season to tie the Dodgers, who had led by 13 $^1/_2$ games in mid-August . . .

And the one play that may have turned around the whole year for both teams came on August 15. The Giants' streak had just about started—four in a row—and they were playing Brooklyn at the Polo Grounds. It was a 1-1 ball game, eighth inning, one out, Billy Cox on third, Ralph Branca on first and Carl Furillo up. In the stands there were 21,007 fidgety fans.

I lived with my Aunt Sarah and her family. I was born, May 6, 1931, not in Fair-field but in a nearby place with almost the same name—Westfield—but the marriage of my father and mother didn't last much more than a year after that, and then I went to live at Aunt Sarah's house in Fairfield.

They were kids themselves, my mother and father—no more than 18, either one of them, when I was born. But he was a baseball player, and my mother was a wonderful athlete herself—a star runner who held a couple of women's track records in that part of the country . . .

Furillo hit a fly ball into right center field. Mays, playing over in left-center for the notorious pull-hitting Furillo, had to come a long distance to make the catch. Make it he did, on the dead run, gloved hand extended and that was the second out. But Cox on third had tagged up and was heading home with the lead run. And Cox could run like a deer. When Mays caught the fly ball, running full speed toward the right field foul line, he was moving away from the play. If he stopped dead and threw, he couldn't possibly get any zip on the ball . . .

> . . . STRAIGHTWAY HE DREW ALL EYES UPON HIMSELF, WHEN THEY BEHELD HIS FRAME, SUCH PROMISE OF GREAT DEEDS WAS THERE.

. . . So he improvised. He caught the ball, planted his left foot and pivoted away from the plate . . .

What I did, though, was catch the ball and kind of let its force in my glove help spin me completely around.

. . . so that he threw like a discus thrower . . .

The art of throwing from a circle 8 ft. 2 1/2 in. in diameter to the greatest distance, and so that it falls within a 90° sector marked on the ground, an implement weighing 8 lb. 6.4 oz. known as a discus. The sport was common in the days of Homer, who mentions it repeatedly. It formed part of the pentathlon, or quintuple games, in the ancient Olympic games . . .

Fans in the bleachers must have wondered what in the world their boy was doing.

. . . The discus must be slung out and not really thrown at all; the athlete's difficulty lies in controlling an implement which can be retained under and against the hand and wrist only by centrifugal force and such slight pressure as the tips of the fingers are able to exert.

AT ONCE, THEN, CONFIDENT IN HIS POWERS HE
MEASURES, NOT THE ROUGH ACRES OF THE PLAIN,
BUT THE SKY'S EXPANSE WITH HIS RIGHT ARM, AND
WIOTH EITHER KNEE BENT EARTHWARD HE GATHERS
UP HIS STRENGTH AND WHIRLS THE DISK ABOPVE HIM
AND HIDES IT IN THE CLOUDS.

One time, outside of a flower store, I saw an emblem
of this guy with wings that said you could send flowers
by wire. And when the wind blew on the overhead
utility lines and made the wires sing, I'd always think to
myself that must be flowers going through the
wires, somebody sending them to somebody else . . .

. . . WHAT POWER HAS THIS MAN AGAINST THE GODS?

Preparatory to making a throw the athlete holds the discus in the right (best)
hand so that the edge rests against the joints of the fingers nearest to the tips.
He takes up his position in the rear half of an 8 ft. 2½ in. circle with the feet
about 18 in. apart and his left side turned in the direction in which the throw
is to be made. The discus is swung up above the head, where it is met and
supported by the fingers of the left hand. The right arm next swings back until
it reaches a point behind and higher than the right shoulder. From this position,
after two or three preliminary swings have been made and the right hand is at
its highest point, the athlete commences a 1¼ turn in a kind of dancing time
with the right arm hanging loosely down. The first pivotal movement is upon the
left foot; when a half turn has been made the weight is transferred to the right
foot, upon which the turning movement continues. As the left foot again takes
the ground, at the front edge of the circle, the right leg begins to push the body
forward and there is a violent turn of the right shoulder, but the arm is still kept
trailing behind and the actual throwing movement does not commence until
the right arm is well off the right shoulder. The left leg forms a point of resis-
tance as the throw is made and the discus departs through the air mounting
upwards . . .

But Willie, making a complete whirling pivot on the dead run, cut
loose with a tremendous peg . . .

. . . AND HOLDING IT ALOFT SUMMONS UP THE
STRENGTH OF HIS UNYIELDING SIDE AND VIGOROUS

ARMS, AND FLINGS IT WITH A MIGHTY WHIRL, SPRING-
ING FORWARD AFTER IT HIMSELF. WITH A TERRIFIC
BOUND THE QUOIT FLIES THROUGH THE EMPTY AIR,
AND EVEN IN ITS FLIGHT REMEMBERS THE HAND THAT
FLUNG IT AND KEEPS IT TO ITS DUE PATH, NOR
ATTAINS A DOUBTFUL OR A NEIGHBORING GOAL . . .

The throw came to the plate as a bullet and Whitey Lockman, the cut-off man . . .

(. . . the good Lord willin' and the creeks don't rise . . .)

. . . let it go through and Wes Westrum, the catcher, caught it belt-high and slapped a tag on a desperately sliding Cox. For a long time . . . the stands were silent, not quite certain they had seen right. Then they exploded when they realized Mays had turned a certain run into a miracle inning-ending double play.

. . . AND MAKES TREMBLE THE GREEN BUTTRESSES AND SHADY
HEIGHTS OF THE THEATER . . .

EDDIE BRANNICK: *The finest play I ever saw.*
CHARLIE DRESSEN: *He'll have to do it again before I'll believe it.*
CARL FURILLO: *The play is impossible. And that's that.*

THE BOX SCORE

BROOKLYN

	A.B	R.	H.	P.	A.
Furillo rf	4	0	1	5	0
Reese ss	4	1	1	1	2
Snider cf	4	0	0	2	0
Pafko lf	4	0	0	1	0
Campan'la c ..	3	0	1	5	0
Hodges 1b	3	0	0	8	0
Cox 3b	3	0	2	1	1
Ter'l'ger 2b ...	2	0	0	1	3
Robinson 2b ..	1	0	0	0	0
Branca p	3	0	1	0	2
TOTALS ...	31	1	6	24	8

NEW YORK

Stanky 2b	3	0	1	1	3
Dark ss	4	1	1	1	1
Mueller rf	3	0	0	2	0
Irvin lf	3	0	1	2	0
Lockman 1b .	3	0	0	10	0
Mays cf	3	1	1	3	1
Westrum c ..	3	1	1	7	1
Hearn p	3	0	0	0	2
TOTALS ...	28	3	5	27	11

BROOKLYN	000	000	100	—1
NEW YORK	100	000	02x	—3

RBI–Irvin, Campanella, Westrum 2. 2b–Dark. HR–Westrum. DB–Branca, Rees & Hodges; Mays & Westrum. LOB–Brooklyn 3, New York 2. BB–Off Branca 1. SO—Branca 5, Hearn 5. WP–Hearn. Balk–Hearn. Hearn–(W, 11-7). Branca–(L, 10-4). Umpires–Warneke, Goetz, Jorda, & Dascoli. T–2:10. A–21,007.

DR. UHLEY: *According to the textbooks every human being has a kind of layer of fat on his back . . .*

WILLIE: *So?*

DR. UHLEY: *So?*

WILLIE: *I mean, what's the problem?*

DR. UHLEY: *The problem is you don't have any fat.*

WILLIE: *I thought you said everybody does.*

DR. UHLEY: *I didn't say everybody does. The book says everybody does. Up till now, the book's been right.*

WILLIE: *Well, if I don't have the fat, what do I have?*

DR. UHLEY: *Willie, all you've got for a back is one continuous muscle.*

Bibliography

Carmichael, John P., editor. *My Greatest Day in Baseball*. New York, 1968.

Encyclopedia Britannica. Chicago, 1943 edition.

Mays, Willie & Charles Einstein. *Willie Mays: My Life in and out of Baseball*. New York, 1966.

New York Times. August 16, 1951.

Statius, Publius Papinus. *Thebaid* J.H. Mozeley, trans. 2 Vol., London & Cambridge, 1961.

BOTH

"He was so much against slavery that he had begun to include prose and poetry in the same book, so that there would be no arbitrary boundaries between them."

—ISHMAEL REED

POE

David Poe, Jr., a letter to his cousin, eighteen o nine:

"Sir, *You* promised *me* on your honor to meet me at the Mansion house on the 23d—*I* promise *you* on *my* word of honor that if you will lend me 30, 20, 15 or even 10$ I will *remit* it to you immediately on my arrival in Baltimore. Be assured I will keep my promise at least as well as you did yours and that nothing but extreme distress would have *forc'd* me to make this application—Your answer by the bearer will prove whether I yet have 'favour in your eyes' or whether I am to be despised by (as I understand) a rich relation because when a *wild boy* I join'd a profession when I then thought and now think an honorable one. But which I would most willingly quit tomorrow if it gave satisfaction to your family provided I could do *any thing* else that would give bread to mine—Yr. Politeness will no doubt enduce you to answer this note from Yrs &c

D. POE JR."

. . . left a career in the law, to follow the disreputable profession of acting . . .

. . . married an actress, Elizabeth Hopkins (nee Arnold), "a lovely little creature" "with the aura of unreality which the stage imparts" . . .

. . . raised a family, trouped the eastern seaboard, in six years on the stage played one hundred and thirty-seven roles . . .

. . . but was less than a successful actor, suffering as he did from "sudden indispositions" which sent him to the stage staggering . . .

. . . was reviewed once as "sur un POE de chambre."

. . . left his young wife, disappeared . . .

. . . and she trouped alone, with the infants . . .

. . . she was delicate, tubercular, and in Richmond, in her boarding house room . . . in the presence of her young son Edgar, who was less than three years old . . . she spit blood, and died . . .

*   *   *

. . . the child remembered:

"The sight of blood inflamed its anger into phrensy" and the garments of the men who came to cart his mother away were

"nigrum nigrius nigro"

*   *   *

To attain the hypnagogic state, between sleep and reason, between death and life . . .

> "The boundaries which divide Life from Death
> are at best shadowy and vague."

To depart the life of this earth, and to be interred—but still alive!

> "It may be asserted, without hesitation, that *no*
> event is so terribly well adapted to inspire the
> supremeness of bodily and of mental distress,
> as is burial before death. The unendurable
> oppression of the lungs—the stifling fumes of
> the damp earth—the clinging to the death
> garments—the rigid embrace of the narrow
> house—the blackness of the absolute Night—
> the silence like a sea that overwhelms . . ."

To become one "whose pleasure lies in arousing and bearing anxiety, through loss of balance, stability and contact with firm earth."

*   *   *

The infant Edgar, adopted by the John Allans of Richmond, was educated in England and Virginia, enrolled in the University at Charlottesville . . .

> (" . . . debts were accummulated, and money borrowed of Jews in Charlottesville at extravagant interest . . . It was then that I became dissolute, for how could it be otherwise?")

enlisted in the army,
was appointed to West Point
. . . . and court-martialed

lived in Baltimore with his aunt Mrs. Clemm
. . . was disowned by Allan . . .
grubbed a meager literary living

. . . 1835, married his first cousin Virginia Clemm
(age 14)
and, with her mother,
set up housekeeping:

Eddie, Sissy and Muddy

Young Virginia: slender, delicate, prone to weakness of the lungs . . .

". . . a picture of a young girl just ripening into womanhood."

"The portrait, I have already said, was that of a young girl. It was a mere head and shoulders . . . The arms, the bosom, and even the ends of the radiant hair melted imperceptibly into the vague yet deep shadow which formed the background of the whole."

"In time the crimson spot settled steadily upon the cheek, and the blue veins upon the pale forehead became prominent; and, one instant, my nature melted into pity, but, in the next, I met the glance of her meaning eyes, and then my soul sickened and became giddy with the giddiness of one who gazed into some dreary and unfathomable abyss."

* * *

To attain the spirit's outer world . . .

" . . a gay and motley train of rhapsodical and immethodical thought."

> "*All* that we see or seem
> Is but a dream within a dream."

> "Would to God I could awaken

> For I dream I know not how . . ."

> "And all my days are trances . . ."

* * *

> "I really believe that I have been mad . . ."

* * *

"At no period of my life was I ever what men call intemperate. I never was in the *habit* of intoxication. I never drank drams, &c. But, for a brief period, while I resided in Richmond, and edited the *Messenger* I certainly did give way, at long intervals, to the temptation held out on all sides by the spirit of Southern conviviality. My sensitive temperament could not stand an excitement which was an everyday matter to my companions. In short, it sometimes happened that I was completely intoxicated."

"... the occasional use of cider, with the hope of relieving a nervous attack."

"During these fits of absolute unconsciousness I drank, God only knows how often or how much."

"All was hallucination, arising from an attack which I had never before experienced—an attack of mania-a-potu."

("No man is safe who drinks before breakfast!")

"I call God to witness that I have never loved dissipation ..."

"I have been taken to prison once since I came here for getting drunk ..."

"I have fought the enemy manfully ..."

"I am resolved not to touch a drop as long as I live."

"I am done forever with drink."

"My *habits* are rigorously abstemious and I omit nothing of the natural regimen, requisite for health:—i.e.—I rise early, eat moderately, drink nothing but water ..."

"... the causes which maddened me to the drinking point are no more, and I am done drinking forever."

"Will you be kind enough to put the best possible interpretation upon my behavior in N-York? You must have conceived a *queer* idea of me—but the simple truth is that Wallace would insist upon the *juleps,* and I knew not what I was either doing or saying."

"... humming-stuff ..."

("Poe is not in Richmond. He remained here about 3 weeks, horribly drunk and discoursing 'Eureka' every night to the audiences of the Bar Rooms.")

* * *

"Happiness is [Man's] purpose. The sources of that, he may be told, are in himself—but his eye will fix on the external means, and these he will labor to obtain. Foremost among these, and the equivalent which is to purchase all the rest, is property. At this all men aim ..."

"... to combine the ideas of an agility astounding, a strength superhuman, a ferocity brutal, a butchery without motive, a *grotesquerie* in horror absolutely alien from humanity, and a voice foreign in tone to the ears of men of many nations, and devoid of all distinct or intelligible syllabification."

"There were a great many women and children, the former not altogether wanting in what might be termed personal beauty. They were straight, tall, and well formed, with a grace and freedom of carriage not to be found in civilized society. Their lips, however, like those of the men, were thick and clumsy . . ."

"In the calm, and, as we would call it, the healthful condition of the public mind . . . we find each quietly enjoying his own property, and permitting to others the quiet enjoyment of theirs . . . Peace reigns, the arts flourish, science extends her discoveries, and man, and the sources of his enjoyments, are multiplied."

"Each animal, if you will take the pains to observe, is following, very quietly, in the wake of its master. Some few, to be sure, are led with a rope about the neck, but these are chiefly the lesser or timid species. The lion, the tiger, and the leopard are entirely without restraint. They have been trained without difficulty to their present profession, and attend upon their respective owners in the capacity of *valets-de-chambre.*"

"A very short while sufficed to prove that this apparent kindness of disposition was only the result of a deeply laid plan for our destruction, and that the islanders for whom we entertained such inordinate feelings of esteem, were among the most barbarous, subtle, and bloodthirsty wretches that ever contaminated the face of the globe."

"Fifty years ago, in France, this eccentric comet, 'public sentiment,' was in its opposite node . . . it should be remembered now, that in that war against property,

"It was quite evident that they had never before seen any of the white race—from whose complexion, indeed, they appeared to recoil."

the first object of attack was property in slaves . . ."

"We speak of the moral influences flowing from the relation of master and slave, and the moral feelings engendered and cultivated by it."

". . . unless we take into consideration the peculiar character (I may say the peculiar nature) of the negro."

"Let us reason upon it as we may, there is certainly a power, in causes inscrutable to us, which works essential changes in the different traces of animals . . . The color of the negro no man can deny, and therefore it was but the other day, that they who will believe nothing they cannot account for, made this manifest fact an authority for denying the truth of holy writ. Then comes the opposite extreme —they are, like ourselves, the sons of Adam, and must therefore, have like passions and wants and feelings and tempers in all respects. This, we deny . . ."

"In truth, from everything I could see of these wretches, they appeared to be the most wicked, hypocritical, vindictive, blood-thirsty, and altogether fiendish race of men upon the face of the globe."

"Their complexion a jet black, with thick and long wooly hair. They were clothed in skins of an unknown black animal, shaggy and silky . . ."

"The bottoms of the canoes were full of black stones . . ."

". . . a black albatross . . ."

". . . black gannets . . ."

". . . brown celery . . ."

"blackfish . . ."

"Our theory is a short one. It was the will of God it should be so. But the means—how was this affected? We will give the answer to anyone who will develope the causes which might and should have blackened the negro's skin and crisped his hair into wool."

". . . he who is taught to call the little negro 'his,' in this sense and *because he loves him,* shall love him *because he is his.*"

"Nothing is wanting but manly discussion to convince our own people at least, that in continuing to command the services of their slaves, they violate no law divine or human . . ."

". . . a species of bittern, with jet black and grizzly plumage . . ."

". . . a very black and shining granite . . ."

"The marl was also black; indeed, we noticed no light colored substances of any kind upon the island."

"He . . . made use of only idiotic gesticulations, such as raising with his forefinger the upper lip, and displaying the teeth which lay beneath it. These were black."

"We noticed several animals . . . covered with a black wool."

"Nature had endowed him with no neck, and had placed his ankles (as is usual with that race) in the middle of the upper portion of the feet."

"Seizing him furiously by the wool with both hands, I tore out a vast quantity of black, and crisp, and curling material, and tossed it from me with every manifestation of disdain."

*   *   *

Virginia Clemm Poe: slender, delicate, with a tendency toward
weakness of the lungs . . .

> "She was a good girl, and told me very
> sweetly that I might have her (plum
> and all) . . .

> > (The pendulum, "messy and
> > heavy, tapering," swinging to the
> > circular pit . . .)

> > ". . . but the fires were not of Eros, and
> > bitter and tormenting to my spirit was
> > the gradual conviction that I could in no
> > manner define their unusual meaning,
> > or regulate their vague intensity . . ."

> "The forehead was high, and very pale, and singularly
> placid; and the once jetty hair fell partially over it, and
> overshadowed the hollow temples with innumerable
> ringlets, now of a vivid yellow, and jarring discordantly,
> in their fantastic character, with the reigning melan-
> choly of the countenance. The eyes were lifeless, and
> lustreless, and seemingly pupilless, and I shrank
> involuntarily from their glassy stare to the contempla-
> tion of the thin and shrunken lips. They parted; and
> in a smile of peculiar meaning, *the teeth* of the
> changed Berenice disclosed themselves slowly to my
> view . . . for these I longed with frenzied desire."

> > (But the pendulum, swinging:
> > "Could I resist its glow? or if
> > even that, could I withstand its
> > pressure?")

1842, Edgar Allan Poe was at last out of debt. He was employed, and content with home and family: Eddie, Sissie, and Muddy. "In the evening, after the plentiful dinner that Mrs. Clemm now could supply without stint, the occupants of the little clapboard house were happy together. Edgar would play the flute, and Virginia would sing to her harp."

> But, early that year: "Suddenly Virginia's voice broke and died: blood streamed from her throat."

> She lay shivering in bed, Eddie's old army coat thrown over her—Catarina, the family cat, draped around her throat.

"But at length, as the labor drew nearer to its conclusion, there were admitted none into the turret; for the painter had grown wild with the ardor of his work, and turned his eyes from the canvas rarely, even to regard the countenance of his wife. And he *would* not see that the tints which he spread upon the canvas were drawn from the cheeks of her who sat beside him. And when many weeks had passed, and but little remained to do, save one brush upon the mouth and one tint upon the eye, the spirit of the lady again flickered up as the flame within the socket of the lamp. And then the brush was given, and then the tint was placed; and, for one moment, the painter stood entranced before the work which he had wrought; but in the next, while he yet gazed, he grew tremulous and very pallid, and aghast, and crying with a loud voice, 'This is indeed *Life* itself!' turned suddenly to regard his beloved:—*She was dead!*"

*   *   *

". . . it is clear that a poem now written will be poetic in the exact ratio of its dispassion. A passionate poem is a contradiction in terms."

"[The poet] recognizes the ambrosia which nourishes his soul, in the bright orbs that shine in Heaven—in the volutes of the flower —in the clustering of low shrubberies—in the waving of the grain-fields—in the slanting of tall, Eastern trees—in the blue distance of mountains—in the grouping of clouds—in the twinkling of half-hidden brooks—in the gleaming of silver rivers—in the repose of sequestered lakes—in the star-mirroring depths of lonely wells. He perceives it in the songs of birds—in the harp of Æolus—in the sighing of the night-wind—in the repining voice of the forest—in the surf that complains to the shore—in the fresh breath of the woods—in the scent of the violet—in the voluptuous perfume of the hyacinth—in the suggestive odor that comes to him, at eventide, from far-distant, undiscovered islands, over dim oceans, illimitable and unexplored."

"With the *passions* of mankind—although [a poem] may modify them greatly—although it may exalt, or inflame, or purify, or control them—it would require little ingenuity to prove that it has no inevitable, and indeed no necessary co-existence."

* * *

". . . Tellmenow Isitsöornot . . ."

"Most of them [the stories] were *intended* for half banter, half satire —although I might not have fully acknowledged this to be their aim even to myself."

"The Atlantic has been actually crossed in a Balloon! and this too with-out difficulty—without any great apparent danger—with thorough control of the machine—and in the inconceivably brief period of seventy-five hours from shore to shore!"

("Some few persons believe it—but *I* do not—and don't you. P.S. 'The Valdemar Case' was a hoax, of course.")

("Of course, there is not one word of
truth in it from beginning to end . . .
please *do not let out the secret."*)

. . . filled his stories with spurious quotations from foreign languages
. . . "makes quotations from the German, but he can't read a word of
the language."

. . . codes, ciphers, and anagrams . . . acrostics, hieroglyphics,
the kabbala . . .

"I believe that demons take advantage of the night to mislead the
unwary—although you know, I don't believe in them."

". . . Tellmenow Isitsöornot . . ."

*   *   *

Worried about his appearance:

"I have been invited out a great deal—but could seldom go, on
account of not having a dress coat."

"My clothes are so horrible . . ."

Cultivated his moustache—the mark of the actor—"that was to
become his trademark . . ."

(until, near the end (1849), "Poe, pale and
haggard, burst into John Sartain's office. He
begged Sartain to protect him from two men
who, he said, were going to kill him. They had
followed him on the train, but he had got off
and returned to Philadelphia to avoid them. He
insisted that Sartain cut off his moustache, so
he could not be recognized . . .")

"His voice, I remember, was very pleasant in its tone and well modulated, almost rhythmical" . . . "he spoke with great precision" . . . "his voice seemed attenuated to the finest golden thread; the audience became hushed, and, as it were, breathless; there seemed no life in the hall but his; and every syllable was accentuated with such delicacy, and sustained with such sweetness, as I have never heard equally by other lips . . . I felt that we had been under the spell of some wizard" . . . "he seems to have chanted his verses instead of reading them in the ordinary sense" . . . "His voice was rich, his enunciation clear, and he read poems with a dramatic, almost histrionic power" . . .

Mrs. Clarke, who heard him read in Richmond, remembered the richness and mellowness and sweetness of Poe's voice, noting a resemblance to that of the actor Edwin Booth . . .

*   *   *

Margaret Fuller thought "he always seemed shrouded in an assumed character."

. . . actor and character, role and player, interfused, the other become his own, his own another . . .

Performing out of shyness: the theater—self-exhibition—the final retreat of the secretive . . .

"Richmond & the U. States were too narrow a sphere & the world shall be my theatre—"

*   *   *

Accused just about everyone, particularly Longfellow, of plagiarism . . .

("I am particularly anxious for a paper on . . . the subject of the Laws of Libel in regard to Literary Criticism . . .")

(accused Fenimore Cooper of "mental leprosy")

. . . wrote a book, *The Conchologist's Text Book*, which was a paraphrase of another's original . . .

> ". . . and the more you put in your book that is not your own, why the better your book will be:—but be cautious and steal with an air."

*   *   *

"Pure gold can be made at will, and very readily from lead in connection with certain other substances . . ."

John Sartain: "I asked him how he came to be in Moyamensing Prison, and he said he has been suspected of trying to pass a fifty-dollar counterfeit note . . ."

*   *   *

". . . Tellmenow Isitsöornot . . ."

. . . to banish uncertainty, to interfuse, to blend . . .

. . . to marry one's cousin, to tell tales of incest . . .

. . . at various times gave his date of birth as 1809, 1811, 1813 . . . at 37, called himself 33 . . .

. . . enlisted in the army as Edgar A. Perry, at other times became Henri le Rennet, Edward S. T. Grey, E. S. T. Grey Esqre., and Thaddeus K. Peasley . . .

*   *   *

Poe, the actor, playing his role, and Edgar, watching him play . . .

> (Gertrude Stein: "I said and I said it well I said an actor sees what he says. Now think a little how he looks and how he hears what he says. He sees what he says.")

"The orange ray of the spectrum and the buzz of the gnat . . . affect me with nearly similar sensations."

*   *   *

"but I am still *very* unwell . . ."

"I am getting better, however, although slowly, and shall get *well.*"

"I am still dreadfully unwell . . ."

> (". . . congestion of the brain . . .")

Mrs. Shew: "I made my diagnosis, and went to the great Dr. Mott with it; I told him that at best, when Mr. Poe was well, his pulse beat only ten regular beats, after which it suspended, or intermitted (as doctors say). I decided that in his best health he had lesion of one side of the brain . . ."

On his deathbed: ". . . tremor of the limbs . . . a busy but not violent or active delirium—constant talking—and vacant converse with spectral and imaginary objects on the walls . . . a violent delirium, resisting the efforts of two nurses to keep him in bed . . ."

. . . died—October 7, 1849—of "chronic inflammation of the meninges."

*   *   *

In 1860—long after Poe's burial in an unmarked grave—Judge Neilson Poe ordered a marble slab, properly inscribed. "It was lying in the yard with other monuments ready for delivery when a train of the Northern Central Railroad accidentally jumped the track and, of all slabs, shattered Poe's beyond repair."

"It was not until a quarter of a century after Poe's death that a group of Baltimore schoolteachers, aided by the citizenry, succeeded in raising enough money to honor the poet with a monument, and commissioned Sir Moses Ezekiel to execute it . . . The sculptor had finished his clay model and had sent it to the foundry to be cast into bronze when it was destroyed by fire."

"He modeled it for the second time, only to have an earthquake demolish it, together with the studio that housed it."

"The third time Sir Moses managed to get it cast before another intervention."

WATERWORLD

ONE

The Indian tribes of the Canadian Plains believed that all buffalo emerged from under a lake, and however recklessly the white man might slaughter, they would never be exterminated . . .

According to the Hopi, all bodies of water are parts of one great ocean underlying the earth . . . the springs are mere openings, or eyes, as the Spanish call them, peering through the earth crust, out of the waterworld.

* * *

Adam Seaborn:

"In the year 1817, I projected a voyage of discovery, in the hope of finding a passage to a new and untried world. I flattered myself that I should open the way to new fields for the enterprise of my fellow-citizens, supply new sources of wealth, fresh food for curiosity, and additional means of enjoyment; objects of vast importance, since the resources of the known world have been exhausted by research, its wealth monopolized, its wonders of curiosity explored, its every thing investigated and understood!"

"I remembered the misfortune of the discoverer SINBAD, whose ship, when he approached the magnetic mountain, fell to pieces, in consequence of the iron being all drawn out of it. To guard against a similar disaster, I fastened my vessel first with tree-nails, and then throughout with copper bolts firmly rivetted and clenched."

"Confident that, with this vessel, I could reach any place to which there was a passage by water, whether on the external or internal world, I named her the EXPLORER."

"On the 4th of September, we entered the harbour of West Point, Falkland Islands. Here I had determined to pass a month for the benefit of my health, which a short passage by water had not completely restored, from the debility occasioned by the vexations and anxieties of business in those retrograde times, and the pernicious habits of living, common among civilized men, upon food rendered palateable by a skilful admixture of poisons."

"I concurred in the opinion published by Capt. Symmes, that seals, whales, and mackerel, come from the internal world through the openings at the poles; and was aware of the fact, that the nearer we approach these openings, the more abundant do we find seals and whales."

> earth opening, polar cleft,
> source and passage of earth's
> unending watery abundance!
>
> birth-channel of whales and seals:
> southern polar orifice

"This will give the polar region seven months constant day, with a continual stream of light and heat pouring upon the same spot, without any interval of night to cool the earth and air. I think if we can but find our way to the polar region, we shall be in much more danger of being roasted alive, than of being frozen to death."

> erogenous!

"Slim: 'How will you justify yourself to the world, to our families, or to your own conscience, if we should, after effecting a passage through this 'icy troop' you speak of, find it closed against our return, and be thus forever lost to our wives, our children, and society?'

A plague upon your lean carcass, thought I . . . I could not tell him of my belief of open poles, affording a practicable passage to the internal world, and of my confident expectations of finding comfortable winter quarters inside; for he would take that as evidence of my being insane . . ."

"I edged away to the eastward, intending to keep near the ice, and hauled to the southward, when a clear sea would permit. The first day, we kept the 'blink of the ice' * in sight, and found it to trend nearly East and West."

"After a comfortable meal, and a sound nap of four hours, I descended the precipice to ascertain whether the river was an arm of the sea, or a fresh water stream. It proved to be pure potable water, and the existence of a continent near the south pole, was thus established."

"I was now convinced of the correctness of Capt. Symmes's theory, and of the practicability of sailing into the globe at the south pole, and returning home by way of the north pole, if no land intervened to obstruct the passage.

> an open passage,
> a clear sail,
> into earth internal!

"Having anchored the Explorer in a safe situation, I landed with a boat's crew at one of the open spaces, to examine the productions of the land, and see if I could discover any indications of inhabitants. I found the timber to be mostly different from that which I was acquainted with, excepting a species of fir resembling our spruce . . . All fears of the consequence of wintering in this region were now done away. Where trees could live, I could live."

---

*an arch formed upon the clouds by the reflection of light from the packed ice.

the mound of delight
is piligerous!

". . . I was well aware that when they (the crew) would suppose we
were sailing northward on the other side of the globe, we should in
fact be sailing directly into it through the opening."

a song,
a geode,
to earth penetrated!

"I, Adam Seaborn, mariner, a citizen of the United States of Amer-
ica, did, on the 5th day of November, Anno Domini one thousand
eight hundred and seventeen, first see and discover this southern
continent, a part of which was between 78° and 84° south latitude,
and stretching to the N.W., S.E., and S.W., beyond my knowledge;
which land having never before been seen by any civilized people,
and having been occupied for the full term of eighteen days by
citizens of the said United States, whether it should prove to be in
possession of any other people or not, provided they were not
Christians, was and of right ought to be the sole property of the said
people of the United States, by right of discovery and occupancy,
according to the usages of Christian nations."

("I had it engraved on a plate of sheathing copper, with a spread
eagle at the top, and at the bottom a bank, with 100 dollar bills
tumbling out of the doors and windows, to denote the amazing
quantity and solidity of the wealth of my country.")

"I was perfectly aware that if the poles were open, of which I had no
doubt, we must . . . on turning the edge of the opening have a ver-
tical sun, an equal division of day and night, and all the phenomena
of the equator."

"The compass was now of no manner of use; the card turned
round and round on the slightest agitation of the box, and the
needle pointed sometimes one way and sometimes another,

changing its position every five minutes . . . My best seamen appeared confounded . . . and a degree of alarm pervaded the whole ship's company."

"We had a regular recurrence of day and night, though the latter was very short, which I knew was occasioned by the rays of the sun being obstructed by the rim of the earth, when the external side of the part we were on turned towards the sun."

"I walked the deck all night, and was very impatient for the morning of that day which was to disclose to me the wonders of the internal world."

> sliding,
> sliding,

"I named this island, which was in 81° 20' internal south latitude, Token Island, considering its discovery as a token or premonition of some great things to come."

> sliding. . . *in!*

"I found the latitude this day, carefully computed from the sun's altitude, with due allowance for refraction, to be 65° 17' south internal."

"My imagination became fired with enthusiasm, and my heart elated with pride. I was about to secure to my name a conspicuous and imperishable place on the tablets of History, and a niche of the first order in the temple of Fame. I moved like one who trod air; for whose achievements had equalled mine? The voyage of Columbus was but an excursion on a fish pond, and his discoveries, compared with mine, were but trifles . . . His was the discovery of a continent, mine of a new World!"

> penetrating, invading,
> violating
> the gentle virgin,
> Earth

"The soft reflected light of the sun, which was now no longer directly visible, gave a pleasing mellowness to the scene, that was inexpressibly agreeable, being about midway between a bright moonlight and clear sunshine. I had great cause to admire the wonderful provision of nature, by which the internal world enjoyed almost perpetual light, without being subject at any time to the scorching heats which oppress the bodies and irritate the passions of the inhabitants of the external surface."

   ·   Mother Earth,
       internal—

       o perfect paradise!

TWO

Donald McCormick:

"One spring morning in 1884, two men stood on the banks of the river Blackwater in Essex [England] and gazed silently and admiringly at a small craft which promised them the chance of fulfilling their separate dreams and ambitions.

The elder was the owner of the craft, and already thinking of the day he would sail her in and out of the thousands of coral islands which comprise the Great Barrier Reef. The other was the man on whom the owner was pinning his hopes of making this dream cometrue—the seasoned seaman whom he had selected as his prospective captain."

"'Well,' inquired the owner, 'and what do you think of her?'

His accent proclaimed him to be an Australian, and he exuded the enthusiasms of that buoyant and exuberantly extrovert nation.

It was obvious from the tone of his voice that he thought the yacht was a veritable gem from the builder's yard, a thing of beauty and a joy to be. But the long pause before the other spoke suggested equally that he had reservations on the subject and was not quite so enthusiastic.

At last he managed to speak: 'She's certainly grand to look at and I'm thinking that she's a sturdy 'un,' he muttered cautiously. 'She needs to be. But I'm also thinking she's a titch of a craft to go to Australia under her own sail.'

Obviously the enthusiastic owner was taken aback. He seemed distinctly annoyed.

'Come, come, Captain, I expected you to say something different from that. Don't you agree she's in first-class condition?'

'Oh, her condition is all right. But she's sixteen years old, don't forget. No chicken as yawl-rigged yachts go. I warrant she's had a fair share of the sea already. A first-rate job for cruising in home waters, but a trip to Australia poses a good many problems. You hadn't thought of shipping her out as deck cargo?'

'Mr. Dudley,' replied the other testily, 'if I had, I certainly shouldn't have sent for you. I chose you from a list of many applicants for this job because I understand you have the qualities and experience for this trip.'

'It's my experience that tells me this is a risky proposition. And I've had enough experience to tell me that one thing a seaman can't tell for sure is what the weather is going to be like a thousand miles away in two months' time. We're going to need good luck and good weather for this trip, especially when we're approaching the Cape.'

'If you accept my proposition, you are absolutely free to pick your own time for making the voyage and you can stop whenever you think it's desirable.'

'There won't be many stops after Madeira, I'm thinking.'

'You couldn't make a coastal trip, hugging the shore of Africa to the Cape?'

'It would take too long and there would be just as many risks with on-shore gales. Not many worthwhile ports we could call at south of the Equator on the African coast. Fact is, what with the blackamoors and cannibals, we'd be safer off at sea.'

Both men laughed at this.

'I bet you could tell some tales of cannibals, Captain.'

'Happen I could. But that's beside the point. If I take this job on, it will have to be the quickest route on the chart—as direct a straight line as sailing will permit. Anyhow, it's a challenge and I've never funked a challenge yet. Nor shall I now.'

'Splendid! Then it's agreed that you will be skipper and find a crew as quickly as possible?'

'If I can get the crew I want, I'll accept. But they'll take some finding, sir. You see, the best sailors know too much about the sea and they don't fancy the risks of getting becalmed a thousand miles from land in a tiny yacht.'

'How many men will you require?'

'We don't want too many. First, because we couldn't carry the provisions for 'em; second, because too many sailors, like too many cooks, get in each other's way. I want a few good men, that's all. I'd settle for a mate, one able seaman and a boy.'"

"The craft of which we have been speaking was the *Mignonette,* a yawl-rigged vessel built at Brightlingsea in 1867. She was a small yacht of only nineteen tons, with a length of fifty-two feet, a beam of twelve feet one inch, and a draught of seven feet four inches. The vessel was listed in Lloyd's first *Register of Shipping* in 1878 and continued to be shown until 1884 under the ownership of Mr. Thomas Hall, of Barnard's Inn, London. But in 1882 Mr. Hall had sold her to a fellow barrister, Mr. Henry J. Want, of Sydney, New South Wales.

Mr. Want had been born in Australia in 1846 and educated partly in France. He was an able and eloquent barrister who had just embarked on a political career. Indeed, it was the prospect of politics which now made it necessary for him to hurry home ahead of the yacht he had bought.

Henry Want felt that a craft with so relatively low a draught would be ideal for cruising around the islands of the Great Barrier Reef and it was his ambition to take *Mignonette* on a summer cruise from Sydney, up the eastern coast of Australia, among the 80,000 square miles of warm, tropical seas dotted with thousands of pine-covered islands to spear turtles and hunt for the dugong. Previously his yachting had been mainly confined to short trips out from Sydney.

With this end in view he had selected Captain Thomas Dudley, then stationed at Colchester, to sail *Mignonette* from Tollesbury in Essex to Sydney. It is true that he had been warned this was a hazardous enterprise, and that the considered opinion of experts was that she should travel as deck cargo rather than under her own sail. But he felt quietly confident that a first-class seaman could carry out the operation and Dudley was a natural choice for the assignment for he came from a family of sea-faring people, his father and brothers all being sailors. He was a tall, impressive man of thirty-one, with a striking personality and a mahogany-hued face that gave evidence of many years spent at sea, and, according to his testimonials, 'a man of exemplary character,' 'thoroughly depend-able and trustworthy' and 'able to tackle any job requiring skilled seamanship, courageous and with real power of command.'"

"The pay for this voyage to Australia was good—well above the average, for Mr. Want was a wealthy man—and in addition the Australian had promised Dudley and the other members of the crew a substantial bonus if the yacht was delivered safely before the end of September. It was an operation not without risks, but, given luck as far as the weather was concerned, and careful seamanship, the ultimate rewards more than outweighed the disadvantages.

Want took a liking to Dudley, despite the latter's contemptuous reference to the 'titch of a craft.' He lost no time in engaging him as captain and Dudley set about finding a crew. But this, as Dudley feared, proved far from easy. Potential crew were apt to dwell upon the disadvantages rather than the financial rewards. To many the idea of being cooped up in a small craft on meagre rations for so long a voyage was somewhat of a nightmare."

"Finally the crew was completed by the signing on of Richard Parker, a seventeen-year-old boy who lived in the neighborhood of Southampton.

It was a small and young crew. Brooks, the third hand, was the eldest at thirty-eight and the mate, Edwin Stephens, was thirty-six.

They were tough, seasoned men, though, with the possible excep-
tion of Parker, who had no previous experience of ocean sailing. But
Parker, like Dudley, had the tradition of the sea in his family."

"Dudley had carefully chosen young Parker as being an intelligent,
high-spirited and well-behaved lad, to whom the prospect of a long
voyage to Australia was something of an adventure.

Mignonette completed her refitting, provisioned, and on May 19
she sailed away from Southampton, passed the Isle of Wight and
out into the English Channel on the first leg of her lengthy voyage."

"For the first three weeks of their trip the weather favoured them.
At times they made fifteen knots and Dudley began to feel that
Mignonette fully justified her owner's praises.

In these early days they kept to the main trade routes and hardly
a day passed without their sighting a ship, or another yacht. With
the Atlantic as calm as a pond their duties were not onerous, and off
watch they spent their time reading, playing poker and sun-
bathing. Brooks acted as cook and occasionally added to their stock
of food with some catches of fish. As they approached Madeira
shoals of dolphins were frequently encountered and one shoal
followed the yacht for five days. They swam astern of *Mignonette* in
a precise, battle fleet formation, from shortly after dawn until just
before noon; then, as though their leader had given a signal, they
swiftly and in unison dived out of sight and were not seen again
until late afternoon. Ostensibly the dolphins were on the look-out
for flying-fish which appeared to be their favourite form of food."

"'You should take a look at the book I've been reading,' interposed
Dudley rather sternly. 'Then you might not joke about such things.'

'Oh, what's it about? Cannibals?!'

'In a way, yes,' replied Dudley. 'It's called *The Narrative of Arthur
Gordon Pym*, by a chap named Edgar Allan Poe.'

The conversation changed abruptly for at that moment the isles
of Madeira were sighted and Dudley ordered Stephens to make out
a list of stores required."

"'So far luck has been with us,' Dudley told the others when they put in at Funchal. 'But the real dangers lie ahead. We could stay here for four days and still be a day ahead of schedule when we leave. But I don't want to do that. Once we cross the Line we must expect storms this time of the year. We shall be going straight from summer into winter and in the South Atlantic it isn't easy to hold a course when storms blow up. We need to have five days in hand when we leave Madeira as we shall surely lag behind for a while somewhere between here and the Cape. But our first job is to stock up with sufficient stores to see us to the Cape even if we do get becalmed on the way.'

So their stay in Madeira was brief enough."

"On the morning of the day they sailed from Madeira, the crew of the *Mignonette* took a flagon of wine and some sandwiches down to one of the beaches for a picnic lunch. With the knowledge that this was to be their last visit ashore for possibly months to come they were anxious to savour every moment of it—the narrow stretch of gleaming-silver-smooth beach jutting inland like an eager tongue out of the waves, the hibiscus and bougainvillaea growing on a terrace just above them and the itinerant guitarist in the distance.

Suddenly a shriek came from the direction of the sea. Stephens pointed to a barely discernible figure frantically struggling in the Atlantic waves some fifty yards away.

'It's a girl, or a boy,' he shouted. 'In real trouble by the look of things.'

'She's in worse trouble if she loses her nerve like that,' added Brooks. 'Wonder if it is a girl.'

Dudley said nothing, but quietly took off his coat and trousers and dashed into the water. There was quite a heavy sea running and swift cross currents; even for a strong swimmer like Dudley the attempt at rescue was extremely risky, the more so as the struggling person appeared to be in a state of panic. Dudley carved his way towards her with long, powerful overarm strokes and he was breathless himself when he reached the nearly demented figure. It was a girl, thought Dudley, though she has a boy's features. At first she resisted his efforts to keep her afloat. It took him all his time to calm her down, turn her on her back and get a firm hold of her arms just above the elbows. Dudley was skilled in life-saving, for which he held a certificate, and he knew exactly how to prevent the girl from turning around and struggling. Even so he was almost exhausted himself when eventually he brought her ashore and gently laid the limp, unconscious figure on the beach.

'Then it is a girl,' chortled Brooks. 'What a salvage prize! She's a good looker, too, but in a queer sort of way.'

'Don't stand there joking,' retorted Dudley angrily. 'If we don't do something quickly, she'll die. Give me a hand at bringing her round.'

For several seconds Dudley feared she was dead. He placed the girl face downwards, knelt astride her and, with his fingers spread out on each side of her body over the lowest ribs, leaned forward so that his weight produced a firm downward pressure. Backwards and forwards, slowly and gently, he swung in an effort to drive the water out of her lungs. After six minutes there was still no sign of life and Stephens, who was also trained in artificial respiration, took over.

The feverish efforts of the two men, each taking it in turns of five minutes at a time, continued for what seemed hours, but was actually less than half an hour. Finally Dudley bent over the inanimate figure and pressed his lips against hers, tugging at his lungs to breathe life into her.

'She's dead,' said Stephens laconically. 'There's nothing more we can do.'

'I refuse to believe it,' replied Dudley. 'I'm going to have one more try.'

Sweating hard in the sub-tropical sun, his lungs aching with every breath he took, Dudley again pressed his lips against those of the girl. By this time a crowd had gathered on the beach and Stephens had sent one of them running to fetch a doctor.

Suddenly Dudley realized with fierce joy and pride in his heart that she was faintly breathing. He continued to massage her back until she opened her eyes and gazed around in frightened bewilderment.

'No,' she murmured in Portugese. 'It is not true. I am dead.'

'You are alive,' replied Dudley. 'You must keep telling yourself that. You are alive and safe.'

An interpreter was found among the crowd and, having questioned the onlookers, he told the English sailors that the girl was Otilia Ribeiro, a seventeen-year-old orphan from Funchal. Someone recalled that she sold flowers and had a passion for ships and the sea.

'But what was she doing so far out from shore?' asked Dudley, somewhat puzzled.

The onlookers shrugged their shoulders. When she had recovered a little, the interpreter questioned the girl closely, but she declined to reply.

'If you ask me, *senhor*, she wanted to do away with her life,' he added.

'Strange that so young and attractive a girl should want to die,' commented Dudley. 'Very strange, for surely she has much to live for.'

'She is an orphan, *senhor*, and life can be very hard for an orphan.'

'She is mad,' said another. 'She has no friends. She's in love with the sea.'

There was laughter among the crowd and Dudley inquired the reason for this.

'They say,' explained the interpreter with a smirk, 'that her amigo is the sea.'

'And what's so funny about that?' asked Dudley, frowning. 'Certainly she struggled hard when I tried to rescue her. She might have had both of us drowned. Still I should like to persuade her that life is worth living. There is not much point in rescuing somebody if she's going to kill herself again within a few days.'

'*Senhor*, there is not much one can do about it.'

'Well, I intend to try,' replied Dudley. 'Where does she live? We will take her home.'

After a doctor had arrived and treated her somewhat perfunctorily and brusquely demanded payment from Dudley, payment for which he, Stephens and Brooks had a whip-around, they discovered that Otilia lived by herself in a drab room in a Funchal tenement. The *concierge*, an unsympathetic old harridan, spat contemptuously when she heard of the girl's escapade.

'She is mad. Quite mad. She keeps to herself and her flower stall. She has no friends, not even a man. All she does is to talk about the sea and ships. She is always trying to sign on as a sea-cook, but nobody will listen to her. They know she is mad.'

'Hm,' said Dudley, 'she might be just as useful as young Parker, but I'm afraid the *Mignonette* is no place for a woman.'

'Then, watch your ship, captain,' advised the *concierge*. 'No doubt she will try to stow herself away in it. She has been known to do so before, but always they bring her back to land.'

They took the girl out for a drink and some food in one of the harbor-side cafes and at length she told them her story. She was the daughter of a fisherman who had been drowned; her mother had died in childbirth and she had been brought up aboard fishing vessels, often doing a man's job. She had always been treated more like a boy than a girl. After her father's death she was educated in a convent for three years. She had learned a smattering of English there and picked up some other phrases from English tourists while plying her trade as a flower-girl. She settled in Funchal to sell flowers because it was the only work she could get. But always her dream was to return to the sea and to sail round the world. She was not well-educated, but she had read a great deal, especially travel books and stories about the sea.

By a strange quirk of fate Australia was the country she most wanted to visit. She had read all about it and it sounded a new, exciting country where one could feel free and enjoy vast, open spaces. She hated being 'shut up' and in Funchal she felt a prisoner. The island was too small. She loved the sea because of its vastness; she would never feel alone at sea. Her grandfather had emigrated to Australia and he had written her letters full of the wonderful life of that then under-developed country. But, alas, her grandfather had died, so he could not help her to fulfil her wish.

So she rambled on, words tumbling out of her mouth in a wild enthusiasm that seemed so different from her despairing mood of only several hours previously. The *Mignonette* was going to Australia? *Si?* That was almost unbelievable. Never before, as far as she could remember, had a ship bound for Australia called in at Madeira. Possibly such a chance would never come again. Could *el capitan* take her? She would work hard, if he agreed. 'I can cook simple meals, I can mend sails—you see, my fingers are proof of that work—and I can scrub decks as well as any man.'

'No,' said Dudley, finally but not unsympathetically, for he felt a certain comradeship for this girl with the call of the sea in her blood. 'I am sorry, but I can't take you. It would not be fair. One girl and four men would make big problems on a long voyage.'

'I would not worry the crew. I should just work and sleep. I do not eat much.'

Then Dudley thought of his employer. Mr. Want could do something for this girl. He had plenty of money. He might even help her to emigrate to Australia.

'But I will do something for you, Otilia, if you promise faithfully not to try to end your life again. You were trying to die in those waves, weren't you?'

She hung her head, then tossed it back proudly and said: 'I was and I wasn't. I love the sea and when I'm unhappy I always go for a swim. Maybe I felt one moment I didn't wish to live any more, but the next I was struggling to escape from death. That was when you heard me scream. Then when you came over to me I wanted to die again.'

'Then, listen to me. Here is my address when I get to Sydney —care of Mr. J. H. Want. If you still feel you would like to emigrate there, write to me and I'll see if Mr. Want, my boss, can help you.'

With the aid of the interpreter, who had cunningly insinuated himself into the party to lunch and drinks, Otilia was made to understand what might be done to help her. She burst into tears and expressed her deepest gratitude to Dudley."

"'But the funny thing is she wasn't really what you'd call beautiful,' said Brooks. 'She was a good looker, but I wouldn't call her beautiful. More like a boy than a girl.'

'Right now I'd say she was the most beautiful girl in the world,' said Stephens. 'After all these weeks at sea, I wouldn't say no to a mermaid.'

'Women are all you two think about,' remarked Dudley. 'I must say I sometimes feel sorry I didn't bring her with us, but I'd have had a heap of trouble keeping your mauling hands off her.'

Richard Parker had said nothing during this conversation. Then, blushing somewhat, he interrupted nervously: 'You very nearly did have her, skipper, whether you liked it or not. Before she tried to drown herself she swam out to the yacht.'

'She what?' chorused the men.

'It was when you were ashore and I was on anchor watch. I caught her trying to sneak aboard and I shoved her off with a boathook.'

'Why didn't you tell me this before?' inquired Dudley.

'I thought you might be angry. Also I lost my head a bit because she had swum out quite far and I wondered afterwards whether she would reach the shore safely. You see, I hit her with the boathook.'

'You bloody young fool, you might have killed her,' said Dudley, his face white with anger.

'I only meant to carry out my instructions—to see nobody got aboard. I thought she might be a thief.'

Dudley knew that Parker was right; the lad had merely carried out his duty, even if he had been a bit officious about it. But, for some reason he could not explain, even to himself, he was bitterly resentful of Parker's action.

'You may have driven her to suicide, or to try to take her life,' he muttered reproachfully.

'Yes, sir. It's been on my conscience a long time. I kind of feel responsible for what happened. That's why I kept quiet about it.'

'I'm still not sure we were right in refusing her passage,' said Dudley. 'I only hope she doesn't try to drown herself again. She was mad keen on the sea.'

'Well,' said Stephens, 'it's the last chance we shall get of seeing a woman for some time.'"

*　*　*

"Thomas Dudley had taken a calculated risk. He had decided to leave the main sea route for ships bound for the Cape of Good Hope and instead to keep between the southeast trades and the westerly winds, in the hope of finding calmer weather in what was mid-winter in those latitudes. On June 25, however, the wind changed to north-west, and for five days the yacht was able to continue on her desired

course. But on the thirtieth day of the month
the wind veered around again to south-west,
beginning to blow with gale force and churning
up the sea so that the craft was buffeted into an
uncertain, drunken puppet in the South
Atlantic. Dudley's face was caked with salt,
blistered and reddened by the tropical sun,
which had beaten down on them relentlessly
despite the storm clouds which scudded swiftly
by. For the first few days of the gale the yacht
had withstood the elements magnificently,
calmly swinging up her bows and riding sky-
wards with confidence while the seas swept
over her. But gradually the storm had gained
the mastery, causing leaks to spring and rigging
to collapse. Under close-rigged canvas the
yacht was rolling wildly."

from Narrative of A. Gordon Pym,
by Edgar Allan Poe
(written some forty years earlier):

*"It was now about one o'clock in the morning,
and the wind was still blowing tremendously.
The brig evidently labored much more than
usual, and it became absolutely necessary that
something should be done with a view of easing
her in some measure. At almost every roll to lee–
ward she shipped a sea . . ."*

"When July 2 dawned, the gale had blown
itself out and the yacht was becalmed until
shortly before sunset, when a slight west-
south-westerly breeze blew up. Dudley had
expected the lull would be succeeded by
another gale and for this reason remained on
the bridge. His judgement was not at fault; by

midnight the wind had increased in force, cutting the rigging with fierce blasts. The captain ordered reduced canvas.

On July 4 the storm had worsened. Great mountains of sea, topped with snow-white foam, loomed high above the tiny yacht. The situation was so bad that Dudley decided to heave-to until the storm blew itself out. All hands were summoned to take in the square-sail and place the canvas cover on the afterskylight.

By sunrise on July 5 Dudley calculated by his sextant that *Mignonette* was about 1,600 miles from the Cape of Good Hope. Her exact position was 27 degrees south, 10 west. Even if the storm abated, they were well off the normal trade routes and far from getting the assistance they so urgently needed."

"The entire range of bulwarks to larboard had been swept away as well as the caboose, together with the jolly-boat from the counter. The creaking and working of the mainmast, too, gave indication that it was nearly sprung."

"To add to our distress, a heavy sea, striking the brig to the windward, threw her off several points from the wind, and, before she could regain her position, another broke completely over her, and hurled her full upon her beam-ends."

"We had scarcely time to draw breath after the violence of this shock, when one of the most tremendous waves I had then ever known broke right on board of us, sweeping the companion-way clear off, bursting in the hatchways, and filling every inch of the vessel with water."

"The captain's plan was to remain hove-to and to keep afloat with the aid of the sea-anchor. But before this could be done the yacht was unexpectedly pooped. Stephens had been the first to realize their danger. It was his sudden shout which caused the others to look astern. An Everest of a wave was bearing inexorably down on them; it rushed on, its peak curling disdainfully as it advanced. For a moment it seemed to halt on the edge of the craft, towering precipitously above them. Then it struck like a blast of lightning, shattering the tiny craft to her keelson.

Dudley was flung across the bridge and the others were hurled down the decks into the stern. For a fleeting moment the yacht was perched crazily in what seemed like midair. Then, as she crashed down on the sea, there was a terrific thud which left Stephens half stunned as his head hit a bollard. *Mignonette*'s starboard quarter was completely stove in and, turning slowly over, the yacht capsized."

"Our chief sufferings were now hunger and thirst, and when we looked forward to the means of relief in this respect, our hearts sunk within us, and we were induced to regret that we had escaped the less dreadful perils of the sea."

"'I doubt if any castaways could have been set adrift less prepared than we are,' said Dudley. 'Two tins of turnips and no water, and nearly 1,600 miles before we can hope to spot land.'"

"We endeavored, however, to console ourselves with the hope of being speedily picked up by some vessel, and encouraged each other to bear with fortitude the evils that might happen."

"It was Brooks who spoke up at last: 'There may be other ships who have headed out into the ocean to escape the storm and are, like us, away from the trade route.'"

"The gnawing hunger which I now experienced was nearly insupportable, and I felt myself capable of going to any lengths in order to appease it. With my knife I cut off a small portion of the leather trunk, and endeavored to eat it, but found it utterly impossible to swallow a single morsel, although I fancied that some little alleviation of my suffering was obtained by chewing small pieces of it and spitting them out."

"'If anyone had told me I should eat raw turtle meat, I would have said he was a liar,' exclaimed Stephens. 'Now I just don't care. I'm only too happy to have something to munch away at. Just munching takes the edge off one's hunger.'"

"Shortly after this period I fell into a state of partial insensibility, during which the most pleasing images floated in my imagination; such as green trees, waving meadows of ripe grain, processions of dancing girls . . ."

"About noon Parker declared that he saw land off the larboard quarter, and it was with the utmost difficulty I could restrain him from plunging into the sea with the view of swimming toward it . . . Upon looking in the direction pointed out, I could not perceive the faintest appearance of the shore—indeed I was too well aware that we were far from any land to indulge in a hope of that nature. It was a long time, nevertheless, before I could convince Parker of his mistake. He

*then burst into a flood of tears, weeping like a
child, with loud cries and sobs, for two or three
hours, when, becoming exhausted, he fell asleep."*

"'. . . perhaps an uninhabited island, skipper,'
cried Parker, laughing uncontrollably: he was
the first to show signs of cracking up. Seasick-
ness and fever had taken its toll of him."

"Parker still had delirious moments when he
dreamed of coral islands and babbled about
oranges and apples growing on trees."

*". . . my chief distress was for water, and I was
only prevented from taking a draught from the
sea by remembering the horrible consequences
which thus have resulted to others who were
similarly situated with ourselves."*

"On the morning of the seventeenth day Parker,
crazed by thirst, failed to abide by the rule
Dudley had laid down—that, twice a day, each
man might gargle with sea water, provided he
spat it out. Parker just lent over the side and
drank in large quantities of sea water. Tem-
porarily assuaged, he immediately fell asleep
only to find within an hour or two that the salt
water had made his thirst more acute and he
was so ill and sick that he fell insensible."

*"Parker turned suddenly toward me with an ex-
pression of countenance which made me shudder.
There was about him an air of self-possession
which I had not noticed in him until now, and
before he opened his lips my heart told me what he
would say. He proposed, in a few words, that one of
us should die to preserve the existence of the others."*

"When yachtsmen were entirely dependent on sail, those of them who ventured far from land not infrequently courted death by becoming becalmed for long periods. Among yachts' crews, as distinct from sailors of the Merchant Navy, there had for centuries been a tradition that in such circumstances, with no immediate prospects of rescue, or of food and drink, cannibalism was permissible."

"Then there flashed across his mind the memory of the book he had been reading, *The Narrative of Arthur Gordon Pym*, by Edgar Allan Poe. Vividly the words of Pym came back to him. Pym and others were castaways in a boat and perishing by starvation. They drew lots to determine who should be sacrificed to become food for the rest."

"He licked his sore lips nervously and almost exulted in the idea of just sucking soft, pliable, warm flesh."

"Revulsion had been changed to a wild, libidinous urge to eat human flesh."

". . . there was something almost sexual in the feeling . . ."

"At length delay was no longer possible, and, with a heart almost bursting from my bosom, I advanced to the region of the forecastle, where my companions were awaiting me. I held out my hand with the splinters, and Peters immediately drew. He was free—his, at least, was not the shortest; and there was now another chance against my escape. I summoned up all my

*strength, and passed the lots to Augustus. He
also drew immediately, and he also was free;
and now, whether I should live or die, the
chances were no more than precisely even. At
this moment all the fierceness of the tiger
possessed my bosom, and I felt toward my poor
fellow creature, Parker, the most intense, the
most diabolical hatred. But the feeling did not
last; and, at length, with a convulsive shudder
and closed eyes, I held out the two remaining
splinters toward him. It was fully five minutes
before he could summon resolution to draw,
during which period of heartrending suspense I
never once opened my eyes. Presently one of the
two lots was quickly drawn from my hand. The
decision was then over, yet I knew not whether
it was for me or against me. No one spoke, and
still I dared not satisfy myself by looking at the
splinter I held. Peters at length took me by the
hand, and I forced myself to look up, when I
immediately saw by the countenance of Parker
that I was safe, and that it was he who had been
doomed to suffer. Gasping for breath, I fell sense-
less to the deck.*

*I recovered from my swoon in time to behold
the consummation of the tragedy in the death of
him who had been chiefly instrumental in
bringing it about. He made no resistance what-
ever, and was stabbed in the back by Peters,
when he fell instantly dead.*"

"'Richard,' he said in a voice that was trembling
with emotion, 'your time is come.'

'What? Me, sir?' replied the lad in a feeble
whisper, probably guessing that the captain
meant he was near to death, but not realizing in
what manner the end would come to him.

'Yes, my boy,' Dudley answered.

He took the pen-knife from his pocket and with a short, sharp blow plunged it into the side of the boy's neck . . . The blood spurted out and within a minute he was dead."

"I must not dwell upon the fearful repast which immediately ensued. Such things may be imag-ined, but words have no power to impress the mind with the exquisite horror of their reality. Let it suffice to say that, having in some measure appeased the raging thirst which consumed us by the blood of the victim, and having by common consent taken off the hands, feet, and head, throwing them together with the entrails, into the sea, we devoured the rest of the body, piecemeal . . .

"'We caught the blood in the baler and drank it while it was warm,' he said, referring to the mate and himself. 'We then stripped the body, cut it open and took out the liver and heart and we ate the liver while it was warm.'"

"Parker's heart was put to dry in the sun."

The men urinated in their clothes, that the moisture might be absorbed back into the bodies, not wasted, and they went to the body of Parker furtively, eyes averted, or at night.

*   *   *

The German barque, *Montezuma*, bound from Rio de Janeiro to Hamburg, altered course near the island of Trinidad, in a whim-sical search for mermaids. July 28, 1884, Brooks, at the tiller of the dinghy of the *Mignonette*, sighted the German barque, a speck on the horizon . . . roused Dudley and Stephens—exhausted on the boat's bottom . . . the men took oars, and with last strength rowed, until they were in turn sighted. At 24° South, 27° West, the dinghy drew to the ship's side . . . the men's eyes glazed and bright, hair and beards caked, legs and arms swollen and red . . . in the boat's bottom, undisguised, the mutilated carcass of Parker, heart and liver missing, blood stains on the boat's sides.

* * *

The dinghy was hoisted aboard, the bodily remains examined by ship's doctor. Wrapped in weighted canvas, with a prayer, Parker was committed to the waters. Dudley, Brooks, and Stephens made slow recovery, below . . .

* * *

September 6, the *Montezuma* sailed into Falmouth harbor. Stephens, Brooks, and Dudley, at Falmouth Police Court, before the Mayor and seven magistrates, were charged with the murder of Parker "on the high seas, within the jurisdiction of the Admiralty." Bail was denied, then, following public outcry, granted. Dudley returned to the comfort of his wife . . . she committed her life savings to her man's defense. (Years after, a memorial tablet to Richard Parker appeared at Pear Tree Churchyard, Itchen Ferry, and was annually maintained and cleaned through funds provided, furtively, by Dudley.)

* * *

Brooks was acquitted. But at a special trial, before the Queen's Bench Division, Dudley and Stephens—December 4—were found guilty of murder. ". . . Lord Coleridge, without putting on the black cap, proceeded to pass sentence of death." December 10, the Home Secretary advised the Queen to suspend capital sentence "until the further significance of Her Majesty's pleasure." December 14, sentence was commuted to six months in prison, without hard labour.

* * *

(Later, Stephens, a morose and lonely figure, became deranged . . .)

* * *

Mr. Henry Want, owner of the lost *Mignonette*, returned to England, sought an interview with Dudley.

"I am as much to blame for young Parker's death as you," Want told Dudley. "You must try to feel that we are both in some measure responsible."

Want offered to pay Dudley's passage out to Australia, and those of his family as well.

"I can't think why you should dream of doing this for me," said Dudley.

"A letter came for you, addressed care of my Sydney office," Want replied. "It had a Madeira postmark and, knowing you had stopped at Madeira on the voyage, I opened it, thinking it might concern the *Mignonette* . . . it told me how you had rescued a young girl from drowning in Madeira and I reckoned that put you right up top in my estimation."

1885, the Dudleys sailed to Australia.

* * *

It was Otilia Ribeiro, flower-girl from Funchal, who had written the letter opened by Want, telling again her gratitude to Dudley for saving her life, for giving her new hope and purpose, and telling that she had already begun her voyage to Australia—had booked as a cook on a ship bound for Luanda . . . the letter innocent of all knowledge of the fate of the *Mignonette*, the death of Parker, trial and conviction of Dudley . . . but filled with warm confession: that as a flower-girl she had been frail and helpless, a prey to all men, but "it is as though the sea is my father and lover. I belong to the sea. I do assure you I am in love with the sea, not with the men who sail her." Otilia's letter turned the heart and mind of Want—who had been disgusted with the wreck of the *Mignonette*, the cannibalism that followed—turned Want to Dudley, to give Dudley a new life in Australia.

* * *

Landed at Luanda, Otilia shipped as stewardess aboard a ship bound for Goa . . . spent time in Portuguese India, and finally (1886) to Bombay.

*   *   *

In a port near Sydney, Dudley set up as ship's chandler, and settled his family, his past buried from all save his wife Philippa, and from Want. But he still looked to the sea, and now and then set out for a short sail, alone. His sleep churned with nightmares: he would dream that Parker came back to life, and forgave him. Hurled awake, in the late night, he turned to Philippa, who urged him "to lead a Christian life," and to pray. But prayer did not bring sleep.

*   *   *

Somewhere, Otilia heard of the *Mignonette*, the death of Parker, trial of Dudley. She wrote Want, furiously defended Dudley, urged Want to do all possible for the man who had saved her life. There was little Want could do—he and Dudley could not associate, lest their names be linked—the past, through gossip, ventilated. The flower-girl from Funchal, the barrister from Sydney, corresponded, agreed tacitly that Dudley should not be told Otilia now knew his story.

In Bombay, Otilia cut her hair short, dressed as a man, passed as a sailor. As a man, she worked passage to Ceylon, then to Java, where her gender was unmasked. Once more a girl, she shipped to Sydney, where Want secured her a berth as stewardess on a friend's yacht.

But the urge to help Dudley, and the urge to once more be a man, do a man's work on the sea, joined forces in the flower-girl. She sometimes heard voices, telling her what to do, and she told Want that her plan came to her in a dream: to cut her hair short, dress as a man, secure berth as a cabin-boy—and to call on Dudley, befriend him, under the new name of *Richard Parker*. Want thought her crazy, the plan dangerous—but she urged and persuaded—and Want consented, turning a blind eye to the adventure.

*   *   *

"She prepared very carefully for her transformation into the role of Richard Parker. Her sleek, black hair was cut short; round her slender breasts she wound a tight bandage and she wore a seaman's cap at a jaunty angle. Her eyebrows were singed off and, speaking English quite fluently now, though with a foreign accent, she spent much time in low dives on the Sydney waterfront, learning and practicing the jargon, the habits and recreations of sea-faring men, cursing and swaggering in an exaggerated fashion and drinking hard liquor with the rest. She was accepted as a man and that gave her the confidence to continue her masquerade. Developing a fondness for low company, she was more at ease among the roughest seamen than anyone else.

For days she watched the ship chandler's shop, partly to discover what times of the day Dudley was entirely alone, partly to make up her mind on how she should approach him. She knew there was no chance of his recognizing her unless she made herself known. Even then, panic seized her. Supposing Dudley thought she was a blackmailer and that he refused to believe she could be a woman. She had given up her job as a stewardess, cut herself off from all who had known her as a woman and secured casual work at the docks.

One day, when Dudley was alone, she walked boldly in.

'You are Thomas Dudley, aren't you?' she inquired, harshly and bluntly because, though fortified by some hard liquor, she was in reality afraid.

Dudley looked aghast at first. So at last his secret was out. Someone had tracked him down. Consternation showed in his face so that Otilia softened her voice when she spoke again.

'Please do not be afraid. I am a friend—perhaps, who knows, your best friend. Captain, I owe my very existence to you. You saved my life. Do you remember?'

'No, I'm afraid I don't,' replied Dudley curtly and with confused feelings of puzzlement and suspicion. If this was somebody come to blackmail him, it was an odd way of setting about it. And at the back of his mind he had a feeling there was something familiar about this strange visitor.

'Do you remember calling at Madeira in the yacht *Mignonette?* Do you remember rescuing a girl from drowning? I was that girl.'

'Are you mad?' asked Dudley. 'You aren't a girl.'

'Not in spirit any longer. But I am a girl and that very same girl, as I can prove to you.'

She took off her sailor's cap and pointed to her hair. 'That has all been cut off. I was Otilia Ribeiro, the girl you rescued. I have now taken the name of Richard Parker, the cabin boy who died. I want you to feel that I am that lad come back to life to pay my debt to you. You may think I'm crazy, but I was never saner. Captain, you must believe me and know that I want to help you.'

'I have never heard a madder story. I can't believe you.'

'You can't, or you won't, Captain? I swear to you that nobody except Mr. Want knows who I am, or anything about you or me. I promise I shall always keep your secret. You have nothing to fear from me as long as you live.'"

"... he sank down in a chair and put his head in his hands and wept uncontrollably.

She put an arm on his shoulder. 'If you wish for further proof, you can ask Mr. Want. Now will you admit you are Thomas Dudley?'

'There seems no point in denying it any longer. But, for my family's sake, promise me you won't talk about these things.'

'I have promised that already. Captain, you saved my life, you gave me the will to do what I always wanted, to be a seaman and to come to Australia. Always, ever since I was a girl, I wished to be free to roam the world, to sail where I wanted. In Madeira I felt in a prison. The sea was so close and yet there was no escape. The night after you arrived in Funchal I swam out to the yacht and kissed her hull. I tried to get aboard as a stowaway, but poor Parker ordered me off.'

'Why do you call yourself Richard Parker? To torment me? I suppose I can't blame you. What must you think of me?'

'Only this, Captain, that I admire your spirit and courage, that I have never forgotten you. No, I am not wishing to torment you, or to bring back terrible memories. I can't say exactly why I want to be Richard Parker, but I want you to feel that you saved my life and that, as a reward from heaven, I have taken his soul on earth. When I was in Goa and Java I learned a great deal about the way a soul can never die, but must always enter another body. Richard Parker's soul is not dead. It lives on in me. Of that I feel sure. Believe that and it may make you feel better.'

'You are a strange girl, Otilia.'

'You must not call me that. From now on I am Richard, a young sailor, looking for work. I now know quite a lot about the sea and ships. I can mend a sail, stitch canvas, lay out hawsers, splice a sword mat. In Funchal it was true I understood a fisherman's work, but since then I have learned much else as well.'

'But to me you are still the little flower-girl at Funchal. I must call you Otilia. I have often thought about you . . . When I was in *Mignonette* I sometimes wished I had allowed you to come, too. I feared you might try to end your life again.'

'Have no fear of that now, as long as you accept me as Richard Parker.'

'That is asking a lot. If only I could understand what your aim is.'

'Soon you will forget that I am Otilia.'

'But why should I? Is this some awful punishment? Why have you come to see me? My mind is all confused. You say you are Otilia Ribeiro and that you are grateful to me. You have no need to be grateful. I only did what many other men would have done. You say you will keep my secret, yet you insist on this mad presence of being Richard Parker. What is it you really want of me?'

'I hardly know myself. I only know I want to help you and Mr. Want told me you had suffered cruelly from remorse. Then I had the idea—call it mad, if you wish—of becoming Richard Parker, of willing his lost soul into my body, of being to you a kind of brother of the sea, a shipmate who wants you to feel that all is understood.'"

"Dudley was bitter. He felt that fate was playing him a crueller trick than ever. The incident at Funchal had always stood out in his memory as something romantic that he cherished. He was not in love with the girl, but he was in love with the idea of having been her rescuer, of having put his lips against hers and breathed life back into her. Damn it, he thought, one can't help being a bit mawkish about a thing like that. Dudley was not a sentimental man, but he felt cheated that the girl had now turned herself into a man and wanted to be regarded as such.

Otilia paused for a moment before replying. 'If Parker had lived, I can't say how I should have felt. But I do know that half of me is always a man. Oh, don't misunderstand me; I'm not a freak. In all ways physically I am like a woman. I just don't want you to be complicated by having another woman in your life. Of course I remember you as a man who has kissed my lips and and breathed life into me. Half of me cherishes that memory. But the other half clamours to be free, asks nothing of you, but to accept me as Richard Parker. If you can't accept that, then we must part and I will never see you again. If you don't like to call me Richard, then call me Ricardo. As I am, I would pass for my brother if I had one. You can tell your family that Otilia's brother came to say 'thank you'.'

'What if I still say I want to see you dressed up as a flower-girl and to call you by your own name?'

'Then, as I have said, it is the end. But if you try you can accept me as a boy. It's better that way. You have a wife and a family. You owe them a duty.'"

*   *   *

Otilia Ribeiro was a mystic, versed in eastern versions of the transmigration of souls. Otilia had died—the flower-girl who had tried to drown herself in Funchal—and Richard Parker, cabin-boy, was reborn. But Dudley was a simple man, who disliked disorder. He was proud to see again this girl whose life he had saved—but how forget that she was a girl, a girl whom he had kissed? His marriage to the pious Philippa was a mere formality, his job as ship's chandler a dull routine, after the sea. He did not want to fall in love with her, but . . .

But better accept her as a boy, than to see her once more disappear. By little, he found even her boyishness stirring his sex—to share a man's work, a man's life, with Ricardo . . .

He found her an old ship's life-boat, together they converted it into a small cabin-cruiser—christened her the *Sanctuary*. Following a day's work, they frequented shorefront taverns, drinking with the sailors.

Otilia lived aboard *Sanctuary,* at Wooloomooloo . . . did odd jobs for Dudley, made fishing expeditions, hauled small cargoes. On some of these trips, Dudley joined her.

Sailors in the taverns taunted her—why didn't she chase women, like the rest of them? She lost her temper, replied that she hated women ... she generally avoided brawls, but the men were afraid of her—she had learned ju-jitsu, could fling a man over her head.

She memorized the seacoast, all bays and capes, could sail without charts ...

* * *

1905, Henry Want died. There was a secret bequest in his will: if Ricardo Parker would become once more Otilia Ribeiro, flower-girl from Funchal, she would receive an annuity.

* * *

Otilia longed for an island, an island of her own, where she could settle in solitude, live simply from land and sea. As stewardess on Want's friend's yacht, she had explored the Great Barrier Reef, from New Guinea in the north, to Breaksea Spit to the south—and she had found her island: uninhabited, but with a supply of fresh water, with pisonia scrub, pandanus palms, tournefortia and casuarina —and in the luminous and prismatic coral were mackerel, snapper, tuna, bonito, coral trout, crabs, gropers, game-fish, swordfish, and lobster.

She determined to settle the island, at least set up a base for trading contacts. It was a risky voyage for a craft as small as *Sanctuary* ... she asked Dudley—would he go with her?

'It seems like tempting the fates,' he said bitterly, 'for Thomas Dudley to go sailing with Richard Parker.'

'You are happier since we met again,' she said. 'You look better, more at peace with yourself ...'

'But it's an unnatural life,' replied Dudley heatedly. 'I'm a man and you're not. No amount of pretending will alter that. Do you think I've ever really made myself feel you're a boy? Oh, yes, at first I tried hard enough. In many ways you seemed like a boy and we could talk of the things seamen talk about. I honestly believed at first that this was the answer to my problems. I could be a faithful husband and father, stand by my family and keep you as just a friend. It seemed to work.

'Then gradually I found myself thinking of you again as a woman. I wanted to beg you to stop this stupid game of being a boy, but I was afraid if I did you would only go away. And I knew that I couldn't bear that. I would rather have you as a friend than nothing at all. But I'm flesh and blood like you and now that we've got to know each other so well, sometimes I—well—want to see your hair grow again—to be something more than just a pal.'

'It wouldn't work, Tom,' said Otilia vehemently. 'I would just lose myself again as a woman. I should be back where I was—helpless and afraid.'

'Afraid of what?'

'Afraid of life.'

'Well, we won't talk about it again, at least not yet. But if I come with you, I must know I have your complete trust. It isn't going to be an easy voyage, for we shall have a lot of stores to take and not much freeboard. If I come, I come as skipper of *Sanctuary*. And I give the orders. Is that agreed?'

'It is agreed, because you've got to feel I trust you. But remember I'm still Ricardo.'"

"A mad urge seized Dudley.

In the night, while Otilia slept, he altered course. There was a strong offshore wind blowing and within a few hours the tiny craft was far out of sight of land. Now Dudley felt better and more in command of himself. He began to plan how this new adventure would shape itself, the adventure of persuading Otilia he was a man who wanted her love and intended somehow to win it.

When she awoke, Otilia expressed her surprise at the sudden change in the weather and the fact that they were out of sight of land.

'The going will be better farther out,' said Dudley laconically. 'It's too risky close inshore in this gale.'

'But surely we needn't be so far out?'

'Oh, yes, it's quite all right. We can alter course soon and head in to leeward of Lady Elliot Island. But the gale may delay us, so we must start rationing ourselves. As from today, until we sight land again, I'm going on a strict diet—one tin of beans a day and no water.'

'But that's nonsense. It's not necessary. We have plenty of rations.'

'Maybe now, but we'll need plenty when we land. And if the gale delays us for three days as it easily may, our rations will look pretty scant.'

'But we were going to stock up again at the next port.'

'Well, we shan't do that now. Our next stop will be when we land at your island.'

'Why have you changed your mind?' asked Otilia suspiciously. 'I thought you were afraid of getting too far from the coast in *Sanctuary.*'

'You said I was captain for this trip, didn't you? You said you trusted me?'

'Why, yes, of course.'

'Then shut up and don't argue.'

He had never spoken to her like that before and Otilia was shocked and hurt. For a long time they didn't speak. When it came to meal-time Dudley handed out her normal rations and took for himself a single tin of beans. She opened her mouth to remonstrate, but he silenced her with a curt: 'No arguments. It's an order.'

Silently they ate, but Otilia no longer had any appetite. She knew that something was going on in Dudley's mind, but couldn't fathom what it was.

He handed her the water barrico, then leaned over the side and scooped up with a spoon some of the sea-water. She was horrified to see him drink it.

'Have you taken leave of your senses?' she asked, now thoroughly alarmed.

'No, I'm just being prudent. Remember I've learned a lot about how little a man can live on at sea. I didn't make that twenty-four-day voyage without finding out a good deal I didn't know before. Since then doctors have explained that sea-water need not be the menace to seamen which we always imagined. Oh, yes, if I could re-live that twenty-four days I should act very differently.'

'Sea-water will only make you ill and increase your thirst. It becomes like hard liquor. You start drinking it and you crave for it.'

'Yes, if you gulp it down in large quantities. That's what sends men mad. But there's nourishment in the plankton in the sea and if I take one spoonful every hour, it will be as much as I need.'

'And supposing you get ill?'

'I shall survive,' replied Dudley, 'and so will you. As long as I'm in command I shall see you safe.'"

"For three more days and nights he maintained his diet of sea-water and beans. It was part bravado, he admitted to himself, because, if his courage failed him, he could always drink from the water barrico. A pitiful fool he would look, if he did so! But somehow his self-imposed abstinence made him feel good, even though at times hunger gnawed at his stomach and the sea-water left his mouth with a dry, brackish taste. He wanted to win this battle over hunger and thirst as much as he had wanted to live when drifting in the dinghy. At least he was now able to convince Otilia that the strong wind had thrown them off course and that they would take much longer to reach their island, so therefore he had been right to insist on rationing.

"For a day and a half more they sailed on, mostly in silence. Otilia was seasick and suffered so much herself that she hardly realized how ill Dudley was. Perhaps that was fortunate, mused Dudley. The fact she's ill makes me feel better."

"His fever was mounting and his tongue like a piece of leather, but he hung grimly on to the wheel, for Otilia was racked with seasickness and unable to take her trick. During a lull in the gale he heard her moaning softly, like a puppy dog in pain. Lashing the wheel into a fixed position, he left his post to take a look at her. She lay motionless with eyes shut and hands stretched across her head. To make her more comfortable Dudley pulled off the seaman's jacket and unwrapped the tight bandage of coarse canvas which was wound round the upper part of her body. She'll faint, if I don't remove it, Dudley told himself, and he marvelled how she would live in such a straight-jacket. At last the canvas was unwound and there she lay, inert, unprotesting and uncaring, a helpless bundle of femininity, despite her boyish looks, the small rounded breasts scored with the harsh imprint of the canvas."

"This was the moment he had hoped and waited for: the ending of the masquerade and the revelation of the girl who hid behind a seaman's clothing.

Dudley was delirious, but he did not care any longer. He exulted in his delirium which was now a joyous fever that pulsed through his veins. Back he went to the wheel, once again heading on the right course, supremely confident that now he was the master and that soon they would make a landfall.

"Dudley picked his way through the breaking surf and nosed the boat into the placid lagoon which lay ahead."

*   *   *

He dropped anchor, stepped ashore, stretched his legs on the beach. Otilia lay asleep in *Sanctuary*. Opening a flask of brandy, he placed it under her nose, and she stirred.

"Drink some of this," he urged.

"Why didn't you wake me sooner?"

"It was best that you slept."

Suddenly she realized the canvas bandage was gone . . . her hands rushed to her breasts.

"What have you done to me?"

"Otilia, this is how I have always wanted you to be—just as I found you in the sea off Funchal. I haven't done anything to harm you . . ."

She sobbed bitterly, tears of anger, of impotence and helplessness. She said nothing, and Dudley held her tight, pressed her head against his shoulder, as Ricardo, Richard, the boy-man in Otilia, wavered . . .

*   *   *

Otilia kept a diary: "Arrived in Paradise, February 2 . . . Tom takes charge."

For two weeks, Tom and Otilia shared their island, man and woman—slept, bathed, caught turtles, went fishing.

"If I died tomorrow, I should be content for never can I have a happier day."

The rains came, they gave up their shelter, returned to *Sanctuary*.

Then, this diary entry: "Tom promises to give up the pipe." In the middle of the month, they set sail for the mainland—and caught the tail of a cyclone. *Sanctuary* was battered and holed, her rigging torn, leaking badly.

Sanctuary never went to sea again.

Nor did Otilia Riberio.

Nor did Thomas Dudley.

*   *   *

Dudley returned to his ship chandler's, to Philippa, his family.

Otilia left Sydney, left Dudley, went to Brisbane—became a fortune teller: "Miss Jack Tar." She wore a seaman's cap, smoked a pipe, and mixed her knowledge of the occult, of the secret cults of the East, that she had learned in India, or in Java, with her studies of the stars and signs of the Zodiac, and with her encyclopedic knowledge, committed to memory, of the Great Barrier Reef and all its islands, of the entire eastern and southern coasts of Australia—so that sailors who drifted to her tent and crystal ball, seafarers and captains, about to set sail and seeking guidance, were astonished at her knowledge and wisdom.

*   *   *

"Tom promises to give up the pipe."

When Tom Dudley had emigrated from England, opened his shop in Australia, he had been nervous, distraught, plagued with night-mares . . . and he discovered opium. In the back room of a tavern, he put a pellet of the drug on a needle, held it in the flame of a spirit lamp until it sizzled, then plugged it into his pipe—smoked, and became calm. It was Tom's secret, unknown to Philippa, or Otilia.

When Tom and Otilia sailed on *Sanctuary* to the Great Barrier Reef, to the island she called Paradise, Tom smuggled opium and pipe aboard, smoked when she was asleep, when the wind would carry the scent from her nostrils. One night, when she slept and he smoked, he dreamed of slashing a morsel of flesh from his buttocks, bandaging himself with the canvas he had removed from her breasts, cooking the meat in the galley, and serving it to her when she woke.

Arrived at the island, she discovered his habit, discovered the opium—or he confided it—and perhaps they smoked together . . .

*   *   *

Years later, Dudley resumed his own name, made no effort to hide his past. Stories circulated that he had once eaten a boy, and he was known at times as "Cannibal Tom" . . . but it was all too long ago, no one cared.

*   *   *

1900, bubonic plague came, for the first time, to Australia. Its origin was traced to rats in the loft of Dudley's shop.

Thomas Dudley was the first man in Australia to die of the plague.

His casket was towed down the Parramutta River.

*   *   *

When Tom died, Otilia took heavily to opium, became a hermit, had "visions." Many years later, she returned to Sydney. "I'm too old to tell fortunes any more. Too old and tired. I shall just sell flowers."

Miss Jack Tar, with sailor cap and pipe, flower-seller, was on the streets of Sydney—as late as 1925.

*   *   *

July 28, 1884, the German barque *Montezuma*, under Captain Simonsen, had altered course near the island of Trinidad, "in a whimsical search for mermaids"—and, so doing, had discovered the survivors of *Mignonette*.

Otilia knew this story, from Dudley—knew it was the quest for mermaids that had saved Tom.

Secretly, she had someone take a photograph of a dugong—that seagoing mammal of the Australian islands, with female breasts, now and then mistaken by sailors for a mermaid—and she secured Captain Simonsen's address. She sent the photo to him.

For years the Captain kept it in his wallet, brought it out for friends—the mammal that breathed air, but took to the sea.

BOOTH

ONE

London, early eighteen-hundreds, Richard Booth, advocate, established his son, Junius Brutus, as clerk in his office of law. Junius was bored, fled the law, joined a troupe of strolling players—tramping the country, eluding the sheriff, sleeping by the road, eating the vegetables thrown at them onstage.

1815, young Booth appeared at Covent Garden, was an instant success . . . played Iago, Richard III, Hamlet, Lear, Shylock, Sir Giles Overreach.

Crossed to America, 1821, played the great theaters of the Atlantic seaboard . . .

* * *

Junius Brutus Booth: "Rise early, walk or use some exercise in the open air, and, when going to bed drink a warm liquid—either weak grog, gruel, or even water; drink nearly or quite a pint at one draught. Lie down directly, and in fifteen minutes you will sink into a comfortable lethargy. Coffee and tea, however, must be avoided, as they prevent sleep. A slice of bread-and-butter, and an onion or lettuce for supper, prior to this potation, is good—much opium, and of a harmless quality, being contained in the latter vegetable."

. . . revived himself after the play with a pint of porter or a glass of brandy . . . then, a drink or two beforehand, to brace himself . . . finally, to act when drunk . . .

locked in his hotel room, before the play, he bribed a passing bellboy to bring mint juleps, which he sucked through the keyhole with a straw . . .

. . . thrown into jail in Albany by his manager, to keep him sober, he bribed the chore boy to bring brandy, which he sipped through a Shaker pipe stuck through the cell's close grating . . .

. . . walked about the streets in full costume . . .

. . . in Natchez, climbed a ladder into the flies, during Ophelia's mad scene: crowed like a rooster . . .

"I can't read! Take me to the lunatic asylum!" he shouted in Boston: was hustled offstage, simpering and screeching with laughter . . . was later seen walking to Providence in his underwear, shaking his head, gesticulating . . .

"I must cut somebody's throat today. Whom shall I take?" he demanded at rehearsal, and whipped out a dagger . . .

. . . in the duel scene in *Richard III,* he chased Richmond through the stage door and into the street . . .

. . . as Othello, nearly suffocated Desdemona with a pillow . . .

*   *   *

Age 26, Junius Brutus Booth suddenly tired of the theater, "where nothing is but what is not." He applied for the job of lighthouse keeper at Cape Hatteras . . . but his business managers, not wishing to lose so valuable a property, made sure he was turned down . . . thereby performing a great service to those who navigate the waterworld . . .

*   *   *

Booth sought solitude, bought Maryland land, with a spring of sweet water, in the wilderness of Belair . . .

. . . worked in the fields, grubbing the soil and sowing the seed, in his bare feet . . .

. . . bought a log cabin, unpainted and unplastered, moved it to his new land, near the spring, among the oak and beech trees, at the skirts of the dense forest—and decorated the spring with granite steps and ledges.

Loved all animals, believing, with Pythagoras, that Men's souls are born again in animals' bodies . . . he refused to drown the little creatures that infested his mattresses . . .

*   *   *

When a black servant died, Booth preached the sermon, and buried the remains—outside the family plot. He loved their music . . .

*   *   *

May 10, 1851—twelfth birthday of their son, John Wilkes—Junius Brutus Booth and Mary Ann Holmes were married.

*   *   *

An infant daughter died, and Booth returned from tour, had the body disinterred and brought into the house, hoping thereby to restore the child to life . . . when his old horse died, he had Mrs. Booth lie across the creature's body, and pray . . .

*   *   *

Junius Brutus Booth died in 1852. He looked so natural the family was afraid to bury him, until assured by Physicians he was not just in a trance . . .

TWO

The Booth children grew up in Belair—the infants, on a winter evening, in wicker cradles, before the great stone fireplace . . .

The child John Wilkes ran wild through the woods, hurling himself to the ground, sniffing the earth's breath, nibbling the sweet roots and twigs. "Life is so short—and the world is so beautiful. Just to breathe is delicious."

The children put on theatricals, and young Johnnie stood at a window, mimicking . . . later, he studied dance, practiced elocution in the Belair woods . . .

. . . muttered to himself, frightened the servants, brandishing his Mexican saber, raving in recitations and rehearsings . . .

Was an expert marksman, went on hunting expeditions, in defiance of his father . . . could shoot through the open neck of a bottle, at some distance, and blast out the bottom . . .

Rode horseback into Belair . . . before a crowd of villagers, dropped his handkerchief to the ground, rode off, and, returning at a gallop, swept the linen gracefully into his hand . . .

At thirteen, he ran away to Baltimore, to become an actor, or an oyster pirate . . .

*   *   *

According to neighbors, the Booth family had "dirty British blood, and being mixed up with southern ideas and niggers made it dirtier" . . .

The family was disliked because they were so secretive *(theatre —self-exhibition—is the final retreat of the secretive)*

Everyone knew that John Wilkes' sister Rosalie was "a little queer" . . . and there were those around who thought that all the Booths were "cracked" . . .

* * *

In Baltimore there were meetings of the Blood Tubs and the Plug-Uglies . . . John Wilkes joined the Know-Nothings: to save the Southern Way of Life from the Irish . . .

* * *

John Wilkes Booth: ". . . he was a perfect man; his chest being full and broad, his shoulders gently sloping, and his arms as white as alabaster, but hard as marble. Over these, upon a neck which was its proper column, rose the cornice of a fine Doric head, spare at the jaws, and not anywhere over-ripe, but seamed with a nose of Roman model . . . which gave to the thoughtfully stern sweep of two direct, dark eyes, meaning to women, snare, and to men, a search warrant . . ."

". . . the lofty square forehead, and square brows were crowned with a weight of curling, jetty hair, like a rich Corinthian capital."

"His profile eagleish, and afar his countenance was haughty. He seemed full of introspections, ambitious self-examinings, eyestrides into the figure, as if it withheld him something to which he had a right."

"His coloring was unusual: the ivory pallor of his skin, the inky blackness of his densely thick hair, the heavy lids of his glowing eyes were all Oriental and they gave a touch of mystery to his face when it fell into gravity; but there was generally a flash of white teeth behind his silky mustache and a laugh in his eyes."

"He was handsome as a young god, with his clear, pale, olive complexion, classically regular features, and hair and mustache literally black as night . . ."

"John Wilkes Booth cast a spell over most men with whom he came in contact, and I believe all women without exception."

". . . ladies wrote him scented notes . . . the stage door was always blocked with silly women waiting to catch a glimpse . . ."

. . . in Albany, a young actress dashed into his room, cut his face with a dirk, then stabbed herself . . . the cause is said to have been "disappointed affection" . . .

*　*　*

According to the critics: ". . . every nerve quivers with the passion which his words give vent to . . ." ". . . the climax of the play was never given with such desperate energy . . ." ". . . Mr. Booth has far more action, more life . . ." ". . . The effect produced upon the audience was absolutely startling and bordered nearly upon the terrible . . ." ". . . J. W. Booth has that which is the grand constituent of all truly great acting, intensity . . ." ". . . Mr. Booth seems to me too energetic, too positive, earthly real and tangible . . ."

As Othello, rushing to the murdered Desdemona, his body and scimitar slammed against her—and she held her breath . . .

In Romeo's final struggle with Juliet, he sprained his thumb, tore her clothes, lifted her out of her shoes . . .

As Richard iii, he leapt over the footlights, dueled Richmond down the center aisle . . . or tumbled him into the orchestra pit, dislocating his shoulder . . .

. . . stabbed himself in the armpit, bound his right arm to his side, fenced with his left . . .

. . . following the performance, he slept smothered in oysters or raw steak, to heal the bruises . . .

*   *   *

Booth may have had a liasion with a Confederate spy, one Izola D'Arcy, who traveled under invented names: Oriana Collier, Eleanore St. Clare, Hero Strong, Izola Violetta . . .

He may have visited France, met a French girl, who said "he was a madman; that he arose at night in his sleep in order to converse with spirits, and that she was so afraid that she was fleeing . . ."

A Washington tavern keeper: ". . . now sometimes drank at my bar as much as a quart of brandy in less than two hours . . ." ". . . he could absorb an astonishing quantity and still retain the bearing of a gentleman . . ."

Booth: "When I want to do something that I know is wrong, or that I haven't time for, no surer way of being rid of the temptation than just to pretend it a reality . . ."

. . . he had his own initials—J.W.B.—pricked in India ink, on his right hand—perhaps to help him know who he was . . .

*   *   *

Spoke with a nasal quality—or with "a mongrel sound in the back of the mouth or top of the throat" . . .

. . . hadn't the patience, as an actor, to reach deep into his lungs and diaphragm, to truly "create" the sound . . . mistrusted the unreal, for fear it wouldn't become real, was too rushed—too anxious to get the meaning out . . .

1865, his career was already blighted by "bronchial trouble" . . .

THREE

Booth hated Lincoln, was personally offended that a man so gross and ugly could be in the White House. A clown, a gorilla, a niggerloving railsplitter . . . the big hands, gnarled and powerful, were hands that had done manual labor . . . the sparse, shaggy body, on which clothes hung loosely and seemed ill-fit, was the body of a peasant, grotesque and brutalized by toil . . .

The Vice-President, Andy Johnson, was a treacherous, traiterous Tennessee tailor . . .

*   *   *

The theater! the theater!
the final act,
to make the unreal real,

actor and character,
role and player,
interfused,

the other become his own,
his own another,

the actor in the theater
searching final measure
for the acts
of his imagination!

Booth: ". . . the country was formed for the white, not for the black man. And looking upon *African slavery* from the same standpoint held by the noble framers of our constitution, I, for one, have ever considered it one of the greatest blessings (both for themselves and us) that God ever bestowed upon a favored nation. Witness heretofore our wealth and power; witness their elevation and enlightenment above their race elsewhere. I have lived among it most of my life, and have seen *less* harsh treatment from master to man than I ever beheld in the North from father to son . . ."

"O, my friends, if the fearful scenes of the past four years had never been enacted, or if what has been was a frightful dream, from which we could now awake, with what overflowing hearts could we bless our God . . ."

. . . waiting until it was too late, until only ragtag Confederate remnants held out in Virginia, at Guinea's Station and Louisa Court House . . . Lee had surrendered, the war, and the cause for which it was fought, were buried . . .

> *("it may be asserted, without hesitation, that no event is so terribly well adapted to inspire the supremeness of bodily and mental distress, as is burial before death.")*

. . . when a cause is no longer supportable, it will be supported in theater . . .

* * *

Always, and from the beginning, the plot focused on Ford's . . . for a time, Booth kept two horses and a buggy in a stable at the rear: Lincoln was to be kidnapped, carried to Richmond, and held a hostage . . . Samuel Arnold was to catch the President when he was thrown out of his box at the theater . . .

The sound of the gunshot that killed the President was thought to be "an introductory effect preceding some new situation in the play."

Booth leapt from box to stage, his spur catching in the presidential bunting, throwing him off balance . . . his ankle collapsed under him, the bone broken, and he hopped, no longer the graceful actor, but ugly! like a bullfrog!

. . . nevertheless crossing the full width of the stage, savoring his exit . . .

*   *   *

A poster:

THE MURDERER

of our late beloved President, Abraham Lincoln

IS STILL AT LARGE

———————

$50,000 REWARD

Will be paid by this Department for his apprehension. BOOTH is Five Feet 7 or 8 inches high, slender build, high forehead, black hair, black eyes, and wore a heavy black moustache, which there is some reason to believe has been shaved off.

At Dr. Mudd's: " 'Davy,' he whispered, 'ask the lady of the house to let me have some hot water and soap—and the doctor's razor, if she will. I'm going to shave off my mustache. That's one identifying mark I can get rid of easily.' "

. . . the mark of the actor . . .

Following the assassination, and before the capture, Booth was seen on a train from Reading to Pottsville; at Tamaqua; at Greensburg; at Titusville, where he was almost lynched—all of the above being in Pennsylvania; as J. L. Chapman of Pittsfield, Mass.; in a Brooklyn saloon; on the stage of McVicker's theater in Chicago; as a railway official in Urbana, Ohio; near Point Lookout, Maryland; in Norfolk, Virginia; en route from Detroit to St. Mary's, Ontario (he was followed by a detective); 15 miles south of Baltimore; at Eastport, Maine, where he was almost lynched; concealed in an upstairs closet in Washington; walking the streets of Washington disguised as a Negro; in New York, in bed, disguised as a female.

*   *   *

Booth was cornered in the barn at Garrett's farm: the hay was fired, the flames flickered and flared—like footlights!

Beyond the glare, the audience: the attacking soldiers, and Boston Corbett, who shot him—unseen . . .

FOUR

In various collections, there are more than 200 pistols "with which Lincoln was killed"—some manufactured since 1865.

Booth shot Lincoln because they had squabbled over a woman.

Lincoln's coffin in Springfield, Illinois, is empty.

Following his capture and death, Booth was sighted in hiding in Ceylon; as captain of a pirate vessel in the China seas; playing *rouge et noir* at Baden-Baden; attending the opera in Vienna; driving in the Bois de Boulogne; visiting St. Peter's in Rome; on the Pelew Islands in the Pacific; in hiding in Washington; wandering in Mexico, South America, Africa, Turkey, Arabia, Italy, and China; fighting in China, with great distinction, against the Taiping rebels; playing Richard III in an amateur dramatics club in Shanghai; performing sleight-of-hand tricks for students at the University of Tennessee; off the New Guinea coast, in a lorcha; as a theatrical preacher, with a love of theater, in Richmond and Atlanta; in delirium in Wartburg, Morgan County, Tennessee; living out his life in England; shipping on a schooner from Havana to Nassau; running a saloon, without a license, in Glen Rose, Texas; living with the Apaches in Indian Territory; teaching school in a log schoolhouse, Bosque County, Texas; as a soldier in the army of Emperor Maximilian; on Raccoon Creek in Friendville, Kentucky; as a cabinet maker in Sewanee, Tennessee; as a mill hand in Memphis . . .

. . . as a drunken housepainter in Enid, Oklahoma: called himself John St. Helen . . . committed suicide January 13, 1903 . . . his remains were embalmed with arsenic, rented out to carnivals . . . acquired by the Jay Gould Million Dollar Spectacle, toured the Midwest for years . . . Jay Gould died September 23, 1967, and the mummy disappeared . . . one of Gould's sons, now living (1977) in Barberton, Ohio, claims an interest . . .

FIVE

In 1858, Boston Corbett—the man who shot Booth—had castrated himself, after being approached by a prostitute. 1887, he went berserk, tried to shoot up the Kansas State Legislature. He disappeared, but was traced to Enid, Oklahoma . . .

SIX

A visitor to Greenmount Cemetery, in Baltimore:

"As I walked after an attendant along the myrtle-bordered winding path that led to the Dogwood area, there seemed to be only one living thing in the old cemetery, a large black raven which flew ahead of us, lighting on one monument after another, performing some part of a mystic ritual as it were. Its presence there was so in keeping with the occasion, so like a fitting 'prop' for the scene, that it only seemed a touch of dramatic art when it finally arrived at the Booth plot ahead of me, and perched on top of the tall marble shaft."

Bibliography

POE

Asselineau, Roger. *Edgar Allan Poe*. Univ. of Minnesota Press, Minneapolis, Minn., 1970.

Bittner, William. *Poe*, Boston, Mass., 1962.

Fagin, N. Bryllion. *The Histrionic Mr. Poe*. Johns Hopkins Press, Baltimore, Md., 1949.

Harrison, James A., editor. *The Works of Edgar Allan Poe*. 17 Vol., New York, N.Y., 1902.

Hoffman, Daniel. *Poe, Poe, Poe, Poe, Poe, Poe, Poe*. Garden City, N.J., 1973.

Kaplan, Sydney. "Introduction" to *The Narrative of Arthur Gordon Pym*. New York, N.Y., 1960.

Krutch, Joseph Wood. *Edgar Allan Poe; A Study in Genius*. New York, N.Y., 1965.

Lawrence, D.H. "Edgar Allan Poe," in *Studies in Classic American Literature*. Garden City, 1953.

Miller, Perry. *The Raven and The Whale*, New York, N.Y., 1956.

Mottram, Eric. "Poe's Pym and the American Social Imagination," in *Artful Thunder*, edited by Robert J. DeMott and Sanford E. Marovitz. Kent, Ohio, 1975.

Ostram, John Ward, editor. *The Letters of Edgar Allan Poe*. Cambridge, Mass., 1948.

—Supplement to "The Letters of Poe," *American Literature*, XXIV. 1952, pages 358-366.

—Second Supplement to "The Letters of Poe," *American Literature*, XXIX. 1957, pages 79-86.

Poe, Edgar Allan. *The Works of Edgar Allan Poe*, "The Richmond Edition." New York, N.Y., no date.

Quinn, Arthur Hobson. *Edgar Allan Poe*. New York, N.Y., 1969.

Southern Literary Messenger, II. April, 1836, pages 336-339.

Stein, Gertrude. *Four in America*. New Haven, Conn., 1947.

Wagenknecht, Edward. *Edgar Allan Poe, The Man Behind the Legend*. New York, N.Y., 1963.

Wilbur, Richard. "The House of Poe," in *Poe, A Collection of Critical Essays*, edited by Robert Regan. Englewood Cliffs, N.J., 1967.

Williams, William Carlos. "Edgar Allan Poe," in *In the American Grain.* Norfolk, Conn., 1925.

Winwar, Frances. *The Haunted Palace.* New York, N.Y., 1959.

WATERWORLD

Dary, David A. *The Buffalo Book.* New York, N.Y., 1974.

Gifford, Barry, editor. *The Portable Curtis: Selected Writings of Edward S.Curtis.* Berkeley, 1976.

McCormick, Donald. *Blood on the Sea.* London, 1962.

Seaborn, Adam. *Symzonia: A Voyage of Discovery.* Scholars' Facsimiles & Reprints, Gainesville, Fla., 1965.

BOOTH

Bryan, George S. *The Great American Myth.* New York, N.Y., 1940.

Clarke, Asia Booth. *The Unlocked Book, A Memoir of John Wilkes Booth.* New York, N.Y., 1938.

DeWitt, David M. *The Assassination of Abraham Lincoln.* New York, N.Y., 1909.

Ferguson, Wm. J. *I Saw Booth Shoot Lincoln.* New York, N.Y., 1930.

Forrester, I.L. *This One Mad Act.* Boston, Mass., 1937.

Grossman, E.B. *Edwin Booth.* London, 1894.

Jones, Thomas A. *J. Wilkes Booth.* Chicago, Ill., 1893.

Kimmel, Stanley. *The Mad Booths of Maryland.* Indianapolis, Ind., & New York, N.Y., 1940.

Lewis, Lloyd. *Myths After Lincoln.* New York, N.Y., 1929.

Mahoney, Ella V. *Sketches of Tudor Hall and the Booth Family,* Belair, 1925.

Ruggles, Eleanor. *Prince of Players.* New York, N.Y., 1953.

Skinner, Otis. *Last Tragedian.* New York, N.Y., 1939.

Stern, Philip Van Doren. *The Man Who Killed Lincoln.* New York, N.Y., 1939.

Weichmann, Louis J. *A True History of the Assassination of Abraham Lincoln and of 1865.* New York, N.Y., 1975.

Wilson, Francis. *John Wilkes Booth.* Boston & New York, N.Y., 1929.

THE ISLAND

ONE

"The Indians told him that on that route he would find the island of Matinino, which it was said was inhabited by women without men, which the Admiral much wished [to see], in order to bring, he says, 5 or 6 of them to the Sovereigns . . ."

> Columbus, first voyage, return . . .
>
> (Was this the Island of Women, the Feminea of Marco Polo, visited only annually by men, for the rendering of services?)

Fourth voyage, outbound:

"On the following night we departed for the Indies, with fair weather as it pleased Our Lord. So, without ever lowering the sails, on the morning of Wednesday 15 June we arrived at the island . . ."

> (And he asked his Indian guide
> the name of the unknown land,
> and the names of those marve-
> lous shapes;
> the Indian answered that the
> name of the island was Madiana;
> that those peaks had been
> venerated
> from immemorial time
> by the ancient peoples of the
> archipelago as the birthplace
> of the human race;
> and that, driven from their
> natural heritage

by the cannibal Caribs of the
south,
the first brown habitants of
Madiana remembered and mourned for
their sacred mountains)

"...There, according to the use and custom
of those who go out from Spain, the Admiral gave orders to the
people to take on fresh water and wood and to wash their linen..."

* * *

1635, the *Compagnie des Îles d'Amérique* settled the island, and the
cannibal Caribs retreated inland ...

1654, 300 Jews, expelled from Brazil, landed ...

1658, there were 5,000 inhabitants (and the Caribs were extermi-
nated) ...

1666 and '**67,** the British attacked ...

1674, the Dutch ...

1693, the British again ...

And again, **1762,** the British (the island captured by Rodney) ...

1763, Louis xv yielded Canada for the French West Indies, prefer-
ring the tropic isles to "a few snowy acres" in North America ...

1793, the British again seized the island ...

And yielded in **1801** ...

1804, the British landed cannon, supplies, and 110 men on the *Rocher
du Diamant,* a rocky fortress jutting out of the sea at the south ...

1805, the French stormed the rock, and the British surrendered ...

1809, the British again . . .

But the French took final possession of Martinique, 1814 . . .

*   *   *

1685, Louis XIV enacted the *Code Noir:*

> Jews and Protestants are not wanted in the colony.
> All slaves are to be baptized and instructed in the Catholic faith.
> The children of non-Catholics are bastards.
> No labor or sales to take place on Sundays.
> Slaves are forbidden to assemble, to sell goods, to hold office, to carry arms, to own property.
> Owners are required to feed their slaves, and may not torture, mutilate, or put them to death.
> Government officials, however, may scourge, brand, clip the ears, hamstring and execute slaves (either on the wheel or by burning).

Pere Labat, 1695: "One would see nothing but mulattoes in our islands, were it not that the King has imposed a fine of 2,000 pounds of sugar if a man be convicted of being the father of one of them. If the father be a master who has debauched his slave, in addition to the fine, both mother and child are confiscated and given to the hospital, and they can never be redeemed under any pretext. One cannot praise sufficiently the zeal of His majesty for this ordinance."

(Saccatra and Sangmêlé . . .)

"According to their charter the Guinea and Senegal companies have to bring, I believe, two thousand slaves every year to the Islands."

By 1736, the Governor, to France: "The need that we have of Negroes is only too real and too pressing."

* * *

1822, whites were massacred, their homes pillaged and burned, by slaves

1831, a white judge was forced to resign, for sitting at a table with persons of color . . .

1848 (March 3): slavery in Martinique was abolished.

TWO

"Another hour; and Martinique looms before us. At first it appears all gray, a vapory gray; then it becomes bluish-gray; then all green."

"It is another of the beautiful volcanic family: it owns the same hill shapes with which we have already become acquainted; its uppermost height is hooded with the familiar cloud; we see the same gold-yellow plains, the same wonderful varieties of verdancy, the same long green spurs reaching out into the sea,— doubtless formed by old lava torrents. But all this is now repeated for us more imposingly, more grandiously;—it is wrought upon a larger scale than anything we have yet seen. The semicircular sweep of the harbor, dominated by the eternally veiled summit of the Montagne Pelé (misnamed, since it is green to the very clouds), from which the land slopes down on either hand to the sea by gigantic undulations, is one of the fairest sights that human eye can gaze upon. Thus viewed, the whole island shape is a mass of green, with purple streaks and shadowings here and there: glooms of forest-hollows, or moving umbrages of cloud."

"The roads of Martinique unroll a gorgeous and fantastic panorama. Volcanic peaks and lava dikes luxuriantly overwhelmed with densest greenness. Hanging gardens flung across the face of precipices; yellow green in the sunlight against the luminous haze of azure shadows; black green in the depths and blacker in the depths beyond. Deep torrent-hewn valleys hung with tree-ferns and great golden aigrettes of bamboo. Emerald valleys stretching far under the flame of the sun to a sapphire sea."

"East, west, and north the horizon is almost wholly hidden by surging of hills: those nearest are softly shaped and exquisitely green; above them loftier undulations take hazier verdancy and darker shadows; farther yet rise silhouettes of blue or violet tone, with one beautiful breast-shaped peak thrusting up in the midst;— while, westward, over all, topping even the Piton, is a vapory huddling of prodigious shapes—wrinkled, fissured, horned, fantastically tall . . . Such at least are the tints of the morning . . . Here and there, between gaps in the volcanic chain, the land hollows into gorges, slopes down into ravines;—and the sea's vast disk of turquoise flames up through the interval."

". . . verdure, in soft and enormous undulations,—in immense billowings of foliage. Only, instead of a blue line at the horizon, you have a green line; instead of flashings of blue, you have flashings of green,—and in all the tints, in all the combinations of which green is capable: deep green, light green, yellow-green, black-green."

". . . the idea of green fire . . ."

". . . the great green trance of the land . . ."

"The absolutism of green does not, however, always prevail in these woods. During a brief season, corresponding to some of our winter months, the forests suddenly break into a very conflagration of color, caused by the blossoming of the lianas—crimson, canary-yellow, blue, and white. There are other flowerings, indeed; but that of the lianas alone has chromatic force enough to change the aspect of a landscape."

"How gray seem the words of poets in the presence of this Nature! ... The enormous silent poem of color and light—(you who know only the North do not know color, do not know light!)—of sea and sky, of the woods and the peaks, so far surpasses imagination as to paralyse it—mocking the language of admiration, defying all powers of expression. That is before you which never can be painted or chanted, because there is no cunning of art or speech able to reflect it."

". . . little by little this naked nature, warm, savage, loving, succeeds in persuading you that work and strain are senseless and that without them life can still be very sweet."

* * *

"It had been one of those tropic days whose charm interpenetrates and blends with all the subtler life of sensation, and becomes a luminous part of it forever,—steeping all after-dreams of ideal peace in supernal glory of color,—transfiguring all fancies of the pure joy of being. Azure to the sea-line the sky had remained since morning; and the trade-wind, warm as a caress, never brought even one gauzy cloud to veil the naked beauty of the peaks."

"And the sun was yellowing,—as only over the tropics he yellows to death. Lilac tones slowly spread through the sea and heaven from the west;—mornes facing the light began to take wondrous glowing color,—a tone of green so fiery that it looked as though all the rich sap of their woods were phosphorescing. Shadows blued;—far peaks took tinting that scarcely seemed of earth;—iridescent violets and purples interchanging through vapor of gold."

"Sunset, in the tropics, is vaster than sunrise . . . The dawn, upflaming swiftly from the sea, has no heralding erubescence, no awful blossoming—as in the North: its fairest hues are fawn-colors, dove-tints, and yellows,—pale yellows as of old dead gold, in horizon and flood. But after the mighty heat of day has charged all the blue air with translucent vapor, colors become strangely changed, magnified, transcendentalized when the sun falls once more below the verge of visibility. Nearly an hour before his death, his light begins to turn tint; and all the horizon yellows to the color of a lemon. Then this hue deepens, through tones of magnificence unspeakable, into orange; and the sea becomes lilac. Orange is the light of the world for a little space; and as the orb sinks, the indigo darkness comes— not descending, but rising, as if from the ground—all within a few minutes. And during those brief minutes peaks and mornes, purpling into richest velvety blackness, appear outlined against passions of fire that rise half-way to the zenith,—enormous furies of vermilion."

"Through the further purpling, loftier altitudes dimly loom; and from some viewless depth, a dull vast rushing sound rises into the night . . . Is it the speech of hurrying waters, or only some tempest of insect voices from those ravines in which the night begins?"

"In the rapidly changing light, the shadows grow blacker under the green cascades of foliage. Rushing torrents flash in the light a moment at the little bridges before they plunge again into blackness."

"The road is now over-arched in the smothering embrace of the heavy growth enclosing us in the utter blackness of the tropical jungle at night."

"Night in all countries brings with it vagueness and illusions which terrify certain imaginations;—but in the tropics it produces effects peculiarly impressive and peculiarly sinister. Shapes of vegetation that startle even while the sun shines upon them assume, after his setting, a grimness,—a grotesquery,—a suggestiveness for which there is no name . . ."

"From the high woods, as the moon mounts, fantastic darknesses descend into the roads,—black distortions, mockeries, bad dreams . . ."

"Tropical night is full of voices;—extraordinary populations of crickets are trilling; nations of tree-frogs are chanting; the *Cabri-des-bois,* or *cra-cra,* almost deafens you with the wheezy bleating sound by which it earned its creole name; birds pipe: everything that bells, ululates, drones, clacks, gurgles, joins the enormous chorus; and you fancy you see all the shadows vibrating to the force of this vocal storm."

* * *

"The city of St. Pierre, on the edge of the land, looks as if it had slided down the hill behind it, so strangely do the streets come tumbling to the port in cascades of masonry,—with a red billowing of tiled roofs over all, and enormous palms poking up through it,—higher even than the creamy white towers of its cathedral."

"We are ashore in St. Pierre, the quaintest, queerest, and the prettiest withal, among West Indian cities: all stone-built and stone-flagged, with very narrow streets, wooden or zinc awnings, and peaked roofs of red tile, pierced by gabled dormers. Most of the buildings are painted in a clear yellow tone, which contrasts delightfully with the burning blue ribbon of tropical sky above; and no street is absolutely level; nearly all of them climb hills, descend into hollows, curve, twist, describe sudden angles. There is everywhere a loud murmur of running water,—pouring through the deep gutters contrived between the paved thoroughfare and the absurd little sidewalks . . ."

"Everything is bright and neat and beautiful; the air is sleepy with jasmine scent and odor of white lilies; and the palm—emblem of immortality—lifts its head a hundred feet into the blue light."

"And everywhere rushes mountain water,—cool and crystal clear, washing the streets;—from time to time you come to some public fountain flinging a silvery fountain to the sun, or shining bright spray over a group of black bronze tritons or bronze swans."

"Looking towards the water through these openings from the Grande Rue, you will notice that the sea-line cuts across the blue space just at the level of the upper story of the house on the lower street-corner. Sometimes, a hundred feet below, you see a ship resting in the azure aperture,—seemingly suspended there in sky-color, floating in blue light."

"The bay settles to rest in blue smoothness. Dolphins are playing in the distance. They love to play in the bay of St. Pierre and here they play with wonderful spirit. They toss their great bodies in smashing somersaults. Without a perceptible effort, they rise with the curving crests of the waves . . ."

"Whoever stops for a few months in St. Pierre is certain, sooner or later, to pass an idle half-hour in that charming place of Martinique idlers,—the beautiful Savane du Fort,—and, once there, is equally certain to lean a little over the mossy parapet of the river-wall to watch the *blanchisseuses* at work. It has a curious interest, this spectacle of primitive toil: the deep channel of the Roxelane winding under the palm-crowned heights of the Fort; the blinding whiteness of linen laid out to bleach for miles upon the huge bowlders of porphyry and prismatic basalt; and the dark bronze-limbed women, with faces hidden under immense straw hats, and knees in the rushing torrent . . ."

"In the simplicity and solidity of the quaint architecture,—in the eccentricity of bright narrow streets, all aglow with warm coloring, in the tints of roof and wall, antiquated by streakings and patchings of mould greens and grays,—in the startling absence of window-sashes, glass, gas lamps, and chimneys,—in the blossom tenderness of the blue heaven, the splendor of tropic light, and the warmth of the tropic wind,—you find less the impression of a scene of to-day than the sensation of something that was and is not. Slowly this feeling strengthens with your pleasure in the colorific radiance of costume,—the semi-nudity of passing figures,—the puissant shapeliness of torsos ruddily swart like statue metal,—the rounded outline of limbs yellow as tropic fruit,—the grace of attitudes,—the unconscious harmony of groupings,—the gathering and folding and falling of light robes that oscillate with swaying of free hips,—the sculptural symmetry of unshod feet. You look up and down the lemon-tinted streets,—down to the dazzling azure brightness of meeting sky and sea; up to the perpetual verdure of mountain woods—wondering at the mellowness of tones, the sharpness of lines in the light, the diaphaneity of colored shadows; always asking memory: 'When? . . . where did I see all this . . . long ago?' . . ."

* * *

"Surely never was fairer spot hallowed by the legend of man's nursing-place than the valley blue-shadowed by those peaks,—worthy, for their gracious femininity of shape, to seem the visible breasts of the All-nourishing Mother,—dreaming under this tropic sun."

THREE

"At the end of the small hours, my father, my mother, and over them the house which is a shack splitting open with blisters like a peach tree tormented by blight, and the roof worn thin, mended with bits of paraffin cans, this roof pisses swamps of rust on to the grey sordid stinking mess of straw, and when the wind blows these ill-matched properties make a strange noise, like the sputter of frying, then like a burning log plunged into water with the smoke from the twigs twisting away . . . And the bed of planks on its legs of kerosene drums, a bed with elephantiasis, my grandmother's bed with its goatskin and its dried banana leaves, and its rags, a bed with nostalgia as a mattress and above it a bowl full of oil, a candle-end with a dancing flame . . ."

> *"and the nigger each day more base, more cowardly,*
> *more sterile, less profound, more exteriorized,*
> *more separated from himself, more shrewd*
> *with himself, less immediate with himself"*

"... *the sudden grave animality of a peasant woman urinating on her feet, stiff legs apart.*"

        ("the monkey never finds his child ugly")

        "The flogged Negro who says 'Sorry, Master' and the twenty-nine legally permitted strokes of the whip and the cell four feet high and the branched yoke of iron ..."

        ("nigger-smell-makes-the-cane-grow")

        "Where's the gentle witch-doctor to unwind from your ankles
        the clammy warmth of the deadly iron rings?"

        ("You must sleep on the river-bank to understand the language of the fish.")

       *   *   *

        "and far from the sea which breaks under the suppurating syzygy of blisters, the body of my country marvelously bent in the despair of my arms, its bones shaken and in the veins the blood hesitating ..."

        "Islands that are scars upon the water"

"... *the corruptions of the dusk that are paced day and night by a damned venereal sun.*"

        "Everything is salty, everything is viscous and heavy like the life of plasmas."

        ("Hills never meet ...")

       *   *   *

"My pride is that my daughter should be very beautiful
when she gives orders to the blackwomen, my joy, that
she reveals a very-white arm among her black hens . . ."

> *("The eyes of the white man burn the eyes*
> *of the negro.")*

"and the light in those days, fecund in purer feats,
inaugurated the white kingdom where I led, perhaps,
a body without a shadow . . ."

> *("If you would eat the ox's head you must*
> *not fear the eyes.")*

". . . How beautiful your mother was, how pale, when
so tall and so languid . . ."

> *"Listen to the white world*
> *appallingly weary . . ."*

"Reverently, my father's boat brought tall white forms:
really, wind blown angels perhaps; or else wholesome
men dressed in good linen . . ."

* * *

. . . The painter Gauguin writes to his wife from Martinique (1887):
". . . Europeans are treasured like white blackbirds." . . . and tells her
of the native girl who squashed a fruit on her breast and offered it
to him . . .

> *"to prescribe at last this unique race free to produce from*
> *its tight intimacies the succulence . . ."*

* * *

"And now suddenly strength and life attack me like a bull, the wave of life streams over the nipple of the Morne, veins and veinlets throng with new blood, the enormous lung of cyclones breathing, the fire hoarded in volcanoes, and the gigantic seismic pulse beats the measure of a living body within my blaze."

"And the voice declares that for centuries Europe has stuffed us with lies and bloated us with pestilence.

> *for it is not true that the work of man is finished*
> *that we have nothing to do in the world*
> *that we are parasites in the world*
> *that we have only to accept the way of the world*

But the work of man has only begun."

"bullets in the mouth thick saliva
our heart daily bursts with meanness
the continents break the frail moorings of isthmuses
lands explode along the fatal division of rivers
and now it is the turn of these Heights
which for centuries have stifled back their cry
to quarter the silence
and the people"

"come wolves who graze in the savage orifices
of the body
when my moon meets your sun at the ecliptic inn"

> *("Although the serpent has little eyes he sees very clearly.")*

> *("Who lives will see")*

> *("Who dies will know")*

* * *

("Crazy ants are not so crazy. They are
in a hurry because they are in a hurry.")

"the soil works
and among the branches heady sweet blossoms of
haste"

* * *

. . . at a Martinique wake, there are music and jokes, the rum flows, the corpse is sometimes lifted from the coffin for a whirl around the dance floor in the arms of anyone able to remain afoot . . .

"There's no denying it: he was a good nigger . . ."

FOUR

"Then, perhaps, your gaze is suddenly riveted by the vast and solemn beauty of the verdant violet-shaped mass of the dead Volcano,—high-towering above the town, visible from all its ways, and umbraged, maybe, with thinnest curlings of cloud . . ."

"This evening, as I write, La Pelée is more heavily coiffed than is her wont. Of purple and lilac cloud the coiffure is,—a magnificent Madras, yellow-banded by the sinking sun."

"Even in bulk, perhaps, Pelée might not impress those who know the stupendous scenery of the American ranges; but none could deny it special attractions appealing to the senses of form and color. There is an imposing fantasticality in its configuration worth months of artistic study: one does not easily tire of watching its slopes undulating against the north sky,—and the strange jagging of its ridges,—and the succession of its terraces crumbling down to the other terraces, which again break into ravines here and there bridged by enormous buttresses of basalt: an extravaganza of lava-shapes overpitching and cascading into sea and plain. All this is verdant wherever surfaces catch the sun: you can divine what the frame is only by examining the dark and ponderous rocks of the torrents. And the hundred tints of this verdure do not form the only colorific charms of the landscape. Lovely as the long upreaching slopes of cane are,—and the loftier bands of forest growth, so far off they look like belts of moss,—and the more tender-colored mosses above, wrinkling and folding together up to the frost-white clouds of the summit,—you will be still more delighted by the shadow-colors,—opulent, diaphanous. The umbrages lining the wrinkles, collecting in the hollows, slanting from sudden projections, may become before your eyes almost as unreally beautiful as the land-scape colors of a Japanese fan;—they shift most generally during the day from indigo-blue through violets and paler blues to final lilacs and purples; and even the shadows of passing clouds have a faint blue tinge when they fall on Pelée."

"For the moment it appears to sleep; and the clouds have dripped into the cup of its higher crater till it has become a lake, seven hundred yards in circumfrance. The crater occupied by this lake—called L'Étang, or 'the Pool'—has never been active within human memory."

"Some day there may be a great change in the little city of St. Pierre . . ."

*　*　*

Early April, 1902:

Mont Pelée emitted low rumbling sounds, and a series of sharp tremors. A scouting party climbed the volcano, reported a new emission of lava filling the crater floor. The report was generally ignored, as there was an election forthcoming in St. Pierre: Governor Mouttet's Progress Party, the party of the whites, faced stiff competition from the Black-backed Radicals, and the governor wished to prevent an exodus of whites from the city, which would leave the votes to the Blacks. The newspaper, *Les Colonies,* was ordered to say that the theory of panic was a "fear-mongering technique of the Radicals."

> (The Blacks replied: "The mountain will sleep only when the whites are out of office.")

April 27, a second scouting party: Messieurs Boulin, Waddy, Décord, Bouteuil, Ange, and Berte ascended the mountain. ". . . these investigators found to their surprise that the normally dry bed of the Étang Sec or Soufrière . . . was now in a condition of ferment . . . long trains of steaming vapor . . . a brilliantly shimmering surface beneath the crowning vapor . . . the noise of boiling water . . ."

Again the report was suppressed. Instead: *"La position relative des cratères et des vallées débouchant vers la mer permet d'affirmer que la securité de Saint Pierre reste entière."*

An excursion to the summit was planned, a holiday: "If the weather be fine, the excursionists will pass a day that will long be kept in remembrance."

Early May, light falls of ashes covered the streets, giving St. Pierre an alpine look. "The beautiful Jardin des Plantes . . . lay buried with its palms, its ravenalas, rubber-trees, and mangos, its giant cactuses and red hibiscus, beneath a cap of gray and white." Blacks on the streets turned white, "as if hoar-frost had fallen over them."

Little birds lay asphyxiated, the farm animals were restless— bleating, neighing, bellowing. A plague of insects moved down the mountainside, the deadly *fer-de-lance* invaded farms and homes.

Some of the whites tried to escape, the governor ordered troops to block all roads leading away . . .

The night of May 7:

". . . the most extraordinary pyrotechnic display: at one moment a fiery crescent gliding over the surface of the crater, at the next long, perpendicular gashes of flame piercing the column of smoke, and then a fringe of fire, encircling the dense clouds rolling down the furnace of the crater. Two glowing craters from which fire issued, as if from blast furnaces, were visible during half an hour, the one on the right a little above the other."

"I distinguished clearly four kinds of noises; first, the claps of thunder, which followed the lightning at intervals of twenty seconds; then the mighty muffled detonations of the volcano, like the roaring of many cannon fired simultaneously; third, the continuous rumbling of the crater, which the inhabitants designated the 'roaring of the lion'; and then last, as though furnishing the bass for this gloomy music, the deep noise of the swelling waters, of all the torrents which take their source upon the mountain, generated by an overflow such as had never yet been seen. The immense rising of thirty streams at once, without one drop of water having fallen on the seacoast, gives some idea of the cataracts which must pour down upon the summit from the storm clouds gathered around the crater."

Next morning—May 8—dawned bright and sunny, and Pelée was still, with only a vapor column rising into the air. "Not a ripple was to be seen on the face of the sea. Not a breath of air was stirring, which made it more difficult for us to breathe."

. . . the air dead, floating volcanic dust undisturbed.

FIVE

seven fifty ante meridian may the eighth nineteen hundred and two:

> Pelée shuddered,
> the crater moaned
>
> seven luminous points
> on Pelée
>
> and
>
> four deafening reports:
>
> a rending, crashing, grinding
> all the world's machinery broken
>
> a mighty hand
> playing the strings of a harp
> greater than the world
>
> not siege-guns, nor thunder,
> but as though explosions
> from high in the clouds
>
> a frightful fracas
>
> Pelée blew a hole in her side
>
> a flash more blinding than lightning
>
> two clouds:
> the first huge and black and laced with lightning
> shot straight up
> the second, lighter,
> traced through with glowing red lines,

shot down the slope,
clinging to the ground

the cloud roaring,
with a galloping sound

a black cloud,
backpowder smoke,
shot from the world's gun

black coils,
unrolling, expanding

a black cloud,
heavily charged with ashes
and blocks of lava,
shot through with incandescent flashes

irradiated by a faint glow,
dull red, incandescent,

shot with bursts of smoke,
but no flame

lightning in and out,
broadly forked,
electric scintillations
playing in the vapors

air charged with ashes,
sun blocked,
darkness absolute,
only flashes from
Pelée illuminating

the cloud, the vapors,
black and violet-gray,

clinging to the ground,
to the valley of the Roxelane,
shot for St. Pierre

struck the city,
a heavy gas,
firedamp,
without flame

lifted, revealing a second cloud,
yellow, sulphurous

both lifted,
like rising blankets,

and roadstead, city, surrounding country
flashed to fire,
in one instant

seawater tore into whirlpools,
boiled in clouds of steam

by the light of the burning city
people like ants scrambled on the beach

volcanic dust,
in fineness impalpable,
floated unseen

and mixed with a violent rain,
a downpour of sodden plaster

flowing mud,
snowdrifted

*   *   *

a storm wind,
counter to the force of the volcano,
blew inward to the crater,
violent, centripetal,
imploding,
un vent impétueux,
une véritable bourrasque,

the gentle clouds of the atmosphere
drawn to the source

SIX

casks of rum exploded,

     hot spirits poured out,

ignited,

     the rum aflame,

rum tumbling down the streets,

     fiery,

pouring through the alleys,

     the gutters and gullies.

burning in the body of the city,

     St. Pierre aflame and reeling,

rum roiling,

     pouring, spreading, at last

into the harbor,

                              aflame, still

flagrant liquors

                              tumbling over the roadstead,

to fire the

                              stricken anchored shipping

SEVEN

"The explosive phenomena associated with slow extrusive eruptions
often assume destructive dimensions, since the internal gas pressure
must attain a very high value before it can overcome the resistance
of the viscous masses of lava. The gases then break through with
terrific force, tearing away still incandescent blocks, stones, and
finer particles. As a result of the rapid release of pressure, the gases
held inside such blocks are suddenly freed, and there forms a pecu-
liarly mobile suspension of solid, partly incandescent fragments of
all sizes dispersed in the hot expanding gases. This suspension is so
dense that it cannot rise into the air, but rushes down the slopes of
the volcano and in a few seconds annihilates every living thing in
its path."

"The condition of explosion may then be stated as follows: A volume
of steam with intense exploding energy rising to the crater-mouth,
blowing out in its first paroxysm a part of the crater-floor, and then
exploding in free air under a heavily depressing cushion of ascending
steam and ash, and with surrounding walls of rock on three sides and
more to form an inner casing to nature's giant mortar. The blast was
forced through the open cut, or lower lip of the crater . . ."

"The magmas involved are extremely viscous. No liquid extrusions
of lava take place. Instead, the vent of the volcano becomes plugged

by a slowly rising column of stiff, semisolid magma which solidifies in the conduit, producing a seal of rock. The rising magma becomes supersaturated with withheld gases, and the molten material builds to a pressure head beneath the blocked vent."

"In this variety of eruption, an emulsion cloud of superheated gases, dust, ash, and larger incandescent particles is formed and due to its high density follows downhill slopes rather than rising. The cloud travels at speeds of more than one hundred miles per hour, leveling everything in its path."

"The vapours . . . were . . . seemingly very dense, for although endowed with an almost inconceivably powerful ascensive force, they retained to the zenith their rounded summits."

A *Nuée ardente,* a fiery cloud, a scorching swarm . . .

". . . an incandescent mass of solid fragments, buoyed up by the rush of expanding, heated gases. The escaping gases rise upwards, form-ing a turbulent, dynamic wall, while the denser part, containing most of the solid material, hugs the ground and rolls rapidly over it, traveling at great speed, since each particle of the solid material is in a more or less floating condition, cushioned by escaping gas . . ."

volcanic ejectamenta

fine and coarse lapilli

bread-crust bombs

EIGHT

trees buried under ashes,
or standing dry and stripped,

sap from the twigs
sucked out,

the few leaves remaining,
scorch-blasted . . .

> Objects carbonized,
> become charcoal,
> without combustion

On most of the bodies the flash passed so quickly that clothing
would not kindle, remained untouched. Instead, the skin blistered,
skulls parted, split open, at the sutures. One fiery breath and the
lungs shriveled. The barometric pressure plunged and bodies
exploded, burst at the abdomen, spongy tissues distended, all bodily
fluids turned to steam.

Pelée, lush green,
rested,

> covered with ash,
> a winter's landscape;

the atmosphere hung thick
in smoke and ash,

the sun broke through,
dim, wan,
as he never is . . .

Off Martinique, an intense lilac, the roseate light commingling with the blue of the sky . . . five great shadow-beams, with broadening ends directed to the zenith . . .

West of St. Lucia, a green sunset . . .

At Barbados, brilliant orange . . .

In Europe, at Berlin, remarkable coloring . . .

Streaked radiations in northern Italy . . .

At Morges, Switzerland, a brilliant disk of whitish-yellow light, appearing above the sunset point a quarter of an hour after the setting of the sun, as if the whole of the west of Switzerland were on fire . . .

> In St. Pierre,
> fresh water
> continued to flow
> from the spigots and fountains
> pipes and hydrants
> of the burned and buried city,
>
> water emanating
> from the wellsprings
> on the slopes
> of Pelée

NINE

Of thirty thousand, one survived:

Auguste Ciparis—or his name may have been, more properly, Samson Sil-Barice—a Black stevedore, age nineteen, and a convicted murderer. He was lodged in an underground dungeon beneath the city jail . . . the only opening to the outside was a tiny grated aperture high on the dungeon door. May 8, in the morning, he awaited his last breakfast: he was to be hanged.

The cell suddenly darkened, and a blast of hot air, mixed with fine ashes—the stevedore described it as "hot, dry sand"—penetrated the grating. He was dressed at the time in hat, shirt, and trousers, and these remained untouched. Nor were his hair and face scorched. But neck, back, and legs were horribly burned, his feet swollen, his hands covered with yellow, offensive matter. Blood oozed from his burns.

Four days he spent in agony, until rescuers—or possibly looters—heard his feeble cries. Saved from the gallows, and nursed back to health, his death sentence commuted, he became famous:

August Ciparis toured with Barnum and Bailey Circus until his death in 1929, his days spent displayed in a replica of his jail cell.

TEN

there were
small paroxysmal eruptions,
May 26,
June 6,
July 9,
August 30.

In October,
from the crater of the *Étang Sec,*
a spine or pillar,
a mass of solidified lava
slowly rose,
to form an obelisk,
a monolith,
a tower.

Semi-rigid, curled over,
with a sharp crest,
forced upward by the pressure
of magma below,
it grew at the rate of
thirty-three feet a day,
to reach, finally,
a height of a thousand feet!

The core was liquid,
one side smooth and slickensided
. . . a horn-like form!

Vapor clouds blowing
from the vast base,
and from the cone,
blue sulphur smoke . . .

1904,
the spine cooled,
cracked, started to break up.

responding, still,
to fresh pulses of lava,
from below

Bibliography

Allen, Troy. *Disaster.* Chatsworth, California, 1974.

Andersen, Wayne. *Gauguin's Paradise Lost.* New York, 1971.

Césaire, Aimé. *Return to my Native Land.* Baltimore, 1969.

Cornell, James. *The Great International Disaster Book.* New York, 1976.

Cotton, C.A.. *Volcanoes as Landscape Forms.* Wellington, N.Y., 1944.

Edson, Wesley. *Terry's Guide to the Caribbean.* Garden City, N.Y., 1970.

Francis, Peter. *Volcanoes.* London, 1976.

Hearn, Lafcadio. *Two Years in the French West Indies.* 1890.

Heilprin, Angelo. *Mont Pelée and the Tragedy of Martinique.* Philadelphia, 1903.

Hovey, E.O. *Preliminary Report on the Martinique and St. Vincent Eruptions. Bulletin.* American Museum of Natural History, October 11, 1902.

Howes, Barbara, editor. *From the Green Antilles.* New York, 1966.

Kennan, George. *Tragedy of Pelée.* New York, 1902.

Labat, Pere. *The Memoirs of Pere Labat, 1693-1705.* Trans. by John Eaden. London, 1970.

Léger, Alexix Saint-Léger. *Collected Poems of St. John Perse.* Princeton, 1971.

McCloy, Shelby T. *The Negro in the French West Indies.* Lexington, Ky. 1966.

Morison, Samuel Eliot. Admiral of the Ocean-Sea. Boston, 1942.

Morison, Samuel Eliot. *Journals and Other Documents on the Life and Voyages of Christopher Columbus.* New York, 1963.

Morris, Charles. *Volcano's Deadly Work.* 1902.

Morton, Benjamin Alexander. *The Veiled Empress.* New York & London, 1923.

Rittman, A. *Volcanoes and their Activity.* New York, 1962.

WATERS OF
POTOWMACK

*Being a gathering of the waters of several states of mid-Atlantic—
Pennsylvania, Maryland, Virginia, West Virginia—waters of
Potomac's North and South Branches, of Shenandoah, and others of
influence—flowing from the heights of Allegheny, cleaving through
the Blue Ridge, absorbing from* Pain de Sucre *and the Catoctins
across the foot of the mountains—broadening, finally, and commin-
gling below Federal City with waters of Chesapeake Bay and the
ocean beyond . . .*

*And being, further, a flowage and commingling of peoples in this
great basin, from the red man, Susquehannock, Piscataway, Nanti-
coke, from the wellsprings of Potomac habitation—to the first white
eyes to view, the first white feet to walk upon this green valley—
Jesuit, John Smith, Lord Calvert—the trickle growing to a flood tide
of whites and the blacks they brought with them—exploring, settling,
inhabiting, tilling, fighting, building, polluting, revolting, rebelling,
governing, designing, cultivating, conserving, rioting . . . these peoples
flowing as the Potomac's waters flow from sources to the sea—flowing
from the wellsprings of history, cleaving through the tangible past,
into the present . . .*

*the whole being writ and limned with scholarly grace and wisdom by
the many who took pains to record—with pen, graver, brush,
machines for typing and the making of photographs—their several
journies.*

Potomac's Valley shall become
a domain we create, an inchoate
scene where snows wane
and bulbs burn under the winter ground.

—Jonathan Williams

IMPRIMIS

they are coming by water, drawing near in crafts and canoes   the river full of swarms of small fry, where fishes spawn in shoals   bushy or brushy river   traveling traders   river of swans   the burning pine, resembling a council fire

Such are the suggested meanings of the Indian word *Potomac* (and the name itself, *Potomac,* may be found in twenty or more different spellings).

Above Great Falls, the river was known as *Cohongarootan* or Goose River, from the multitude of geese which frequented it in winter. *Shenandoah,* tributary to *Potomac,* may be Silver Water, River of High Mountains, River Through the Spruces, or still others, while Potomac's South Branch was called by Blue Ridge Indians *Wappatomika,* or River of Wild Geese.

———————

Three major streams—the North and South Branches and the Shenandoah—converge to form the single river and tidal estuary now known as the Potomac. Bounded on the north by the watershed of the Susquehanna, on the west by that of the Ohio, on the south by the James and Rappahanock, and on the east by Chesapeake Bay, into which it flows, the Potomac River and basin cover an area of over one hundred thousand square miles—four percent of the continental United States. Parts of Pennsylvania, Maryland, Virginia, and West Virginia, and the entire District of Columbia, are included in this area.

———————

Near Forty Three, between Brown and Backbone Mountains, not far from Blackwater Falls (where river waters run dark through coal beds and laurel thickets), a spring bubbles to the surface, flows northeastward, to Kempton, Difficult Creek, and Glade Run: the headfountains of Potomac. Wolfden Run and Elklick Run flow in; the waters pass Pee Wee and Horserock Hills, flow between Dans and Big Savage mountains, turn eastward and then southeastward around Piney Mountain, to Cumberland, Knobly Mountain, and the furthest northwestward diggings of the C&O Canal. Beyond Warrior Mountain to Oldtown . . .

> Shawnee old Town, where Thomas Cresap settled in 1741 on an Indian wartrack, treated the Indians well, fed them generously.

The river embraces the South Branch, Sawpit and Purslane Runs, and turns northeast again, to meander in the Paw Paw Bends. Past Doe Gully and Sideling Hill, to take in the wild Great Cacapon, and flow not far from Berkeley Springs . . .

> . . . where the Indians gathered, before the time of whites, at the warm springs, and observed the valley as a neutral area: Tuscarora, Shawnee, Delaware, Iroquois, Catawba, and Huron, some of them bitter enemies, coming from great distances, camping side by side on Cacapon and Sleepy Creek mountains, bathing together in the springs, without animosity.

The waters turn southeast again, passing near Broadfording on the Conococheague, and Falling Waters, circling around Terrapin Neck to flow not far from Bardane and Bolivar, then to burst from the mountains at Harper's Ferry and the embouchure of Shenandoah. Strongly southeastward, now, bubbling over Bullring Falls, past Catoctin Mountain, Stumptown and Point of Rocks, Sugarloaf Mountain and Ball's Bluff, to Blockhouse Point, the river enturbulates over Great Falls, and gentles again, beyond Stubblefield and Little Falls . . .

. . . where the Indians maintained fishing villages, on the terraced bluffs overlooking the river, or on the floodplain just above the current, the villages swept freely by every spring freshet.

. . . Cabin John, Horsepen Run, Snakeden Branch, and Difficult Run, in the broadening tidal estuary, flowing due south beyond the Federal City, then meandering in the wider reaches, absorbing creeks and runs *where the edge of the hill is   at the end of the hill twisting in the lands   at the end of water   where one goes pleasantly   at the long tidal stream.*

Past Bull Run, Bull Town Cove, Blue Banks, and Bull Bluff, downstream with the *stream that scoops out banks,* to the tidal run where *it flows in the opposite direction.* Then *one goes on downward   the jutting of water inland   at the big tidal river.*

Winkedoodle Point is *pleasant or fair.* Piccowaxen Creek is *ragged, pierced, or broken shoes.* At Manahowic Creek, *they are merry people,* and Chaptico Bay is a *big broad river.*

To Honest Point. Thicket Point. Tippity-Wichity Island. Yeocomico: *he, that is floating on water, tossed to and fro.*

to Smith Point,
Point Lookout . . .

to the open Bay:

Waters of Potowmack

ONE

DISCOVERY AND INDIANS

Amerigo Vespucci, 1497 . . . John Cabot, 1498 . . . Quexos, 1521 and 1525 . . . Verrazano, 1524 . . . Estevan Gómez, 1525 . . . John Rut, 1527 . . .

These and others, sailing in the Atlantic north or south, may have seen and not reported—or failed to see, hidden in fog or darkness—the opening of Bahía de Madre de Dios: Chesapeake Bay.

But in 1507 brothers and novices of the Society of Jesus, together with an Indian, coasted northward from Santa Elena (South Carolina), and entered the bay.

Juan de la Carrera:

> Our Fathers and Brothers disembarked in a great and beautiful port, and men who have sailed a great deal and have seen it say it is the best and largest port in the world. So, if I remember rightly, the pilot remarked to me, It is called the Bay of the Mother of God, and in it there are many deep-water ports, each better than the next. I saw this port myself when I went with the Governor, as I will narrate later. It seemed to me (for as it looked to me and I was given to understand), it was about 3 leagues at the mouth, and in length and breadth it was close to 30. They say that at the end of it the other sea begins.

The Jesuit fathers and brothers sailed up the River James,

landed

settled,

and were wiped out by Indians.

In 1588 Vicente Gonzales, Captain, bearing with him one Luis Gerónimo de Oré, sailed north from San Augustín (Florida), rounded capes Hatteras and Henry, entered the Bay of the Mother of God, and followed the westerly shore northward.

> As they continued to sail north, the land from the east jutted into the bay . . . They discovered inlets and coves as well as rivers along the western shore. Then they came upon a large freshwater river, which, where it entered the bay, was more than 6 fathoms deep. To the north there was very high land, with ravines, but without trees, delightful and free, which has the aspect of a green field and was pleasant to behold. On the south shore of this river the beach is very calm and is lined with small pebbles. Farther up on the south bank of the same river there appeared a delightful valley, wooded, and pleasant land which seemed to be fertile and adaptable to stock-raising and farming. The river was located in a latitude of 38°. They named it San Pedro.

Potomac's first white sighting . . .

———————————

For many thousands of years before Captain Gonzales, fishing, hunting, wandering Indians roamed Potomac shores, one tribe succeeding another, until Piscataways, Nacostines, Nanticokes, and Potopacos settled on the Maryland side, and tribes of the Powhatan Confederacy on the Virginia shore. All were of Algonquin stock, and of a peaceful nature. They made permanent settlements or villages near the water, cultivated the soil, raised maize, beans, and tobacco, and ate massively of the oysters (a shell midden near Pope's Creek, Maryland, covers 30 acres). They killed game with a throwing stick—*atlatl*—as well as with bow and arrow, and dined on bison, elk, bear, wolf, skunk, swan, eagle, hawk, and buzzard. Settlements, except for hunting camps, were confined to the shores of river and tributary, from the river mouth to the Great Falls. Inland there was forest, with an open growth of hardwoods, the browsing deer reducing underbrush.

Tidewater Indians were adept at the manufacture of stone implements. W. H. Holmes, archeologist, 1897:

> The primitive inhabitants of the crystalline highlands had to make use of massive forms of rock or of rude angular or slightly water-worn fragments, and the reduction of these to available sizes and forms was a difficult work. But the inhabitants of the lowlands were born to more fortunate conditions. The agents of nature—the floods—had with more than human intelligence and power selected the choice bits of rock, the tough quartzite, the flinty quartz, the tough and brittle lavas, the indurated slates, the polished jasper, and the beautiful flints, from all the cliffs and gorges of the mountains, and had reduced them to convenient sizes and shapes, and had laid them down in the beds of the shallow estuaries where through the subsequent rising of the land and the cutting of valleys they were found at the door of the tidewater lodge . . .
>
> The greatest aboriginal bowlder quarry known, and the most important implements shops yet observed on the Atlantic slope, are located on Fourteenth street 2½ miles from the President's house. One of the most interesting native soapstone quarries in the great series extending along the eastern base of the highland from Massachusetts to Georgia is on Connecticut avenue extended, barely beyond the city limits; and the most important ancient village-site in the whole tidewater province is situated on Anacostia river within the city and little more than a mile from the capitol.
>
> The capital city is paved with the art remains of a race who occupied its site in the shadowy past.

Rhyolite from South Mountain, soapstone from Bull Run, quarries on Piny Branch of Rock Creek, at the mouth of Wicomico, on Potomac Creek on the island of Chopawomsic . . . Fracturing or flaking, battering or pecking, incising or abrading, to make celts, axes, pestles, arrowheads, drills, knives, hoes, picks, chisels, pipes, and foolish ornaments . . .

Many of the villages were stockaded for defense with posts of honey locust, the thorny branches intertwined. Although at peace with one another, the Powhatans lived in fear of the Monocans and Manahoacs from the upland; and the Piscataways were crowded by Susquehannocks and Senecas from the north.

According to George Alsop, 1666, the Susquehannocks were "a people cast into the mold of a most large and warlike deportment, the men being for the most part seven foot high in latitude, and in magnitude and bulk suitable to so high a pitch; their voice large and hollow, as ascending out of a Cave, their gate strait and majestick."

An Iroquoian tribe, the Susquehannocks were hunters, living on the fresh-water streams, descending in spring and summer to salt water for fish and oysters, and to prey on sedentary Piscataways. By the seventeenth century, they had reached Great Falls and were moving down both sides of Chesapeake Bay.

One of the Five Nations, the Senecas (no doubt reinforced by others of the Five), ranged and raided through eastern America, from their home in upper New York to the Mississippi and to Florida, attacking Susquehannock and Piscataway alike.

The lower Potomac Indians huddled on the tidewater shores, "a mere selvage woven upon the fabric of the wilderness."

Sherds, spalls, and shells by a spring of sweet water . . . mortars of quartzite, pestles of felsite . . . 618 skulls, found in an Accokeek ossuary . . .

To this day [1935], a very considerable number of people reside about Port Tobacco River, who are designated locally as "Wesorts," who claim Indian origin, and who evince, in many cases, Indian physical characteristics, and who are evidently of mixed ancestry, Indian, negro, and white.

April 10, 1607, John Smith and company departed the West Indies, heading for Virginia. April 21, they were struck by a storm, and floundered four days, out of sight of land and with no bottom. At dawn April 26, they sighted land—Cape Henry—and sailed into Chesapeake Bay. Search was made for a site for permanent settlement. May 13, the ships, standing in six fathoms of water in the James River, were tied to trees on the shore, and the next morning men and supplies went ashore, to establish Jamestown.

The following year, Smith explored Chesapeake Bay.

The second of June 1608. Smith left the fort, to performe his discoverie: with this company.

Ralp Morton.			Anas Todkill.	
Thomas Momford.			Robert Small.	Sould.
William Cantrill.	Gent		James Watkins.	
Richard Fetherstone.			John Powell.	
James Bourne.			James Read, blacke smith.	
Michael Sicklemore.			Richard Keale, fishmonger.	
			Jonas Profit, fisher.	

These being in an open barge of two tunnes burthen, leaving the *Phenix* at Cape Henry, we crossed the bay to the Eastern shore, and fell with the Iles called Smith Iles. The first people we saw were 2. grimme and stout Salvages upon Cape-Charles, with long poles like Javelings, headed with bone. They boldly demanded what we were, and what we would, but after many circumstances, they in time seemed very kinde . . . Passing along the coast, searching every inlet and bay fit for harbours and habitations: seeing many Iles in the midst of the bay, we bore up for them, but ere wee could attaine, such an extreme gust of wind, raine, thunder, and lightning happened, that with great daunger, we escaped the raging of that ocean-like water. The next day . . . brought us to the river Wighcocomoco. The people at first with great furies seemed to assault us, yet at last with songs, daunces, and much mirth, became very tractable . . . In crossing over from the maine to other Iles, the wind and waters so much increased with thunder lightning and raine, that our foremast blew overbord, and such mightie waves overwrought us in that smal barge, that with great labour wee kept her from sinking, by freeing out the water. 2 daies we were forced to inhabit these uninhabited Iles, which (for the extremities of gusts, thunder, raine, stormes, and il weather) we called Limbo. Repairing our fore sail with our shirts, we set saile for the maine . . . But finding this easterne shore shallow broken Iles, and the maine for most part without fresh water, we passed by the straights of Limbo, for the weasterne shore. So broad is the bay here, that we could scarce perceive the great high Cliffes on the other side. 30 leagues we sailed more Northwards, not finding any inhabitants, yet the coast well watred, the mountains very barren, the vallies very fertil, but the woods extreame thicke, full of Woolves, Beares, Deare, and other wild beasts . . . When we first set saile, some of our gallants doubted nothing, but that our Captaine would make too much hast home. But having lien not above 12 daies in this smal Barge, oft tired at their oares, their bread spoiled with wet, so much that it was rotten (yet so good were their stomacks that they could digest it), did with continuall complaint so importune him now to returne, as caused him bespeake them in this manner.

Gentlemen . . . what shame would it be for you (that have beene so suspitious of my tendernesse) to force me returne with a months provision, scarce able to say where we have bin nor yet heard of that wee were sent to seeke. You cannot say but I have shared with you of the worst is past; and for what is to come, of lodging, diet, or whatsoever, I am contented you allot the worst part to my selfe. As for your feares, that I will lose my selfe in these unknowne large waters, or be swallowed up in some stormie gust, abandon those childesh feares, for worse than is past cannot happen, and there is as much daunger to returne, as to proceed forward. Regaine ther fore your old spirits; for returne I wil not, (if God assist me) till I have seen the Massawomekes, found Patawomeck, or the head of this great water you conceit to be endlesse.

3 or 4 daies we expected wind and weather, whose adverse extreamities added such discouragements to our discontents as 3 or 4 fel extreame sicke, whose pitiful complaints caused us to returne, leave the bay some 10 miles broad at 9 or 10 fadome.

The 16 of June, we fel with the river of Patawomeck. Feare being gon, and our men recovered, wee were all contente to take some paines to knowe the name of this 9 mile broad river. We could see no inhabitants for 30 myles saile . . . The cause of this discovery was to search a glistering mettal, the Salvages told us they had from Patawomeck . . . also to search what furres, metals, rivers, Rockes, nations, woods, fishings, fruits, victuals, and other commodities the land afforded, and whether the bay were end-lesse, or how farre it extended. The mine we found 9 or 10 myles up in the country from the river, but it proved of no value. Some otters, Beavers, Martins, Luswarts, and sables we found and, in diverse places, that abundance of fish lying so thicke with their heads above the water, as for want of nets (our barge driving amongst them) we attempted to catch them with a frying pan.

Lord De-La-Ware, 1611:

This is a goodly River called Patomack, upon the borders where-of there are growne the goodliest Trees for Masts, that may be found elsewhere in the World: Hempe better then English, growing wilde in aboundance: Mines of Antimonie and Leade.

1621, George Calvert, the first Lord Baltimore, established a colony in Newfoundland, called Avalon. 1623, he secured a charter, but on visiting the settlement in 1627 he found the climate unsuitable, and sailed for Virginia.

June 20, 1632, a charter was issued to his son, Cecilius Calvert, the second Lord Baltimore:

> Unto the true meridian of the first fountain of the river Pattowmack, thence verging towards the south, unto the farther bank of the said river, and following the same on the west and south, unto a certain place called Cinquack, situate near the mouth of the said river, where it disembogues into the aforesaid bay of Chesapeake . . .
>
> Also, We do GRANT, and likewise CONFIRM, unto the said Baron of BALTIMORE, his heirs and assigns, all islands and islets within the limits aforesaid, all and singular the ports, harbors, bays, rivers and straits belonging to the region of islands afore-said, and all the soil, plains, woods, mountains, marshes, lakes, rivers, bays and straits, situate, or being within the metes, bounds and limits aforesaid, with the fishings of every kind of fish, as well of whales, sturgeons, or other royal fish.

Father Andrew White:

> On the Twenty Second of the month of November, in the year 1633, being St. Cecilia's day, we set sail from Cowes in the Isle of Wight, with a gentle east wind blowing . . .

The first Maryland colonists, in the *Ark,* of 300 tons, and the *Dove,* of 50 tons . . .

> On the 3 of March came unto Chesapeake Bay, at the mouth of Patomecke. This baye is the most delightful water I ever saw, between two sweet landes, with a channell 4 : 5 : 6 : 7 : and 8 fathoms deepe, some 10 leagues broad, at time of yeare full of fish, yet it doth yeeld to Patomeck, wch we have made St Gre-gories. This is the sweetest and greatest river I have seene, so that the Thames is but a little finger to it. There are no marshes or swamps about it, but solid firme ground, with great variety of woode, not choaked up with undershrubs, but commonly so farre distant from each other as a coach and fower horses may travele without molestation.

Having now arrived at the wished-for country, we allotted names according to circumstances. And indeed the Promontory, which is toward the south, we consecrated with the name of St. Gregory, naming the northern one St. Michael's in honor of all the angels. Never have I seen a larger or more beautiful river . . .

For the rest, there are such numbers of swine and deer that they are rather an annoyance than an advantage. There are also vast herds of cows, and wild oxen, fit for beasts of burden and good to eat, besides five other kinds of animals unknown to us.

The soyle, which is excellent so that we cannot sett downe a foot, but tread on Strawberries, raspires, fallen mulberrie vines, acchorns, walnutts, saxafras etc: and those in the wildest woods.

Birds diversely feathered there are infinite, as eagles, swans, hernes, geese, bitters, duckes, partridge read, blew, partie coloured, and the like . . .

That night, fires blazed through the whole country, and since they had never seen such a large ship, messengers were sent in all directions, who reported that a *Canoe,* like an island had come with as many men as there were trees in the woods. We went on, however, to Heron's Islands, so called from the immense number of these birds.

geography

The North and South Branches of the Potomac come together just below Oldtown, Maryland, and some 75 miles further downstream the Shenandoah enters at Harpers Ferry, where Virginia, West Virginia, and Maryland converge. Other major tributaries are the Cacapon, Monocacy, and Anacostia Rivers, and Conococheague Creek.

Although not a major system, like the Mississippi and other western rivers, the Potomac is second in size only to the Susquehanna among United States rivers of the North Atlantic slope.

EARLY SETTLEMENT

So that he, who out of curiosity desires to see the Landskip of the Creation drawn to the life, or to read Natures universal Herbal without book, may with the Opticks of a discreet discerning, view *Mary-Land* drest in her green and fragrant Mantle of the Spring. Neither do I think there is any place under the Heavenly altitude, or that has footing or room upon the circular Globe of this world, that can parallel this fertile and pleasant piece of ground in its multiplicity, or rather Natures extravagancy of a superabounding plenty. For so much doth this Country increase in a swelling Spring-tide of rich variety and diversities of all things, not only common provisions that supply the reaching stomach of man with a satisfactory plenty, but also extends with its liberality and free convenient benefits to each sensitive faculty, according to their several desiring Appetites.

For fiſh the Riuers are plentifully ſtored, with *Sturgion, Porpuſſe, Baſe, Rockfiſh, Carpe, Shad, Herring, Ele, Catfiſh, Perch, Flatfiſh, Troute, Sheepes-head, Drummers, Iarfiſh, Creuiſes, Crabbes, Oiſters* and diuerse other kindes . . .

Eagles, wilde Turkeis much bigger then Engliſh, *Cranes, Herons* white and ruſſet, *Hawkes, wilde Pigeons* (in winter beyond number or imagination, my felfe haue feene three or four hourse together flockes in the aire, so thicke that even they haue ſhaddowed the skie from vs), *Turkie Buſſards, Partridge, Snipes, Owles, Swans, Geeſe, Brants, Ducke* and *Mallard, Droeis, Shel Drakes, Cormorants, Teale, Widgeon, Curlewes, Puits,* befides other small birds, as Blacke birde, hedge ſparrowes, Oxeies, woodpeckers, and in winter about Chriſt-mas many flockes of *Parakertoths.*

For my part I rather impute their fecundity to the prouidence of God, who for euery mouth prouideth meate, and if this increaſe were not, the Naturalls would aſſuredly ſtarue: for the Deere (they kill as doe wee Beeves in *England)* all the yeer long, neither fparing yong nor olde, no not the Does readie to fawne, nor the yong fawnes, if but two daies ould), *Beauers, Otters, Foxes, Racounes,* almoſt as big as a *Fox,* as good meat as a lamb, hares, wild Cats, muske rats, Squirills flying, and other of three or foure ſorts, *Appoſſumes,* of the bigneſſe and likeneſſe of a Pigge, of a moneth ould, a beaſt of as ſtrange as incredible nature . . .

There are wooſels or blackbirds with red shoulders, thrushes, and diverse sorts of small birds, some red, some blew, scarce so bigge as a wrenne . . .

The wood that is most common is Oke and Walnut . . . There is also some Elme, some black walnut tree, and some Ash . . . of walnuts there is 2 or 3 kindes: there is a kinde of wood we called Cypres . . . By the dwelling of the Savages are some great Mulbery trees . . . In some parts, were found some Chesnuts whose wild fruit equalize the best in France, Spaine, Germany, or Italy, to their tasts that had tasted them all. Plumbs there are of 3 sorts. The red and white are like our hedge plumbs: but the other, which they call *Putchamins,* grow as high as a Palmeta. The fruit is like a medler; it is first greene, then yellow, and red when it is ripe: if it be not ripe it will drawe a mans mouth awrie with much torment; but when it is ripe, it is as delicious as an Apricock.

Near the Anacostia, the bison were "found to be very good and wholesome meate, and are very easie to be killed," and on the estuary, "myriads of canvass back ducks which literally blackened the surface of the water."

The Air and Temperature of the Seasons is much govern'd by Winds in *Virginia,* both as to heat and cold, driness and moisture . . . . the Nore and Nore-West are very nitrous and piercing, cold and clear, or else stormy. The South-East and South hazy and sultry hot: Their Winter is a fine clear Air, and dry, which renders it very pleasant: Their Frosts are short, but sometimes very sharp,

that it will freeze the Rivers over three Miles broad; now, the
Secretary of State assured me, it had frozen cleer over *Potomack*
River, over against his House, where it is near nine Miles over: I
have observed it freezes there the hardest, when from a moist
South East, on a sudden the Wind passing by the Nore, a nitrous
sharp Nore-West blows; not with high Gusts, but with a cutting
brisk Air; and those Vales then that seem to be shelter'd from the
Wind, and lie warm, where the Air is most stagnant and moist,
are frozen the hardest, and seized the soonest; and there the
Fruits are more subject to blast than where the Air has a free
Motion. Snow falls sometimes in pretty Quantity, but rarely
continues there above a Day or two; Their Spring is about a
Month earlier than in *England;* In *April* they have frequent Rain,
sometimes several short and suddain Gusts. May and June the
Heat encreases, and it is much like our Summer, being mitigated
with gentle Breezes that rise about nine of the clock, and decrease
and incline as the sun rises and falls. *July* and *August* those
Breezes cease, and the Air becomes stagnant that the Heat is
violent and troublesome. In September the Weather usually
breaks suddenly, and there falls generally very considerable Rains.

From the journal of Henry Fleet,

Here I was tempted to run up the river to the heads, there to
trade with a strange and populous nation, called Mowhaks,
man-eaters, but after good deliberation, I conceived many
inconveniences that might fall out.

On Monday, the 25th of June, we set sail for the town of Tohoga,
when we came to an anchor two leagues short of the Falls, being
in the latitude of 41, on the 26th of June. This place without all
question is the most pleasant and healthful place in all this coun-
try, and most convenient for habitation, the air temperate in
summer and not violent in winter. It aboundeth with all manner
of fish. The Indians in one night commonly will catch thirty
sturgeons in a place where the river is not above twelve fathom

broad. And as for deer, buffaloes, bears, turkeys, the woods do swarm with them, and the soil is exceedingly fertile, but above this place the country is rocky and mountainous like Cannida.

The 27th of June I manned my shallop, and went up with the flood, the tide rising about four feet in height at this place. We had not rowed above three miles, but we might hear the Falls to roar about six miles distant, by which it appears that the river is separated with rocks.

A note for the Adventurers memory, of such things as hee may (if he please) carry with him, either for his owne better accommodation (on Ship-board, or for some time after his arrivall in Maryland) or for trade, according to his abilitie.

Provision for Ship-board.
Fine Wheate-flower, close and well packed, to make puddings, etc. Clarret-wine burnt. Canary Sacke. Conserves, Marmalades, Suckets, and Spices. Sallet Oyle. Prunes to stew. Live Poultry. Rice, Butter, Holland-cheese, or old Cheshire, gammons of Bacon, Porke, dried Neates-tongues, Beefe packed up in Vinegar, some Weather-sheepe, meats baked in earthen posts, Leggs of Mutton minced, and stewed, and close packed up in tried Sewet, or Butter, in earthen pots: Juyce of Limons, etc.

Provision for trade in Virginia or Maryland.
If he be minded to furnish himself with Cattell in Virginia, his best way is to carry a superfluitie of wollen, or linnen cloth, callicoes, sayes, hatts, shooes, stockings, and all sorts of clothing; of Wine, Sugar, Prunes, Raisins, Currance, Honey, Spice, and Grocery wares, with which hee may procure himself cattell there, according to the stocke he dealeth withall. About 4. or 5. Pound laid out heere in commodities, will there buy a Cow; and betweene 20. and 30. shillings, a breeding Sow. The like Commodities will furnish him with there, or in Maryland, with Hogges, Poultry, and Corne. Hee may doe well to carry a

superfluity of Knives, Combes, and Bracelets, to trade with the women Natives; and some Hatchets, Howes, and Axes, to trade with the men for Venison, Fish, Turkies, Corne, Fawnes to store a Parke, etc.

Provisions for his House.

Iron, and Locks, and Hinges, and bolts; etc. Mustard-seede, Glasse and Leade for his windows, Mault for beere, a Hogshead of Beefe or Porker; Two or three Firkins of Butter, a hundred or two of old Cheeses; a gallon of honey, Soape and Candles, Iron wedges, Pookes for Rennet to make cheese: a good Mastiffe, etc.

Provision for Husbandry.

Seede Wheate, Rie, Barley, and Oates (the best way to preserve it from heating at sea, is to carry it in the eare) Kernells of Peares and Apples (especially of Pepins, Pearemaines, and Dusons) for the making hereafter of Cider, and Perry; the stones and seedes of all those fruits and rootes, and herbes, which he desireth to have. Good store of claver grasse seede, to make good meadow.

Provision for Fishing and Fowling.

Imprimis, necessaries for a boate of 3. or 4. Tunne; as Spikes, Nayles, Pitch, Tarre, Ocome, Canvis for a sayle, Ropes, Anchor, Iron for the Ruther: Fishing-lines for Cod and Macrills, etc. Cod-hookes, and Macrill-hookes, a Seane or Basse-net, Herring-netts, Leade, Fowling-pieces of sixe foote; Powder and Shott, and Flint Stones; a good Water-Spaniell, etc.

A direction for choice of servants.

In the taking of servants, he may doe well to furnish himselfe with as many as he can, of usefull and necessary Arts: A Carpenter, of all others the most necessary; A Mill-wright, Shipwright, Boate-wright, Wheele-wright, Brick-maker, Bricklayer, Potter: one that can cleave Lath and Pale, and make Pipestaves, etc. A Joyner, Cooper, Turner, Sawyer, Smith, Cutler, Leather-dresser, Miller, Fisherman, and Gardiner. These will be of most use; but any lusty young able man, that is willing to labour and take paines, although he have no particular trade, will be beneficial enough to his Master.

North America is naturally a very beautiful country, & as for Virginia & Maryland, if you but glance across the plains you will see them covered with lofty trees & lovely orchards of apples, pears, cherries, apricots, figs & peaches. Where there is no timber, there are fine pastures, or land planted with tobacco, grain, vegetables, & all the necessaries of life. You will see the four great rivers meandering along, & from their tranquil, peaceful course be unable to discern from whence they rise.

Nothwithstanding, we finde by them of best experience, an industrious man not other waies imploied, may well tend foure akers of Corn, and 1000. plants of Tobacco; and where they say an aker will yeeld but three or foure barrels, we have ordinarily foure or five, but of new ground six, seven, and eight, and a barrell of Pease and Beanes, which we esteeme as good as two of Corn, which is after thirty or forty bushels an aker, so that one man may provide Corne for five; and apparell for two by the profit of his Tobacco. They say also English Wheat will yeeld but sixteene bushels an aker, and we have reaped thirty; besides to manure the Land, no place hath more white and blew Marble than here . . .

[Tobacco is] generally made by all the Inhabitants of this Province, and between the months of *March* and *April* they sow the seed (which is much smaller than Mustard-seed) in small beds and patches digg'd up and made so by art, and about *May* the plants commonly appear green in those beds: in *June* they are transplanted from their beds, and set in little hillocks in distant rowes, dug up for the same purpose: some twice or thrice they are weeded, and succoured from their illegitimate Leaves that would be peeping out from the body of the Stalk. They top the several Plants as they find occasion in their predominating rankness: About the middle of *September* they cut the Tobacco down, and carry it into houses (made for that purpose) to bring it to its purity.

Having for 19. yeare served *Virginia* the elder sister, I casting my
eye on Mary-land the younger, grew in amoured on her beauty,
resolving like Jacob when he had first served for Leah, to begin
a fresh service for Rachell.

Two years and upward have I enjoyed her company with
delight and profit . . .

Hath she been deflowered by her own Inhabitants, stript,
shorne and made deformed; yet such a naturall fertility and
comeliness doth she retain that she cannot but be loved.

It is (not an Island as is reported, but) part of that maine
adjoyning to *Virginia,* only separated from *Virginia,* by a river
often miles broad, called *Patomack* river, the commodities and
manner of living as in *Virginia,* the soyle somewhat more
temporate (as being more northerly) many stately and navigable
rivers are contained in it, plentifully stored with whol some
springs, a rich and pleasant soile, and so that its extraordinary
goodnes hath made it rather desired than envied, which hath
been fatall to her (as beauty is often times to those that are
endued with it).

Settlers attacking new ground, with a hoe tillage scarcely less prim-
itive than that of the Indians, releasing topsoil to swamp the inlets,
silt the estuary . . .

Following John Smith's discovery of the river, patents for land were
taken out, 1,000 or more acres at a time, as far up as the Great Falls,
the "ffreshes of Petomack." Settlers came in, indentured servants,
and, "about the last of August came in a dutch man of warre that
sold us twenty Negars." (John Smith)

Houses, courthouses, and churches were built, and there were
parsons, "such as wear black coats, babble in a pulpit and roar in a
tavern."

Settlement, however, was slow, and many of the patents expired,
"the lands lapsing for wante of Seating." There were Indians:

Few or none had bin the Damages sustained by the English from the Indians, other than occasionally had happen'd sometimes upon private quarrells and provocations, untill in July, 1675, certain Doegs and Susquahanok Indians on Maryland side, stealing some Hoggs from the english at Potomake on the Virginia shore (as the River divides the same), were pursued by the English in a Boate, beaten or kill'd and the hoggs retaken from them; whereupon the Indians, repairing to their owne Towne, report it to their Superiors, and how that one Mathews (whose hoggs they had taken) had before abused and cheated them, in not paying them for such Indian trucke as he had formerly bought of them, and that they took his hogs for Satisfaction. Upon this (to be Reveng'd on Mathews) a warr Captain with some Indians came over to Potomake and killed two of Mathewes his servants, and came also a second time and Kill'd his sonne.

Depradations continued; the settlers employed rangers:

A Journiall of our Ranging, Given by me, David Strahane, Lieut. of the Rangers of Pottomack.
   June 9th, 1692: We ranged on Ackoquane & so back of the Inhabitants & thence South. We returned & discovered nothing.
   June, the 17th: We ranged over Ackoquane & so we Ranged Round Puscattaway Neck & ther we lay that night.
   And on the 18th came to Pohike & ther we heard that Capt. Mason's Servt. man was missing. Then we sent to see if we could find him & wee followed his foot about halfe a mile, to a house that is deserted, & we took the track of a great many Indians & we followed it about 10 miles & our horses being weary & having no provisions, we was forced to returne.
   June the 26th: We Ranged up to Jonathan Mathew's hs. along with Capt. Masone, & ther we mett with Capt. Housely & we sent over for the Emperour, but he would not come & we went over to the towne & they held a Mascomacko [council] & ordered 20 of their Indians to goe after the Indians that carried away Capt. Masone's man, & so we returned.

July the 3rd: We Ranged up Neapsico, and so back of the Inhabitants, &c.

July 11th: We Ranged up to Brent-towne & ther we lay &c.

The 19th: We ranged up Ackotink & discovered nothing &c.

So we Ranged once in the week till the 20th Septbr: then we marcht to Capt. Masone's & ther we mett with Capt. Housely & his men, so we drawed out 12 of our best horses: & so we ranged up Ackotink & ther we lay that night.

Sept. the 22nd: We Ranged due North till we came to a great Run that made into the suggar land, & we marcht down it about 6 miles & ther we lay that night.

Sept. the 23d: We marcht to the suggar land and the 24th we Ranged about to see if we could find the trace of any Indians but could not see any fresh sign. The 26th marcht to Capt. Masone's & there I dismissed my men till the next march.

The sugar land!

Taking their Range through a Piece of low Ground about Forty Miles above the inhabited Parts of Patowmeck River and resting themselves in the Woods . . . observed an inspissate Juice, like Molasses, distilling from the Tree. The Heat of the Sun had candied some of this juice, which gave the Men a Curiosity to taste it. They found it Sweet and by this Process of Nature learn'd to improve it into Sugar. But these Trees growing so far above the Christian Inhabitants, it hath not yet been tried whether for Quantity or Quality it may be worth while to cultivate this Discovery . . . yet it has been known among the Indians longer than any now living can remember.

Beyond Great Falls, sugar maples: the first taste of upland . . .

(spruce knob)

Rising high in the Alleghenies, the North Fork of the South Branch drains Spruce Knob, in West Virginia, at an elevation of 4,860 feet.

UPRIVER EXPLORATION

John Smith, speaking to an Indian, 1613: "When we asked him what was beyond the mountaines, he answered the Sunne: but of anything els he knew nothing."

Robert Beverley spoke of the Blue Ridge as an horizon of mystery, distant mountains known to the average planter only because they "shew themselves over the tops of the trees."

Durand of Dauphiné, 1686, "went fifty leagues into the country & from there could see high mountains, like the Alps, covered with eternal snows . . . From thence the lovely rivers watering Virginia flow."

Smith again: "Beyond the mountaines from whence is the head of the river Patawomeke, the Savages report, inhabit their most mortall enimies, the Massawomekes upon a great salt water, which by all likelyhood is either some part of Commada, some great lake, or some inlet of some sea that falleth into the South sea."

John Clayton reported to the Royal Society, 1688:

> The Heads of the Branches of the Rivers interfere and lock one with another, which I think is best expressed after the Manner that an *Indian* explained himself once to me, when I enquired how nigh the Rivers of *Carolina, Virginia* and *Maryland* arose out of the Mountains, from those that ran Westerly on the other Side of the Mountains, he claps the fingers of one Hand 'twixt those of the other, crying, they meet thus; the Branches of different Rivers rising not past a hundred Paces distant one from another: So that no Country in the World can be more curiously watered.

———

John Lederer, 1669:

> The fourteenth of March, from the top of an eminent hill,
> I first descried that Apalataean mountains, bearing due west
> to the place I stood upon: their distance from me was so great,
> that I could hardly discern whether they were mountains or
> clouds, until my Indian fellow travelers prostrating themselves
> in adoration, howled out after a barbarous manner, *Okée paeze*
> i.e. God is nigh.

> The eighteenth of March, after I had in vain assayed to ride
> up, I alighted, and left my horse with one of the Indians, whilst
> with the other two I climbed up the rocks, which were so
> incumbered with bushes and brambles, that the ascent proved
> very difficult: besides the first precipice was so steep, that if
> I lookt down I was immediately taken with a swimming in
> my head . . . The height of the mountain was very extraordinary
> . . . but to the north and west, my sight was suddenly bounded
> by mountains higher than that I stood upon . . .

> The ascent was so steep, the cold so intense, and we so tired,
> that having with much ado gained the top of one of the high-
> est, we drank the king's health in brandy, gave the mountain his
> name, and agreed to turn back again, having no encouragement
> from that prospect to proceed to a further discovery; since from
> hence we saw another mountain, bearing north and by west to
> us, of a prodigious height.

September 1716, the Huguenot John Fontaine accompanied Gover-
nor Alexander Spotswood and the Knights of the Golden Horseshoe
on an expedition to the Blue Ridge:

> *3d.*—About eight we were on horseback, and about ten we
> came to a thicket, so tightly laced together, that we had a great
> deal of trouble to get through; our baggage was injured, our
> clothes torn all to rags, and the saddles and holsters also torn.

4th.—We crossed one of the small mountains this side the Appalachian, and from the top of it we had a fine view of the plains below. We were obliged to walk up the most of the way, there being abundance of loose stones on the side of the hill.

5th.—A fair day. At nine we were mounted; we were obliged to have axe-men to clear the way in some places . . . In some places it was very steep, in others, it was so that we could ride up. About one of the clock we got to the top of the mountain; . . . We drank King George's health, and all the Royal Family's, at the very top of the Appalachian mountains. About a musket-shot from the spring there is another, which rises and runs down on the other side; it goes westward, and we thought we could go down that way, but we met with such prodigious precipices, that we were obliged to return to the top again. We found some trees which had been formerly marked, I suppose, by the Northern Indians, and following these trees, we found a good, safe descent. Several of the company were for returning; but the Governor persuaded them to continue on. About five, we were down on the other side, and continued our way for about seven miles further, until we came to a large river, by the side of which we encamped . . . We saw, where we were over the mountains, the footing of elks and buffaloes, and their beds.

6th.—We crossed the river, which we called Euphrates. It is very deep; the main course of the water is north; it is four-score yards wide in the narrowest part. We drank some healths on the other side, and returned; after which I went a swimming in it. We could not find any fordable place, except the one by which we crossed, and it was deep in several places. I got some grasshoppers and fished; and another and I, we catched a dish of fish, some perch, and a fish they call chub. The others went a hunting, and killed deer and turkeys. The Governor had graving irons, but could not grave anything, the stones were so hard. I graved my name on a tree by the river side; and the Governor buried a bottle with a paper inclosed, on which he writ that he took possession of this place in the name and for King George the First of England. We had a good dinner, and after it we got the men together, and loaded all their arms, we drank the King's health in Champagne, and fired a volley—the Princess's health in Burgundy, and fired a volley, and all the rest of the Royal Family in claret, and a volley. We drank the Governor's health and fired another volley. We had several sorts of liquors, viz., Virginia red wine and white wine, Irish usquebaugh, brandy, shrub, two sorts of rum, champagne, canary, cherry, punch, water, cider, &c.

. . . celebrating thus the Shenandoah.

Ascending the North Fork of South Branch to Mouth of Seneca, up Seneca Creek and across the Alleghenies to the head of Cheat, northward by way of Backbone: the Seneca or Shawnee Trail, a trail along the Blue Ridge, a trail in the Valley. The Conestoga Path: southward out of Pennsylvania, across Great and Little Pipe Creeks to Monocacy, westward over the mountains, across Antietam Creek, fording the Potomac below Shepherdstown: a trade route, Potomac to Susquehanna, via Conococheague Creek and The Carolina Road: fording the Potomac at the mouth of Monocacy, passing east of the Catoctins and Bull Run Mountain to the branches of Occoquan, and continuing southwest.

There were Shawnees, "the Strange Indians that are at the head of Potomocke neare the mountaines," at Shawnee Old Town, where Thomas Cresap settled. Toward the south, the Valley was a Shawnee hunting ground. Old Town was on "the Track of Indian Warriors, when going to War, either to the Noward, or Soward." Delawares from the north and Catawbas from the south traveled this track, and there was a great battle at the mouth of Antietam Creek, another at Slim Bottom on the South Branch, and another at Hanging Rocks. In still another, at Painted Rock, near Harper's Ferry, the Catawbas buried a Delaware chief alive; later, they said that Swearingen's spring flowed from the pulsing of his heart.

At the Smoke Hole on the South Branch, Indians fished and hunted, burned fires to dry their meat on the ledges and in the shallow shelter caves in the cliffs. The smoke, protected by the high walls, hung motionless over the gorge, in a flat canopy.

The Iroquois chief Tachanoontia said, 1742: "We have the Right of Conquest, a Right too dearly purchased and which cost us too much Blood to give up without any reason at all . . . All the World knows we conquered the several Nations living on the Susquehanna, Cohongoronto and on the back of the great Mountains in Virginia. They feel the effects of our conquests, being now a part of our Nation and their lands at our disposal." Champlain's map of New France (1632) shows the correct topography of the Shenandoah Valley: no doubt the work of Jesuits accompanying the Iroquois on hunting parties.

There were burial mounds in the Shenandoah Valley: near Luray, skeletons of an Indian and a buffalo, side by side; in the alluvial bottom of Pass Run, a human skull and eight shark's teeth; on the South Branch of Potomac near Brandywine, seven skeletons arranged like the spokes of a wheel; and near Martinsburg, the skeletons of giants, seven feet long, with three-foot thighs.

––––––––––

REPORT OF THE COMMISSIONERS TO
LAY OUT THE BOUNDS OF THE NORTHERN NECK

To the Honble William Gooch Esq, his Majestys Lieutenant Governor and Commander in Chief of the Colony and Dominion of Virginia

The Underwritten Commissioners appointed by your Honour in obedience to the orders of his Majesty in his Privy Council of the 29th of November 1733 for Surveying and settling the Boundaries of that Tract of Territory of Land granted by the Crown to the Ancestors of the Right Honourable Thomas Lord Fairfax and under whom his Lordship now claims, Do humbly beg Leave to lay before your Honour the following Report of their Proceedings . . .

. . . .

We desired to know of my Lords Commissioners what they demanded in his Lordships Name as the Bounds of his grant? To which they answer'd, that he claimed all the land contain'd within the South Branch of Rappahannock River, and the main branch of Potowmack as high as the head Springs thereof.

. . . .

Then in Conjunction with my Lords Commissioners We directed the main Branch of Powtomack River called Cohaungorooton to be Survey'd to the head Spring thereof, and appointed Mr Mayo and Mr Brookes whom we thought Equal to the difficult Service on the part of His Majesty; To these were join'd Mr Winslow and Mr Savage for the Lord Fairfax. These being all first sworn, were order'd by their Several Warrants to begin at the Confluence of that River with Sharando, and from thence to run the Courses, and Measure the Distances thereof to its first Spring; and of all this to return an Exact Plat, shewing all the Streams runing into the same on either side, together with a fair Copy of their Field-Notes. We also directed them to take the Latitude, and observe particularly where the said River intersects the 40th Degree.

And to enable them to perform this arduous Work, We allotted them a Sufficient Number of Men for their Assistance and Defence, and a Competent Quantity of Provisions for their Subsistence

. . . .

The Lands at and near the Falls, were not granted till about the year 1709, nor can we find by any Evidence, that it was so much as known that the River ran thro' the great Ridge of Mountains till several Years after that

By the Map, you may please to observe that the River Potowmack divides itself into two Branches, just beyond the blue Mountains, there the main River loses its name, and the North Branch, which is much the larger, is call'd by the Indians Cohungorooton, and the other Sharando, as therefore the name of Potowmack ceases at this Confluence, and the Branches into which its Waters are divided have quite other Names, The Fork may not improperly be called the head thereof.

In the Year 1709 a Good Number of foreign Protestants were encouraged by the Government to settle beyond the

Mountains, in order to strengthen our Frontiers on that Side; And they discover'd some distance up each of the aforemention'd branches, But none of thes discoverys very far, till the Surveyor sent out by us the last Fall, trac'd the River Cohungorootun quite up to the Head Spring, which he found according to the Meanders thereof to be above two hundred Miles from its confluence with Sharando.

. . . .

But if his Lordship be allow'd to extend his Boundary from the head of Conway River to the Head Spring of Cohungorootun, including the great and little Fork of Rappahannock, he will then have at least five Millions two hundred eighty two thousand Acres within his Grant . . .

> All which is most humbly submitted by
>   Sir   Your Honours most humble Servants
>   w. byrd
>   john robinson
>   john grymes
>   *Williamsburgh*, August 10th 1737

From a letter by William Byrd,

> And here I think I ought to do Justice not only to the uncommon Skill, but also to the Courage and Indefatiguable Industy of Majr. Mayo and two of the other Surveyors, employ'd in this long and difficult Task. Neither the unexpected Distance, nor the Danger of being doubly Starved by Hunger and excessive Cold, could in the least discourage them from going thro' with Their Work, tho' at one time they were almost reduced to the hard necessity of cutting up the most useless Person among them, Mr. Savage, in order to Support and save the lives of the rest. But Providence prevented that dreadful blow by an unexpected Supply another way, and so the Blind Surveyor escapt.

The field notes of this survey, to the headwaters of the Potomac, are lost. A second survey was made in 1746 by one Thomas Lewis, who made notes with a quill pen, in a tiny notebook, $3\frac{1}{2}$ by $5\frac{5}{8}$ inches:

JOURNAL 1746

From head Rappahannock to
head of Potomak running
Fairfax Boundary

. . . .

    Wenesday September 10th 1746

Set out from home in order to wait on
his majestys & the Right Hounrable Thomas
Lord Fairfax Comisioner at Capt Downs
from Thence to proceed to Run the Dividing
Line Between his majesty and Ld Fairfax
from the head Spring of Rappahonock to
the head Spring of the North Branch
of Potowmack. Lay at Michael Wood
this night having Rod about 20 miles

    Tuesday 16th   Spent the Day
in preparing for our Journey &c
in the Evening Retired to our Camp
where we spent our hours with
a great Deal of pleasure & meriment
was taken Ill in the night violent
Vomiting &c

    Wensday 17th . . . . . .
. . . . .This night
we were alarmed with a Quarrall
that happened in Capt Downs lane
amongst a Crowd of Drunken peple
the Rails & Staks of Capt Downs
fence Supply'd the want of Cudgels
which they apply'd with tolerable
good Sucses

Saturday 20th   the mountains made
Such a Dismal appearance that John
Thomas one of our men took Sick on
the Same & So Returned home.

. . . . Returned to
our Camp very much Fautaug'd
Several horss very much hurt amongst
the Rocks on the mountain.

N 22½ (18) pole the Fork of the midle
    Branch 34 poles &
N 10 W. 126 poles

. . . .

N 10 E 60 po to the higest water near
    the top of the mountain

1000 X a Br. Call'd the fountain of life
    from the Seasonable Relive it was to us
    the Day Being Exceding hot ye mountain
    very high & Steep we were allmost over
    -come & Ready to faint for want of
    Water

Friday 3d Began at ye End of 1640
pole Run the Day Before Thence
604 pole ye top of y Divels Back Bone
alias the north mountain a Chestnut oak
md 31 miles.
824 X a Br. of Shand Runs to left
1104 pole left off & Encampd on ye
Comisioners & Baggage Could Come up
this Day Several of the horses had like Been
killd. tumbling over Rocks and precipices
& ourselves often in the outmost Danger
this tirable place was Call'd Purgatory

. . . we at length got to the Bottom nor
was our Case then much Better there Being
a large Water Course the Banks Extremly
Steep wc the neightborhood of the mountn
obliged us to Cross very often at places or
Banks allmost perpendicular. afer
a great Whiles Dispair we at length got
    about 10 oClock
to our camp. hardly any of us Escaping
without Broken Shins or Some other miss
-fortune.

        Being
along the mountains   prodigiously full of
fallen Timber & Ivey as thick as it Could
grow So Interwoven that horse or man Could
hardly force his way through it. So that we
had very Difficult access to the top of the Alleg-
haney mountain where was a precipice about
16 feet high & were very hard Set to get a place
where there was any probeability of our ascending
when we had gain'd the Sumit there was a
Level as fur as we Could see to Right & left
Clear of timber about a Quarter of a mile wide
Covered with Large flat Rocks & marshey
tho on the tope of the highest mountain I ever
Saw

. . . Roots together with the pines are Spread
over the Rocks & under the moss like arches In
what Danger must we be, in such a place all
Dangerous places being obscured under a
Clock of moss Such thickets of Loral to Strugle
with whose Branches are all most as Obstinate
as if Composed of Iron.

    Thursday 16   Lay By in order to Rest
and Refresh our Selves & horses who were very

much Fatigued & Cripled one of our men
kill'd a Deer.

884 poles through the Swamp
1014 pole another Swamp Begins
1054 poles aLarge Creek Runs to the
Right which we Concluded to be the
Waters of Potowmack
1094 Total for the Day & fare Side the
    Swamp. here we Encamp'd

    The land or Soil on the N.W. Side the
River is Black & very moist a great
many Small Springs and Ouzey places
& prety Stoney & hilley Exceding well
timbred with Such as very Large
Spruce pines great multitude of Beach
and Shugartrees Chery trees the most
and finest I ever Saw Some three or
four foot Diameter thirty or forty
foot without a Branch. Some few
oaks Chestnuts and Locusts tho'
not maney &c

East 26 poles
s 71 E 31 poles
s 83 E 27 poles
s 80 E 6 poles to the Spring head
where we found the Following old
marks to (viz.) aSpruce pine
md RB. BW. IF. BL. FF. 1736
A Beach P.G. 1736 A Beach JS. &a
Black aBeach W.MAYO. two
Beaches & two Spruce pines markd
with three notches three way Each
& one Large Spruce pine Blazed
three Ways

We Dined on a Loyn Roasted Vension
about three O'Clock at the Spring head
Drank his Majestys health.

> Philip Kennedy, 1853: "[We] rode on down the middle
> of the wild meadow, through green grass, knee-high,
> and waving gently in the summer wind, until we
> reached a small stream, whose banks were overgrown
> with osiers and other delicate shrubs. This was the
> infant Potomac."

Never was any poor Creaturs in
Such ᵃ Condition ᵃˢ we were in nor Ever
was a Criminal more glad By having
made his Escape out of prison as
we were to Get Rid of those Accursed
Lorals.

———

George Washington, 1748 (age 16):

Saturday March 12   This morning Mr. James Genn ye. sur-
veyer came to us we travell'd ofer ye Blue Ridge to Capt. Ashby
on Shannondoah River, Nothing remarkable happen'd

Sunday March 13   . . . We went through most beautiful Groves
of Sugar Trees and spent ye. best part of y. Day in admiring ye.
Trees and richnes of ye Land

Monday 14th . . . (The Land exceeding Rich and Fertile all ye.
way produces abundance of Grain Hemp Tobacco &ca.) . . .

Fryday 18th We Travell'd up about 35 Miles to Thomas
Barwicks on Potomack where we found y. River so excessively
high by Reason of y. Great Rains that had fallen up about y.
Allegany Mountains as they told us which was then bringing
down y. melted Snow and that it would not be fordable for

several Days it was then above Six foot Higher than usual and was rising we agreed to stay till Monday we this day call'd to see y. Fam'd Warm Springs we camped out in y. field . . .

Sunday 20th   Finding y. River not much abated we in y. Evening Swam our horses over and carried them to Charles Polks in Maryland for Pasturage till y. next Morning

Monday 21st   We went over in a Canoe and travell'd up Maryland side all y. Day in a Continued Rain to Collo Cresaps right against y. Mouth of y. South Branch about 40 Miles from Polks I believe y. worst Road that ever was trod by Man or Beast

Wednesday 23d   Rain'd till about two oClock and Clear'd when we were agreeably surprised at y. sight of thirty odd Indians coming from War with only one Scalp   We had some Liquor with us of which we gave them Part it elevated there Spirits put them in y. Humour of Dauncing . . .

Tuesday 28th   This Morning went out and Survey'd five Hundred Acres of Land and went down to one Michael Stumps on y. So Fork of ye. Branch on our way Shot two Wild Turkies.

March 31st   . . . Lot 4th   this Lot survey'd myself Beginning at a Pine by a Rock . . .

APRIL

Sunday 3 d   Last Night was a much more blostering night than ye. former we had our Tent Carried Quite of with ye. Wind.

———

To the Right Honourable the Lords Commissioners of Trade and Plantations

The humble Petition of Jacob Stauber, John Ochs, Ezekiel Harlan and Thomas Gould

Sheweth

That the said Jacob Stauber and Ezekiel Harlan having lived upwards of twenty years in Pennsilvenia, following Husbandry of which they have a perfect understanding, and also are well acquainted with the nature of the land in those parts, and what it is most capable of producing.

That the said Jacob Stauber hath lately taken a Journey into Virginia on purpose to make a search after some uninhabited Land behind the Mountains of that Province, which are about thirty Miles over, and but one place fit to make a road, after he had passed these Mountains with much pains, great difficulty and hazard of Life without any Company or seeing any Indian in all his Travells, he spent three Months time to View the Soyl and Situation of the Land lying Westward to the said Mountains towards Missisipy River, which Land he found to be good Pasture Ground fitt for planting of Vineyards on the side of the Mountains and a very good Soyle for Hemp, Flax, and all sorts of Grain, a proper climate to produce Silk . . .

In Consideration of these Advantages, if Your Lordships would be pleased to approve off yᵉ same and influence that the Government would be graciously pleased to grant a Joint Patent for a Free Grant for the following Tract of Land to your Petitioners and their Heirs for ever, to begin at the double Top Mountain by Hawks Bill Creek including the Mountains through which the road is to be made, to go thence Northwards in a line to the Borders of Pensilvania and behind the same, to make the whole breadth 200 Miles, thence in a Straight West line to the River Missisipy . . .

Also the great Expences of making a Road 30 Miles long through the Mountains . . . the same must be Cutt in a Rock . . .

March 30th 1731

August 21, 1751, Colonel Burwell, president of the Council and Commander-in-Chief of Virginia, wrote to the Board of Trade:

"Notwithstanding the Grants of the Kings of England, France or
Spain, the Property of these uninhabited Parts of the World must
be founded upon prior occupancy according to the Law of Nature;
and it is the seating and cultivating the soil and not the bare travel-
ling through a Territory that constitutes Right; and it will be politic
and highly for the Interest of the Crown to encourage the seating
the Lands Westward as soon as possible."

1699, Giles Vandercastel and Burr Harrison set out from Stafford,
in Tidewater, for Conoy Island and Point of Rocks:

> The Distance from the inhabitance is about seventy miles, as
> we conceave by our Journeys. The 16th of this Instance Aprill
> we set out for the Inhabitance and ffound a good track ffor five
> miles all the rest of the daye's Journey very Grubby and hilly,
> Except some small patches; but very well for horse, tho nott
> good for cartes, and butt one runn of any danger in a fresh and
> then very bad. That night lay at the sugar land, which Judge to
> be fforty miles.
>
> The 17th day we sett the River by a small Compaise, and
> found itt lay up N.W. by N. and afterwards sett it ffoure times
> and alwayes ffound itt neere the same corse. We generally kept
> about one mile ffrom the River.
>
> About seven or eight miles above the sugar land we came to
> a broad Branch of about fifty or sixty yards wide: a still or small
> streeme; itt took oure horses up to the Belleys, very good going
> in and out.
>
> About six miles ffarther came to another greate branch
> of about sixty or seventy yeards wide with a strong streeme
> making ffal with large stones, that caused our horses sometimes
> to be up to their Belleyes and sume times nott above their
> knees; so we conceave it a ffresh than not ffordable.
>
> Thence in a small Treck to a smaller Runn, about six miles,
> Indeferent very.
>
> And soe held on till we came within six or seven miles of the
> forte or Island, and then very Grubby and greate stones stand-
> ing Above the ground like heavy [hay] cocks; then hold for

three or ffoure miles, and then shorte Ridgges with small Runns untill we came to the forte or Island.

In 1712, Christopher de Graffenried "visited those beautiful spots of the country, those enchanted islands in the Potomac River above the falls. And from there, on our return, we ascended a high mountain standing alone in the midst of a vast flat stretch of country, called because of its form Sugar Loaf which means in French Pain de sucre."

Meshach Browning, when a small child, emigrated to western Maryland:

> We went on in good order until we reached Sideling Hill, where the road was very rough and rocky: by and by we arrived at a very sideling place, with a considerable precipice on our left—the wheels struck a rock on the other side, and away went wagon, horses, and all down the hill, rolling and smashing barrels of rum, hogsheads of sugar, sacks of salt, boxes of dry-goods, all tumbling through one another, smashing the bed of the wagon, and spilling the rum, molasses, sugar, and all.
>
>   My frightened mother called out, "Where is Meshach?"— knowing that I was riding in the wagon when it turned the dreadful somerset. All was bustle and alarm, until at length I was found under some straw and rubbish, stunned breathless, mangled, and black with suffocation . . . The wagon was broken to pieces, the left hind-wheel smashed, and entirely useless. The man applied the spilling rum to us in handsful, until life began to return; and as mother saw hopes of my returning to her bosom again, she became quieted.

1747, one James Caudy—or Coddy—settled on the Cacapon River, near "Caudy's Castle":

> A fragment of the mountain, separated from and independent of the neighboring mountains, forming, as it were, a half cone, and surrounded with a yawning chasm . . . the eastern side is a

solid mass of granite, directly perpendicular . . . From its west-
ern side it may be ascended by a man on foot to within about
ninety or one hundred feet of its summit. From thence the rock
suddenly shoots up something in the form of a comb, which is
about ninety or one hundred feet in length eight or ten feet in
thickness, and runs about north and south. On the eastern face
of the rock, from where the comb is approached, a very narrow
undulating path is formed, by pursuing which, active persons
can ascend to its summit . . . Along the path a few laurel shrubs
have grown out of the fissures of the rock.

. . . During Indian raids early settlers, led by Caudy, would
race up the rock and lie in wait near the top ready to push
Indians over the edge of the precipice into the gorge below as
they struggled up in single file.

The first Germans to reach the Potomac were at the mouth of Anti-
etam Creek in 1726. Fording the river, they moved up the Shenan-
doah Valley, but a few—"an eddy of emigration"—followed an old
Iroquois trail, east of the Catoctins, up the North Fork of Goose
Creek and into the Blue Ridge.

Early settlers on the South Branch were Red Ike Pancake, Uriah
Blue, and Colonel Thomas Cresap, who settled at Shawnee Old
Town on the Maryland shores of the Potomac, 1741—acquired
land, built roads, traded with the Indians. They called him "Big
Spoon." Cresap traveled to London, age 70 . . . took a second wife,
age 80 . . . and survived to the age of 105.

(estuary)

The main river is nearly 400 miles long, and the tidal estuary on the lower reaches covers 117 miles, with 200,000 acres of water surface. Although heavily silted through the years, the estuary is navigable to Alexandria and Washington, with a 24-foot channel maintained by the U. S. Army Corps of Engineers.

TIDEWATER COLONIAL

From the journal of Philip Vickers Fithian, tutor to the children of Councillor Robert Carter at Nomini Hall, Westmoreland County, Virginia, 1773-74: "The broad beautiful Potowmack looks smooth & unbroken as tho' it was fettered in Ice."

George Washington's diary, January 1760:

> Friday, 18th . . . The Misting continuing till noon, when the Wind got Southerly, and being very warm occasioned a great thaw. I however found Potomk River quite covered with Ice . . .
> Sunday, 20th . . . The wind continued Southerly the whole day, the Ground very soft and rotten.
> Tuesday, 22nd . . . The weather clear and cold. the ground hard and froze and the River block'd up again.
>
> Kill'd 17 more Hogs . . .
>
> Monday, 28th. The River clos again and the ground very knobby and hard.

Again, Washington:

> 1770 [JANUARY]
> *Where & how my time is spent*
> 1. At home all day alone.
> 2. At home all day. Mr. Peake dined here.
> 3. At home all day alone.
> 4. Went a hunting with Jno. Custis and Lund Washington. Started a Deer and then a Fox, but got neither.
> 5. Rid to Muddy hole and Doeg Run. Carrd. the Dogs with me, but found nothing. Mr. Warnr. Washington and Mr. Thruston came in the Evening.
> 6. The two Colo. Fairfax's and Mrs. Fairfax dined here, as did Mr. Alexander and the two Gentn. that came the day before. The Belvoir Family returned after Dinner.

7. Mr. Washn. and Mr. Thruston went to Belvoir.

8. Went a huntg. with Mr. Alexander, J. P. Custis and Ld. W—n. Killd a fox (a dog one) after 3 hours chase. Mr. Alexr. went away and Wn. and Thruston came in ye aftern.

9. Went aducking, but got nothing, the Creeks and Rivers being froze. Mr. Robt. Adam dined here and returnd.

10. Mr. W-n. and Mr. Thruston set of home. I went a hunting in the Neck and visited the Plantn. there. Found and killd a bitch fox, after treeing it 3 times and chasg. it abt. 3 Hrs.

11. At home all day alone.

Fithian again:

Tuesday 14.
The Weather vastly fine! There has been no rain of consequence nor any stormy or disagreeable Weather, since about the 10.th of last Month! From the Window, by which I write, I have a broad, a diversified, and an exceedingly beautiful Prospect of the high craggy Banks of the River *Nominy!* Some of those huge Hills are cover'd thick with *Cedar,* & Pine Shrubs; A vast quantity of which seems to be in almost every part of this Province—others are naked, & when the Sun Shines look beautiful! At the Distance of about 5 Miles is the River Potowmack over which I can see the smoky Woods of Maryland . . . Between my window and the potowmack, is Nominy Church, it stands close on the Bank of the River Nominy, in a pleasant agreeable place.

Sunday 3.
The country begins to put on her Flowery Garment, & appear in *gaity*—The *Apricots* are in their fullest Bloom; Peaches also, & Plumbs, & several sorts of Cheries are blossoming; as I look from my Window & see Groves of Peach Trees on the Banks of Nomini: (for the orchards here are very large) and other Fruit Trees in Blossom; and amongst them interspers'd the gloomy Savin; beyond these at great distance the blue Potowmack; and over this great River, just discern the Woods of Maryland.

From the journal of John Mercer, kept at his plantation at Marlborough, Stafford County, Virgina, 1767:

	Temp.		
March			
21	64-63	Daffodil	
		Hyacinths 6	
		Violet	
		Narcissous	
22	60-69	Almond	
		Apricot	
23	45-48	May Cherry	
		Cucumber hotbed	
31	44-52	Beans	
		Pease	
April			
1	47-48	Dwarf Iris	
2	41-52	Cowslips	
3	44-50		rain all night & morn
7	44-50	Wild curran	
9	48-32	Asparagus	
		Radishes	
13	54-62	Pear	
		Wall flower	
15	48-53	Frittillary	
16	46-60	Green Sagia	
17	48-55	Prickson	
20	34-60	Catchfly Julia	
30	64-70	Parrot Tulip	
May			
3	53-57	Mourng bride	rain in the night
4	55-63	Purple Stocks	Do in the night & Morn.
8	59-72	Horsechestnut	
		Snow drop	

| 15 | 60–76 | Corn Hay | fine rain in the night |
| 21 | 75–80 | Sm'bl. Iris | |

June
5	70–64	Jessamine	fine rain
17	75–82	Yucca	
		African Marigold	

July
5	70	Coxcomb	rain all day
16	73–76	Marvel of Peru	
23	76–85	Sunflower	

Fithian:

I had the pleasure of walking to day at twelve o-Clock with Mrs Carter; She shewed me her stock of Fowls & Mutton for the winter; She observed, with great truth, that to live in the Country, and take no pleasure at all in Groves, Fields, or Meadows; nor in Cattle, Horses, & domestic Poultry, would be a manner of life too tedious to endure.

J. F. D. Smyth visited Tidewater Virginia, 1784:

Several rich, moift, but not too wet fpots of ground are chofen out, in the fall, each containing about a quarter of an acre, or more . . .

Thefe fpots, which are generally in the woods, are cleared, and covered with brufh or timber, for five or six feet thick and upwards, that is fuffered to remain upon it until the time when the tobacco feed must be fowed, which is within twelve days after Chriftmas.

The evening is commonly chofen to fet thefe places on fire, and when everything thereon is confumed to ashes the ground is dug up, mixed with the ashes and broken very fine; the tobacco-feed, which is exceedingly fmall, being mixed with afhes alfo, is then fown, and juft raked in lightly; the whole is immediately covered with brufh for fhelter to keep it warm . . .

In this condition it remains until the frofts are all gone, when the brufh is taken off, and the young plants are expofed to the nutritive and genial warmth of the fun, which quickly invigorates them in an aftonifhing degree, and foon renders them ftrong and large enough to be removed for planting, efpecially if they be not fown too thick . . .

The foil for tobacco muft be rich and ftrong . . .

In the firft rains, which are here called feafons, after the vernal equinox, the tobacco plants are carefully drawn while the ground is foft, carried to the field where they are to be planted . . .

After the plants have taken root, and begun to grow, the ground is carefully weeded, and worked either with hand hoes or the plough . . .

When it is ripe, a clammy moifture or perfpiration comes forth upon the leaves . . . and they are then of a great weight and fubstance.

When the tobacco is cut it is done when the fun is powerful . . .

As the plants advance in curing the fticks are removed from the fcaffolds out of doors into the tobacco house . . . being placed higher as the tobacco approaches a perfect cure . . .

The weight of each hogfhead muft be nine hundred and fifty pounds neat, exclufive of the cafk.

Tobacco: grown on the plantations, cured, packed in hogsheads, rolled down the rolling roads to the waterside, where every family dock was an Atlantic port of call.

> Washington, to a London merchant: "I must once again beg the favor of you never to send me any Goods but in a Potomack Ship, and for this purpose let me recommend Captn. John Johnson . . . Johnson is a person I am acquanted with, know him to be very careful and he comes past my door in his Ship."

Andrew Burnaby, 1759, remarked on "the cheapness of land and the commodiousness of navigation: for every person may with ease procure a small plantation, can ship his tobacco at his own door, and live independent."

William Byrd: "Indeed people sail all these rivers with merchantmen and arrive in front of the houses of the merchants and planters in order to load and unload, which serves commerce splendidly."

In Tidewater Potomac there are 98 navigable bays or creeks: 49 on the Maryland shore, 49 on the Virginia shore . . .

Burnaby:

The fruits introduced from Europe succeed extremely well; particularly peaches, which have a very fine flavour, and grow in such plenty as to serve to feed the hogs in the autumn of the year. Their blossoms in the spring make a beautiful appearance throughout the country.

Lord Adam Gordon, 1764-65:

They live on their Estates handsomely, and plentifully, raising all they require, and depending for nothing on the Market . . . The houses are larger, better and more commodious than those to the Southward . . .

They assist one another, and all Strangers with their Equipages in so easy and kind a manner, as must deeply touch a person of any feeling and convince them that in this Country, Hospitality is everywhere practiced . . . Their provisions of every kind is good, their Rivers supply them with a variety of Fish, particularly Crabs and oysters,—their pastures afford them excellent Beef and Mutton, and their Woods are Stocked with Venison, Games and Hogs . . . The Women make excellent Wives, and are in general great Breeders.—It is much the fashion to Marry young.

Tobias Lear:

> The number of inhabitants living in the several counties of Virginia and Maryland, bordering upon the Potomack or its branches, amount to upwards of three hundred thousand, according to the census taken by order of the general government, in the year 1791.—They are all, or so nearly so, that not one fiftieth part can be excepted, cultivators of the soil. It is, therefore, easy to conceive, that they must send an immense quantity of produce to the shipping ports on the river. But, still so extensive is the country through which the Potomack and its branches pass, that it is yet but thinly settled.

———

Fithian:

> Sup'd on Crabs & an elegant dish of Strawberries & cream —How natural, how agreeable, how majestic this place seems!
> . . . we supt on Artichoks, & huckleberries & Milk—The toasts, after Supper, were the King; Queen & Royal Family, the Governor & his family, & then young Ladies of our acquaintance . . .
> Dined with us to day Captain Walker, Colonel Richd Lee; and Mr Lancelot Lee. Sat after dinner till Sunset, drank three Bottles of Medaira, two Bowls of Toddy!

Lord Gordon:

> Poultry is as good as in South Carolina, and their Madeira Wine excellent, almost in every house; Punch and small Beer brewed from Molasses is also in use, but their Cyder far exceeds any Cyder I ever tasted at home—It is genuine and unadulterated, and will keep good to the age of twelve years and more.

(It became necessary for the Maryland assembly to pass legislation that indentured servants and slaves would be fed food other than oysters and terrapins several days each week.)

Durand:

> We decided to pass the night at Colonel Fichoux [Fitzhugh's],
> whose houses stand along the banks of the great Pethomak
> river . . .
>
> He treated us royally, there was good wine & all kinds of
> beverages, so there was a great deal of carousing. He had sent
> for three fiddlers, a jester, a tight-rope dancer, an acrobat who
> tumbled around, & they gave us all the entertainment one could
> wish for. It was very cold, yet no one ever thinks of going near
> the fire, for they never put less than a cartload of wood in the
> fireplace & the whole room is kept warm.
>
> The next day, after they had caroused until afternoon, we
> decided to cross this river. The Colonel had a quantity of wine
> & one of his punch-bowls brought to the shore.

And elsewhere, "It is a common law country. The laws are so wise
that there are almost no law-suits . . .When a man squanders his
property he squanders his wifes also, & this is fair, for the women
are foremost in drinking and smoking."

Fithian:

> There were several Minuets danced with great ease and propri-
> ety; after which the whole company joined in country-dances,
> and it was indeed beautiful to admiration . . .
>
> Mrs *Carter*, & the young Ladies came Home last Night from
> the Ball, & brought with them Mrs *Lane,* they tell us there were
> upwards of Seventy at the Ball; forty-one Ladies; that the com-
> pany was genteel.

Burnaby:

> Towards the close of an evening, when the company are
> pretty well tired with country dances, it is usual to dance jigs; a
> practice originally borrowed, I am informed, from the negroes.
> These dances are without method or regularity: a gentleman

and lady stand up, and dance about the room, one of them retiring, the other pursuing, then perhaps meeting, in an irregular fantastical manner.

Fithian:

The Dinner was as elegant as could be well expected when so great an Assembly were to be kept for so long a time.—For Drink, there was several sorts of Wine, good Lemon Punch, Toddy, Cyder, Porter &c. About Seven the Ladies & Gentlemen begun to dance in the Ball-Room—first Minuets one Round; Second Giggs; third Reels; And last of All Country-Dances; tho' they struck several Marches occasionally—The Music was a French-Horn and two Violins—The Ladies were Dressed Gay, and splendid, & when dancing, their Skirts & Brocades rustled and trailed behind them!—But all did not join in the Dance for there were parties in Rooms made up, some at Cards; some drinking for Pleasure; some toasting the Sons of america; some singing "Liberty Songs" as they call'd them, in which six, eight, ten or more would put their Heads near together and roar . . .

Mrs *Carter* informed me last Evening that this Family one year with another consumes 27000 Lb. of Pork; & twenty Beeves. 550 Bushels of Wheat, besides corn—4 Hogsheads of Rum, & 150 Gallons of Brandy.

Danced till half after two . . . We got to Bed by three after a Day spent in constant Violent exercise, & drinking an unusual Quantity of Liquor; for my own part with Fatigue, Heat, Liquor, Noise, Want of sleep, and the exertion of my Animal spirits I was almost brought to believe several times that I felt a Fever fixing upon me, attended with every Symptom of the Fall Disorders—.

Advertisement in the *Virginia Gazette*, April 18, 1766:

> The well known Horse
> R A N T E R
> WILL cover MARES this ſeaſon
> at *Marlborouglh*, in *Stafford*
> county, *Virginia*, at 40 s.
> the leap, 4 1 . for the ſeaſon,
> and $1. to enſure a colt, *Virginia*
> currency

Smyth:

There are races eſtabliſhed annually, almoſt at every town and conſiderable place in Virginia; and frequent matches on which large ſums of money depend; the inhabitants, almoſt to a man, being quite devoted to the diverſion of horſe-racing.

Very capital horſes are ſtarted here, ſuch as would make no deſpicable figure at Newmarket: nor is their ſpeed, bottom, or blood inferior to their appearance; the gentlemen of Virginia ſparing no pains, trouble or expence in importing the beſt ſtock, and improving the excellence of the breed by proper and judicious croſſing.

The gentlemen of fortune expend great ſums on their ſtuds . . . even the moſt indigent perſon has his ſaddle horſe, which he rides to every place, and on every occasion . . . indeed a man will frequently go five miles to catch a horſe, to ride only one mile upon afterwards.

Burnaby:

The horses are fleet and beautiful; and the gentlemen of Virginia, who are exceedingly fond of horse-racing, have spared no expence or trouble to improve the breed.

Lord Gordon:

> Their Breed of Horses extremely good, and in particular those
> they run in their Carriages, which are mostly from thorough
> bred Horses and country Mares,—they all drive Six horses . . .
> going frequently Sixty Miles to dinner.

Fithian:

> Loud disputes concerning the Excellence of each others
> Colts—Concerning their Fathers, Mothers (for so they call the
> Dams), Brothers, Sisters, Uncles, Aunts, Nephews, Nieces,
> & Cousins to the fourth Degree!—All the Evening Toddy
> constantly circulating—Supper came in, & at Supper I had a
> full, broad, sattisfying View of Miss Sally Panton—I wanted
> to hear her converse, but poor Girl anything she attempted to
> say was drowned in the more polite & useful Jargon about
> Dogs & Horses.

Beverley:

> There is yet another kind of sport which the young people take
> great delight in and that is the Hunting of wild Horses which
> they pursue sometimes with Dogs and sometimes without.
> You must know that they have many Horses foaled in the
> Woods of the Uplands that never were in hand and are as shy as
> any Savage Creature. These having no mark upon them belong
> to him that first takes them.

In 1694, 1695, 1699, and 1712, acts were passed in the Maryland
assembly "to prevent the great evil of the multiplicity of horses in
the province."

Fithian:

> Rode to Ucomico Church—8 Miles—Heard Parson Smith. He
> shewed to us the uncertainty of Riches, and their Insufficiency
> to make us happy . . .

The three grand divisions of time at the Church on Sundays, Viz. before Service, giving & receiving letters of business, reading Advertisements, consulting about the price of Tobacco, Grain, &c. & settling either the lineage, Age or qualities of favourite Horses. 2. In the Church at Service, prayrs read over in haste, A Sermon seldom under & never over twenty minutes, but always made up of sound morality, or deep studied Metaphysicks. 3. After Service is over three quarters of an hour spent in strolling round the Church among the Crowd, in which time you will be invited by several different Gentlemen home with them to dinner. The Balls, the Fish-Feasts, the Dancing-School, the Christnings, the Cock fights, the Horse-Races, the Chariots, the Ladies Masked.

A Mr. Davis, teacher, circa 1800:

About eight miles from Occoquan Mills is a place of worship called Poheek Church. Thither I rode on Sunday and joined the congregation of Parson Weems, a Minister of the Episcopal persuasion, who was cheerful in his mien that he might win men to religion. A Virginian Churchyard on Sunday resembles rather a race-course than a sepulchral ground. The ladies come to it in carriages and the men make their horses fast to the trees . . . . I was confounded on first entering the Churchyard at Poheek to hear 'Steed threaten Steed with high and boastful neigh.' Nor was I less stunned with the rattling of carriage wheels, the cracking of whips and vociferations of the gentlemen to the Negroes who accompanied them.

The building of Pohick Church:

ARTICLES OF AGREEMENT made this seventh day of April in the year 1769. Between the Vestry of Truro Parish in County of Fairfax, of the one part, and Daniel French of Fairfax Parish in the County aforesaid, Gent. of the other part, as follows, Vizt. The said Daniel French doth undertake and agree to build and finish in a workmanlike manner a Church, near the forks of the road above Robert Boggess's, to be placed as the Vestry shall hereafter direct . . . to be built of good bricks well burnt . . . The corner of the House, the Pedistals, and Doors with the Pediment heads to be of good white freestone, and the Returns and Arches of the Windows to be of rubbed brick. The Doors to be made of pine plank, two inches thick, moulded and raised pannells on both sides, and the frames thereof to be of pine clear of sap, with locust sills. The Window frames to be of pine clear of sap, with locust sills; the sashes to be made of pine plank one inch and three quarters thick; the Lights to be of the best Crown Glass, eighteen in each Window, eleven inches by nine; the Window and Door Cases to be made with double Archatraves . . . The frame of the Roof to be of pine, except the King-Posts which are to be of oak; and the scantling to be of a size and proper proportion to the building. The Roof to be covered with inch pine plank well seasoned, and cyphered and lapt one inch and a half, and then with cypress shingles twenty inches long, and to show six inches . . .

The Floors to be framed with good oak clear of sap, and laid with pine plank inch and a half thick, and well seasoned . . . The Isles to be laid with flaggstone, well squared and jointed.

The Pews to be wainscoted with pine plank an inch and a half thick, well seasoned, to be quarter-round on both sides, and raised pannel on one side the seats to be of inch and a half pine plank, fourteen inches broad and well supported. The Altar Piece to be twenty feet high and fifteen feet wide, and done with wainscot after the Ionic order. The floor of the Communion Place to be raised twenty inches higher than the floor of the House, with hand-rails and Bannisters of pine, and a Communion-Table of Black Walnut of a proper size. The Apostles Creed, the Lords-Prayer, and the ten Commandments to be neatly painted on the Alter-piece in black letters . . .

The inside of the Church to be Ceiled, Plaistered and White-Washed; no Loam or Clay to be used in the Plaistering. The outside Cornice, and all the Wooden-Work on the inside of the House (except the floors) to be neatly painted of the proper colours. Stone Steps to be put to the Doors, and locks and hinges; and hinges to the Pews, Pulpit and Communion Place.

The whole Building to be compleated and finished by the first day of September, which shall be in the year of our Lord, one thousand seven hundred and seventy two.

William Byrd:

Because navigation in Virginia is so easy and convenient, every year many hundred English ships come there from all points of the earth, in order to trade and bring, among other very useful things, many Negroes or black slaves to sell.

Fithian:

When I am on the Subject, I will relate further, what I heard M.r George Lees overseer, one Morgan, say the other day that he himself had often done to Negroes, and found it useful: He said that whipping of any kind does them no good, for they will laugh at your greatest Severity; But he told us he had invented two things, and by several experiments had proved their success.—For Sullenness, obstinacy, or Idleness, says he, Take a Negro, strip him, tie him fast to a post; take then a sharp Curry-Comb, & curry him severely til he is well scraped; & call a Boy with some dry Hay, and make the Boy rub him down for several Minutes, then salt him, & unlose him. He will attend to his Business, (said the inhuman Infidel) afterwards!—But savage Cruelty does not exceed His next diabolical invention— To get a Secret from a Negro, says he, take the following method—Lay upon your Floor a large thick plank, having a peg about eighteen Inches long, of hard wood, & very Sharp, on the upper end, fixed fast in the plank—then strip the Negro, tie the Cord to a staple in the Ceiling, so as that his foot may just rest on the sharpened Peg, then turn him briskly round, and you would laugh (said our informer) at the Dexterity of the Negro, while he was relieving his Feet on the sharpened Peg!

George Washington:

> Monday, 28th . . . Found the new Negro Cupid ill of a pleurisy at Dogue Run Quarter and had him brot. home in a cart for better care of him.
>
> Tuesday, 29th . . . Darcus, daughter to Phillis, died, which makes 4 negroes lost this Winter; viz, 3 Dower Negroes namely—Beck,—appraised to £50, Doll's Child born since, and Darcus— . . . , and Belinda, a Wench of mine.

From Virginia laws and statutes:

> I. FOR the better settling and preservation of estates within this dominion.
>
> II. *Be it enacted, by the governor, council and burgesses of this present general assembly, and it is hereby enacted by the authority of the same,* That from and after the passing of this act, all negro, mulatto, and Indian slaves, in all courts of judicature, and other places, within this dominion, shall be held, taken, and adjudged, to be real estate (and not chattels;) and shall descend unto the heirs and widoes of persons departing this life, according to the manner and custom of land of inheritance, held in fee simple . . .
>
> XXXVII. And whereas, many times, slaves run away and lie out, hid and lurking in swamps, woods, and other obscure places, killing hogs, and committing other injuries to the inhabitants of this her majesty's colony and dominion, *Be it therefore enacted, by the authority aforesaid, and it is hereby enacted,* That in all such cases upon intelligence given of any slave lying out, as aforesaid, any two justices (Quorum unus) of the peace of the country wherein such slave is supposed to lurk or do mischief shall be and are empowered to issue proclamation . . . Which proclamation shall be published on a Sabbath day, at the door of every church and chapel, in the said county, by the parish clerk, or reader, of the church, immediately after divine worship: And in case any slave, against whom proclamation hath been thus issued, and once published at any church or chapel, as aforesaid,

stay out, and do not immediately return home, it shall be lawful for any person or persons whatsoever, to kill and destroy such slaves.

Thomas Jefferson, writing in 1785:

> There must doubtless be an unhappy influence on the manners of our people produced by the existence of slavery among us. The whole commerce between master and slave is a perpetual exercise of the most boisterous passions, the most unremitting despotism on the one part, and degrading submissions on the other. Our children see this and learn to imitate it; for man is an imitative animal . . . The parent storms, the child looks on, catches the lineaments of wrath, puts on the same airs in the circle of smaller slaves, gives loose to the worst of passions, and thus nursed, educated, and daily exercised in tyranny, cannot but be stamped by it with odious peculiarities. The man must be a prodigy who can retain his manners and morals undepraved by such circumstances. And with what execration should the statesman be loaded, who, permitting one half the citizens thus to trample on the rights of the other, transforms those into despots, and these into enemies, destroys the morals of the one part, and the *amor patriae* of the other. For if a slave can have a country in this world, it must be any other in preference to that in which he is born to live and labor for another; in which he must lock up the faculties of his nature, contribute as far as depends on his individual endeavors to the evanishment of the human race, or entail his own miserable condition on the endless generations proceeding from him.

Burnaby:

> From what has been said of this colony, it will not be difficult to form an idea of the character of its inhabitants. The climate and external appearance of the country conspire to make them indolent, easy, and good natured; extremely fond of society and

much given to convivial pleasures. In consequence of this, they
seldom show any spirit of enterprise, or expose themselves
willingly to fatigue. Their authority over their slaves renders
them vain and imperious.

Jefferson:

With the morals of the people, their industry is also destroyed.
For in a warm climate, no man will labor for himself who can
make another labor for him. This is so true, that of the propri-
etors of slaves a very small proportion indeed are ever seen to
labor.

Smyth:

In ſhort, take them all together, they form a ſtrange combina-
tion of incongruous contradictory qualities, and principles
directly oppoſite; the beſt and the worſt, the moſt valuable
and the moſt worthleſs, elegant accomplishments and ſavage
brutality, being in many of them moſt unaccountably blended.

———————

Byrd:

It is to be wondered at, that the Virginians devote themselves to
nothing else but tobacco trade, since they could plant many
more useful things.

Douglas Southall Freeman:

Mount Vernon has a sandy surface, and below that a heavy soil.
At a depth of eighteen inches to two feet, approximately, is the
clay pan. This accentuates both wetness and dryness. Precisely
the "right year" is required for good growing conditions. This is
not soil for wheat, and is still worse for tobacco.

Fithian:

And their method of farming is slovenly, without any regard to
continue their Land in heart, for future Crops—They plant

large Quantities of Land, without any Manure, & work it very hard to make the best of the Crop, and when the Crop comes off they take away the Fences to inclose another Piece of Land for the next years tillage, and leave this a common to be destroyed by Winter & Beasts till they stand in need of it again to plough—The Land most commonly too is of a light sandy soil, & produces in very great quantities shrubby *Savins & Pines.*

Johann David Schoepf, traveling in Virginia, 1783-84:

The Virginians of the lower country are very easy and negligent husbandmen. Much and very good land, which would yield an abundant support to an industrious family, remains unused when once a little exhausted, no thought being given so far to dunging and other improvements. New land is taken up, the best to be had, tobacco is grown on it 3-4 years, and then Indian corn, so long as any will come. And in the end, if the soil is thoroughly impoverished, they begin again with a new piece and go through the rotation. Meantime wood grows again on the old land, and on the new is at pains to be cleared off; and all this to avoid dunging and all the trouble involved in a more careful handling of their cattle, if dung is to be had.

Isaac Weld traveled in Maryland, 1796:

From Port Tobacco to Hoe's Ferry on the Potowmac River, the country is flat and sandy and wears a most dreary aspect. Nothing is to be seen here for miles together but extensive plains that have been worn out by the culture of tobacco, overgrown with yellow sedge and interspersed with groves of pine and cedar trees, the dark green colour of which forms a curious contrast with the yellow of the sedge. In the midst of these plains are the remains of several good houses.

Abandoned tobacco lands—"old fields"—grown up in sedge, sassafras, and pine. There were also "poisoned fields"—land burned by the Indians, to improve the game.

On the Virginia side, the port of Dumfries grew, briefly flourished, and died; the inlet silted up, the land was abandoned.

Fithian:

> The School consists of eight—Two of Mʳ Carter's Sons—one Nephew—And five Daughters—The eldest Son is reading Salust: Grammatical Exercises, and latin Grammar—The second Son is reading english Grammar & Reading English: Writing and Cyphering in Subtraction—The Nephew is Reading and Writing as above; and Ciphering in Reduction—The eldest daughter is Reading the Spectator; Writing; & beginning to Cypher. . . .
>
> Miss Nancy is beginning on the *Guitar.* Ben finished reading Salusts Cataline Conspiracy.
>
> Spent most of the Day at the great house hearing the various Instruments of Music.
>
> Mʳ *Stadley* played on the Harpsichord & harmonica . . .
>
> Mʳ Carter has an overgrown library of Books of which he allows me the free use. It consists of a general collection of law books, all the Latin and Greek Classicks, vast number of books on Divinity chiefly by writers who are of the established Religion; he has the works of almost all the late famous writers, as Locke, Addison, Young, Pope, Swift, Dryden, &c.

And in the library of John Mercer at Marlborough, Stafford County:

> Alian's Tactick's of War
> Smith's Distilling & Fermentation
> Greek Grammar
> Greek Testament
> Colgrave's French Dictionary
> The Sum of Christian Religion
> The Country Parson's Advice
> History of the Turks 4th vol
> Bradley's Hop Garden
> Monarchy of the Bees

A Discourse of Sallets
Pocket Farrier
Acc^t of Society for Reformation of Manners
Atkinson's Epitome of Navigation
Salmon's Herbal 2 vol
Strother on Sickness & Health
Wiseman's Surgery 2 vol
Arbuthnot of Aliment
Andrey on Worms
Shakespears Plays 8 vol
Robert's Map of Commerce
The Musical Miscellany 6 vol
Mead on Poysons
Ovid's Art of Love

————————

Fithian: "We had an elegant dinner; Beef & Green; roast-Pig; fine boil'd Rock-Fish, Pudding, Cheese &c—Drink: good Porter-Beer, Cyder, Rum, & Brandy Toddy. The Virginians are so kind."

TURNING POINT: 1776

St. Mary's County, July 15th, 1776

Gentlemen:

This to inform you that there is now lying, off the mouth of the St. Mary's River, between seventy and eighty sail of vessels. I am now at Leonard Town on my way down with part of the 6th Battalion under my command, where I received an Express from Col. Barnes (who is now at St. Inegoe's Neck with the lower Battalion) informing me that this morning Ten Boats full of men landed on St. George's Island and had returned for more. I expect to be opposite the island some time this night and shall endeavor to get the best intelligence I can of their numbers and give the earliest notice. We shall want more powder and lead and also flints, if they are to be had . . .

Gentlemen: Your mo;obedt Servt

Jeremiah Jordon, colonel in the Maryland Militia, reported the appearance of the seventy-two vessels of the fleet under Lord Dunmore, Royal Governor of Virginia. Writing again, July 17:

I think from all appearances the Fleet will continue some time, if so, some Cannon and Swivels will be absolutely necessary to dislodge the men they have landed on the Island. With what assistance we can give in this quarter, I think 500 of the Militia of the upper Battalions will be full enough to oppose the enemy. We have now at different posts about 600 men . . . Col. Barnes with his Battalion is on the other side of the river, watching the motions of the enemy there.

Major Thomas Price, reporting July 23 and 26:

Three or four large ships went up the river the evening before I got here, since which a number of cannon have been fired as I suppose near the mouth of Nanjemoy. I have ordered the other two pieces of Cannon to the Lower Camp and shall as soon as the nine pounder arrives order that there and if intrenching tools which I have sent after can be had thro up an entrenchment . . .

By the best advice I can get from the Prisoners and many deserters the whole fleet does not intend to stay here longer than those up Potowmack comes down which they expect everyday.

Lord Dunmore's invasion was part of a larger plan. British Loyalists were to incite the Indians to raise an army in Detroit, attack and seize Pittsburg, and raid the back settlements of Virginia from there. A stronghold was to be established at Cumberland, and Alexandria was to be seized. Dunmore, with a fleet of ships and body of runaway slaves, would meet them at Alexandria. The colonies would be split, north and south, along the line of the Potomac.

Major Price wrote, "We have several Deserters from the Enemy most of them in the small pox . . . The shores are full of Dead Bodies chiefly negroes. I think if they stay here any time they must be ruined, for by Deaths Desertions and the Worm I think their business must be done compleatly."

The western action did not materialize. Lord Dunmore raided as far as Quantico, but he was harassed by local militia—and a violent summer storm on the Potomac. The British fleet never reached Alexandria.

For the remainder of the Revolution, the British raided waterfront plantations:

> We have for some time past been ravaged in this County by the enemy. They on Friday last landed and plundered several families on Smith's Creek . . .

> Two of the enemy's vessels came up the Potomac on Thursday last in the Evening. They dispatched two of their barges in the night to plunder; the men from these landed at Port Tobacco Warehouse . . . From thence they crossed over to Mr. Walter Hanson's and robbed him of all effects to considerable value.

On Friday morning they landed at Captain George Dent's before the militia could be collected in sufficient force to oppose them and burnt all his houses.

On the 13th a Brig with two Schooners appeared off the mouth of St. Clement's Bay, and landed two barges loaded with men at Mr. Herbert Blackestone's House, which they burned and carried Blackestone with them, where he has continued.

The Americans offered suicide barges:

These barges were loaded with explosives and drifted down on the anchored British fleet at night, which annoyed the British no end. The men in the barges had little chance of escape because the fuses could not be lit until the boats had made contact with the fleet.

For many years after, the American Revolution was known in southern Maryland as Lord Dunmore's War.

TWO

UPRIVER SETTLEMENT

Andrew Burnaby, 1759, at the Great Falls:

> The channel of the river is contracted by hills . . . It is clogged moreover with innumerable rocks; so that the water for a mile or two flows with accelerated velocity. At length coming to a ledge of rocks, which runs diametrically across the river, it divides into two spouts, each about eight yards wide, and rushes down a precipice with incredible rapidity . . . These two spouts, after running in separate channels for a short space, at length unite in one about thirty yards wide; and as we judged from the smoothness of the surface and our unsuccessful endeavors to fathom it, of prodigious depth. The rocks on each side are at least ninety or a hundred feet high; and yet, in great freshes, the water overflows the tops of them, as appeared by several large and entire trees, which had lodged there.

David Baillie Warden, 1816:

> The wild and romantic scenery of the Great Falls, which are to be seen most to advantage from the Virginia side is scarcely to be equalled. There is a stupendous projecting rock covered with cedar, where one may sit and gaze at the waters dashing with impetuosity over the rugged surface. At the close of winter vast masses of ice, rolling over the rocks with hideous crash, present a scene truly sublime.

. . . Several delicious springs issue from a neighboring hill which commands an enchanting prospect . . . the yellow jessamine is of a prodigious size. The prickly pear grows on the banks . . . White hore-hound and sweet fennel, . . . the odour of aromatic plants, . . . wild cherries and strawberries.

George Washington, writing from Harper's Ferry, 1785:

In my ride from George Town to this place, I made the following observations: The land about the first, is not only hilly, and a good deal mixed with flint stone, but is of an indifferent quality 'till we left the great Road (3 Miles from G:Town) . . . The quality of the land then improves, and seems well adapted to the culture of small grain, but continues broken and by no means in a high state of cultivation . . . That about the Maryland Sugar Lands . . . which is five miles above Seneca, is remarkably fine, and very level. From thence to Monocasy about 12 miles further they are less level and of much inferior quality. That from Monocasy to Frederick Town (distant 12 or 13 Miles) nothing can well exceed them for fertility of Soil, convenient levelness, and luxuriant growth of Timber. The farms seem to be under good cultivation . . .

Frederick Town stands on a branch of Monocasy, and lyes rather low. The Country about it is beautiful and seems to be in high cultivation.

J. F. D. Smyth, 1784:

The land around Frederick Town is heavy, ftrong, and rich, well calculated for wheat, with which it abounds; this being as plentiful a country as any in the world.

The face of the country here fwells into beautiful hills and dales, and twelve miles beyond the town it arifes into mountains, named the South Mountain. The foil is generally of a deep rufty brown colour.

Burnaby, crossing the Blue Ridge:

> When I got to the top, I was inexpressibly delighted with the
> scene which opened before me. Immediately under the moun-
> tain, which was covered with chamoe-daphnes in full bloom,
> was a most beautiful river: beyond this an extensive plain, diver-
> sified with every pleasing object that nature can exhibit; and, at
> the distance of fifty miles, another ridge of still more lofty
> mountains, called the Great, or North Ridge, which inclosed
> and terminated the whole.
>
> The river Shenandoah rises a great way to the southward
> from under this Great North Ridge ... it is exceedingly roman-
> tic and beautiful, forming a great variety of falls, and is so trans-
> parent, that you may see the smallest pebble at the depths of
> eight or ten feet.

Smyth, in the Shenandoah Valley:

> This valley is about thirty miles wide, extending many hundred
> miles in length, and contains a body of the richest land in the
> world. It abounds with the moſt clear and pellucid watercourſes.

Washington, in the Paw Paw Bends:

> This tract, though small, is extremely valuable. It lyes on
> Potomac River about 12 miles above the Town of Bath (or
> Warm Springs) and is in the shape of a horse Shoe: the river
> running almost around it. Two hundred Acres of it is rich
> low grounds; with a great abundance of the largest and finest
> Walnut trees . . . [on the South Branch] the Road . . . to
> Patterson's Ck. is Hilly down the Ck. on which is good Land,
> Sloppy to Parker's, and from Parker's to Turner's Hilly again.

Smyth:

> I croſſed May's Creek, and Wills's Creek, . . . paſſed by old Fort
> Cumberland, which is in a beautiful and romantic ſituation, on
> the north ſide of the Potomack, amidſt vaſt mountains and

mighty torrents of water, that break through the mountains in dreadful and tremendous chaſms. . . .

Here I began to aſcend the mighty Alleghany, and . . . after having . . . waded through a black and diſmal river named Savage River, and a number of large and dangerous watercourſes beſides, I arrived at Gregg's habitation, in the midſt of the mountain; where I remained all night amidſt the dreadful ſcreamings and howlings of multitudes of every ſpecies of wild beaſts.

The emigration from Tidewater westward began in the early part of the eighteenth century. "The meaner sort of the people (in whom consists the strength of all Countrys), are daily moving higher up."

1724 or 1725, a 535-acre grant was taken by one William Hawlin "above Goose Creek on Potowmack river side"—"below the Yaller rocks"—"on both sides Red Rock Run." Later, Hawlin's widow took up a grant of 416 acres "about two miles below the Kitchen Mountain."

And Samuel Skinker took up 672 acres on the south side of Pignut.

1753, a group of Moravian brethren journeyed from Pennsylvania to North Carolina:

> *Oct. 15.* We started at 2:30 A.M. had moonlight and a good road . . . . We had a little work done on our wagon, as the pole had been injured. The smith charged a big price and his work did little good. We saw the Blue Mts. some 8 to 10 miles to our right, and had unusually fine weather. We stopped for noon eight miles further on by the Kanikatschik . . . A couple of miles beyond we stopped for the night by Corrnell Chimpersen's mill, where we had good water. Br. Nathanael held the evening service.
>
> *Oct. 16.* Br. Grube conducted morning prayers, and we set out at 4 A.M. On the way we bought 10 bushels of oats, and after driving five miles had breakfast by a creek where Irish people live. Two

miles further we found good water, also three miles beyond, where a house stands back a little on the left. One mile brought us to a Tavern. We could again see the Blue Mts. quite plainly. In another mile we reached a German inn, where we bought some hay and spent the noon hour. Two miles from the inn we passed the boundary between Pennsylvania and Maryland, it is said that Maryland is here only six miles wide. From the Susquehannah here the residents are chiefly Irish, and they have good lands, but one can buy little or nothing from them. Two and a half miles further we came to an old Swiss, where we bought some hay. He was very friendly and asked that we come to see him again. One mile beyond we bought some kraut from a German named Fende Kra, which tasted very good to us. We went on and camped for the night two miles from the Patomik, putting up our tent by a creek. The man on whose land we were came to see us, was very friendly, and took supper with us . . . . Br. Gottlob held the evening service . . .

Oct. 17. We started at five o'clock and had two miles to go to the Patomik which we reached at daybreak. Br. Jac. Losch rode in first to find the ford which makes a decided curve between the banks. We crossed safely but it was very difficult to drive out at the other end and we had a great deal of trouble to get up the bank. The river . . . in flood . . . runs far over the high banks, and flows swiftly,—toward the south-east . . . For supper we cooked chicken, which tasted very good. Br. Nathanael conducted evening prayer.

Oct. 18. . . . We turned our horses out to graze in a meadow as we had no feed for them . . . Br. Gottlob held evening prayers . . . we sang several sweet verses of blessing . . . Then we lay peacefully down to rest under our tent.

Oct. 19. . . . We had a good trip to-day; we could plainly see the Blue Mountains on our right. Some high mountains were directly in front of us. Br. Nathanael held the evening service, and then we went to sleep.

Oct. 20. Very early the Brn. brought in our horses from pasture. Br. Grube waked the other Brn. by singing a few verses, and after eating our broth we set out about five o'clock

... We traveled eight miles this afternoon, and put up our tent near the Shanidore Creek ... We had a pretty camping place tonight, and felt happy, and thankful to the Lord for bringing us safely so far. Br. Nathanael held evening prayers.

Meshach Browning settled in western Maryland:

October being the beginning of the hunting season, my uncle commenced his task of laying in the winter's provisions: some days he would hunt deer, other days for bees; and, as he was most successful in bee-hunting, he spent more of his time in hunting bees than he did in pursuing the deer. Soon our table was abundantly supplied with venison and honey; and the high, fresh tame grass caused our cows to give large quantities of milk, from which aunt, who was a very industrious woman, made plenty of butter; and frequently a fat turkey being added to our table store, we began to think that there was not such a place to be found in all creation ...

I kept my stand perhaps five or six minutes, when I saw something slipping through the bushes, which I took to be one of the deer; but I soon found that it was coming toward me. I kept a close look out of it; and directly, within ten steps of me, up rose the head and shoulders of the largest panther that I ever saw, either before or since ... I aimed my rifle at him as well as I could, he looking me full in the face; and when I fired he made a tremendous spring for me, and ran off through the brush and briers with the dog after him.

As soon as I recovered a little from my fright, I loaded again and started after them. I followed them as fast as I could, and soon found them at the foot of a large and very high rock; the panther, in his hurry, having sprung down the cleft of rock fifteen or twenty feet; but the dog, being afraid to venture so great a leap, ran around, and the two had met in a thick laurel swamp, where they were fighting the best way they could. I stood on top of the rock over them, and fired at the base of the panther's ear, when down he went; and I ran round the rock ... But when I got near him I found he was up and fighting again, and consequently I had to hurry back for my gun, load it again, creep slyly up, take aim at his ear, as before, and give him another shot, which laid him dead on the ground. My first shot had broken his shoulder; the second pierced his ear, passing downward through his tongue; the last entered one ear, and came out the other, scattering his brains all around. He measured eleven feet three inches from the end of his nose to the tip of his tail. This was the largest panther I ever killed . . .

Mary and myself proposed to walk a little through the beautiful glade, which was covered with grass knee-high, and intermixed with wild flowers of all the kinds and colors that nature had ever produced. All that fancy could desire was here to be seen at a single glance.

. . . A fine snow fell, when off I started again to hunt bears. I saw several tracks, but took the largest one, which I followed rapidly, as the snow was still falling fast; and I had every advantage of the bear, for he could neither hear nor see me. I pushed on after him, until I arrived at a small branch, which the bear was compelled to cross, and in which he had stopped to take a drink. The bank was very high, I did not see him till he bounded up the opposite side into the thick bushes. I could not get a good sight of him till he was at some distance; but knowing that would be my last chance, as he reached the top of the hill, I fired at him, hit or miss. I reloaded my gun, and went to where I last saw him, when I discovered he was badly wounded, there being a great quantity of blood along his trail.

. . . The bear was obliged to retreat about a mile through cleared ground, where I could not only run as fast, if not faster than him, but also where I had a fair chance for a hand-to-hand fight. I followed the trail, running with all my might. Observing him making all the head-way he could, I increased my speed till within gun-shot, when I fired at him a second time; but seeing no change in his speed, I loaded as I ran, in order to lose no ground and, coming still closer to him, I gave him a third shot. Still, on he went; but as I saw he was failing, I loaded again as I ran, and poured in a fourth fire, which I found made him stagger considerably in his gait. I then saw that one of his thighs was broken. By this time he had entered a small ravine, having steep banks on each side, where I could run round and head him off; in doing which, I saw a large tree laying across the branch he was traveling up. I went out on this log till I got about the middle of the branch, where I stood, unseen by the bear, till he was almost under me, when I notified him that I was there, by saying, 'Old fellow, you are mine at last.' He stopped to see what was the matter, when I took the fifth shot at his head, and down he went into the water. In the twinkling of an eye I sprang from the log, knowing that I could cut his throat before he recovered from the effect of the shot. I seized him by the ear, and holding his head up, I slashed his neck through to the bone, and from ear to ear, in a couple of cuts.

...The dogs started off in full cry after what we were pretty certain was a bear, and in a short time we heard the fighting begin. The dogs would run awhile, and fight awhile; and after a chase of at least three miles, all the time coming nearer home, the bear at last ran into a large glade, in full view of Colonel Lynn's house. It so happened that General Lee, . . . who fought with General Washington, was on his road to the West, and had stopped with Colonel Lynn a few days. When the dogs and the bear came in sight, the whole family, together with General Lee, came out to see the sport. Hugh and I came into the glade, and commenced hostilities at once; and after three rounds fired at him, the bear yielded to superior numbers, there being four to one; and he died like a hero, fighting till the last breath left him.

I turned to follow the dog; but all again becoming quiet, I listened with anxiety, when I heard something moving behind me. I looked around, and beheld the panther coming toward me, but not near enough for me to shoot. He made a short turn, which brought him opposite me, and within ten steps; but he went on the off side of a rock, that covered him from my shot. As I saw he would have to come from behind the rock, and be exposed to my view, I held my fire till he came out; and as soon as he made his appearance, I let him have a shot, which I directed as near as I could for his heart. As the gun cracked he sprang into the air, snapping at the place where the ball had struck him; and then turning towards me, he came on till within about five steps of me, put his paws on a small fallen tree, and looked me full in the face. While he stood looking at me, I saw the blood streaming from both sides of his body . . .

As I went on, walking fast, I came to some shelly rocks, where the snakes began to rattle; the weeds seemed to be shaking all around me, and I could see them twisting themselves in every direction . . .

I then followed the trail, with great difficulty, till it became fresher; when off went the dogs, and immediately they were on the old fellow in a hollow tree; and such fighting, and cutting with teeth, I never saw before or since. He was the largest and strongest wolf I ever met in my life. He remained in the tree, with his mouth wide open; and every time a dog came within reach, he would sink every tooth into him. I encouraged the dogs to make another set at him; when the strongest took a deep hold on one of the wolf ears, while the other seized the remaining one. He then bounded from the tree, and the two dogs threw him on the ground. He tried again and again to recover his feet, but they tumbled him down, until they were all tired; when I took a club and beat him on the head until he was dead. I took off his scalp and hide, which were worth nine dollars.

I was once making wild Hay in a glade . . .

In the morning, when I saw such a beautiful snow on the ground, I told Mr. Little that I would try to find where the old panther had her residence . . . I had not made more than half my circuit, when I found her track, where she had come out of a swamp and was taking a straight course for the Savage river, which ran through a very mountainous country, covered with almost impenetrable thickets.

Traveling on with a light foot and willing mind, I presently found a fine large doe, which she had killed, and sucked its blood. The body being still warm, I skinned it, took the track again, and followed it over the Meadow Mountain down to the Savage river, and on to the steep hills along its border . . .

When I got my eyes on her, she was looking me in the face, and distant not more than five steps. I took careful aim between her eyes, let her have the whole load in her brains, and down she dropped, without scarcely making a struggle. I skinned and scalped her . . .

All the settlers lived in cabins, and fed their children on bread, meat, butter, honey, and milk; coffee and tea were almost out of the question, being only used by a very few old ladies who had been raised in other parts of the country . . .

Hellebore is the first weed that shoots up in the spring, and it grows to the height of two feet, with a stalk somewhat resembling that of corn, and a strong, broad leaf. It grows in marshy ground and this place, being a narrow muddy branch, was full of it. The bear had got into the mud, and was amusing himself by biting off the hellebores and slinging them out of his way.

This he continued to do until I was on the bank of the run, and within thirty steps of him. I then knew that he was my prize, and I stood quietly looking at him playing; for I had never before seen a grown bear play . . .

Seeing that he [the bear] was still biting the dog severely, and that I could effect nothing with the knife, I ran up suddenly, seized him by the wool on his hips, and gave him a hard jerk, which as he was very weak, threw him flat on the ground. He then gave a long groan, which was so much like that of a human being, that it made me feel as though I had been dealing foully with the beast; but there I had to stand, and hear his heavy groans, which no person could have distinguished from those of a strong man in the last agonies of death.

I stood looking calmly at him, until the sport was marred by the thought of the brave manner in which he had defended himself against such unequal numbers, and it really seemed to me that I had committed a crime against an unoffending animal.

––––––––––

In 1803, a book was published:

A

TREATISE

on

PRACTICAL FARMING;

EMBRACING PARTICULARLY

THE FOLLOWING SUBJECT, VIZ.

The USE of PLAISTER of PARIS, with Directions for Using it; and GENERAL OBSERVATIONS on the USE of OTHER MANURES.

ON DEEP PLOUGHING; THICK SOWING of GRAIN; METHOD OF PREVENTING FRUIT TREES from DECAYING, and

Farming in General.

––––––––––

BY JOHN A. BINNS,

OF LOUDON COUNTY, VIRGINIA, FARMER

––––––––––

FREDERICK-TOWN, MARIAND,

Printed by JOHN B. COLVING - Editor of

the REPUBLICAN ADVOCATE.

1803

Binns's "plaister of paris" was actually gypsum, and its use revolutionized Piedmont agriculture. Jefferson: "The county of Loudon . . . had been so exhausted and wasted by bad husbandry that it began to depopulate, the inhabitants going Southwardly in quest of better lands . . . It is now become one of the most productive Counties of the State of Virginia and the price given for the lands is multiplied manifold."

In the Piedmont and in the naturally fertile Shenandoah Valley, German settlers from Pennsylvania established small farms—50 to 100 acres, planted grasses, fenced and housed their stock, introduced a varied family husbandry, and quickly became richer than the landpoor Tidewater colonists.

Burnaby, on the Shenandoah Germans:

> I could not but reflect with pleasure on the situation of these people: and think if there is such a thing as happiness in this life, that they enjoy it. Far from the bustle of the world, they live in the most delightful climate, and richest soil imaginable; they are everywhere surrounded with beautiful prospects and sylvan scenes; lofty mountains, transparent streams, falls of water, rich valleys, and majestic woods; the whole interspersed with an infinite variety of flowering shrubs, constitute the landscape surrounding them: they are subject to few diseases; are generally robust; and live in perfect liberty: they are ignorant of want.

Captain Ferdinand Marie Bayard, writing in 1791:

> It is a magnificent country about Winchester. The men are tall, well-made, of strong constitutions, and ruddy. The horses and cattle have the eye and the gait of health.

Smyth:

> Many of the Irish here can fcarcely fpeak in English and thou-fands of the Germans underftand no language but High Dutch however they are all very laborious, and extremely induftrious, having improved this part of the country beyond conception; but they have no idea of focial life, and are more like brutes than men.

And Kercheval:

> There was soon a mixed population of Germans, Irish, and a few English and Scotch. The national prejudices which existed between the Dutch and Irish produced much disorder and

many riots. It was customary for the Dutch, on St. Patrick's Day, to exhibit the effigy of the saint, with a string of Irish potatoes around his neck.

The fenfible, and this I flatter myfelf, is the greater part of this nation, feem to be fully perfuaded, that it is impoffible for a country to flourifh and become powerful, without country Manufactures . . .

I know by experience, that one of the wifeft Princes now in Europe preferred a plain but industrious Manufacturer at his Levee, fpoke with him above an hour, when at the fame time, he did not look at a number of the greateft and richeft of the Nobility of his dominions, whose principal occupation is to opprefs their farmers and hunt foxes . . .

   I have purchafed an advantageoufly fituated tract of land on Patowmack, not far from the mouth of Monocafy, of two thousand one hundred acres, which except a fmall balance, is paid— on this land I have erected all the neceffary buildings for the Manufactory, as glafs ovens for bottles, window and flint glafs, and a dwelling house for one hundred and thirty-five now living fouls—I have made a beginning of glafs making.

Johann Friedrich Amelung, German glass-maker of New Bremen, who purchased 2100 acres north and east of Sugarloaf Mountain, later added another 900 acres. Some of his land purchases were as follows:

Part of Gantt's Garden	1570	acres
Adam's Bones	194	"
Tobacco Hook	71	"
I Don't Care What	51	"

Amelung raised money in Germany and America, and with sixty-eight trained glass workers, their families, a pastor, and two teachers, as well as a few other tradesmen, sailed from Bremen in June, 1784.

Within two years, he spent more money than he had raised. Congress refused him a loan.

The real reason for Amelung's failure was probably the fact that he could not adjust himself to the demands of the new country. He had high-flown, artistic notions; he apparently wanted to produce artistic glass products in the style of the Venetian and Bohemian glass blowers and realized too late that the time for this sort of thing had not yet arrived in America. The country needed window-panes and medicine bottles, not delicate wine glasses and flower vases.

Jefferson:

The passage of the Potomac through the Blue Ridge is, perhaps, one of the most stupendous scenes in nature. You stand on a very high point of land. On your right comes up the Shenandoah, having ranged along the foot of the mountain an hundred miles to seek a vent. On your left approaches the Potomac, in quest of a passage also. In the moment of their junction, they rush together against the mountain, rend it asunder, and pass off to the sea. The first glance of this scene hurries our senses into the opinion, that this earth has been created in time, that the mountains were formed first, that the rivers began to flow afterwards, that in this place particularly, they have been dammed up by the Blue Ridge of Mountains, and have formed an ocean which filled the whole valley; that continuing to rise they have at length broken over at this spot, and have torn the mountain down from its summit to its base. The piles of rock on each hand, but particularly the Shenandoah, the evident marks of their disrupture and avulsion from their beds by the most powerful agents of nature, corroborate the impression. But the distant finishing which nature has given to the picture, is of a very different character. It is a true contrast to the foreground. It is as placid and delightful as that is wild and tremendous. For the mountain being cloven asunder, she presents to your eye, through the cleft, a small catch of smooth blue horizon, at an infinite distance in the plain country, inviting you, as it were, from the riot and tumult roaring around, to pass through the breach and participate of the calm below. Here the eye ultimately composes itself; and that way, too, the road happens actually to lead. You cross the Potomac above the junction, pass along its side through the base of the mountain for three miles, its terrible precipices hanging in fragments over you, and within about twenty miles reach Fredericktown, and the fine country round that. This scene is worth a voyage across the Atlantic.

(geology)

*A geological section of the State of Maryland, from the top of Savage
Mountain to Point Lookout at the mouth of the Potomac, exhibits in
miniature a section of the geology of the world, from the most recent ter-
tiary deposits to the most ancient rock formations. Penetrating this
area, the Potomac flows through the five distinct physiographic regions
of the eastern seaboard: the Allegheny Plateau, the Ridge and Valley
Province, the Blue Ridge, the Piedmont and the Coastal Plain—each
with its characteristic geology, terrain, and forest cover. Headwaters
originate in the first three of these regions; only one major tributary—
the Monocacy—rises in the Piedmont Plateau.*

*A heavily dissected peneplain, the Allegheny Plateau is composed
of nearly flat-lying carboniferous rocks—the coal country—and is
bounded on the southeast by the Allegheny Front or Allegheny Escarp-
ment. Southeastward lies the Ridge and Valley Province, fifty to sixty
miles wide: this is the Valley, the Great Valley, the Hagerstown Valley
(Maryland), the Cumberland Valley (Pennsylvania), the Shenandoah
Valley, the Valley of Virginia. Bounded on either side by an abrupt scarp
of shales and sandstones, the valley floor is generally level or gently
rolling, and consists largely of decomposed limestones. It is intensely
fertile, and the soft limestone is honeycombed with caverns. Some of the
oldest rocks known on earth—of Archeozoic and Lower Cambrian
times—are the granitic gneisses occasionally exposed in the Blue Ridge
Province, notably in the banks and islands of the Potomac River, and
on the Ridge itself (as old Rag Granite). Antietam quartzite and
Harper's shale are similarly ancient. Now a large uphold of crystalline
rocks, dipping in parts beneath the Valley, the Ridge was formed
originally deep beneath the surface, as molten lava. A major fault
probably extends along its full length. Lithologically akin to the Blue
Ridge in its western areas is the Piedmont Province, composed of
granites, gneisses and schists, greenstone, soapstone, and marble, creat-
ing a heavy, fertile soil. Like the Blue Ridge, the grain or strike of the
Piedmont is from Northeast to southwest. In its lower areas, toward the*

southeast, it is covered in places by an outwash deposit of gravel and sand, spread by the Potomac, and here the materials of the Piedmont have been so altered that their original structures and evidences of origin have been obliterated. Southeasternmost, where the Potomac becomes a tidal estuary, lies the Coastal Plain—beginning roughly at the Great Falls, and extending to Chesapeake Bay and beyond, one hundred miles beneath the surface of the Atlantic ocean. Composed of clays, sandstones, greensands, shell marl, coarse and cobbly gravels, formed by the washing down of soil and rocky debris from crystalline Piedmont rocks (on whose eastward continuation the material is super-imposed), the Coastal Plain dips gently seaward. The boundary between Piedmont and Plain is best defined at Great Falls and the Palisades, where the Potomac leaves the last of the upland rock. Elsewhere, across the land it is a sinuous and ill-defined border, the softer Plain formations feathering out as they lap onto the obdurate crystalline rocks.

FEDERAL CITY

George Washington, 1790:

> July
> Monday, 12th. Exercised on Horseback between 5 and 6 in the morning.
>
> Sat for Mr. Trumbull from 9 until half after ten. And about Noon had two Bills presented to me by the joint Committee of Congress—The one 'An Act for Establishing the Temporary and permanent Seat . . .'

An Act for establishing the temporary and permanent seat
of the Government of the United States

SECTION I. *Be it enacted by the Senate and House of Representatives of the United States of America in Congress assembled,* That a district of territory, not exceeding ten miles square, to be located as hereafter directed on the river Potomac, at some place between the mouths of the Eastern Branch [Anacostia River] and Connogochegue, be, and the same is hereby, accepted for the permanent seat of the government of the United States.

Washington considered various sites: the vicinity of the Conococheague . . . at the mouth of the Monocacy . . . in the Georgetown area . . .

Georgetown property owners offered their land: "It is conceived that the hilliness of the country, far from being an objection, will be thought a desirable circumstance, as it will at once contribute to the beauty, health and security of a city intended for the seat of Empire. For a place merely commercial, where men willingly sacrifice health to gain, a continued flat might perhaps be preferred."

The location was chosen, and Washington wrote from Philadelphia, February 3, 1791, to William Deakins, Jr., and Benjamin Stoddert:

> Gentlemen: In asking your aid in the following case permit me at the same time to ask the most perfect secrecy.
>
> The federal territory being located, the competition for the location of the town now rests between the mouth of the Eastern branch, and the land on the river, below and adjacent to Georgetown. In favour of the former, Nature has furnished powerful advantages. In favour of the latter is its vicinity to Georgetown, which puts it in the way of deriving aids from it in the beginning, and of communicating in return an increased value to the property of that town. These advantages have been so poised in my mind as to give it different tendencies at different times. There are lands which stand yet in the way of the latter location and which, if they would be obtained, for the purposes of the town, would remove a considerable obstacle to it, and go near indeed to decide what has been so long on the balance with me . . .
>
> The object of this letter is to ask you to endeavor to purchase these grounds of the owners for the public . . . but as if for yourselves, and to conduct your propositions so as to excite no suspicion that they are on behalf of the public.

Later—December 1791—Washington wrote:

> Potomac River then, is the centre of the Union. It is between the extremes of heat and cold. It is not so far to the south as to be unfriendly to grass, nor so far north as to have the produce of the Summer consumed in the length, and severity of the winter. It waters that soil, and runs in that climate, which is most congenial to English grains, and most agreeable to the Cultivators of them.
>
> It is the River, more than any other, in my opinion, which must, in the natural progress of things, connect by its inland navigation . . . the Atlantic States with the vast region which is populating (beyond all conception) to the Westward of it. It is

designated by law for the seat of Empire; and must, from its extensive course through a rich and populous country become, in time, the grand Emporium of North America. To these reasons may be added that, the lands within, and surrounding the district of Columbia are as high, as dry, and as healthy as any in the United States.

And Tobias Lear, 1793:

The whole area of the City consists of upwards of four thousand acres.—The ground, on an average, is about forty feet above the water of the river. Although the whole, when taken together, appears to be nearly a level spit, yet it is found to consist of what may be called wavy land; and is sufficiently uneven to give many very extensive and beautiful views from various parts of it, as well as to effectually answer every purpose of cleansing and draining the city.

Thomas Jefferson would have preferred a site near the Great Falls, for, among other reasons, "remoteness from the influence of any overgrown commercial city." However, he accepted the site chosen:

November 29, 1790
Proceedings to be had under the Residence act.
a territory not exceeding 10. miles square (or, I presume, 100 square miles in any form) to be located by metes and bounds.
   3. commissioners to be appointed
     I suppose them not entitled to salary.
the Commissioners to purchase or accept 'such quantity of land on the E. side of the river as the President shall deem *proper for the U. S.'* viz. for the federal Capitol, the offices, the President's house & gardens, the town house, Market house, publick walls, hospital ...
    The Comissioners should have some taste in architecture, because they may have to decide between different plans.
    They will however be subject to the President's direction in every point.

He wrote on January 29, 1791:

> The President having thought Major L'Enfant peculiarly qualified to make such a draught of the ground as will enable himself to fix on the spot for the public buildings, he has been written to for that purpose.

Major of Engineers Pierre Charles L'Enfant enjoyed the unofficial position of Advisor in Aesthetics to the new government. "Whenever, during the war or after, something in any way connected with art was wanted, L'Enfant was as a matter of course appealed to." He relieved the monotony at Valley Forge with his quick pencil sketches, and even Washington sat for his likeness to be drawn by the man he called "Monsieur Langfang."

It was said of L'Enfant that he always saw things "en grande."

Jefferson to L'Enfant, March 1791:

> *Sir,* You are desired to proceed to Georgetown, where you will find Mr. Ellicott employed in making a survey and map of the Federal territory. The special object of asking your aid is to have drawings of the particular grounds most likely to be approved for the site of the federal town and buildings. You will therefore be pleased to begin on the eastern branch, and proceed from thence upwards, laying down the hills, valleys, morasses, and waters between that, the Potomac, the Tyber, and the road leading from Georgetown to the eastern branch, and connecting the whole with certain fixed points of the map Mr. Ellicott is preparing. Some idea of the height of the hills above the base on which they stand, would be desirable.

From the *Georgetown Weekly Ledger*, March 12, 1791:

> Some time last month arrived in this town Maj. Andrew Ellicott, a gentleman of superior astronomical abilities. He was appointed by the President of the United States to lay off a tract

of land ten miles square on the Potomac for the use of Congress. He is now engaged in this business and hopes soon to accomplish the object of his mission. He is attended by Benjamin Banniker, an Ethiopian . . .

Wednesday evening arrived in this town Major Longfont.

Washington's notes for the federal city:

> Quary Stone to be raised by Skilful People.
>
> The buildings, especially the Capitol, ought to be on a scale far superior to any thing in *this* Country; the House for the President should also (in the design though not executed all at once) be upon a Commensurate scale.

Washington to the secretary of state, March 31, 1791:

> The terms agreed on between me, on the part of the United States, with the Land holders of Georgetown and Carrollsburg are. That all the land from Rock Creek along the river to the Eastern-branch and so upwards to or above the Ferry including a breadth of about a mile and a half, the whole containing from three to five thousand acres, is ceded to the public, on condition That, when the whole shall be surveyed and laid off as a city, (which Major L'Enfant is now directed to do) the present Proprietors shall retain every other lot; and, for such part of the land as may be taken for public use for squares, walks, &ca., they shall be allowed at the rate of Twenty five pounds per acre. The Public having the right to reserve such parts of the wood on the land as may be thought necessary to be preserved for ornament &ca. The Land holders to have the use and profits of all their ground until the city is laid off into lots, and sale is made of those lots which, by this agreement, become public property. No compensation is to be made for the ground that may be occupied as streets or alleys.

Washington's diary, June 1791:

> Tuesday, 28th. Whilst the Commissioners were engaged in preparing the Deed to be signed by the Subscribers this afternoon, I went out with Majr. L'Enfant and Mr. Ellicot to take a more perfect view of the ground, in order to decide finally on the spots on which to place the public buildings and to direct how a line which was to leave out a Spring (commonly known by the name of the Cool Spring) belonging to Majr. Stoddart should be run.

And July 20, 1791:

> I am now happy to add that all matters between the Proprietors of the soil and the public are settled to the mutual satisfaction of the Parties, and that the business of laying out the city, the grounds for public buildings, walks &c. is progressing under the inspection of Major L'Enfant with pleasing prospects.

L'Enfant to Washington, September 1789:

> Ser;
> The late determination of Congress to lay the foundation of a city which is to become the Capital of this vast Empire offers so great an occasion . . .
>
> No nation, perhaps, had ever before the opportunity offered them of deliberately deciding on the spot where their Capital City should be fixed . . . And, although the means now within the power of the Country are not such as to pursue the design to any great extent, it will be obvious that the plans should be drawn on such a scale as to leave room for that aggrandizement and embellishment which the increase of the wealth of the nation will permit it to pursue at any period, however remote.

To Hamilton:

> I feel a sort of embarrassment how to speak to you as advantageously as I really think of the situation determined upon. I become apprehensive of being charged with partiality when I

assure you that no position in America can be more susceptible of grand improvement.

To Jefferson, Georgetown, March 11, 1791:

Sir:

I have the honor of informing you of my arrival at this place where I could not possibly reach before Wednesday last and very late in the evening after having travelled part of the way on foot and part on horse back leaving the broken stage behind.

On arriving I made it my first care immediately to wait on the mayor of the town in conforming with the direction which you gave me—he appeared to be much surprised and assured me he had received no previous notice of my coming nor any instruction relating to the business I was sent upon . . . I am only at present to regret that an heavy rain and thick mist which has been incessant ever since my arrival here has put an insuperable obstacle to my wish of proceeding immediately to the survey. Should the weather continue bad as there is every appearance it will I shall be much at a loss how to make a plan of the ground you have pointed out to me and have it ready for the President at the time when he is expected at this place. I see no other way if by Monday next the weather does not change, but that of making a rough draft as accurate as may be obtained by viewing the ground in riding over it on horse back, as I have already done yesterday through the rain to obtain a knowledge of the whole. I put from the eastern branch towards George-town up the heights and down along side of the bank of the main river and along side of Goose and Rock creeks as far up as their springs.

As far as I was able to judge through a thick fog I passed on many spots which appeared to me raly beautiful and which seem to dispute with each other who command. In the most extensive prospect of the water the gradual rising of the ground from Carrollborough toward the Ferry Road, the level and extensive ground from there to the bank of the Potomack as far as Goose Creek present a situation most advantageous to run streets and prolong them on grand and far distant point of view the water running from spring at some distance into the creeks, appeared also to me possible to be conducted without much labour so as to form pounds for watering every part of that spot . . .

No proof of the ground between the eastern branch and Georgetown can be say to be of a commanding nature, on the contrary it appear to first sight as being itself surrounded, however in advancing toward the eastern branch these heights seem to sink as the waves of a tempestuous sea.

L'Enfant to Jefferson:

jeorgetown april the 4th. 1791

Sir.

. . . The number and nature of the publick building with the necessary appendix I should be glad to have a statement of as speedily as possible—and I would be very much obliged to you in the meantime if you could procure for me what Ever may fall within your reach—of any of the different grand city now existing such as for example—as London—madry—paris—Amsterdam—naples—venice—genoa—florence together with particular maps . . . For notwithstanding I would reprobate the Idea of Imitating and that contrary of Having this Intention it is my wish and shall be my Endeavor to delineate on a new and original way the plan the contrivance of which the President has left to me without any restriction soever—yet the contemplation of what exist of well improved situation, given the parrallel of these, with deffective ones, may serve to suggest a variety of new Ideas and is necessary to refine and strengthen the Judgement.

From L'Enfant's notes:

. . . there were the level ground on the water and all round were it decend but most particularly on that part terminating in a ridge to Jenkins Hill and running in a paralell with at half mile off from the river Potowmack separated by a low ground intersected with three grand streams—many of the most desirable

position offer for to Erect the Publique Edifices thereon—
from these height every grand building would rear with a
majestied aspect over the Country all around and might be
advantageously seen from twenty miles off which Contiguous
to the first setlement of the City they would there stand to ages
in a Central point to it, facing on the grandest prospect of both
branch of the Potowmack with the town of Alexandry in front
seen in its fullest extend over many points of land projecting
from the Mariland and Virginia shore in a manner as add much
to the perspective . . .

Thus in every respect advantageously situated, the Federal City
would soon grow of itself and spread as the branches of a tree
do . . .

After much menutial search for an elligible situation, prompted
I may say from a fear of being prejudiced in favour of a first
opinion I could discover no one so advantageously to greet the
congressional building as is that on the west end of Jenkins
heights which stand as a pedestal waiting for a monument, and
I am confidant, were all the wood cleared from the ground no
situation could stand in competition with this . . .

It is not the regular assemblage of houses laid out in square and
forming streets all parrallel and uniform that is so necessary for
such plan could only do on a well level plain and were no sur-
rounding object being interesting it become indifferent which
way the opening of street may be directed.
     but on any other ground a plan of this sort must be defective
and it never would answer for any of the spots proposed for the
Federal City, and on that held here as the most eligible it would
absolutely annihilate every advantage enumerated and the see-
ing of which will alone injure the success of the undertaking.
     such regular plan indeed however answerable as they may
appear upon paper or seducing as they may be on the first aspect
to the eyes of some people most even when applyed upon the
ground the best calculated to admit of it become at last tiresome

and insipide and it never could be in its orrigine but a mean continuance of some cool imagination wanting a sense of the real grand and truly beautifull only to be met with were nature contribut with art and diversify the objects.

having first determined some principal points to which I wished making the rest subordinate I next made the distribution regular with the streets at right angle *north-south* and *east west* but afterwards I opened others on various directions as avenues to and from every principal places, wishing by this not merely to contrast with the general regularity nor to afford a greater variety of pleasant seats and prospect as will be obtained from the advantageous ground over the which the avenues are mostly directed but principally to connect each part of the city with more efficacy by, if I may so express, making the real distance less from place to place in managing on them a resiprocity of sight.

[t]hose avenues which will afford a variety of pleasant rides, and become the means for a rapid intercourse with all parts of the city, to which they will serve as does the main artery in the animal body . . .

A fall which issuing from under the base of the Congress building may there form a cascade of forty feet heigh or more than one hundred wide which would produce the most happy effect in rolling down to fill up the canall and discharge itself in the Potowmack of which it would then appear as the main spring when seen through that grand and majestic avenue intersecting with the prospect from the palace . . .

. . . to procure to the palace and all other houses from that place to congress a prospect of the Potowmack the which will acquire new swiftness being laid over the green of a field well level and made brilliant by shade of few trees artfully planted.

L'Enfant prepared a map of his plan, but he refused to release it to the Commissioners, who wished to proceed with the sale of lots. L'Enfant feared that they only wanted to accommodate speculators and were not anxious to cooperate in establishing his plan. The Commissioners complained to Washington, who replied:

> It is much to be regretted, however common the case is, that men who possess talents which fit them for peculiar purposes should almost invariably be under the influence of an untoward disposition or are sottish idle, or possessed of some other disqualification by which they plague all those with whom they are concerned. But I did not expect to have met with such perverseness in Major L'Enfant as his late conduct exhibited . . .
>
> I have no other motive . . . than merely to shew that the feelings of such Men are always alive and where their assistance is essential; that it is policy to humor them or to put on the appearance of doing it.

But L'Enfant held onto the map for a while.

> In the fall of 1791, Mr. Daniel Carroll, prominent local citizen and a relative of one of the Commissioners, started to build a house across one of L'Enfant's surveying lines. L'Enfant warned him that, if the house were built, he would order it taken down. Construction continued.

L'Enfant to the Commissioners, November 21:

> Respecting the house of Mr. Carroll of Duddington . . . I directed yesterday forenoon a number of hands to the spot and employed with them some of the principal people who had worked in raising the house to the end that every possible attention be paid to the interests of the gentleman as shall be consistent in forwarding the public object.
>
> The roof is already down with part of the brickwork and the whole will I expect be leveled to the ground before the week is over.

Commissioners to Washington, November 25:

> We are sorry to be under the disagreeable necessity of men-
> tioning to you an occurance which must wound your feelings.
> On our meeting here today, we were to our great astonishment
> informed that, Maj^r. L'Enfant, without any Authority from us,
> & without even having submitted to our consideration, has
> proceeded to demolish, M^r. Carroll's house. M^r. Carroll who
> had received some letters from the Maj^r. on the subject, fearing
> the consequences obtained an injunction from the Chancellor,
> for him to desist; with a summons to Maj^r. L'Enfant to attend
> the Court of Chancery in December, to receive his decision
> on the subject, but before his return the house was in part
> demolished . . . Anticipating your feelings on this subject, and
> fully apprised of the Maj$^{r.s}$ fitness for the work he is employed
> in, we cannot forbear expressing a hope that the affair may be
> still so adjusted that we may not Lose his services.

Commissioners to L'Enfant, November 26:

> On our meeting this day were equally surprised and concerned
> to find that you had proceeded to demolish Mr. Carroll's house.
> We were impelled by many considerations to give immediate
> directions to those acting in your absence to desist . . . Our
> opinion ought to have been previously taken on a subject so del-
> icate and so interesting.

Washington wrote to Jefferson, November 30, requesting that he

> Judge from the complexion of things how far [L'Enfant] may be
> spoken to in decisive terms without losing his services; which,
> in my opinion would be a serious misfortune.—At the same
> time, *he must know,* there is a line beyond which he will not be
> suffered to go.

Jefferson to L'Enfant, December 1:

> I have received with sincere concern the information from yourself as well as others, that you proceeded to demolish the house of mͬr Carrol of Duddington, against his consent, and without authority from the Commissioners, or any other person. in this you have laid yourself open to the laws, & in a country where they will have their course, to their animadversion will belong the present case.—in future I must strictly enjoin you to touch no man's property, without his consent, or the previous order of the Commissioners. I wished you to be employed in the arrangements of the federal city. I still wish it: but only on condition that you can conduct yourself in subordination to the authority of the Commissioners, to the laws of the land, & to the rights of it's citizens.

L'Enfant appealed to the Commissioners:

> He erected that House on ground he knew was not his . . . and that it was questionable when he proceeded to build if the whole Spote he possessed himself of should not be thus appropriated.

Commissioners to Jefferson, December 8:

> As the house was nearly demolished before the Chancellors injunction arrived, Mr. Carroll did not think it worth while to have it served, trusting perhaps, that our directions expressly forbidding their further proceedings in it would have been attended to—We are sorry to mention that the Majr. who was absent at the time we issued them, paid no attention to them but completely demolished it on his return, this instance has given fresh alarm . . . The Majr. has indeed done us the honour of writing us a letter justifying his conduct—We have not noticed it.

From Jefferson's notes, December 11:

> I confess, that on a view of L'Enfant's proceedings and letters latterly, I am thoroughly persuaded that, to render him useful, his temper must be subdued.

Washington to L'Enfant, December 13:

> Sir: I have received your letter . . . and can only once more, and
> now for all, inform you that every matter and thing which has
> relation to the Federal district, and the City within it, is com-
> mitted to the Commissioners appointed . . .
>
> Were it necessary, I would again give it to you as my opinion
> that the Commissioners have every disposition that can be
> desired to listen to your suggestions, to adopt your plans, and to
> support your authority for carrying the latter into effect, as far
> as it shall appear reasonable, just and prudent to them, and
> consistent with the powers under which they act themselves.
> But having said this in more instances than one it is rather
> painful to reiterate it. With esteem and regard I am etc.

Washington to the Commissioners, December 18:

> His aim is obvious. It is to have as much scope as possible for
> the display of his talents, perhaps for his ambition . . . I submit
> to your consideration whether it might not be politic to give
> him pretty general, and ample powers for defined objects; until
> you shall discover in him a disposition to abuse them.
>
> His pride would be gratified, and his ambition excited by
> such a mark of your confidence. If for want of these, or from any
> other cause he should take amiss and leave the business, I have
> no scruple in declaring to you (though I do not want him to
> know it) that I know not where another is to be found, who
> could supply his place.

January 18, 1792, Washington to Jefferson:

> The conduct of Majr. L'Enfant and those employed under him,
> astonishes me beyond measure!

Jefferson to L'Enfant, February 22:

> I am charged by the President to say that your continuance would
> be desirable to him; & at the same time to add that the law
> requires it should be in subordination to the Commissioners.

L'Enfant's reply, February 26:

> My desire to conform to the judgement and wishes of the Pres-
> ident have really been ardent. and I trust my actions always have
> manifested those desires more uncontrovertable . . . to change a
> wilderness into a city, to erect and beautify buildings etc. to that
> degree of perfection necessary to receive the seat of Govern-
> ment of a vast empire . . . If there the law absolutely requires
> without any equivocation that my continuance shall depend
> upon an appointment from the Commissioners—I cannot nor
> would I upon any consideration submit myself to it.

Jefferson to L'Enfant, February 27:

> From your letter received yesterday in answer to my last . . . it is
> understood you absolutely decline acting under the authority of
> the present Commissioners, if this understanding of your
> meaning be right, I am instructed by the president to inform
> you that not withstanding the desire he has entertained to pre-
> serve your agency in the business, the condition upon which it
> is to be done is inadmissable & your services must be at an end.

Jefferson to Daniel Carroll, March 1:

> Much time has been spent in endeavoring to induce Major
> Lenfant to continue in the business he was engaged in, in
> proper subordination to the Commissioners. he has however
> entirely refused, so that he has been notified that we consider
> his services as at an end. the plan is put into the hands of an
> engraver, and will be engraved within three or four weeks.

The Georgetown proprietors, greatly upset, petitioned the Presi-
dent to reconsider. But Washington felt that he, not L'Enfant, had
been insulted: "No further overtures will ever be made to this
Gentn. by the Government."

L'Enfant's plans went into execution, without him.

Washington:

> The Plan of the City having met universal applause (as far as
> my information goes) and Major L'Enfant having become a
> very discontented man, it was thought that less than from 2500
> to 3000 dollars would not be proper to offer him for his ser-
> vices: instead of this, suppose five hundred guineas and a Lot in
> a good part of the City was to be substituted? I think it would
> be more pleasing, and less expensive.

The Commissioners officially offered l'Enfant $2,500, which he
refused, and remained silent for eight years.

> Washington: "Did Major L'Enfant assign any reason
> for his rejection of the compensation offered him?"

L'Enfant had started work on the Federal City without contract
or other financial agreement. When his plan was published,
he received nothing for it, having neglected to copyright it.
Starting in 1800, he presented memorials to Congress and the
Commissioners; the small sums they voted him were consumed
by creditors.

> To the Commissioners of the City of Washington
> PHILADELPHIA *August 30th* 1800
> A concurrence of disastrous events rendering my position so diffi-
> cult as to be no longer possible to withstand unless speedily relief
> be obtained by collecting what yet remains my due . . .

He wrote to Jefferson, 1801:

> The peculiarity of my position and the embarrassement
> ensuing from the conduct of the Board of the Commissionaires
> of the City of Washington in regard to requests and communi-
> cations made to them rendering the freedome of a direct
> address to you unavoidable—I hope the necessity will plead my
> excuse and seeing the time near approaches when
> it will be presumable you will wish to call Congress attention
> to the State of things relative to this new Seat of Government;

I now with great dependence on your goodness beg your consideration of the circumstances with me.

. . . I will no more than express—that I after many heavy pecuniary sacrifices occasioned by variety of Situations during the revolution war—I since the peace of 1783 was also differently Encouraged and Invited by many Commissions to the free spending of my own, dependent upon promises of regular reappointment with promotion all which ended to my loss and absolut ruin.—that on the particular Instance of my agency to the Enterprise of the City of Washington I have received no remuneration what ever, that—no kind of precon-vention were for the Service no price agree upon for plans, nor the Copy right conceded to the Commissionaires nor to any ones else, and that—extended as was my Concerns and agency beyond the usual to Architects; although by the grand Combination of new Schems I contributed eminently to the ensurance of the city establishment by which numbers of Individuals and the Country to an immense distance desire a increasing of their wealth I deed by no one opperations nor transactions worked on my own profit.

Acquainted Ser as you necessarily must have become with managements of the City affairs in which my free exertions were not the least usefull to the promotion of the national object—the merite, and that of orriginating of the plan you, doubtless, will readily allow to me and certain I am that—for all what I suffered, the only reproach to which I may be liable . . . is my having been more faithfull to a principle than ambition—too zealous in my pursuits—and too hazardous on a depen-dence on mouth friends.

L'Enfant presented to Congress a bill for his services in the amount of $95,000; this was rejected, and he finally accepted the $2,500 originally offered.

Destitute, he was rescued by a friendly planter, Dudley Digges, who took care of him at his country house, Green Hill, near Silver Spring, not far from Clean Drinking Manor.

L'Enfant died in 1825, leaving personal effects valued at $46.

———————

Nicholas King, surveyor of the City of Washington, to President Thomas Jefferson, September 25, 1803:

> Whether the malignant fever, to which the large towns situated on the navigable waters of the United States are frequently subjected, are of local origin or imported is not, as it relates to this city, a fact of so much importance as that generally conceded of its propogation and virulence, depending on the state of the atmosphere. That it is invariably and most alarming and destructive in those situations which become the receptacle of the filth of the city, whether brought by the rain along the streets, or discharged through the common sewers. It is in the vicinity of the water, where the docks, slips, and other artificial obstruction to the regular and free current or stream of the river, retain the accumulated filth between the wharves that the air is vitiated. The mud and faeces are there exposed to the putrifying heat of the mid-day sun, for even at high water there is no current to carry it off into the stream . . . . The dreadful consequences are now suffered, when a radical cure will be attended with enormous expense. Happy may it be for the future inhabitants of the city of Washington if it profit by the experience of others, and before it is too late, adopt a system of improving; the waters property, which . . . shall effectually remove the impurities brought into the river.

———————

Official Report of Major General Robert Ross, British Commander, August 1814:

> Judging it of consequence to complete the destruction of the public buildings with the least possible delay, so that the army might retire without loss of time, the following buildings were set fire to and consumed: the Capitol, including the Senate-House and the House of Representatives, the arsenal, the dockyard,

(navy-yard), treasury, war office, President's palace, rope-walk, and the great bridge across the Potomac . . . The object of the expedition being accomplished, I determined, before any greater force of the enemy could be assembled, to withdraw the troops, and accordingly commenced retiring on the night of the 25th.

Another British chronicler, Charles Ingersoll:

The army which we had overthrown the day before, though defeated, was far from annihilated; and having by this time recovered its panic, began to concentrate itself on our front, and presented quite as formidable an appearance as ever . . .

Whether or not it was their intention to attack, I cannot pretend to say, because . . . soon after, when something like a movement could be discerned in their ranks, the sky grew suddenly dark, and the most tremendous hurricane . . . came on. Of the prodigious force of the wind, it is impossible for you to form any conception. Roofs of houses were torn off by it, and whisked into the air like sheets of paper; while the rain which accompanied it, resembled the rushing of a mighty cataract, rather than the dropping of a shower. The darkness was as great as if the sun had long set, and the last remains of twilight had come on, occasionally relieved by flashes of vivid lightning streaming through it, which, together with the noise of the wind and the thunder, the crash of falling buildings, and the tearing of roofs as they were strips from the walls, produced the most appalling effect . . . This lasted for nearly two hours without intermission; during which time, many of the houses spared by us, were blown down, and thirty of our men, besides several of the inhabitants, buried beneath their ruins. Our column was as completely dispersed, as if it had received a total defeat. . .

By the time we reached the ground where yesterday's battles had been fought, the moon rose, and exhibited a spectacle by no means enlivening. The dead were still unburied, and lay about in every direction, completely naked. They had been stripped even of their shirts; and, having been exposed in this state to the violent rain in the morning, they appeared to be bleached to a most unnatural degree of whiteness. The heat and rain together had likewise affected them in a different manner, and the smell which arose upon the night air was horrible.

1860:

Drinking water continued to be taken from wells and springs. There were but two little sewers, whose contents most annoyingly backed up into the cellars and shops of Pennsylvania Avenue. Along the northern edge of the rubbish-strewn Mall ran an open ditch, an enlargement of Tiber Creek—"floating," says an eyewitness, "dead cats and all kinds of putridity and reeking with pestilential odors."

Teddy Roosevelt described his joy, when he was president, in going out on rough cross-country walks, "perhaps down Rock Creek, which was then as wild as a stream in the White Mountains."

(interdigitation)

Obedient to geology and climate are the varying plant and animal life of the Potomac, with a major boundary or, more properly, a zone of interdigitation, found in the area of Great Falls and the District of Columbia. In the heart of this area is Plummer's Island, known to the Indians as Winnemana or Beautiful Island, where Upland flora and fauna have been found to mingle with those of Tidewater, and several new species have been discovered.

TRANSPORTATION

1748, Thomas Cresap journeyed from his outpost settlement at Old Town, to Williamsburg: floating with the current in the upper river, avoiding rocks and shoals . . . portaging at Great Falls . . . then, spreading sail for the easy cruise in the estuary and bay.

> Many of the prominent men of the colony were at the time in the Assembly in session at Williamsburg. The intelligent Cresap had no difficulty in interesting them in his view of the political and economic situation over the mountains . . . A strong company was at once formed (1748) for trading with the Indians and establishing settlements in the western country. This was the organization of the Ohio Company.

> *Petition of John Hanbury to the King*
> *on behalf of the Ohio Company, 1748*
> . . . .
> THAT Your Petitioners beg leave humbly to inform Your Majesty that the Lands to the West of the said Mountains are extremely fertile the Climate very fine and healthy and the Water of Mississippi and those of Potomac are only separated by one small Ridge of Mountains easily passable by Land Carriage from thence to the West of the Mountains and to the Branch of the Ohio and the Lake Erie British Goods may be carried at little Expence and afforded reasonably to the Indians in those Parts.

The Ohio Company—John Hanbury, George Mason, three Washingtons, and others—pursued the fur trade to the West.

Beginning at Alexandria—then called Belhaven—goods were carried overland in wagons to the phantom town of Philae, above the Great Falls; thence by water to the mouth of Wills Creek, where a storehouse and fort were built. The fort came to be known as Fort Cumberland.

1752, Cresap was given the task of building a road from Wills Creek to the Monongahela. With an Indian, Nemacolin, he followed the path discovered a year earlier by Christopher Gist: over Wills, Savage and Meadow Mountains, into Little Meadows, over Briery Mountain and into the Great Meadows, thence over Laurel Hill via Red Stone Creek, to the Monongahela. The Road was laid out and marked.

March 1755, the greatest armada ever seen on the river—a British fleet bearing 1,300 soldiers under command of General Braddock —entered the estuary of the Potomac.

Extracts from
A Journal of the Proceedings of the Detachment of Seamen, ordered by Commodore Kepple, to Assist on the late Expedition to the *Ohio* . . .

April 10th: Orders were given to March to Morrow with 6 Companies of Sr P. Halket's Regiment for *Winchester* towards *Will's Creeks;* April 11th: Yesterdays Orders were Countermanded and others given to furnish Eight days Provisions, to proceed to *Rock's Creek* (8 Miles from Alexandria) in the Sea Horse & Nightingale Boats; April 12th: Arrived at *Rock's Creek* 5 miles from the lower falls of *Potomack* & 4 Miles from the Eastern branch of it; where we encamped with Colonel Dunbars Regiment.

April 13th: Employed in loading Waggon's with Stores Provisions and all other conveniences very near *Rock's Creek* a very pleasand Situation.

April 14th: Detachment of Seamen were order'd to March in the Front: arrived at Mr Lawrence Owen's: 15 Miles from *Rock's Creek;* and encamp'd upon good Ground 8 Miles from the Upper falls of *Potomack.*

April 15th: Encamp't on the side of a Hill near Mr Michael Dowden's; 15 Miles from Mr Owen's, in very bad Ground and in 1½ foot Snow.

April 16th: Halted, but found it extremely difficult to get either Provisions or Forrage.

April 17th: March'd to *Fredericks Town;* 15 Miles from Dowden's, the road very Mountainous, March'd 11 Miles, when we came to a River call'd *Monskiso,* which emptied itself into the *Potomack;* it runs very rapid; and is, after hard Rain, 13 feet deep: We ferried over in a Float for that purpose. This Town has not been settled Above 7. Years; there are 200 Houses & 2 Churches 1 Dutch, 1 English; the inhabitants chiefly Dutch, Industrious, but imposing People; Provisions & Forrage in Plenty.

April 18th: Encamp'd with a New York Company under the Command of Captain Gates, at the North End of the Town, upon very good Ground.

April 19th: Exercising Recruits, & airing the Tents: several Waggons arrived with Ordnance Stores, heavy Dews at Night occasion it to be very unwholsome.

April 20th: Nothing Material happen'd.

April 21th: The General attended by Captains Orme, Morris and Secretary Shirley; with Sr John St Clair; arrived at Head Quarters.

April 24th

April 25th: Ordnance Stores Arrived, with 80 Recruits for the 2 Regiments.

April 27th: Employ'd in preparing Harnefs for the Horses

April 29th: March'd to Mr Walker's 18 Miles from Fredericks Town; pafs'd the South Ridge, commonly called the Blue Ridge, or *Shanandoh Mountains* Very easy Ascent and a fine Prospect . . . no kind of Refreshment.

April 30th: March'd to *Connecochiag;* 16 Miles from Mr Walker's Close by the *Potomack,* a very fine Situation, where we found all the Artillery Stores preparing to go by Water to Wills Creek.

May 1st: Employed in ferrying (over the *Potomack)* the Army Baggage into Virginia in 2 Floats and 5 Batteaux; The Army March'd to Mr John Evans, 16 Miles from ye *Potomack* and 20 Miles from Winchester, where we Encamp'd, and had tolerable good living with Forrage; the roads begin to be very indifferent.

May 2nd: Halted and sent the Horses to Grafs.

May 3rd: March'd to Widdow Barringers 18 Miles from Mr Evans; the day was so excessive hot, that many Officers and Men could not Arrive at their Ground until Evening this is 5 Miles from Winchester and a fine Situation.

May 4th: March'd to Mr Pots 9 Miles from the Widdow's where we were refresh^t with Vinison and wild Turkeys the Roads excessive bad.

May 5th: March'd to M^r. Henry Enocks, a place called the *forks of Cape Capon,* 16 Miles from M^r. Pots; over prodigious Mountains, and between the Same we crofs'd a Run of Water in 3 Miles distance, 20 times after marching 15 Miles we came to a River called *Kahepatin* where the Army ferried over, We found a Company of Sr Peter Halkets Regiment waiting to escort the Train of Artillery to *Wills Creek.*

May 6th: Halted, as was the Custom to do every third day, The Officers for pafsing away the time, made Horse Races and agreed that no Horse should Run over 11 Hands and to carry 14 stone.

May 7th: March'd to Mr Cox's by the side of y^e *Potomack* 12 miles from Mr Enock's, and Encamped we cross'd another run of Water 19 Times in 2 Miles. Roads bad.

May 8th: Ferried over the River into *Maryland;* and March'd to M^r. Jacksons, 8 Miles from M^r. Cox's where we found a Maryland Company encamp'd in a fine Situation on the Banks of the *Potomack;* with clear'd ground about it; there lives Colonel Crefsop, a Rattle Snake Colonel, and a D-d Rascal; calls himself a Frontiersman, being nearest the *Ohio;* he had a Summons some time since from the French to retire from his Settlement, which they claim'd as their property, but he refused it like a man of Spirit; This place is the Track of Indian Warriours, when going to War, either to the N^{o}ward, or S^{o}ward He hath built a little Fort round his House, and is resolved to keep his Ground. We got plenty of Provisions &c. The General arrived with Captains Orme and Morris, with Secretary Shirley and a Company of light Horse for his Guard, under the command of Capt Stewart, the General lay at the Colonels.

May 9th: Halted and made another Race to amuse the General.

D^o. 10th: March'd to *Will's Creek;* and Encamp'd on a Hill to the E^tward of the Fort, when the General past the Troops; Colonel Dunbar informed them, that there were a number of Indians at *Wills Creek,* that were Friends to English therefore it was the Generals positive Orders, that they should not be Molested upon any account, upon the Generals Arrival at the Fort, He was Saluted with 17. Guns, and we found 100 Indian Men, Women & Children with 6 Companies of Sr Peter Halketts Regiment, 9 Virginian Companies and a Maryland Company.

May 11th: *Fort Cumberland,* is situated within 200 Yards of *Wills Creek* on a Hill 400 Yards from the *Potomack,* it's greatest length from East to West is 200 Yards, and breadth 40 it is built with Loggs drove into the Ground; and 12 feet above it Embrazures are cut for 12 Guns which are 4. Pounders, though 10 are only Mounted with Loopholes for small Arms; The Indians were greatly surprised at the regular way of our Soldiers Marching and our Numbers.

General Braddock, Fort Cumberland, June 5, 1775:

On the 10th of May I arriv'd at this place, and on the 17th the train join'd me from Alexandria after a March of twenty seven days, having met with many more Delays and Difficulties than I had even apprehended, from the Badness of the Roads, Scarcity of Forage, and a general Want of Spirit in the people to forward the Expedition.

I have at last collected the whole Force with which I propose to march to the Attack of Fort Duquesne, amounting to about two thousand effective Men, eleven hundred of which Number are Americans of the southern provinces, whose slothful and languid Disposition renders them very unfit for Military Service. I have employ'd the properest officers to form and discipline them and great pains has and shall be taken to make them as useful as possible . . .

It would be endless, Sir, to particularize the numberless Instances of the Want of public and private Faith, and of the most absolute Disregard of all Truth, which I have met with in carrying on of His Majesty's Service on this continent.

The Journal again: "June 10th: the last Division of His Majesty's Forces March'd from *Wills Creek* with General Braddock."

Cutting the road as they went, through a "wooden country," the army stretched out to a length of four miles: over Will's Mountain, up Braddock's Run to the forks, into the valley of George's Creek, over Savage Mountain, through dense white pine forests, near the tract known as Shades of Death, to the Little Meadows . . . marching in regular formation, to the Monongahela.

———

Buffalo trace.
          Indian trail.
                    Nemacolin's path . . .
    Braddock's Road,
              The National Road . . .

An act of Congress, April 30, 1802, enabled the people of Ohio to form a state government.

That one-twentieth of the net proceeds of the lands lying within said State sold by Congress shall be applied to the laying out and making public roads leading from the navigable waters emptying into the Atlantic, to the Ohio, to the the said state, and through the same, such roads to be laid out under the authority of Congress with the consent of the several states through which the roads shall pass.

AN ACT TO REGULATE THE LAYING OUT AND MAKING A ROAD FROM CUMBERLAND, IN THE STATE OF MARYLAND, TO THE STATE OF OHIO

SECTION I. *Be it enacted by the Senate and House of Representatives of the United States of America in Congress assembled,* That the President of the United States be, and he is hereby authorized to appoint, by and with the advice and consent of the Senate, three discreet and disinterested citizens of the United States, to lay out a road from Cumberland . . . in the state of

Maryland . . . to the state of Ohio; whose duty it shall be . . . to repair to Cumberland aforesaid, and view the ground, from the points on the river Potomac . . . to the river Ohio; and to lay out in such direction as they shall judge, under all circumstances the most proper, a road from thence to the river Ohio . . .

SEC. 2 And be it further enacted, That the aforesaid road shall be laid out four rods in width, and designated on each side by a plain and distinguishable mark on a tree, or by the erection of a stake or monument sufficiently conspicuous, in every quarter of a mile of the distance at least . . .

SEC. 3 And be it further enacted, That the commissioners shall as soon as may be, after they have laid out the road, as aforesaid, present to the President an accurate plan of the same, with its several courses and distances, accompanied by a written report . . .

SEC. 4 And be it further enacted, That all parts of the road which the President shall direct to be made, in case the trees are standing, shall be cleared the whole width of four rods; and the road shall be raised in the middle of the carriage-way with stone, earth, or gravel or sand . . .

SEC. 5 And be it further enacted, That said commissioners shall receive four dollars per day, while employed as aforesaid, in full compensation . . .

SEC. 6 And be it further enacted, That the sum of thirty thousand dollars be, and the same is hereby appropriated, to defray the expenses of laying out and making said road . . .

Approved March 2, 1806.

TH. JEFFERSON.

The commissioners, December 30, 1806,

beg leave to report to the President of the United states, and to premise that the duties imposed by the law became a work of greater magnitude, and a task much more arduous, than was conceived before entering upon it . . .

The face of the country within the limits prescribed is generally very uneven, and in many places broken by a succession of high mountains and deep hollows, too formidable to be reduced within five degrees of the horizon, but by crossing them obliquely, a mode which, although it imposes a heavy task of hill-side digging, obviates generally the necessity of reducing hills and filling hollows, which, on these grounds, would be an attempt truly quixotic.

The road was finally built, Cumberland to Wheeling, at an average cost of $13,000 per mile.

Wagoners and stage drivers, regulars and sharpshooters, Indians, pony express and mail robbers, all navigated the pike . . . Henry Puffenberger and Jacob Breakiron were wagoners, David Bonebreaker drove a stage, Dumb Ike and Crazy Billy were pike characters.

Taverns were built: the Black Tavern, Thistle Tavern, Temple of Juno, selling "strong waters to relieve the inhabitants," and stogies, four for a penny. Teamsters ate, drank, smoked, danced, bragged and fought . . . slept on the floor, feet to fireplace.

A wagoner recalled,

> I have stayed over night with William Sheets, on Nigger Mountain, when there would be thirty six-horse teams on the wagon yard, one hundred Kentucky mules in an adjacent lot, one thousand hogs in other enclosures, and as many fat cattle from Illinois in adjoining fields. The music made by this large number of hogs, in eating corn on a frosty night, I will never forget.

Geo. Washington, May 4, 1772:

> An Act has passed this session empowering Trustees (to be chosen by ye Subscribers to the Scheme) to raise money by way of Subscription, & Lottery, for the purpose of opening, and

extending the Navigation of Potomack from the Tide Water, to Fort Cumberland.

1784

September

Having found it indispensably necessary to visit my Landed property West of the Apalachean Mountains . . . and having made the necessary preparations for it, I did, on the first day of this Month (September) set out on my journey.

3d. Colo. Warner Washington, Mr. Wormeley, Gen'l Morgan, Mr. Trickett, and many other Gentlemen came here to see me—and one object of my journey being to obtain information of the nearest and best communication between the Eastern and Western Waters; and to facilitate as much as in me lay the inland Navigation of the Potomac; I conversed a good deal with Gen'l Morgan on this subject . . .

10th . . . After leaving the Waters of Wills Creek which extends up the Mountain (Alligany) two or three Miles as the Road goes, we fell next on those of George's Creek, which are small—after them, upon Savage River which are considerable: tho' from the present appearance of them, does not seem capable of Navigation.

26th . . . I could obtain no good acct. of the Navigation of the No. Branch between McCulloch's crossing and Will's Creek (or Fort Cumberland) indeed there were scarce any persons of whom enqueries could be made . . . but in general I could gather . . . that there is no fall in it—that from Fort Cumberland to the Mouth of Savage River the water being good is frequently made use of in its present State with Canoes—and from thence upwards, is only rapid in places with loose Rocks which can readily be removed.

October

4th. The more then the Navigation of Potomack is investigated, duly considered, the greater the advantages . . . appear.

. . . These two alone (that is the South Branch and Shannondoah) would afford water transportation for all that fertile

Country between the Bleu Ridge and the Alligany Mountains; which is immense . . .

Let us open a good communication with the Settlements west of us—extend the inland Navigation as far as it can be done with convenience—and shew them by this means, how easy it is to bring the produce of their Lands to our Markets, and see how astonishingly our exports will be increased . . .

Having gone so far, I will hazard another idea in proof of my opinion of this navigation . . . It is, that the Navigation from the Great Falls and through the Shenandoah falls, will not be opened *five* years before that of the latter River will be improved *at least* 150 miles; and the whole produce of that rich and extensive vale between the Blue ridge and the Alligany Mountains be brought through *it*, and the *South Branch*, as far South Westerly as Staunton into the Potomack; and thence by the Great falls to the place or places of Exportation. Add this to what will be drawn from the upper part of Maryland, and parts of Pensylvania (which at present go to Baltimore by an expensive land transportation) and then annex thereto the idea of what may come (under a wise policy) from the Western waters, and it opens a field almost too extensive for imagination . . .

Let the benefits arising from water transportation, be once felt . . . everything within its vortex . . . will be sucked into, and be transported by water.

Washington to the Marquis de Lafayette:

As the clouds which overspread your hemisphere are dispersing, and peace with all its concomitants is drawing upon your Land, I will banish the sound of War from my letter: I wish to see the sons and daughters of the world in Peace and busily employed in the more agreable amusement of fulfilling the first and great commandment, *Increase and Multiply:* as an encouragement to which we have opened the fertile plains of the Ohio to the poor, the needy and the oppressed of the Earth; any one therefore who is heavy laden, or who wants land to cultivate, may repair thither and abound, as in the Land of promise, with milk and honey: the ways are preparing, and the roads will be made easy thro' the channels of Potomac.

From a notice in the *Virginia Gazette*, December 4, 1784:

At a numerous and respectable meeting held the 12th of last month at Alexandria by gentlemen of this state and Maryland to deliberate and consult on the vast great political and commercial object, the rendering navigable the Potomack River from tide water, it was unanimously resolved that every possible effort ought to be exerted to render those waters navigable to their utmost sources . . . This is perhaps a work of more political than commercial consequence as it will be one of the grandest chains for preserving Federal Union. The western world will have free access to us and we shall be one and the same people.

May 17th, 1785, in Alexandria, the Patowmack Company was formally organized, with George Washington president. Original plans called for opening the river from Tidewater to Fort Cumberland, so that a minimum of fifty barrels of flour could move downstream in even the driest season. Boulders in the stream bed were to be blasted at Seneca and Shenandoah Falls, and a canal built at Great Falls. Washington felt that locks would not be needed, even at Great Falls:

The Water through these Falls is of sufficient depth for good navigation; and as formidable as I had conceived them to be; but by no means impractible. The principal difficulties lye in rocks which occasion a crooked passage. These once removed, renders the passage safe without the aid of Locks.

Later, it was found necessary to build canals at five falls—House's, Shenandoah, Seneca, Little, and Great—with locks at the latter two.

Washington looked for a man to superintend operations: a man "who knows best how to conduct water upon a level, or who can carry it thro' hills or over Mountains, that would be most useful to us."

The name of James Rumsey came to his attention:

> As I have imbibed a very favorable opinion of your mechanical abilities, and have had no reason to distrust your fitness in other respects; I took the liberty of mentioning your name to the Directors, and I dare say if you are disposed to offer your services, they would be attended to under favorable circumstances.

James Rumsey: inventor, before Fulton, of the steamboat. 1784, armed with a testimonial from Washington, he secured from the Virginia legislature an exclusive right to build and navigate boats on Virginia waters, for the next ten years. December 1787, at Steamboat Bend on the Potomac, above Shepherdstown, he fired up the boiler and his first steamer chugged upstream, attaining speeds of three miles an hour. A week later, the pipes froze and burst, but he stuffed them with rags, and got her up to four miles an hour.

Meanwhile, he agreed to take over management of the Patowmack Company.

Washington:

> We expect to begin our operations on the Patowmack Navigation about the 6th of next Month, under the Management of a Mr. James Rumsey. If the Miners therefore, who have been accustomed to the blowing of Rocks under Water, are desirous of employment in this way, I am persuaded he would hire them, were they to apply to him, either at the Seneca falls, or the Falls of Shannondoah.

To Geo. Wm. Fairfax:

> We have commenced our operations on the navigation of this river; and I am happy to inform you, that the difficulties rather vanish than increase as we proceed.

Three classes of labor were secured: hired whites, indentured whites, and Negro slaves—none of whom got along with one another.

Washington:

> We are endeavoring to engage our miners to bore by the foot; rather than by the day; but as yet have not agreed with any in this way; they ask a shilling, which we think is too much to common labourers we pay 40/ per month; and we find paying the workmen every fortnight rather troublesome once a month would do better: as they will be frequently moving, we have provided Tents as most convenient and least expensive, for their accommodation.

For daily rations, laborers received one pound salt pork, or one and a quarter pounds salt beef, or one and a half pounds fresh beef or mutton, one and a half pounds flour or bread, three gills of rum.

The Irish day laborers tended to run away. As for the others—from the *Maryland Chronicle*, February 22, 1786:

> We hear that several servants who had been purchased to work on the Potowmack Navigation lately ran away, but being soon after apprehended, were sentenced to have their heads & eyebrows shaved, which operation was immediately executed.

Rumsey reported to Mr. Hartshorne, company treasurer:

> Great Falls potowmack July 3d 1786. Sir We have Been much Imposed upon the last Two weeks in the powder way (we had two Blowers, One Run off the other Blown up) we therefore was Obliged to have two new hands put to Blowing and there was much attention gave to them least Axedents should happen yet they used the powder Rather too Extravagent, But that was not all they have certainly stolen a Considerable Quantity as we have not more by us than will last until tomorrow noon. Our hole troop is Such Villians.

At Little Falls, the lock pits were dug, and hasty and impermanent wooden locks erected. At Great Falls, Washington insisted that the canal be cut on the Virginia side.

> After an early breakfast at Mr. Fairfax's Gov'r. Johnson and I set out for the Falls (accompanied by Mr. Fairfax) where we met the other Directors and Colo. Gilpin in the operation of levelling the ground for the proposed cut or Canal from the place where it is proposed to take the Water out, to the other where it will be let into the River again. In the highest of which, and for near 70 Rod, it is between five or seven feet higher than the Surface of the Water at the head. After which it descends, and for at least 300 yards at the lower end, rapidly. This cut, upon the whole, does not appear to be attended with more difficulty than was apprehended.

But the cut proved to be through solid rock . . .

> At the Great falls the labour has indeed been great; the water there is taken into a canal about 200 yards above the Cataract and conveyed by a level cut (thro' a solid rock in some places and very stoney ground in others) more than a mile to the lock seats; five in number, by means of which the Craft when these locks are compleated will be let into the River below the fall (which in all is 76 feet).

Five locks were eventually constructed at Great Falls—

> Blown out of the solid rock, the natural rock worked tolerably smooth forming the sides, some mason work being used where the fixtures are inserted for supporting the gates, the sluice gates in these locks as in several of the others that are deep, do not lift but are made of cast iron and turn on a pivot fixed in the center, so that when the sluice is open this little gate or stopper is turned edgewise to the stream, they work very easy and are managed in deep locks much more readily than those of the ordinary construction.

Some of the hewn blocks, of Triassic sandstone, were ferried across the river from Seneca, and into each block the stonecutter carved his trademark: roman numerals, or an indecipherable glyph.

From the president's report, 1801:

> It must appear evident that without some unforeseen accident the great object held out in our last report, that of a free navigation of the Potomac during a considerable portion of the year from the mouth of George's Creek to tide water will be accomplished by the end of the year in time for the ensuing spring water.

The trustees laid out a town at Great Falls to be called Matildaville, with forge, sawmill, grist mill, superintendent's house, etc. (laid out, but never built).

In February 1802, the locks were opened for business.

Attention turned now to improving the riverbed upstream, and on the Shenandoah:

Washington:

> At the foot of these falls the Directors and myself (Govr. Lee having joined us the Evening before) held a meeting. At which it was determined, as we conceived the Navigation could be made through these (commonly called the Shannondoah) Falls without the aid of Locks, and by opening them would give eclat to the undertaking and great ease to the upper Inhabitants . . .
> The Shannondoah will intercept every article 200 miles from its mouth, and water bear it to the Markets.

Channels in the Potomac were to be improved by banking with saplings and brush loaded with stone.

With locks and channels open, farmers moved their crops to market. Water craft were mostly floats or rafts, designed according to the harvest and the size of the locks. On delivery of the cargo at Georgetown, they were broken up and sold for firewood. A few permanent boats were built, seventy feet by ten feet, covered with tarpaulins over hoops, and manned by crews of four. Two gallons of whiskey, four tin cups, thirty pounds of bacon, and twenty feet of rope were standard supplies for a trip from Cumberland to Georgetown. After unloading, the boats were roped and poled back upstream, against the current.

Principal downstream cargoes were flour, whiskey, iron, and tobacco, and trade goods went out from Georgetown, via the Potomac, to points on Lake Erie, the Missouri River and the Gulf of Mexico.

Difficulties for the Potomac Company, however, were endless. Subscribers failed to pay up, revenues were low and loans difficult to secure, the river channels were inconstant, temporary wooden locks had to be replaced with stone and masonry—and there was always either too much or too little water: at times the forty-foot rock at Great Falls was covered, in flood—while at others a flat-boat could scarcely be floated in the channel approaching it.

In 1799, Washington died.

From the report of a Virginia state commission, July 1822:

> ... that the affairs of the Potomac Company have failed to comply with the terms and conditions of the charter; that there was no reasonable ground to expect that they would be able to effect the objects of their incorporation; that they have not only expended their capital stock and the tolls received, with the exception of a small dividend of five dollars and fifty cents on each share declared in 1802, but had incurred a heavy debt which their resources would never enable them to discharge; that the floods and freshets nevertheless gave the only navigation that was enjoyed; that the whole time when produce and goods could be stream bourne on the Potomac in the course of an entire year, did not exceed forty-five days; that it would be imprudent and inexpedient to give further aid to the Potomac Company.

A report by Thomas Moore, Virginia engineer, August 1820:

> But when the powers of art have been exerted to the utmost
> extent to procure an easy navigation in the bed of a stream, still it
> must hold a very inferior grade to that of an independent canal,
> because the natural fall of the river must be overcome by the labor
> of men, and . . . in proportion to the length must be very expen-
> sive compared with a canal furnished with locks, where the
> loaded boats are drawn on level water, by the labor of horses.

Virginia Board of Public Works, to the legislature, 1823:

> The estimates of the probable cost necessary for constructing
> an independent canal along the valley of the Potomac river from
> Cumberland to tide water—185 miles.
>   Total with contingencies $2,000,000

Resolution passed by a convention meeting in Washington,
November 6, 1823:

> Whereas, a connection of the Atlantic and Western waters, by a
> canal, leading from the seat of the general government to the
> river Ohio, regarded as a local object, is one of the highest
> importance to the states immediately interested therein, and,
> considered in a national view, is of inestimable consequence to
> the future union, security, and happiness of the United States:
>   *Resolved, unanimously,* That it is expedient to substitute,
> for the present defective navigation of the Potomac river above
> tide water, a navigable canal, by Cumberland to the mouth of
> Savage Creek, at the eastern base of the Alleghany and to
> extend such canal.

Although constructed, finally, only to Cumberland, the canal was
surveyed through to Pittsburgh, via Wills Creek, Casselman's River,
and the Youghiogheny.

1828, the remaining property of the Potomac Company was
conveyed to the Chesapeake and Ohio Canal Company.

That summer, President John Quincy Adams took part in ground-breaking ceremonies for the canal: "To subdue the earth is preeminently the purpose of the undertaking."

> On the same day—July 4—work was started on the Baltimore and Ohio Railroad . . .

Workmen were hard to find, particularly skilled stonemasons, for construction of the locks. The company advertised in Dublin, Cork, and Belfast, offering "meat three times a day, a reasonable amount of liquor and $8, $10, $12 a week." Beginning in 1829, the Irish laborers poured in, went to work with trowel, ax, chisel, and hammer; horse, cart, scraper, wheelbarrow, drill, and gunpowder . . .

Every summer, the sickly season arrived, the workers associated their aches and fevers with the low waters, the murky, malodorous riverbed.

August 1832, Asiatic cholera appeared, and was soon general from Harper's Ferry, down to Point of Rocks.

> If the Board but imagine the panic produced by a man's turning black and dying in twenty four hours in the very room where his comrades are to sleep or to dine they will readily conceive the utility of separating the sick, dying and dead from the living.

> Before this letter reaches Washington, the whole line of canal from the point of rocks to WmsPort will be abandoned by the Contractors and Laborers—The Cholera has appeared amongst them, and has proved fatal in almost every case. There has been upwards of 30 deaths nearly opposite to us since friday last, and the poor Exiles of Erin are flying in every direction . . . It is candidly my opinion, that by the last of this week you will not have a working man on the whole line.

> They have since been suffering great mortality west of Harper's Ferry, & I fear the work is by this time suspended. The poor

creatures, after seeing a few sudden & awful deaths amongst their friends, straggled off in all directions through the country; but for very many of them the panic came too late. They are dying in all parts of Washington County at the distance of 5 to 15 miles from the river. I myself saw numbers of them in carts & on foot making their way towards Pennsylvania.

Following the cholera came warfare between rival factions:

January 1834, there was a preliminary skirmish between Corkonians from above Williamsport, and the Longfords, or Fardowners, from below the town. Several were killed before militia arrived. Local citizens patrolled the Conococheague aqueduct, while both sides collected weapons, and the countryside took on the appearance of an armed camp. January 24, the Longfords marched in force, 300 strong, armed with guns, clubs, and helves. Crossing the aqueduct, they met 300 Corkonians on a hilltop, near Dam No. 5, and there was a pitched battle, with several casualties. Two companies of U.S. troops finally arrived from Fort McHenry . . .

New Year's Day, 1838, a number of Irish raided their rivals at Old-town, and Nicholas Ryan's tavern was nearly demolished. The men were pursued by a sheriff's posse, but all escaped . . .

———————

When finally completed in 1850, the Chesapeake and Ohio Canal was 184 1/2 miles long, from Rock Creek in the District of Columbia to Wills Creek at Cumberland, Maryland. There were seven rubble or masonry dams in the bed of the river, eleven stone aqueducts over the northern tributaries, seventy-five stone or composition locks with a lift averaging eight feet, many score culverts to carry the smaller streams under the trunk, a quarter-mile long tunnel, and a towpath twelve feet wide, on the river side of the canal. The water-way itself was six to eight feet deep, and fifty to eighty feet wide. Total descent was 578 feet.

Final cost—estimated originally at $2,000,000—came to over $11,000,000.

Service was imperfect, especially during the early years: employees and boatmen were green; construction sometimes proved shoddy; there was too much water—or too little water; and there were leaks—with or without the help of muskrats. Obstructions included fallen rocks, sunken wrecks, loose boats, dead animals . . .

Banks of the canal were built to withstand the worst possible floods, that of 1847 having been the highest in sixty years. But in 1852, the water rose six feet higher, reaching sixty-four feet at Great Falls. Damage was extensive.

1857, a great ice freshet, followed by successive spring floods, flowed down the valley, ripping holes in the dams.

1861-64, Confederates under Lee, Early, Mosby, and White burned boats, stole mules, and sabotaged banks, dams, and locks.

November 1877, came the worst flood in 150 years, the water at Great Falls rose to seventy feet above low-water. Walls, towpath, and even the masonry dams were breached, tools, stores, and cargoes were lost.

> All the floods were the result of rapid deforestation and deep plowing in the Potomac watershed . . .

May 30, 1889, a "cyclone" entered the valley near Martinsburg, crossed the river above Williamsport, and was followed by torrential rains. The river rose, kept on rising, to points in excess of the flood of '77. The junction of Potomac and Conococheague became a lake. At Sandy Hook, opposite Harper's Ferry, water reached a point eight feet higher than the railroad tracks, which were, in turn, seventeen feet above the canal. Frame buildings, roped to trees, broke loose; cargoes, boats, and drowned teams were strewn crazily down the valley . . .

> One of the peculiarities of the freshet of 1889 is that the stonework of the walls, &c., is more generally involved than on any previous occasion of the kind. The telephone wires have

been swept away . . . and every bridge for which the canal company is responsible is down.

Damage was estimated at close to a million dollars. The canal was repaired . . .

    . . . but the flood of '89 marked the beginning of the end.

Regulations
For Navigating the
Chesapeake and Ohio Canal.

1st. Every Boat or Float, navigating the Canal after the 15th day of August next, shall be propelled by a towing line drawn by men or horses, and shall be moreover furnished with strapping or snubbing lines for passing through the locks of the Canal without injury to the same . . .

3d. No Boat or Float shall forcibly strike, or violently rub against any other boat, or against the banks, locks, aqueducts, inside walls, or wastes, or bridges of the Canal.

8th. No Carcaſs, or dead animal, or putrid substance of any kind, shall be thrown into the Canal, or into any basin or feeder connected therewith . . .

11th. No raft or tow of timber paſſing on the Canal, shall consist of more than eight cribs, and when consisting of more than one, they shall be so united, as to conform readily to the curvatures of the Canal banks, and to glide by the same without rubbing against them . . .

15th. . . . As soon as she has opened a passage for the other, so as that the tow-line may sink to the bottom of the Canal, the boat entitled to paſs shall float over the tow-line.

16th. No Boat or Float, unless specially licensed to travel with greater speed, shall move on the Canal . . . with a velocity exceeding four miles an hour.

Boats carrying U.S. mail had the right-of-way over passenger packets, the latter over freight, and all boats over rafts. Boats descending prevailed over boats ascending. Right-of-way was yielded by turning to the berm side, away from the towpath, and slowing to a halt.

Most of the boats came from boatyards along the basin at the head of the canal. They were built of oak and white pine, fine two- and three-inch planks, sixty and seventy-five feet long, cut in the Cumberland hills. Generally, they were ninety-seven by fourteen feet, with five-foot draught, dimensions fixed by the size of the lock chambers. The flat bottoms, curved at bow and stern, were tarred; above the water line the boats were painted white, with green trim. Capacity was 125 tons. There was a stable for the mules at the bow, a hayhouse amidships, and a cabin at the stern.

Steamboats were introduced, but they were costly, burning too much coal in proportion to cargo capacity. Mules, slower but cheaper, were finally used universally. They were broken by hitching them to logs. If a green mule tended to sit down, he was hitched to a couple of trained mules and dragged along, until he found it more comfortable to stand.

> At Point of Rocks, where the Catoctins edge into the river, the Canal and the Railroad had contested for years for a narrow strip of ledge, forty feet wide. The courts finally herded them both through, but required the railroad to build a solid fence, to shield the mules from the steam engines.

An average trip, Cumberland to Georgetown, loaded with coal, took five days. Coming back light, you could make it in three days, sixty to seventy miles a day.

The halfway stake was nailed to a big elm on the four-mile level above Big Slack Water. There was a haunted house on the lower nine-mile level . . .

A lock-keeper, on duty day and night, received his house, an acre for a garden, and $150 a year. Married men with large families were preferred: more hands to do the work. Many supplemented their income selling liquor to the boatmen.

. . . Unless the boatmen were shipping whiskey, in which case they could always tap one barrel for a gallon, and refill with water.

Boatmen were a special breed, living on their boats, wintering in settlements away from towns, marrying from among themselves, so that children grew up knowing no other life . . . It was a family affair: Mrs. Wes Lizer was known up and down the water for her apple dumplings, while Scat Eaton's wife made the best pie, from blackberries picked along the towpath.

Piney Wine, Dent Shupp, Daze Wolf, Rufus Stride, Oth Grove, Rome Mose, John Keysucker and Charlie Shawt, all boated the canal.

And there was Johnny Howard, who got into a fight with his captain and killed him. He was hanged in the Cumberland jail yard, March 17, 1876. A song was written about him; Annie Stride "used to play it on the piano and sing it until people cried. It was so sad. Annie boated, too. She could steer better than Ben could."

Off hours in Cumberland, a boatman headed for Shantytown, for drinkin' and fightin', at Old Aunt Susan Jones's Rising Sun Saloon.

———————

In the Paw Paw Bends, the canal tunneled through the knobby spur of a 2,000-foot mountain. The tunnel was brick lined; wrought-iron posts with chestnut stringers edged the towpath. From a rocky ledge above the towpath, just outside the tunnel, the boats took on drinking water from the finest cold spring.

Negro hands refused to boat through the tunnel, clambering instead over the mountain: they believed the tunnel haunted by a headless man.

Once two boats entered the tunnel at the same time from opposite ends: meeting in the middle, both refused to yield, and they stayed there for days, blocking traffic—until finally the company built a fire in the middle and smoked them out.

1923: The water was let out of the ditch at the end of the boating season.

Many of the locktenders and locktenders' widows stayed on, beside locks ruined by flood and neglect . . . Tom Moore at Mountain Lock, Mrs. Lucy Zimmerman at No. 39, Lewis Cross at Catoctin, and Emma Fulton at Point of Rocks.

Washington's Birthday, 1939, the c&o Canal, comprising 5,250 acres, was dedicated as a public park. A 38-year-old mule named Mutt took part in the ceremonies. The canal was partly restored, but subsequently there were floods . . .

(climate and flow—land use)

*Average annual temperature for the entire Potomac basin is 54°
Fahrenheit, with recorded extremes of 30° below zero and 112° above.
Mean precipitation is 38 inches a year, and snowfall varies from 5
inches on the Coastal Plain to 30 inches on the Allegheny Plateau. The
river is divided into two distinct areas of climate, with separate sources
of storm systems. The Blue Ridge serves as a border: eastward, the
major storms have been associated with the movement northward and
northeastward of low pressure areas, including the West Indian hurri-
canes; whereas west of the Ridge major storms are generally of the
frontal type, producing precipitation of long duration, low intensity,
and even distribution.*

*With such variations in climate, both seasonally and erratically, the
Potomac is subject to great variations in stream flow. During the flood
of March 1936, an estimated 480,000 cubic feet per second flowed past
Point of Rocks; on September 16, 1914, the recorded discharge fell to 540
cubic feet per second. Generally, the flow is heavy in spring, and low in
late summer and early fall.*

*Roughly 12 percent of the population of the United States lives in the
Potomac River basin. Of the land surface, 55 percent is forested, 23
percent is cropland, 16 percent pasture, 2 percent urban, and 4 percent
miscellaneous. For the remainder of this century it is predicted that
forest land will remain nearly stable, but that urban and suburban
areas will gain heavily at the expense of crop and pasture lands.*

CIVIL WAR

JOHN BROWN

May 8, 1858, Chatham, Ontario, the Provisional Constitutional Convention was held. There was a reading of the Provisional Constitution and Ordinance for the People of the United States:

> Whereas, slavery throughout its entire existence in the United States is none other than a most barbarous, unprovoked, and unjustifiable war of one portion of its citizens upon another portion . . .

The following officers were elected:

> Secretary of War—John Henry Kagi
> Secretary of State—Richard Realf
> Secretary of the Treasury—George Gill
> Treasurer—Owen Brown
> Members of Congress—Osborn P. Anderson
>   A. M. Ellsworth
> and,
> Commander-in-Chief: John Brown

Brown, October 2L, 1859:

> I wish to say, furthermore, that you had better—all you people at the South—prepare yourselves for a settlement of that question that must come up for settlement sooner than you are prepared for it . . . This question is still to be settled—this negro question I mean; the end of that is not yet.

July 1859, Brown, with twenty-two associates, rented the Kennedy farm, on the Maryland side, not far from Harper's Ferry. During the day, the men were confined to the loft, to avoid arousing suspicion of the neighbors. Housework was done mostly by Brown's two young daughters-in-law.

Osborn P. Anderson:

> As we could not circulate freely, they would bring in wild fruit and flowers from the woods and fields. We were well supplied with grapes, paw-paws, chestnuts, and other small fruit, besides bouquets of fall flowers, through their thoughtful consideration.
>
> During the several weeks I remained at the encampment, we were under the restraint I write of through the day; but at night, we sallied out for a ramble, or to breathe the fresh air and enjoy the beautiful solitude of the mountain scenery around, by moonlight.

John Brown, October 16:

> And now, gentlemen, let me impress this one thing upon your minds. You all know how dear life is to you, and how dear your life is to your friends. And in remembering that, consider that the lives of others are as dear to them as yours are to you. Do not, therefore, take the life of any one, if you can possibly avoid it; but if it is necessary to take life in order to save your own, then make sure work of it.

Kagi:

> This is just the right time. The year's crops have been good, and they are now perfectly housed, and in the best condition for use. The moon is just right. Slaves are discontented at this season.

October 16, 1859, after dark:

John Brown, commander-in-chief of the Provisional Army: "Men, get on your arms; we will proceed to the Ferry."

Horse and wagon were brought to the door, and pikes, fagots, a sledge-hammer, and a crowbar were loaded. The men buckled on their arms and threw over their shoulders long gray shawls, to conceal the arms. Captain Owen Brown and privates Coppoc and Meriam remained behind, in charge of arms and supplies, and to marshal the runaway slaves that were expected to join them. John Brown put on his battle-worn Kansas cap, mounted the wagon, and led his army of eighteen, marching in double column, down the little lane to the road, and on to Harper's Ferry.

The night was cloudy, damp and dark; the army met no one on the six-mile march.

Captains Cook and Tidd, their commissions signed, sealed, and in their pockets, went on ahead, to destroy telegraph wires on both Maryland and Virginia sides. Following them were Kagi and Stevens, as advance guard. Entering the Maryland bridge at 10:30 P.M., they took William Williams, the watchman, as their first prisoner. Williams thought it all a joke until the gun muzzles were in his face. Crossing the bridge, the men passed the Wager House—combined hotel and railroad station—and came to the armory gate, where Daniel Whelan, second watchman, was taken prisoner. Brown's men forced the lock on the gate with the crowbar: the U.S. Armory at Harper's Ferry had fallen to the Provisional Army.

Brown, to Whelan and Williams:

> I came from Kansas, and this is a slave State: I want to free all the negroes in this State; I have possession now of the United States armory, and if the citizens interfere with me I must only burn the town and have blood.

Meanwhile, a raiding party was on its way up Bolivar Heights. Five miles from the Ferry lived Colonel Lewis W. Washington, great-grandnephew of the president, and possessor of a pistol presented to Washington by Lafayette, as well as a sword, reported to be a gift of Frederick the Great to the first president. Colonel Washington was awakened at midnight by four armed men and taken prisoner. The sword was secured and the colonel was led out to his carriage, behind which stood a farm wagon, with his liberated slaves. The party headed for the Ferry.

1:25 A.M., the B&O night express, Wheeling to Baltimore, arrived at the Wager House on schedule. After the usual stop the engineer started to cross the bridge, but was driven back to the station by gunfire.

Shephard Hayward, free Negro, merely passing by, was shot and killed, when he refused a command to halt.

At dawn, Brown permitted the train to go through. The engineer took it across the bridge and down the line to Monocacy, arriving at 7:05 A.M. Here the telegraph wires were intact, and the alarm was spread.

Brown ordered breakfast for forty-five, sent over from the Wager House. He himself refused to eat, fearing the food had been poisoned.

As the morning shift of workers arrived at the gates, they were taken hostage with the others.

Throughout the morning, Kagi kept urging Brown to escape while escape was possible, but Brown waited, for word of the expected slave uprising.

12 noon: the Jefferson guards reached the Maryland end of the Potomac bridge, drove back Brown's guard, and crossed to the Wager House. There was sporadic brutal street fighting during the

day, but the militia was generally ineffective. Most of them were drunk.

Brown retired with his men and eleven of the most prominent prisoners, including Colonel Washington, to the engine house. At one point, Brown offered to surrender, on his own terms:

> In consideration of all my men, whether living or dead, or wounded, being soon safely in and delivered up to me at this point with all their arms and ammunition, we will then take our prisoners and cross the Potomac bridge, a little beyond which we will set them at liberty; after which we can negotiate about the Government property as may be best.

Terms were rejected, and men and hostages spent a second night in the engine house, without food, shivering in the cold, unable to sleep. Brown's son Oliver had been wounded.

Allstead, a prisoner:

> In the quiet of the night, young Oliver Brown died. He had begged again and again to be shot, in the agony of his wound, but his father had replied to him, "oh you will get over it," and, "If you must die, die like a man." Oliver lay quietly in a corner. His father called to him, after a time. No answer. "I guess he is dead," said Brown.

The second night, October 17, Brevet-Colonel Robert E. Lee, Second United States Cavalry, and First Lieutenant J. E. B. Stuart, First Cavalry, attended a conference at the White House with the president and secretary of war, and then arrived at Harper's Ferry to take command of a detachment of u.s. Marines—who replaced the drunken militia.

Stuart:

> By two A.M., Colonel Lee communicated to me his determination to demand a surrender of the whole party at first dawn, and

in case of refusal, which he expected, he would have ready a few picked men, who were at a signal to take the place at once with the bayonet. He chose to demand a surrender before attacking, because he wanted every chance to save the prisoners unhurt, and to attack with bayonets for the same reason.

Through Stuart, Lee offered his terms to Brown:

> Colonel Lee, United States army, commanding the troops sent by the President of the United States to suppress the insurrection at this place, demands the surrender of the persons in the armory buildings.
>
> If they will peaceably surrender themselves and restore the pillaged property, they shall be kept in safety to await the orders of the President. Colonel Lee represents to them, in all frankness, that it is impossible for them to escape; that the armory is surrounded on all sides by troops; and that if he is compelled to take them by force he cannot answer for their safety.
>
> R. E. LEE
> Colonel Commanding United States Troops.

Brown and Stuart parleyed at the engine house door for some minutes, but could not agree. Stuart gave the signal, and a storming detail of twelve men, under Lieutenant Green, battered down the door. Shots were fired, and there were casualties on both sides, but Brown and his men were easily subdued.

Green:

> . . . the sorriest lot of people I ever saw. They had been without food for over sixty hours, in constant dread of being shot, and were huddled up in the corner where lay the body of Brown's son and one or two others of the insurgents who had been killed.

The attack was over.

———

Richard Realf, Brown's secretary of state:

> [Brown believed that] upon the first intimation of a plan
> formed for the liberation of the slaves, they would immediately
> rise all over the Southern States. He supposed that they would
> come into the mountains to join him, where he proposed to
> work, and that by flocking to his standard they would enable
> him (by making the line of mountains which cuts diagonally
> through Maryland and Virginia down through the Southern
> States into Tennessee and Alabama, the base of his operations)
> to act upon the plantations on the plains lying on each side of
> that range of mountains, and that we should be able to establish
> ourselves in the fastnesses, and if any hostile action (as would
> be) were taken against us, either by the militia of the separate
> states or by the armies of the United States, we proposed to
> defeat first the militia, and next, if it were possible, the troops of
> the United States, and then organize the freed blacks under this
> provisional constitution, which would carve out for the locality
> of its jurisdiction all that mountainous region in which the
> blacks were to be established and in which they were to be
> taught the useful and mechanical arts, and to be instructed in all
> the business of life. Schools were also to be established, and so
> on. That was it . . . The negroes were to constitute the soldiers.
> John Brown expected that all the free negroes in the Northern
> States would immediately flock to his standard. He expected
> that all the slaves in the Southern States would do the same. He
> believed, too, that as many of the free negroes in Canada as
> could accompany him, would do so.

One of the raiders, Charles Tidd, made his escape through the hills,
and eventually to Massachusetts. He reported that "twenty-five
men in the mountains of Virginia could paralyse the whole business
of the South, and nobody could take them."

Brown:

> These mountains are the basis of my plan. God has given the
> strength of the hills to freedom; they were placed here for the

emancipation of the negro race; they are full of natural forts, where one man for defence will be equal to a hundred for attack; they are also full of good hiding-places, where large numbers of brave men could be concealed, and baffle and elude pursuit for a long time. I know these mountains well, and could take a body of men into them and keep them there, despite of all the efforts of Virginia to dislodge them.

Thomas Wentworth Higginson:

There was indeed, always a sort of thrill in John Brown's voice when he spoke of mountains. I shall never forget the quiet way in which he once told me that "God had established the Alleghany Mountains from the foundation of the world that they might one day be a refuge for fugitive slaves."

John Murray Forbes:

Captain Brown was a grim, farmer-like looking man, with a long gray beard and glittering, gray-blue eyes which seemed to me to have a little touch of insanity about them.

Brown:

I may be very insane, and I am so, if insane at all. But if that be so, insanity is like a very pleasant dream to me.

Henry A. Wise, governor of Virginia:

And they are themselves mistaken who take him to be a madman. He is a bundle of the best nerves I ever saw . . . He is cool, collected and indomitable, and it is but just to him to say that he was humane to his prisoners . . . He is a fanatic, vain and garrulous, but firm, truthful and intelligent.

Brown, to his jailor:

> Have you any objection to my writing to my wife to tell her that
> I am to be hanged on the 2d of December at noon?

From his letters:

> *Dear Wife and Children, every one,*—. . . I can trust God with
> both the time and the manner of my death, believing, as I now
> do, that for me at this time to seal my testimony for God and
> humanity with my blood will do vastly more toward advancing
> the cause I have earnestly endeavored to promote, than all I
> have done in my life before.

> I feel no consciousness of guilt in the matter . . . Already dear
> friends at a distance, with kindest sympathy, are cheering me
> with the assurance that posterity, at least, will do me justice.

Following sentencing, and before execution, at Charlestown, there
were constant rumors of invasion, of attempts to free him by force.

> Alarms would be given, the troops would fall into rank, and the
> cavalry would clatter out of town on some wild-goose chase.
> Night after night mysterious fires from burning barns or
> haystacks lighted up the sky, making the perturbed citizens
> believe that the rescue attack had come at last. The fires were
> never explained; perhaps the slaves did set them, as was gener-
> ally believed.

December 2:

> As he came out the six companies of infantry and one troop of
> horse, with General Taliaferro and his entire staff, were deploy-
> ing in front of the jail, whilst an open wagon with a pine box, in
> which was a fine oak coffin, was waiting for him.

> > Brown: "I had no idea that Governor Wise considered
> > my execution so important."

Brown looked around and spoke to several persons he recognized, and, walking down the steps, took a seat on the coffin box along with the jailor, Avis. He looked with interest on the fine military display . . . The wagon moved off, flanked by two files of riflemen in close order.

> Brown: "This is a beautiful country. I never had the pleasure of seeing it before."

On reaching the field where the gallows was erected, the prisoner said, "Why are none but military allowed in the inclosure? I am sorry citizens have been kept out." On reaching the gallows he observed Mr. Hunter and Mayor Green standing near, to whom he said, "Gentlemen, good-bye," his voice not faltering.

The prisoner walked up the steps firmly, and was the first man on the gallows. Avis and Sheriff Campbell stood by his side, and after shaking hands and bidding them an affectionate adieu, he thanked them for their kindness, when the cap was put over his face and the rope around his neck. Avis asked him to step forward on the trap. He replied, "You must lead me; I cannot see." The rope was adjusted, and the military order given, "Not ready yet!" The soldiers marched, countermarched, and took up position as if an enemy were in sight, and were thus occupied for nearly ten minutes, the prisoner standing all the time . . .

He was swung off at fifteen minutes past eleven. A slight grasping of the hands and twitching of the muscles were seen.

> As the trap was sprung, a private of the Richmond Grays turned pale, his knees weak. Those near him asked if he felt ill, and he asked for a stiff drink of whiskey . . . It was John Wilkes Booth, who had come along for the show . . .

Then all was quiet.

The body was several times examined, and the pulse did not cease until thirty-five minutes had passed.

BULL RUN

Colonel William T. Sherman, U.S.A.:

The march demonstrated the general laxity of discipline; for with all my personal efforts I could not prevent the men from straggling for water, blackberries or anything on the way they fancied.

Our men had been told at home that all they had to do was to make a bold appearance, and the Rebels would run.

General Beauregard, CSA:

Of the topographical features of the country thus occupied it must suffice to say that Bull Run is a small stream, running in this locality nearly from west to east, to its confluence with the Occoquan River, about twelve miles from the Potomac, and draining a considerable scope of country from its source in Bull Run Mountain to a short distance of the Potomac Occoquan. At this season habitually low and sluggish, it is, however, rapidly and frequently swollen by the summer rains until unfordable. The banks for the most part are rocky and steep, but abound in long-used fords. The country on either side, much broken and thickly wooded, becomes gently rolling and open as it recedes from the stream . . .

In view of these palpable military conditions, by 4:30 A.M. on the 21st of July [1861], I had prepared and dispatched orders directing the whole of the Confederate forces within the lines of Bull Run, including the brigades and regiments of General Johnston, which had arrived at that time, to be held in readiness to march at a moment's notice.

... The Stone Bridge on the Confederate left was held by Evans with 1 regiment and Wheat's special battalion of infantry, 1 battery of 4 guns, and 2 companies of cavalry.

About 5:15 A.M., Tyler's artillery [Union] opened fire across the Stone Bridge and his infantry deployed over the open farm lands, with Schenck's brigade below and opposite to the bridge, and Keyes' and Sherman's brigades above it.

Beauregard:

As the Federalists had advanced with an extended line of skirmishers in front of Evans, that officer promptly threw forward the two flank companies of the Fourth South Carolina Regiment and one company of Wheat's Louisiana Battalion, deployed as skirmishers to cover his small front. An occasional scattering fire resulted, and thus the two armies in that quarter remained for more than an hour, while the main body of the enemy was marching his devious way through the Big Forest to take our forces in the flank and rear . . .

A fierce and destructive conflict now ensued. The fire was withering on both sides, while the enemy swept our short thin lines with their numerous artillery.

> "George Knoll . . . being in his characteristic mood, but hungry, took from his haversack a chunk of fat bacon, stuffing himself while the artillery fire was in progress."

Beauregard:

Now, however, with the surging mass of over 14,000 Federal infantry pressing on their front, and under the incessant fire of at least twenty pieces of artillery, with the fresh brigades of Sherman and Keyes approaching, the latter already in musket range, our lines gave back.

Fully conscious of this portentous disparity of force, as I posted the lines for the encounter, I sought to infuse into the hearts of my officers and men the confidence and determined spirit of resistance to this wicked invasion of the homes of a free people which I felt.

Now, full 2 o'clock P.M., I gave the order for the right of my line, except for my reserves, to advance to recover the plateau. It was done with uncommon resolution and vigor, and at the same time Jackson's brigade pierced the enemy's center with the determination of veterans and the spirit of men who fought for a sacred cause . . . With equal spirit the other parts of the line made the onset and the Federal lines were broken and swept back at all points from the open ground of the plateau. Rallying soon, however, as they were strongly re-enforced by fresh regiments, the Federalists returned, and by weight of numbers pressed our lines back, recovered their ground and guns and renewed the offensive.

. . . About 3:30 P.M., the enemy, driven back on their left end center, and brushed from the woods bordering the Sudley Road, south and west of the Henry house, had formed a line of battle of truly formidable proportions, of crescent outline . . .

But as Early formed his line and Beckham's pieces played upon the right of the enemy, Elzey's brigade, Gibbon's Tenth Virginia, Lieutenant-Colonel Stewart's First Maryland, and Vaughn's Third Tennessee regiments, Cash's Eighth and Kershaw's Second South Carolina, Wither's Eighteenth and Preston's Twenty-eighth Virginia advanced in an irregular line, almost simultaneously, with great spirit, from their several positions on the front and flanks of the enemy in their quarter of the field. At the same time, too, Early resolutely assailed their right flank and rear. Under this combined attack the enemy was soon forced, first, over the narrow plateau in the southern angle, made by the two roads so often mentioned, into a patch of woods on its western slope, thence back over Young's Branch and the turnpike into the fields of the Dogan farm and rearward, in extreme disorder, in all available directions toward Bull Run.

General Irwin McDowell, commanding u.s. forces:

But our men, exhausted with the fatigue and thirst, and confused by firing into each other, were attacked by the enemy's reserves, and driven from the position we had gained, overlooking Manassas. After this, the men could not be rallied.

Colonel Andrew Porter, Sixteenth u.s. Infantry:

Soon the slopes behind us were swarming with our retreating and disorganized forces, whilst riderless horses and artillery teams ran furiously through the flying crowd. All further efforts were futile; the words, gestures and threats of our officers were thrown away upon men who had lost all presence of mind and only longed for absence of body.

W. W. Blackford, Confederate officer:

The whole field was a confused swarm of men, like bees, running away as fast as their legs could carry them, with all order and organization abandoned. In a moment more the valley was filled with them as far as the eye could reach. They plunged through Bull Run wherever they came to it regardless of fords or bridges, and there many drowned. Muskets, cartridge boxes, belts, knapsacks, haversacks and blankets were thrown away in their mad race, that nothing might impede their flight. In the reckless haste the artillery drove over every one who did not get out of their way. Ambulance and wagon drivers cut the traces and dashed off on the mules.

General McDowell:

The men having thrown away their haversacks in the battle and left them behind, they are without food; have eaten nothing since breakfast. We are without artillery ammunition. The larger part of the men are a confused mob, entirely demoralized.

John O. Casler, Confederate soldier:

I saw three horses galloping off, dragging a fourth, which was dead.

William Howard Russell, reporter for the London *Times:*

The scene on the road had now assumed an aspect which has not a parallel in any description I have ever read. Infantry soldiers on mules and draft horses, with the harness clinging to their heels, as much frightened as their riders; Negro servants on their masters' chargers; ambulances crowded with unwounded soldiers; wagons swarming with men who threw out the contents in the road to make room, grinding through a shouting, screaming mass of men on foot, who were literally yelling with rage at every halt.

A member of the Washington Artillery of New Orleans reported, after the battle:

We live splendidly: Chicken, eggs, vegetables, milk, ice, and claret, paté de fois gras, sardines, etc.

Blackford:

Along a shady little valley through which our road lay the surgeons had been plying their vocation all the morning upon the wounded. Tables about breast high had been erected upon which screaming victims were having legs and arms cut off. The surgeons and their assistants, stripped to the waist and all bespattered with blood, stood around, some holding the poor fellows while others, armed with long bloody knives and saws, cut and sawed away with frightful rapidity, throwing the mangled limbs on a pile near by as soon as removed. Many were stretched on the ground awaiting their turn, many more were arriving continually, either limping along or borne on stretchers, while those upon whom operations had already been performed calmly fanned the flies from their wounds.

D. E. Johnston, Confederate soldier:

Returning to the battle line, we found ourselves groping around in the dark . . . The cries of the Federal wounded, and the groans of the dying, the occasional volleys of musketry fired by some of our troops at imaginary foes, with the hooting of owls, made the night hideous and weird.

General McDowell, reporting from Fairfax Country Courthouse the following day:

I learn from prisoners that we are to be pressed here to-night and tomorrow morning, as the enemy's force is very large and they are elated. I think we heard cannon on our rear guards. I think now, as all my commanders thought at Centreville, there is no alternative but to fall back to the Potomac.

And another voice:

The defeated troops commenced pouring into Washington over the Long Bridge at daylight on Monday, 22d—day drizzling all through with rain. The Saturday and Sunday of the battle (20th, 21st) had been parched and hot to an extreme—the dust, the grime and smoke, in layers, sweated in, follow'd by other layers again sweated in, absorb'd by those excited souls—their clothes all saturated with the clay-powder filling the air—stirr'd up everywhere on the dry roads and trodden fields by the regiments, swarming wagons, artillery, etc.—all the men with this coating of murk and sweat and rain, now recoiling back, pouring over the Long Bridge—a horrible march of twenty miles, returning to Washington baffled, humiliated, panic-struck.

. . . Sidewalks of Pennsylvania Avenue, Fourteenth street, etc., crowded, jamm'd with citizens, darkies, clerks, everybody, lookers-on; women in the windows, curious expressions from faces . . . During the forenoon, Washington gets all over motley with these defeated soldiers—queer-looking objects, strange eyes and faces, drench'd (the steady rain drizzles on all day) and fearfully worn, hungry, haggard, blister'd in the feet . . . Amid the deep excitement, crowds and motion, and desperate eager-ness, it seems strange to see many, very many, of the soldiers sleeping—in the midst of all, sleeping sound. They drop down anywhere, on the steps of houses, up close by the basements of fences, on the sidewalk, aside on some vacant lot, and deeply sleep. A poor seventeen or eighteen year old boy lies there, on the stoop of a grand house; he sleeps so calmly, so profoundly. Some clutch their muskets.

—Walt Whitman

A SMALL ENGAGEMENT

September 24, 1861, at Hanging Rocks on North River—a branch of Cacapon:

. . . The Confederates on the cliffs, rolled stones down upon the advancing Union forces on the road below, and routed them.

BALL'S BLUFF

On the Potomac, October 21, 1861:

Harrison's is one of a number of long narrow islands . . . It is nearly half a mile wide, and more than two miles in length . . . Opposite the island, the Virginia shore rises abruptly; in many places directly from the water's edge, in cliffs or bluffs.

[Union] General Stone ordered a reconnaissance by a few men from the force on Harrison's Island, which was opposite the high bluff at Ball's Bluff. They crossed in the moonlight, advanced a short distance, and retired, reporting to General Stone that they had discovered a Rebel camp, which afterwards proved to be merely openings in an orchard, which looked to their excited eyes like tents. However, the camp was taken for granted, and . . . about 450 men were sent to capture it.

The river was swollen and the current rapid, and there was much labor and delay in making use of the boats.

To convey his battalion to the foot of the bluffs Colonel Devens had one four-oared bateau or "flat boat," and a couple of small skiffs, needing frequent bailing . . . One or two other skiffs were subsequently added, but the transportation was wholly inadequate.

The place for landing upon the Virginia shore was most unfortunately selected, being at a point where the shore rose with great abruptness . . . and was studded with trees, being entirely impassable to artillery or infantry in line . . . In fact, no more unfortunate position could have been forced upon us by the enemy for making an attack, much less selected by ourselves.

The bank is of a miry clay, and the heights almost precipitous, with fallen trees and rocks, making it very difficult to get up the artillery. Arriving by circuitous routes on the summit, we found an open field of six acres, covered with wild grass, scrub oak, and locust trees, and forming a segment of a circle, the arc of which was surrounded with trees.

The Federal position at this time was upon the plateau of the bluff, some 700 yards in front of the river, where there was a cleared field of ten or twelve acres.

. . . formed at the top of the Bluff, afterwards moving forward on the right, where they encountered the picket reserve of the enemy . . .

Colonel Baker . . . brought battalions . . . to reinforce our line, and under direct orders from General Stone, assumed command of the movement.

Lieutenant Bramhall, New York Light Artillery:

I crossed with the first piece . . . arriving upon the island after a half hour's hard labor to keep the boat from floating down the stream. We ascended the steep bank, made soft and sloppy by the passage of the troops, and at a rapid gait crossed the island to the second crossing. At this point we found only a scow, on which we did not dare to cross the piece and the horses together, and thus lost further time by being obliged to make two crossing. Upon arriving on the Virginia shore we were compelled to dismount the piece and carriage and haul the former up by the prolonge, the infantry assisting in carrying the parts of the latter to a point about thirty feet up a precipitous ascent, rendered almost impassable with soft mud, where we remounted the piece, and hitching up the horses dragged it through a perfect thicket up to the open ground above where the fighting was going on.

We had seen but little of the enemy during the day, as they were in the woods while our line was in the open, but they had, nevertheless, very seriously made known their presence to us. We were too ignorant to attempt any sort of cover.

The Virginians and Mississippians being accustomed to the rifle, most of them old hunters, rarely missed their man. Climbing into the tops of trees, creeping through the tall grass, or concealed in the gullies, they plied their weapons with murderous havoc especially among the Federal officers.

By this time there were many dead and wounded, and we used the boats to send them over to the Island. The cannons were useless—since the ammunition was exhausted, and the cannoneers killed or wounded . . . The strength of the forces engaged was about 1600 Federals, against 3200 Confederates. Had there been proper transportation, this difference would have been remedied.

The re-enforcements from the island came up very slowly, and it was evident to all that unless aid in force reached us from the left, we should be driven into the river, as the increasing yells and firing of the enemy indicated their larger number.

. . . a wild, terror stricken yell; then the simultaneous crash of 1,000 muskets, each hurling its leaden contents along the Federal left and centre!

> Colonel W. H. Jenifer, CSA: "I sent my adjutant to you for ammunition and provisions, and if provisions could not be had at once, to send a barrel of whiskey."

Seeing that the crisis was come—as the Confederates were assuming the offensive and closing upon him from three sides, with the river at his back—Colonel Baker turned to the bayonet as the last hope . . . Baker ran forward and at once received a stinging wound . . .

At this moment the hostile lines were within stone's throw, and both advancing. The Federals, seeing the fall of their leader, halted. Some soldiers seized Baker's body and ran with it rearward. This started the rest.

> "Between the physical fear of going forward and the moral fear of turning back, there is a predicament of exceptional awkwardness. . . ."

. . . A general retreat took place . . . All regimental order was lost, and the huddling of the men on the hill rendered the Confederate fire, which was rapidly closing in on all sides, so much the more fatal.

Brigadier General N. G. Evans, CSA:

At about 6 o'clock P.M. I saw that my command had driven the enemy near the banks of the Potomac. I ordered my entire force to charge and drive him into the river. The charge was immediately made by the whole command, and the forces of the enemy completely routed, and cried out for quarter along his whole line.

In this charge the enemy were driven back at the point of the bayonet, and many were killed and wounded by this formidable weapon.

Lieutenant Colonel John McGuirk, Seventeenth Mississippi Infantry:

Above the roar of musketry was heard the command of Colonel Featherston, "Charge, Mississippians, charge! Drive them into the Potomac or into eternity!" The sound of his voice seemed to echo from the vales of Maryland. The line arose as one man from a kneeling position, discharged a deadly volley, advanced the crescent line, and thus encircled the invaders.

Again, the Union side:

> A kind of shiver ran through the huddled mass upon the brow
> of the cliff; it gave way; rushed a few steps; then, in one wild,
> panic-stricken herd, rolled, leaped, tumbled over the precipice!
> The descent is nearly perpendicular, with ragged, jutting crags.
> . . . Screams of pain and terror filled the air. Men seemed
> suddenly bereft of reason; they leaped over the bluff with
> muskets still in their clutch, threw themselves into the river
> without divesting themselves of their heavy accoutrements—
> hence went to the bottom like lead. Others sprung down upon
> the heads and bayonets of those below.

> The scow, which had already carried over many wounded, now
> started on her last trip, but when starting, a number of unin-
> jured men rushed forward, disturbing the trim of the boat, so
> that half way across the river she rolled over, and all were
> thrown out. Only one man is known to have escaped drowning.
> The scow floated down the stream and was lost. The small
> boats were riddled by bullets and disappeared.

Lieutenant Bramhall, artillery:

> Finding that the battle was lost to us, and with but one man left
> to aid me . . . and growing weak and stiff from my wounds . . . I
> caused the piece to be drawn down to the edge of the cliff,
> whence it was afterward thrown down, lodging in the rocks and
> logs with which the descent was cumbered . . . The horses
> belonging to the piece were all shot, . . . five of them lay dead in
> one heap.

One year later:

> We have been to Harrison Island, and in sight of Ball's Bluff,
> which rested as quiet and silently as though blood had not dyed
> its soil. We have countermarched, and our division is near the

Potomac . . . A little fire is burning a few feet before me, and the smoke curls up lazily in the sunshine. The air has the lovely, dreamy haze of autumn. The trees are gently shaking off the ripe leaves. The hum of insects is not yet ended. Near are the strokes of our woodcutters axes. Farther off is the murmur of a rapid.

SPRINGTIME

The Second Massachusetts Infantry, on the Masanutten Range, May 1862:

We climbed the hill. There was no *hard* climbing, however. The road over the gap was as smooth and firm as any in Roxbury or Dorchester . . . Another brigade was bivouacked for a mile or two by the road, and their brilliant fires crackling all along on either side . . . made a bewildering and fascinating scene. At the top we rested, and turning to look, beheld a view of the utmost beauty; a lovely valley, of great breadth, confined by the distant Alleghanies, whose tops the rising sun was just tingeing . . .

Then we returned. Up the hill and down again, and back to camp. On the way up, a few of us took short cuts from angle to angle once or twice to gather wild flowers. There was great abundance of several kinds. Wild cherry was in blossom, and laurel, and what they call dogwood here, which I think is found in Milton, in Massachusetts, and "red bud," without leaves, but gorgeous in its wealth of flowering; and of lowlier plants, the red columbine, mayflower, much like the New Hampshire one, which is more beautiful than that in the Plymouth woods (I have gathered both), the anemone, the iris, far more delicately lovely than any I ever saw wild before; and above all, such profusion of wood violets as one rarely finds, of which many were colored so like pansies that they were easily mistaken for them at a little distance. Sitting upon a rock to rest, the sight of belted men, with swords in their side and pistols ready, gathering flowers, awakened strange sensations.

ANTIETAM

THE MARYLAND CAMPAIGN,
SEPTEMBER 3 TO 20, 1862
INCLUDING THE BATTLES OF
SOUTH MOUNTAIN, CRAMPTON'S GAP AND ANTIETAM,
OR SHARPSBURG.
BY
GENERAL ROBERT E. LEE
Commanding the Army of Northern Virginia
Headquarters, October—, 1862

Not to permit the season for active operations to pass without endeavoring to inflict injury upon the enemy, the best course appeared to be the transfer of the army into Maryland. Although not properly equipped for invasion, lacking much of the material of war, and feeble in transportation, the troops poorly provided with clothing, and thousands of them destitute of shoes, it was yet believed to be strong enough to detain the enemy upon the northern frontier until the approach of winter.

The Confederates forded the Potomac at Botoler's or Blackford's ford, below Shepherdstown, "where the river, from the wash of the dam above, was broad, sandy, and shallow."

On the 3d of September we marched with three days rations and bivouacked at Dranesville, with the whole army. The order was given on the following day for Jackson to cross the Potomac . . .

On the 5th we marched through Leesburg and bivouacked in a half mile of the Potomac, which stream was next morning crossed.

As full of hope as the soldiers of Hannibal going over the Alps . . . the men splashed through the water, too happy to be moving forward to trouble themselves about wet clothing.

It was with a deep heaving of the chest and expansion of the lungs with us all that we stood at last upon the Maryland shore. . . . At all of the farm houses near the river the people appeared hospitable and reb down to their boots, and crazy to see Lee. Adjutant Owen brought back a string of ladies, who overwhelmed the old man with kisses and welcomes.

The columns were soon upon the high road towards Boonesboro, and we were all struck with the beautiful scenery of this part of the country. As we climbed the hills long stretches of valley extended as far as the eye could reach in the direction of the Potomac. How still and peaceful it all looked.

———————

Lee:

The arduous service in which our troops had been engaged, their great privations of rest and food, and the long marches without shoes over mountain roads, had greatly reduced our ranks before the action began. These causes had caused thousands of brave men to absent themselves.

E. P. Alexander, Confederate artillery officer:

About one-half of the small-arms were still the old smoothbore muskets of short range, and our rifled cannon ammunition was always inferior in quality. The lack of shoes was deplorable, and barefoot men with bleeding feet were no uncommon sight. Of clothing, our supply was so poor that it seemed no wonder the Marylanders held aloof from our shabby ranks. For rations, we were indebted mostly to the fields of roasting ears, and to the apple orchards . . . On Sept. 5 the army began to cross the Potomac.

W. M. Owen, Confederate officer:

We reached the vicinity of Sharpsburg early in the morning of September 15, and formed a line of battle along the range of hills between the town and the stream, with our back to the Potomac.

On the opposite shore of the Antietam the banks are quite steep and afford good position for artillery. All the batteries present were placed in position along the ridge. Longstreet said, "Put them all in, every gun you have, long range and short range."

A courier arrived in hot haste, with news that Jackson had captured Harpers Ferry . . .

"This is indeed good news," said General Lee; "let it be announced to the troops"; and staff officers rode at full gallop down the line, and the announcement was answered by great cheering.

September 17:

The battle began with the dawn. Morning found both armies just as they had slept, almost close enough to look into each other's eyes . . . A battery was almost immediately pushed forward beyond the central woods, over a plowed field, near the top of the slope where the cornfield began. On this open field, in the corn beyond, and in the woods which stretched forward into the broad fields, like a promontory into the ocean, were the hardest and deadliest struggles of the day.

Kyd Douglas, Confederate officer:

With me it was a fearful day—one I am not likely ever to forget. With two hundred pieces of artillery turned against us and pouring a continuous fire with fearful accuracy upon our guns as well as our line of battle, I need not explain that I had more work than play, more danger than glory . . . My first horse "Ashby," in his first battle, between fright and excitement was exhausted in a few hours; another and then another became necessary. The day was hot, the battle terrific while it lasted, the suspense racking, the anxiety intense.

John Dooley, Confederate soldier:

About 11 A. M. (I think) the enemy advanced upon our center. We have a good view of our batteries, and as line after line of the blue coats advance to the charge, our guns open at about two hundred yards' distance . . . We can plainly see the earth as it is torn up and scattered wildly about in face of each successive line of infantry that marches up the slope . . .

This was the finest sight we witnessed today.

Another:

From our position on the right we could not see the combatants, but could hear the crash of small arms and the wild rebel yell. As long as we could hear this yell we felt that things were going our way.

Dooley:

In the field below us the enemy are slowly but cautiously approaching, crouching low as they advance behind the undulating tracks in the rich meadows through which they are passing. From the numbers of their flags which are distinctly visible above the rising ground we judge them to be at least two thousand in number. As long as our little battery of two guns is served with tolerable precision the enemy, who appear to be new troops, do not dare to venture close or raise their heads. But in a few minutes the Yankee artillery, far superior to ours, dismounted one of our pieces, killed the horses; and the remaining gunner, fearing capture, hitched the only remaining

horse to the other cannon and made away to the rear as hard as
he could go.

I shall never forget poor Beckham on Kemper's staff. As soon
as our first gun opened on the enemy, he gave a lusty cheer and
rising in his stirrups flung his hat around his head, wild with
enthusiasm. Almost instantly he was hurled from his horse by a
shot and his foot terribly mangled. He was borne from the field
cheering as he went.

The enemy having taken our position appeared to think they
had performed wonders, for instead of pursuing us and shoot-
ing us down, they began to give regular *methodical* cheers, as if
they had gained a game of base ball.

A soldier:

I recall a round shot that came ricochetting over the ground,
cutting little furrows, tossing the earth into the air, as the plow
of the locomotive turns its white furrow after a snowstorm. Its
speed gradually diminished and a soldier was about to catch it,
as if he were at a game of baseball.

General John B. Gordon, CSA:

The predicted assault came. The men in blue filed down the
opposite slope, crossed the Antietam, and formed in my front,
an assaulting column four lines deep. The brave Union Com-
mander, superbly mounted, placed himself in front, while his
band in rear cheered them with martial music. It was a thrilling
spectacle. The entire force, I concluded, was composed of fresh
troops. As we stood looking upon that brilliant pageant,
I thought, "What a pity to spoil with bullets such a scene of
martial beauty." But there was nothing else to do.

Every act of the Union commander clearly indicated his
purpose to depend on bayonets. He essayed to break through
by the momentum of his solid column. It was my business to
prevent this. To oppose man against man and strength against
strength was impossible; for there were four lines of blue to my
one of gray. During the few minutes required for the column to

reach my line, I could not hope to disable a sufficient number of the enemy to reduce his strength to an equality with mine. The only remaining plan was to hold my fire until the advancing Federals were almost upon my lines. I did not believe that any troops on earth, with empty guns in their hands, could withstand so sudden a shock. My men were at once directed to lie down upon the grass. Not a shot would be fired until my voice should be heard commanding "Fire!"

There was no artillery at this point upon either side, and not a rifle was discharged. The stillness was literally oppressive, as this column of Union infantry moved majestically toward us. Now the front rank was within a few rods of where I stood. With all my lung power I shouted "Fire!"

Our rifles flamed and roared in the Federals' faces like a blinding blaze of lightning. The effect was appalling. The entire front line, with few exceptions, went down. Before the rear lines could recover, my exultant men were on their feet, devouring them with successive volleys. Even then these stubborn blue lines retreated in fairly good order.

The fire now became furious and deadly. The list of the slain was lengthened with each passing moment. Near nightfall, the awful carnage ceased; Lee's center had been saved.

A North Carolina soldier:

The sun seemed almost to go backwards, and it appeared as if night would never come.

Major-General John G. Walker, CSA:

To those who have not been witnesses to a great battle like this, where more than a hundred thousand men, armed with all the appliances of modern science and skill, are engaged in the work of slaughtering each other, it is impossible by the power of words to convey an adequate idea of its terrible sublimity.

Douglas Southall Freeman:

> Sharpsburg itself was aflame and under artillery fire; its side
> streets were filled with demoralized soldiers, who had become
> separated from their commands; above it, through the smoke
> and bursting shells, flocks of bewildered pigeons flew round
> and round.

General Hood, CSA:

> Whole ranks of brave men, whose deeds were unrecorded save
> in the hearts of loved ones at home, were mowed down in heaps
> to the right and left. Never before was I so continuously
> troubled with fear that my horse would further injure some
> wounded fellow soldier, lying helpless upon the ground.

General Hooker, USA:

> I discovered that a heavy force of the enemy had taken posses-
> sion of a corn-field (I have since learned about a 30-acre field)
> in my immediate front, and from the sun's rays falling on their
> bayonets projecting above the corn, could see that the field was
> filled with the enemy with arms in their hands ... In the time I
> am writing every stalk of corn in the northern and greater part
> of the field was cut as closely as could have been done with a
> knife, and the slain lay in rows, precisely as they had stood in
> their ranks a few moments before.

> The poor fellow's whole lower jaw had been knocked off;
> carrying tongue and teeth with it, leaving the moustache,
> clotted with blood; arching over a frightful chasm of tangled
> muscles and arteries! The dripping from the aperture ran down
> over his bosom in a sheet of gelid, clotted gore.

Major-General McClellan, USA:

> The enemy was pressed back to near the crest of the hill, where
> he was encountered in great strength posted in a sunken road

forming a natural pit running in a northwesterly direction . . .
Here a terrific fire of musketry burst from both lines.

A Union soldier:

It seemed like merely a hop, skip, and jump till we were at the
lane, and into it, the Confederate breaking away in haste and
fleeing up the slope. What a sight was that lane! I shall not dwell
on the horror of it; I saw many a ghastly array of dead afterward,
but none, I think, that so affected me as did the sight of the poor
brave fellows in butternut homespun that had there died.

George F. Noyes, Union officer:

I was walking down the lines, when a regimental captain thus
accosted me, holding up a great piece of pork on his sword:
"Look here, captain, this is the allowance of pork for my com-
pany, and I shall have to eat it all, for I am the only one left."

As I rode past the barn, a collection of amputated limbs lying
outside the door attested the hurried and wholesale character of
the work going on within.

. . . a fine horse struck with death at the instant when, cut down
by his wound, he was attempting to rise from the ground. His
head was half lifted, his neck proudly arched, every muscle
seemed replete with animal life . . .

Near by stood a wounded battery-horse and a shattered caisson
belonging to one of Hood's batteries. The animal had eaten
every blade of grass within reach. No human being ever looked
more imploringly for help than that dumb animal, wounded
beyond the possibility of moving, yet resolutely standing, as if
knowing that lying down would be the end.

Behind the battery came hobbling as best they could a string of
fearfully mutilated horses which had been turned loose as they
received their wounds, and who had followed their comrades when

they left the spot where they had been in action. After they had all passed, I saw a horse galloping after them and dragging something. Thinking it was his rider as he emerged from the clouds of smoke on the field of battle, I moved to intercept and stop the animal, but to my horror discovered that the horse was dragging his own entrails from the gaping wound of a cannonball, and after passing us a few yards the poor brute fell dead with a piercing scream.

General Lee:

It was now nearly dark and the enemy had massed a number of batteries to sweep the approaches to the Antietam . . . Our troops were much exhausted and greatly reduced in numbers by fatigue and the casualties of battle. Under these circumstances it was deemed injudicious to push our advantage further in the face of fresh troops of the enemy.

Douglas:

I went off the pike and was compelled to go through a field in the rear of Dunker Church, over which, to and fro, the pendulum of battle had swung several times that day. It was a dreadful scene, a veritable field of blood. The dead and dying lay as thick over it as harvest sheaves. The pitiable cries for water and appeals for help were much more horrible to listen to than the deadliest sounds of battle. Silent were the dead, and motionless. But here and there were raised stiffened arms; heads made a last effort to lift themselves from the ground; prayers were mingled with oaths, the oaths of delirium; men were wriggling over the earth; and midnight hid all distinction between the blue and the gray. My horse trembled under me in terror, looking down at the ground, sniffing the scent of blood, stepping falteringly as a horse will over or by the side of human flesh; afraid to stand still, hesitating to go on, his animal instinct shuddering at this cruel human mystery. Once his foot slid into a little shallow filled with blood and spurted a little stream on his legs and boots . . . I dismounted and giving the reins to my courier I started on foot.

Noyes:

> It is a narrow country lane, hollowed out somewhat between the
> fields, partially shaded ... Here they stood in line of battle ... In
> every attitude conceivable—some piled in groups of five or six;
> some grasping their muskets ... ; some, evidently officers, killed
> while encouraging their men; some lying in the position of calm
> repose, all black and swollen, and ghastly with wounds. The air
> grows terribly offensive from the unburied bodies; and a pestilence
> will speedily be bred if they are not put under ground. The most
> of the Union soldiers are now buried, though some only slightly.
>
> The men were now permitted to bring in bundles of straw from
> the neighboring farms, with which they made themselves beds,
> and lay down in line of battle; the tired gunners made them-
> selves similarly comfortable alongside their guns ... No one
> removed even his sword; our horses stood saddled and ready ...
> There was no tree over our heads to shut out the stars.

Casualties at Antietam, killed and wounded: 23,000 ...

Noyes—September 18, the following day:

> The feeling seemed to possess every heart that this day was to
> be crowned with victory; the whole tone of conversation as we
> drank our coffee on the grass was hopeful, nay, almost exultant;
> the hour for crushing the rebellion seemed to have struck; the
> opportunity had come to drive the rebels into the Potomac.
> But sunrise came, hour after hour slipped by, with no orders
> to advance ... and gradually a bitter feeling began to trouble us,
> while the conviction forced itself upon our minds that the
> enemy was to be permitted to escape.

September 19:

> Up again at 3 A.M., we drank our coffee, saw that the division
> had a good breakfast, and made all ready for battle ... Finally,

at 8 A.M., we learned that the rebels had slipped through our fingers and returned across the Potomac. The river, lately in their rear, and forming one side of the angle into which we had driven them, was now their best defense against us.

. . . The campaign must now be transferred to Virginia; the long, weary days of marching and nights of shelterless discomfort were all to be again endured.

Douglas:

On the night of the 18th the Confederate army crossed into Virginia at Blackford's Ford, even taking its debris with it, all its wagons and guns, useless wagons, disabled guns, everything. If a scavenger had gone over the field the next day, he would have found nothing worth carrying off. General Lee watched this crossing, lasting through the night, and gave directions to facilitate it. General Jackson on horseback spent much of his time in the middle of the river, urging everything and everybody to push on.

The scene on the Maryland side on the night of the crossing rivaled Bedlam. The wagon train had to go down a very high and almost perpendicular bank, and except for the still greater danger from behind, was such a descent as no prudent wagoner would ever have attempted to make. Although it was as precipitous as the road to perdition, the teamsters had to make an elbow half way down, at the imminent risk of an overturn— some of the wagons actually meeting with such a calamity. These were set fire to, partly for warmth, partly for the purpose of seeing . . .

The strangest feature of the whole affair, was the grotesque appearance of our army who had stripped off most of their clothes, and who went shuddering and shivering in the cold water . . .

Artillery, infantry, ambulances, wagons, all mixed up in what appeared to be inextricable confusion in the water; and the ford, too, was full of large boulders. Immense fires were blazing on the banks, which had the effect of blinding both men and animals. Staff-officers stood on either bank, shouting to the drivers.

General Walker:

> As I rode into the river, I passed General Lee, sitting on his horse in the stream, watching the crossing of the wagons and artillery. Returning my greeting, he inquired as to what was still behind. There was nothing but the wagons containing my wounded and a battery, all of which were near at hand, and I told him so,
> "Thank God!" I heard him say as I rode on.

Reaching Virginia, many of the stragglers fled up the Shenandoah Valley, those who had shoes throwing them away as they ran, so they would not be reenlisted.

GETTYSBURG

Col. Blackford, csa, rode north with Jeb Stuart, June 1863,

> crossing the Occoquan at Wolf Run Shoals, capturing a small force at Fairfax Court House, passing through Dranesville, and reaching Rowser's Ford of the Potomac on the night of the twenty-seventh. The ford was wide and deep and might well have daunted a less determined man, for the water swept over the pommels of our saddles. To pass the artillery without wetting the ammunition in the chests was impossible, provided it was left in them, but Stuart had the cartridges distributed among the horsemen and it was thus taken over in safety. The guns and caissons went clean out of sight beneath the surface of the rapid torrent, but all came out without the loss of a piece or a man, though the night was dark, and by three o'clock in the

morning of the twenty-eighth of June we all stood wet and dripping on the Maryland shore.

At another ford, R. A. Shotwell:

Thousands of rough voices sang . . . the musicians, nude as Adam, each with a bundle of clothes on top of his head (to keep them dry) tooting with "might and main" on their brass horns . . . Several columns crossing together, with colonels on horseback, flags fluttering, and the forest of bright bayonets glistening in the afternoon sun . . .

Longstreet, addressing Lee, Gettysburg, July 1:

All we have to do is throw our army around by their left, and we shall interpose between the Federal army and Washington. We can get a strong position and wait . . .

"No," said General Lee; "the enemy is there, and I am going to attack him there."

I suggested that such a move as I proposed would give us control of the roads leading to Washington and Baltimore, and reminded General Lee of our original plans. If we had fallen behind Meade and had insisted on staying between him and Washington, he would have been compelled to attack and would have been badly beaten. General Lee answered, "No; they are there in position, and I am going to whip them or they are going to whip me." I saw he was in no frame of mind to listen to further argument at that time, so I did not push the matter, but determined to renew the subject the next morning. It was then about 5 o'clock in the afternoon . . .

When the battle of the 2d was over, General Lee pronounced it a success, as we were in possession of ground from which we had driven the Federals and had taken several field-pieces. The conflict had been fierce and bloody, and my troops had driven back heavy columns and had encountered a force three or four times their number, but we had accomplished little toward victorious results.

I was disappointed when he came to me on the morning of the 3d and directed that I should renew the attack against Cemetery Hill, probably the strongest point of the Federal line. For that purpose he had already ordered up Pickett's division.

"I want you to take Pickett's division and make the attack. I will reenforce you by two divisions of the Third Corps."

"That will give me fifteen thousand men," I replied. "I have been a soldier, I may say, from the ranks up to the position I now hold. I have been in pretty much all kinds of skirmishes, from those of two or three soldiers up to those of an army corps, and I think I can safely say there never was a body of fifteen thousand men who could make that attack successfully."

The general seemed a little impatient at my remarks, so I said nothing more . . .

The plan of assault was as follows: our artillery was to be massed in a wood from which Pickett was to charge, and it was to pour a continuous fire upon the cemetery. Under cover of this fire and supported by it, Pickett was to charge.

———————

A Confederate soldier:

The night before, when we had taken our place for bivouac on the corpse-covered battle field, there rose before us, what we at first thought was a cloud, black and threatening, but which we soon discovered were the mountains behind, or on which the Federal left was posted; protected, we discovered, too, on the morrow, by breastworks. In regarding this we stared at each other in amazement.

Lieutenant Haskell, USA:

The advantages of the position, briefly, were these: the flanks were quite well protected by the natural defenses there, Round Top up the left, and a rocky, steep untraversable ground up the right. Our line was more elevated than that of the enemy, consequently our artillery had a greater range and power than theirs. On account of the convexity of our line, every part of the line could be reinforced by troops having to move a shorter distance than if the line were straight; further, for the same reason, the line of the enemy must be concave, and, consequently, longer, and with an equal force, thinner, and so weaker than ours. Upon those parts of our line which were wooded, neither we nor the enemy could use artillery; but they were so strong by nature, aided by art, as to be readily defended by a small against a very large, body of infantry. When the line was open, it had the advantage of having open country in front, consequently, the enemy here could not surprise, as we were on a crest, which besides the other advantages that I have mentioned, had this: the enemy must advance to the attack up an ascent, and must therefore move slower, and be, before coming to us, longer under our fire, as well as more exhausted. These, and some other things, rendered our position admirable.

A Confederate, surveying the enemy positions:

His troops seemed to be heavily massed right on our only point of attack. Holding an advanced front, almost inaccessible in the natural difficulties of the ground, first by a line of skirmishers, almost as heavy as a single line of battle, in the lower ground; then the steep acclivity of the "Ridge" covered with two tiers of artillery, and two lines of infantry supports. These had to be passed over before reaching the crest of the heights where his heavy reserves of infantry were massed in double column.

Colonel James Arthur Lyon Fremantle of His Majesty's Cold-stream Guards, attached to the Confederates as an observer:

Colonel Sorrell, the Austrian, and I arrived at 5 A.M. at the same commanding position we were on yesterday, and I climbed up a tree in company with Captain Schreibert of the Prussion army. Just below us were seated Generals Lee, Hill, Longstreet, and

Hood, in consultation—the two latter assisting their delibera-
tions by the truly American custom of whittling.

Longstreet: "Never was I so depressed as that day."

As early as three o'clock on the morning of the 3rd of July Pick-
ett's division was under arms and moving to the right and
southeast of the Cashtown and Gettysburg road.

. . . A shady, quiet march . . . we halted for a short time in the
woods, but moved forward pretty soon into a field, near a branch.

Lieutenant Haskell, in the Union position:

Eleven o'clock came. The noise of battle has ceased upon the
right; not a sound of a gun or musket can be heard on all the
field; the sky is bright, with only the white fleecy clouds floating
over from the west. The July sun streams down its fire upon the
bright iron of the muskets in stacks upon the crest and the daz-
zling brass of the Napoleans. The Army lolls and longs for the
shade . . . The silence and sultriness of a July noon are supreme.

A Union soldier:

Shortly after eleven o'clock the firing ceased, and, for over an
hour, there was hardly a picket shot heard. It was a queer sight to
see men look at each other without speaking; the change was so
great men seemed to go on tiptoe, not knowing how to act . . . I
began looking around for something to eat.

John Dooley:

While we are resting here we amuse ourselves by pelting each
other with green apples.

A Confederate:

> As the sun climbed towards the meridian, many of the men drew out their "corn dodgers" and bits of bacon, to make their frugal dinner . . . Others spread their blankets on the gravelly hillside and stretched themselves for a nap. Everything looked quiet, dull and lazy,—as one sees the harvest-hands lolling under the trees at noontime.

Haskell:

> We dozed in the heat, and lolled upon the ground, with half-open eyes. Our horses were hitched to the trees munching some oats. A great lull rests upon all the field. Time was heavy.

Fremantle:

> At noon all Longstreet's dispositions were made. His troops for attack were deployed into line, and lying down in the woods; his batteries were ready to open. The general then dismounted and went to sleep.

At General Meade's headquarters, there was not wanting to the peacefulness of the scene the singing of a bird, which had a nest in the peach tree.

General Alexander, CSA:

> I rode to see Pickett, who was with his division a short distance in the rear . . . He seemed very sanguine, and thought himself in luck to have the chance. Then I felt that I could not make any delay or let the attack suffer by any indecision on my part. And, that General Longstreet might know my intention, I wrote him only this: "GENERAL: When our artillery fire is at its best, I shall order Pickett to charge."

Lieutenant Colonel W. M. Owen, CSA:

> The order to fire the signal-gun was immediately communi-
> cated . . . and the report of the first gun rang out upon the still
> summer air. There was a moment's delay with the second gun,
> a friction-primer having failed to explode. It was but a little
> space of time, but a hundred thousand men were listening.
> Finally a puff of smoke was seen at the Peach Orchard, then
> came a roar and a flash, and 138 pieces of Confederate artillery
> opened upon the enemy's position, and the deadly work began
> with the noise of the heaviest thunder.

Lieutenant Haskell:

> In an instant . . . the report of gun after gun in rapid succession
> smote our ears and their shells plunged down and exploded all
> around us. We sprang to our feet. In briefest time the whole
> Rebel line to the West was pouring out its thunder and its iron
> upon our devoted crest. The wildest confusion for a few
> moments obtained sway among us. The shells came bursting all
> about. The servants ran terror-stricken for dear life and disap-
> peared. The horses, hitched to the trees or held by the slack
> hands of the orderlies, neighed out in fright and broke away and
> plunged riderless through the fields.

And from soldiers on both sides:

> The ground roar of nearly the whole artillery of both armies
> burst in on the silence, almost as suddenly as the full notes of an
> organ would fill a church.

> The armies seemed like mighty wild beasts growling at each
> other.

> The men did not cheer or shout—they growled.

> We thought that at the second Bull Run, at the Antietam, and
> at Fredericksburg . . . we had heard heavy cannonading; they

were but holiday salutes compared with this. Besides the great ceaseless roar of the guns, which was but the background of the others, a million various minor sounds engaged the ear. The projectiles shriek long and sharp. They hiss, they scream, they growl, they sputter; all sounds of life and rage; and each has its different note.

The enemy shot hurtled among us and clipped off the clover heads by our side.

The very earth shook as from a mighty quake. So intense were its vibrations that loose grass, leaves, and twigs arose from six to eight inches above the ground, hovered and quivered as birds about to drop.

Large limbs were torn from the trunks of the oak trees under which we lay and precipitated down upon our heads.

The sun . . . was now darkened . . . In any direction might be seen guns, swords, haversacks, heads, limbs, flesh and bones in confusion or dangling in the air or bounding on the earth.

A small boy of twelve years was riding with us at the time. This urchin took a diabolical interest in the bursting of shells, and screamed with delight when he saw them take effect.

Riderless horses galloping madly through the fields . . . Mules with ammunition, pigs wallowing about, cows in the pasture.

A shell at our right exploded, and a piece cut through the bowels of the off wheel horse, another striking the nigh swing horse . . . on the gambrel joint, breaking the off leg . . . We continued on, the wheel horse trampling on his bowels all the time.

When the cannonade was at its height, a Confederate band of music, between the cemetery and ourselves, began to play polkas and waltzes, which sounded very curious.

Alfred B. Gardner was struck in the left shoulder, almost tearing his arm from his body. He lived a few minutes and died shouting, "Glory to God! I am happy! Hallelujah!"

General Longstreet:

Unwilling to trust myself with the entire responsibility, I had instructed Colonel Alexander to observe carefully the effect of the fire upon the enemy and, when it began to tell, to notify Pickett to begin the assault. I was so impressed with the hopelessness of the charge that I wrote the following note to Alexander:

"If the artillery fire does not have the effect to drive off the enemy or greatly demoralize him, I would prefer that you should not advise General Pickett to make the charge. I shall rely a great deal on your judgement to determine the matter, and shall expect you to let Pickett know when the moment offers."

To my note the colonel replied as follows:

"I will only be able to judge the effect of our fire upon the enemy by his return fire, for his infantry is but little exposed to view, and the smoke will obscure the whole field. If there is an alternative to this attack, it should be carefully considered before opening our fire, for it will take all the artillery ammunition we have left."

Alexander:

I was startled by the receipt of a note from Longstreet, ordering me to judge whether or not the attack should be made at all.

Until that moment, though I fully recognized the strength of the enemy's position, I had not doubted that we would carry it, in my confidence that Lee was ordering it. But here was a proposition that I should decide the question. Overwhelming reasons against the assault at once seemed to stare me in the face . . .

Before the cannonade opened I had made up my mind to give Pickett the order to advance within fifteen or twenty minutes after it began. But when I looked at the full developement of the enemy's batteries, and knew that his infantry was generally protected from our fire by stone walls and swells of the ground, I could not bring myself to give the word. It seemed madness to launch infantry into that fire, with nearly three quarters of a mile to go at midday under a July sun. I let the 15 minutes pass, and 20, and 25, hoping vainly for something to turn up . . .

The enemy's fire suddenly began to slacken . . . I wrote Pickett, urgently: "For God's sake come quick. The eighteen guns are gone; come quick, or my ammunition won't let me support you properly."

Longstreet:

Pickett said, "General, shall I advance?"

The effort to speak the order failed, and I could only indicate it by an affirmative bow. He accepted the duty with seeming confidence of success, leaped on his horse, and rode gayly to his command . . .

General Pickett, a graceful horseman, sat lightly in the saddle, his brown locks flowing quite over his shoulders.

Alexander:

Longstreet said, "I don't want to make this attack. I would stop it now but that General Lee ordered it and expects to go on. I don't see how it can succeed."

I listened, but did not dare offer a word. The battle was lost if we stopped. Ammunition was far too low to try anything else, for we had been fighting three days. There was a chance, and it was not my part to interfere. While Longstreet was still speaking, Pickett's division swept out of the wood and showed the full length of its grey ranks and shining bayonets, as grand a sight as ever a man looked on.

Colonel W. H. Taylor, CSA:

> The charge was made down a gentle slope, and then up to the enemy's lines, a distance of over half a mile, denuded of forests, and in full sight of the enemy, and perfect range of their artillery.

And others:

> Before us lay bright fields and fair landscape.

> . . . a scene of unsurpassed grandeur and majesty . . . As far as eye could reach could be seen the advancing troops, their gay war flags fluttering in the gentle summer breeze, while their sabers and bayonets flashed and glistened in the midday sun.

> . . . here and there an officer motioning with his sword to perfect the alignment, which, as a general thing, is as fine as on a holiday parade.

> In my admiration and enthusiasm I rushed some ten paces in advance and cast my eyes right and left. It was magnificent!

John Dooley:

> I tell you, there is no romance in making one of these charges . . . When you rise to your feet as we did today, I tell you the enthusiasm of ardent breasts in many cases *ain't there* and instead of burning to avenge the insults of our country, families and altars and firesides, the thought is most frequently, *Oh*, if I could just come out of this charge safely how thankful *would I be!*

A Confederate observer:

> As Pickett's Division pressed on by us . . . the fixed look in their face, showed that they had steeled themselves to certain death.

General Franklin Sawyer, USA:

> The front of the column was nearly up the slope . . . when suddenly a terrific fire from every available gun from the Cemetery to Round Top Mountain burst upon them. The distinct, graceful lines of the rebels underwent an instantaneous transformation. They were at once enveloped in a dense cloud of smoke and dust. Arms, heads, blankets, guns and knapsacks were thrown and tossed into the clear air . . . A moan went up from the field, distinctly to be heard amid the storm of battle.

> Lead and iron seemed to fill the air, as in a sleet storm . . .

> Men, or fragments of men, were being thrown in the air every moment, but, closing up the gaps and leaving swaths of dead and dying in their tracks, these brave men still kept up their march.

Alexander:

> We were halted for a moment by a fence, and as the men threw it down for the guns to pass, I saw in one of the corners a man sitting down and looking up at me. A solid shot had carried away both jaws and his tongue . . . He sat up and looked at me steadily.

Captain June Kimble, CSA:

> For five, perhaps ten minutes we held our ground and looked back for and prayed for support. It came not.

Alexander:

> Pickett's men never halted, but opened fire at close range, swarmed over the fences, and among the enemy's guns—were swallowed up in smoke, and that was the last of them. The conflict hardly seemed to last five minutes before they were melted away.

Longstreet:

> When the smoke cleared away, Pickett's Division was gone.
> Nearly two-thirds of his men lay dead on the field, and the
> survivors were sullenly retreating down the hill.

A Confederate:

> Amidst that still continuous, terrible fire, they slowly, sullenly,
> recrossed the plain—all that was left of them . . .

Alexander:

> About that time General Lee, entirely alone, rode up and
> remained with me a long time. He then probably first appreci-
> ated the full extent of the disaster as the disorganized stragglers
> made their way back to us . . . But, whatever his emotions, there
> was no trace of them in his calm, self-possessed bearing.

Longstreet:

> There is no doubt that General Lee, during the crisis of that
> campaign, lost the matchless equipoise that characterized him,
> and that whatever mistakes were made were not so much
> matters of deliberate judgement as the impulses of a great mind
> disturbed by unparalleled conditions.

A Confederate:

> During the whole of this miserable day, and part of the preced-
> ing, the men had nothing to eat, and were very often without
> water. I succeeded at one time, in satisfying the pangs of
> hunger, by eating the fruit from a cherry tree, which either hung
> close to the ground, or whose boughs had been struck off by the
> bullets and shells.

Dooley:

> I begin now to suffer from thirst, for the only water they bring us is from a neighboring run which is warm and muddy and has the additional properties belonging to human blood and dead bodies.

> This is a horrid night . . .

> Here is a poor wounded Confederate who is walking up and down, wandering anywhere his cracked brain directs him. Just on top of his head and penetrating to his brain is a large opening made by a shell in which I might insert my hand. He walks about as if nothing was the matter with him, and pays no attention to any advice given him.

> Another victim and member of my regiment is deliriously moaning and shouting all the night. He begins in a low tone of voice and shouts louder and louder, using only one phrase all the time, until he becomes exhausted. Thus he repeats frantically a hundred times at least the words, "I'm proud I belong to the 1st Va. Regiment!"

Brigadier-General John D. Imboden, CSA, 1 A.M., July 4, the following morning:

> When [General Lee] arrived there was not even a sentinal on duty at his tent, and no one of his staff was awake. The moon was high in the clear sky and the silent scene was unusually vivid. As he approached and saw us lying on the grass under a tree, he spoke, reined in his jaded horse, and essayed to dismount. The effort to do so betrayed so much physical exhaustion that I hurriedly rose and stepped forward to assist him, but before I reached his side he had succeeded in alighting, and threw his arm across the saddle to rest, and fixing his eyes upon the ground leaned in silence and almost motionless upon

his equally weary horse,—the two forming a striking and never-to-be-forgotten group. The moon shone full upon his massive features and revealed an expression of sadness that I had never before seen upon his face.

Lee to Imboden, 2 A.M.:

We must now return to Virginia. As many of our poor wounded as possible must be taken home. I have sent for you, because your men and horses are fresh and in good condition, to guard and conduct our train back to Virginia. The duty will be arduous, responsible and dangerous.

July 4, noon:

The rain fell in blinding sheets; the meadows were soon overflowed, and fences gave way before the raging streams. During the storm, wagons, ambulances, and artillery carriages by hundreds—nay, by thousands—were assembling in the fields . . . in one confused and apparently inextricable mass. As the afternoon wore on there was no abatement in the storm . . . Horses and mules were blinded and maddened by the wind and water.

Imboden, the night of the Fourth:

After dark I set out from Cashtown to gain the head of the column during the night. My orders had been peremptory that there should be no halt for any cause whatever. If an accident should happen to any vehicle, it was immediately to be put out of the road and abandoned. The column moved rapidly, considering the rough roads and the darkness . . . For four hours I hurried forward . . . and in all that time I was never out of the hearing of the groans and cries of the wounded and dying. Scarcely one in a hundred had received adequate surgical aid, owing to the demands on the hard-working surgeons from still worse cases that had to be left behind. Many of the wounded in the wagons had been without food for thirty-six hours. Their torn and bloody clothing, matted and hardened, was rasping the tender, inflamed and still oozing wounds. Very few of the wagons had even a layer of straw in them, and all were without springs, . . . the teams trotted on, urged by whip and shout.

———————

Alexander:

In order to protect his retreat, Lee had maintained a pontoon bridge at Falling Waters, a few miles from Williamsport. But it was weakly guarded, and on June 5 a small enemy raiding party . . . had broken it and destroyed some boats, fortunately not all. The retreat of the army was, therefore, brought to a standstill just when forty-eight hours more would have placed it beyond pursuit. We were already nearly out of provisions, and now the army was about to be penned up on the riverbank and subjected to an attack at his leisure by Meade.

All diligence was used to relieve the situation. The ferryboats were in use by day and by night carrying over, first, our wounded, and next, 5,000 Federal prisoners brought from Gettysburg. Warehouses on the canal were torn down, and from the timber new pontoon boats were being built to repair the bridge at Falling Waters.

A Confederate:

The river was full and past fording when we arrived at it, and the ferryboat was kept busy taking men across and bringing ammunition back for our army. The cavalry were swimming their horses across all the time we were at work, the army lying in line of battle, waiting for us to get the bridge built . . . When the bridge was completed the army commenced crossing the river, but the bridge was kept full all the time with ambulances, medical wagons, ordnance wagons and artillery, and such things as had to be kept dry, consequently there was no room for the infantry to cross, except one division, that was guarding the bridge. The rest waded the river at Williamsport. The greater portion of the wagon train had to ford at the same place. The water came up under the arms of the men.

Blackford:

On either bank fires illuminated the scene, the water reached the armpits of the men and was very swift. By the bright lurid light the long line of heads and shoulders and the dim sparkling of their musket barrels could be traced across the watery space, dwindling away almost to a thread before it reached the further shore. The passage of the wagon trains was attended with some loss, for the current in some cases swept them down past the ford into deep water. It was curious to watch the behavior of the mules in these teams. As the water rose over their backs they began rearing and springing vertically upward, and as they went deep and deeper the less would be seen of them before they made the spring which would bring their bodies half out of the water; then nothing would be seen but their ears above the water, until by a violent effort the poor brutes would spring aloft; and indeed after the waters had closed over them, occasionally one would appear in one last plunge high above the surface.

A Confederate:

On reaching the upper end of the town we could see a long line of men wading in the Potomac river. It was just break of day and it was terrible to see the men in the big river with only their heads above the water . . . the Potomac was rising rapidly.

Longstreet:

The natural difficulties in making such movements were increased by the darkness of the night, a heavy rainstorm flood-ing the road with mud and water, and finally by one of our wagons loaded with wounded running off the bridge, breaking it down and throwing it headlong into the water . . . The rear of my column passed the bridge at 9 o'clock in the morning.

. . . The army on the 13th of July, passed over very quietly— the bridges having been covered with bushes to prevent the rumbling of the wheels.

As the last ones crossed the bridge they cut the cable that held it . . .

PRISONERS OF WAR

QUARTERMASTER-GENERAL'S OFFICE, *Washington, July 20, 1863*

General D. H. Rucker,
Chief Quartermaster, U.S. Army, Washington:
GENERAL: It is proposed, as I am informed, by the General-in-Chief to establish a depot for prisoners of war at Point Lookout . . .
Old tents should be sent from those in depot and necessary camp and garrison equipage, lumber to erect kitchens and storehouses, and large cast-iron boilers for cooking. The labor will be performed by the prisoners themselves.

John R. King:

The 20th of May 1864, we marched through the big gate marked in large letters, "Prisoner's Camp." Now our campaigns were ended . . . The prison at Point Lookout was located on a narrow piece of ground about one quarter of a mile wide at the mouth of the Potomac River. Here the river is ten miles in width.

Anthony M. Keiley:

> The military prison, or rather prisons, at Point Lookout, consisted of two inclosures, the one containing about thirty, the other about ten acres of flat sand, on the northern shore of the Potomac at its mouth, but a few inches above high tide, and utterly innocent of trees, shrub, or any natural equivalent.

THE DIARY OF BARTLETT YANCEY MALONE

Bartlett Y. Malone was borned and raised in North Carolina Caswell County in the Year of our Lord 1838. And was Gradguated in the corn field and tobacco patch: And inlisted in the war June the 18th 1861. And was a member of the Caswell Boys Company . . .

> His purposes will ripen fast
> Unfolding evry hour
> The bud may have a bitter taste
> But sweet will be the flower
>
> May your days be days of pleasure
> May your nites be nites of rest
> May you obtain lifes sweetest pleasure
> And then be numbered with the blest.

> Whar ere you rome
> What ere your lot
> Its all I ask
> Forget me not.
>
> Remember me when I am gon
> Dear friend remember me
> And when you bow befour the throne
> O then remember me.

Candy is sweet
It is very clear
But not half so sweet
As you my dear

———————

One day amidst the plas
Where Jesus is within
Is better than ten thousen days
Of pleasure and of Sin

O for grace our hearts to soften
Teach us Lord at length to love
We alas forget too often
What a friend we have above.

All I like of being a Whale
Is a water Spout and a tail.

———————

A certain cewer for the Toothack if the the tooth is hollow take
a pease of the scale that is on a horses leg and put it in the hol-
low of the tooth   It is a serten cewer so sais J. H. Lyon.

B. Y. M.

THIS IS FOR THE YEAR 1863

... We was then cut off and had to Surender: was then taken
back to the rear and stiad thir untell next morning   The morn-
ing of the 8th we was marched back to Warrenton Junction and
got on the cars about day next morning we got to Washington
we then staid in Washington untel 3 o'clock in the eavning of
the 8th then was marched down to the Warf and put on the
Stemer John Brooks and got to Point Lookout about one
O'clock on the eavning of the 10th day of November 1863 ...

Our rations at Point Lookout was 5 crackers and a cup of
coffee for Breakfast. And for dinner a small ration of meat 2

crackers three Potatoes and a cup of Soup. Supper we have non. We pay a dollar for 8 crackers or a chew of tobacco for a cracker.

A Yankey shot one of our men the other day wounded him in the head shot him for peepen threw the cracks of the planken . . .

The 24th day of Dec. 63 was a clear day but very cool. And Generl Butler the Yankey beast revewed the prisners camp:

The 25th was Christmas day and it was clear and cool and I was both coal and hungry all day only got a peace of Bread and a cup of coffee for Breakfast and a small Slice of Meat and a cup of Soup and five Crackers for Dinner and Supper I had non:

The 26th was clear and cool and dull for Christmas.

The 28th was cloudy and rained a littel   The 28th was a raney day.

The 28th was cloudy in the morning and clear in the eavning. And Jeferson Walker died in the morning   he belonged to the 57th N. C. Regt. The 30th was a beautyful day.

The 31st which was the last day of 63 was a raney day. And maby I will never live to see the last day of 64. And thairfour I will try to do better than I have. For what is a man profited if he shal gain the whole world and loose his one Soul: Or what Shal one give in exchange for his Soul:

B. Y. MALONE

B. Y. MALONE'S BOOK
FOR THE YEAR 1864

I spent the first day of January 64 at Point Lookout M.D. The morning was pleasant but toward eavning the air changed and the nite was very coal.   was so coal that five of our men froze to death befour morning. We all suffered a great deal with coal and hunger too of our men was so hungry to day that they caught a Rat and cooked him and eat it. Thir names was Sergt. N. W. Hester & I. C. Covington.

The 6th was coal and cloudy and we had 9 men to die at the Hospital to day. Our beds at this plaice is composed of Sea feathers that is we geather the small stones from the Bay and lye on them

The 7th was very cool a small Snow fell after nite

The 10 was a nice day and I saw the man to day that makes Coffens at this plaice for the Rebels and he sais that 12 men dies here every day that is averidgs 12

The Commander at this point is named Marsto

The 22th day of January 64 was a very pritty day And it was my birth day which maid me 25 years of age   I spent the day at Point Lookout. M. D. And I feasted on Crackers and Coffee. The two last weeks of January was beautyfull weather . . .

The 18th it was so coal that a mans breath would freeze on his beard going from the Tent to the Cookhouse. O, it was so coal the 18th.

King:

Two days out of every three we were guarded by a gang of ignorant and cruelsome negroes.

Please do not think that I dislike the negroes . . . The negro guard was very insolent and delighted in tantalizing the prisoners for some trifle affair . . . "Look out, white man, the bottom rail is on top now."

Shotwell:

The lower portion of the Pen was occupied by rows of small tents or pretense of tents, they being a lot of condemned canvas, ruined by salt water and mildewed.

. . . From seven to ten men were huddled in each tent like a sweltering nest of pigs.

In rainy weather the rotten canvas served to gather and pour down upon us steady streams of water . . . while within an hour after the rain ceased, great clouds of dry sand began their tireless whirling.

Keiley:

> During the scorching summer, whose severity during the day is
> as great on that sand-barren as anywhere in the Union north of
> the Gulf, and through the hard winter, which is more severe at
> that point than anywhere in the country south of Boston, these
> poor fellows were confined here in open tents, on the naked
> ground, without a plank or a handful of straw between them and
> the heat or frost of the earth.
>
> And when, in the winter, a high tide and an easterly
> gale would flood the whole surface of the pen, *and freeze as it
> flooded,* the sufferings of the half-clad wretches . . . may easily be
> imagined . . .
>
> During all this season the ration of wood allowed to each
> man was an arm-full for five days, and this had to cook for
> him as well as warm him, for at the time there were no public
> cookhouses and mess-rooms.

> I never saw any one get enough of any thing to eat at Point Look-
> out, except the soup, and a teaspoonful of that was *too much* for
> ordinary digestion.
>
> These digestive discomforts were greatly enhanced by the
> villainous character of the water, which is so impregnated with
> some mineral as to offend every nose, and induce diarrhoea
> in almost every alimentary canal. It colors every thing black
> in which it is allowed to rest, and a scum rises on the top of a
> vessel, if it is left standing during the night.

Shotwell:

> The soup was always luke-warm, and garnished with white
> worms half an inch long; while the food was gritty with sand
> and dirt.

> Our rations grow daily worse—the soup more watery, the pork
> fatter and more rancid, the beef leaner and more stringy.

The camp was full of haggard, half-clad men, whose sunken eyes, and tottering gait bespoke them already doomed . . .

Washington, *November 13, 1863*

DR. J. H. DOUGLAS
Associate Secretary, Sanitary Commission:

SIR: In compliance with orders received from the central office to proceed to Point Lookout, Md., and inquire into the condition, &c., of the rebel prisoners there confined, also the sanitary condition of the encampment and its inmates, I hereby submit the following report:

. . . No attention was given to the separating of different diseases. Wounded and erysipelas, fever and diarrhea, were lying side by side. . . . There being no stoves in the hospital, the men complained greatly of cold, and I must admit that for the poor emaciated creatures suffering from diarrhea, one single blanket is not sufficient . . .

The grounds around the hospital have not, according to looks, been policed for a very long time. Filth is gradually accumulating and the sinks are not at all thought of, requiring a little extra exertion to walk to them. They void their excrement in the most convenient place to them, regardless of the comfort of others . . .

They are ragged and dirty and very thinly clad . . . Some are without shirts, or what were once shirts are now hanging in shreds from their shoulders . . . Generally they have one blanket to three men, but a great many are entirely without . . . A great many of the tents have been pitched over old sinks lightly covered . . . They are troubled greatly with the itch . . .

Very respectfully, your obedient servant,
W. F. SWALM.

King:

Bathing in the bay was a source of pleasure granted us . . . it was a great relief to stand on the beach and watch the ships and small craft pass . . . some with a line and net waded in the water waist deep and caught the big crabs. . . . When the tide was coming in the water was delightful, at the dead line we sat on the post until the waves were highest, then we rode them to the shore.

APRIL 1865

Right or wrong, God judge me, not man. For be my motive good or bad, of one thing I am sure, the lasting condemnation of the North. I love peace more than life. Have loved the Union beyond expression. For four years have I waited, hoped and prayed for the dark clouds to break and for a restoration of our former sunshine. To wait longer would be a crime. All hope for peace is dead. My prayers have proved as idle as my hopes. God's will be done. I go to see and share the bitter end.

I have ever held the South were right. The very nomination of Abraham Lincoln, four years ago, spoke plainly war, war, upon southern rights and institutions. His election proved it. "Await an overt act." Yes, till you are bound and plundered. What folly. The South was wise. Who thinks of argument or pastime when the finger of his enemy presses the trigger?

The country was formed for the white, not for the black man. And looking upon *African slavery* from the same standpoint held by the noble framers of our constitution, I, for one, have ever considered it one of the greatest blessings (both for themselves and us) that God ever bestowed upon a favored nation. Witness heretofore our wealth and power; witness their elevation and enlightenment above their race elsewhere. I have lived among it most of my life, and have seen less harsh treatment from master to man than I ever beheld in the North from father to son . . .

When I aided in the capture and execution of John Brown (who was a murderer on our Western border and who was fairly tried and convicted, before an impartial judge and jury, of treason, and who, by the way, has since been made a god) I was proud of my little share in the transaction, for I deemed it my duty that I was helping our common country to perform an act of justice. But what was a crime in poor John Brown is now considered (by themselves) as the greatest and only virtue of the whole Republican party. Strange transmigration. Vice so becomes a virtue, simply because more indulged in . . .

Alas, poor country. Is she to meet her threatened doom? Four years ago I would have given a thousand lives to see her remain (as I had always known her) powerful and unbroken. And even now I would hold my life as naught to see her what she was. O, my friends, if the fearful scenes of the past four years had never been enacted, or if what has been was a frightful dream, from which we could now awake, with what overflowing hearts could we bless our God . . .

My love, (as things stand to-day) is for the South alone. Nor do I deem it a dishonour in attempting to make for her a prisoner of this man to whom she owes so much misery. If success attends me, I go penniless to her side. They say she has found that "last ditch" which the North has so long derided, and been endeavoring to force her in, forgetting they are our brothers, and that it is impolitic to goad an enemy to madness.

A confederate doing duty upon his own responsibility.

J. WILKES BOOTH

FORD'S THEATRE
Tenth Street, above E

Friday Evening, April 14th, 1865

*This Evening
the Performance will be honored
by the presence of*
PRESIDENT LINCOLN

BENEFIT AND LAST NIGHT OF
Miss LAURA KEENE
in
Tom Taylor's Celebrated Eccentric Comedy,
as originally produced in America by Miss Keene,
and performed by her upwards of
one thousand nights,
entitled

OUR   AMERICAN   COUSIN

General and Mrs. Ulysses S. Grant planned to attend the performance with the president's party, but at the last moment the Grants withdrew (Mrs. Grant couldn't stand Mrs. Lincoln), and the president invited instead Major Henry R. Rathbone and his fiancée, Miss Clara Harris.

The performance began at 7:45, but the presidential party didn't appear until 8:30. As Lincoln entered his box, the players halted, the orchestra struck up "Hail to the Chief," and the audience rose, waved handkerchiefs, and cheered. Lincoln bowed, then took his seat and the play resumed.

The president was to be guarded by John F. Parker, special guard, but he and Lincoln's coachman went out for a drink, and when Parker came back he took a seat in the dress circle, so he could see the show.

During the second act, John Wilkes Booth appeared in the alley to the stage door, leading a bay mare. Ordering a stage hand to hold the mare, he entered the theater, passed under the stage to the front of the building, came out on the street, and dropped into the nearest tavern for a drink (he had been drinking heavily recently— a quart of brandy downed in two hours was not unusual).

Later, he emerged. The third act was now playing. He entered the lobby. Passing the doorkeeper, he climbed the stairs to the dress circle and worked his way around the wall to the rear of the private boxes.

Presenting a card to Lincoln's footman, he brushed past him, entered the presidential box, closed the door and barred it from within.

———

Mary Lincoln laughed. Instantly there was a sound like the report of a firearm, muffled but distinct. Hawk [the actor on stage] thought it came from the property room. Then at the front of the President's box he saw a man brandishing a knife.

Shouting words that Hawk did not understand, the man was over the balustrade. He landed upon the stage in a kneeling posture, about two feet out from the lower box next to the foot-lights, making a long rent in the green-baize stage carpet . . . Buckingham, the doorkeeper, . . . got sight of the man crossing toward the "prompt side"—crossing rapidly, with a gait that Mrs. Wright described as "like the hopping of a bull-frog," flourishing the knife as he went.

. . . Smoke drifted out of the President's box. For a moment the greater part of the audience sat as if in a trance.

Abruptly, from within the box, a piercing scream rang out—
and the house became an inferno.

There will never be anything like it on earth. The shouts,
groans, curses, smashing of seats, screams of women, shuffling
of feet and cries of terror created a pandemonium.

There were shouts of "Hang him!" "Kill him!" Chairs were torn
from their fastenings. Many persons were in tears. Actors and
actresses were jumbled in confusion on the stage with those of
the audience who kept mounting it. Some of the musicians had
left their instruments behind them. Mrs. Wright put her foot
through a 'cello that she seems to have been trying to use as a
ladder.

I had never witnesesed such a scene as was now presented.
The seats, aisles, galleries, and stage were filled with shouting,
frenzied men and women, many running aimlessly over one
another; a chaos of disorder beyond control.

Outside, a crowd gathered in the street, shouting "Burn the theater!"

Emerging in the alley, Booth knocked down the man holding his
horse, mounted and spurred the mare, rode up the alley to F Street,
and was seen to turn right.

The ball entered the skull about midway between the left ear
and the median line of the back of the head.

Lincoln tried to rise, lifting his head, "and then it hung back."
    Some called for water, others for brandy and a surgeon. A navy
doctor, in uniform, clambered onto the stage, was lifted into the
box. A pitcher of water was handed up to him.
    Major Rathbone, slashed in the arm, dislodged the bar across the
door, at the back of the box.

The president, still breathing, was lifted from his chair, carried down the stairs from the dress circle, across the street, and into the Petersen House, a private home.

Laura Keene, standing in the lobby, by the ticket window, exclaimed, in full theatrical voice: "For God's sake, try to capture the murderer!"

Sergeant Silas T. Cobb, on duty at the Washington end of the Navy Yard bridge, across the Anacostia, challenged a rider:

"Who are you, sir?"
"My name is Booth."
"Where are you from?"
"The city."
"Where are you going?"
"I'm going home."
"And where is your home?"
"In Charles."
"What town?"
"I don't live in any town."
"Oh, you must live in some town."
"No, I live close to Beantown but not in the town."
"Why are you out so late? Don't you know you're not allowed to pass after nine o'clock?"
"That's news to me. I had business in the city and thought if I waited I'd have the moon to ride home by."

Sgt. Cobb passed him.

In the Petersen house, after midnight: "In rare moments of silence the President's labored breathing sounded through the hall, rising and falling."

Across the Anacostia, Booth took the old T. B. Road, by Silver Hill. He was joined on the way by Davey Herold, co-conspirator.

Together, they arrived at Lloyd's barroom in the Surratt House at Surrattsville—now Clinton—around midnight. Booth did not dismount; his leg was swollen and painful. He had broken it, when his spur caught in the draped flag, as he leaped from the box to the stage.

Herold dismounted, roused the sodden Lloyd, brought Booth a drink of whiskey, and a carbine Booth had arranged to pick up (the murder weapon, a derringer, had been dropped at the theater).

The pain in Booth's leg, aggravated by riding, became unbearable. Leaving Surrattsville, he turned away from the Potomac and the boat awaiting him at Port Tobacco, rode through the village of T.B., across Mattawoman Swamp, to the home of Dr. Samuel Mudd, near Bryantown.

Dr. Mudd:

> I was aroused by the noise, and as it was such an unusual thing for persons to knock so loudly, I took the precaution of asking who were there before opening the door. After they had knocked twice more, I opened the door, but before doing so they told me they were two strangers on their way to Washington, that one of their horses had fallen, by which one of the men had broken his leg. On opening the door, I found two men, one on a horse led by the other man who had tied his horse to a tree near by. I aided the man in getting off his horse and into the house, and laid him on a sofa in my parlor.
>
> After getting a light, I assisted him in getting up-stairs where there were two beds, one of which he took . . .
>
> On examination I found there was a straight fracture of the tibia about two inches above the ankle.

The boot was slit across the instep and removed, and the doctor made a splint by doubling a piece of an old bandbox.

It was now daylight.

At the Petersen house in Washington, "the measured breathing grew slowly fainter and the sound of it ended." April 15, 7:22 A.M.

———————

During the day, Dr. Mudd made the rounds of his patients in Bryantown, while Herold tried unsuccessfully to borrow a carriage in the neighborhood. When Mudd returned in late afternoon, Booth and Herold were gone. Booth carried with him a rough crutch, made for him by a freedman of the place.

Turning again toward the Potomac, they became lost in Zekiah Swamp, tracking and backtracking through the night, until found by Ozzie Swan, a Negro. Swan carried Booth in his wagon and Herold followed with the horses, to the home of Samuel Cox, land owner and Southern sympathizer, not far from Faulkner. It was, again, daybreak.

Cox hid the men in a dense pine thicket, and sent for his foster brother, one Thomas Jones, official Confederate agent in the area.

Jones:

> I have often observed when there is a weighty matter to be discussed between men, how reluctant they seem to approach it. Cox had a most important disclosure to make to me; I knew that he had, and yet, for some minutes, we spoke of any matter rather than that which had brought us together. At length he said to me: "Tom, I had visitors about four o'clock this morning."
> "Who were they, and what did they want?" I asked.
> "They want to get across the river," said Cox, answering my last question first; and then added in a whisper, "Have you heard that Lincoln was killed Friday night?"
> I said, "Yes, I have heard it," ... There was silence between us for a minute, which was broken by Cox.
> "Tom, we must get those men who were here this morning across the river."

The place where Booth and Herold were in hiding was about two hundred yards south of the present village of Cox Station . . . As I drew near the hiding place I saw a bay mare, with saddle and bridle on, grazing in a small open space where a clearing had been made for a tobacco bed. I at first thought that she belonged to some one in the neighborhood and had got away. I caught her and tied her to a tree. I then went on a little further until I thought I was near the place indicated by Cox. I stopped and gave the whistle. Presently a young man—he looked scarcely more than a boy—came cautiously out of the thicket and stood before me. He carried a carbine ready cocked in his hands.

"Who are you, and what do you want?" he demanded.

"I come from Cox," I replied; "he told me I would find you here. I am a friend; you have nothing to fear from me."

He looked searchingly at me for a moment and then said, "Follow me," and led the way for about thirty yards into the thick undergrowth to where his companion was lying. "This friend comes from Captain Cox," he said; and that was my introduction to John Wilkes Booth . . .

I told him that I would do what I could to help him; but for the present he must remain where he was; that it would not do to stir during the hue and cry then being made in the neighborhood. I promised to bring him food every day, and to get him across the river, if possible, just as soon as it would not be suicidal to make the attempt.

He held out his hand and thanked me.

He told me, as he had told Cox, that he had killed President Lincoln. He said he knew the United States Government would use every means in its power to secure his capture. "But," he added, with a flash of determination lighting up his dark eye, "John Wilkes Booth will never be taken alive"; and as I looked at him, I believed him.

He seemed very desirous to know what the world thought of his deed, and asked me to bring him some newspapers.

I mentioned to Booth that I had seen a horse grazing near by, and he said it belonged to him. I told him and Herold that they would have to get rid of their horses or they would certainly betray them; besides, it would be impossible to feed them.

Before leaving, I pointed out to Herold a spring about thirty or forty yards distant, where he could procure water for himself and companion. I advised him to be very cautious in going to the spring, as there was a footpath running near it that was sometimes, though seldom, used. Then promising to see them next day and bring food and newspapers, I mounted my horse and rode home.

Herold led the horses into shallow water, over quicksand, and shot them . . .

Jones:

There were but two boats on this side the river that I knew of, and they were both mine . . .

It need not be said that Booth's only chance for crossing the river depended upon my being able to retain possession and control of one of these two boats.

When I reached home from my visit to Booth that Sunday, I called Henry Woodland, who had continued to live with me after his emancipation, and told him to get out some gill-nets next morning and to fish them regularly every day, and after fishing always to return the boat to Dent's Meadow.

Dent's Meadow was then a very retired spot back of Huckle-berry farm, about one and a half miles north of Pope's Creek, at least a mile from the public road and with no dwelling house in sight. This meadow is a narrow valley opening to the river between high and steep cliffs that were then heavily timbered and covered with an almost impenetrable undergrowth of laurel. A small stream flows through the meadow, widening into a little creek as it approaches the river. It was from this spot I determined to make the attempt of sending Booth across to Virginia.

Immediately after breakfast on Monday morning, I wrapped up some bread and butter and ham, filled a flask with coffee, and put it all in the pockets of my overcoat. I then took a basket of corn on my arm as though I were going to call my hogs that ran at large in the woods surrounding my house, and mounting my horse, set out on my dangerous visit.

Nothing of any especial importance happened at this interview. Booth seemed to be suffering more with his leg than on the previous day, and was impatient to resume his journey so as to reach some place where he could be housed and get medical attention. I told him he must wait. While we were talking I heard the clanking of sabers and tramping of horses, as a body of cavalry passed down the road within two hundred yards of us. We listened with suspended breath until the sound died away in the distance. I then said, "You see, my friend, we must wait."

Tuesday morning, after my visit to the pine thicket, I rode up to Port Tobacco.

Tuesday was then, as it is now, the day for the transaction of public business in our county. I was therefore likely to meet a good many people in the county-town that day, and hear whatever was going on.

I found the men gathered about in little groups on the square . . . The general impression seemed to be that Booth had not crossed the river.

I mingled with the people and listened till I was satisfied that nothing was positively known. Every expression was merely surmise.

Wednesday and Thursday passed uneventfully away. The neighborhood was filled with cavalrymen and detectives. They visited my house several times during that week (as they did every house in southern Maryland) and upon one occasion searched it. They also interviewed my colored man, Henry Woodland, and threatened him with dire penalties if he did not tell all he knew. Henry did not *know* anything because I had told him nothing. I took no one into my confidence.

As the days rolled away, Booth's impatience to cross the river became almost insufferable. His leg, from neglect and exposure, had become terribly swollen and inflamed, and the pain he had to bear was excruciating. To add to his further discomfiture—if that was possible—a cold, cloudy, damp spell of weather, such as we often have in spring, set in and continued throughout the week . . . The only breaks in the monotony of that week were my daily visits, and the food and newspapers I carried him. He never tired of the newspapers.

Booth—from fragments of a diary:

April 13-14   Friday the Ides
I struck boldly and not as the paper say. I walked with a firm step through a thousand of his friends, was stopped but pushed on. A colonel was at his side. I shouted Sic semper *before* I fired. In jumping broke my leg. I passed all his pickets, rode sixty miles that night with the bone of my leg tearing the flesh at every jump. I can never repent it, though we hated to kill. Our country owed all her troubles to him, and God simply made me the instrument of his punishment. The country is not what it *was*. This forced union is not what I have loved. I care not what becomes of me.

Jones:

On Friday evening, one week after the assassination, I rode down to Allen's Fresh . . .

Allen's Fresh, about three miles east of my house, was and still is, a small village situated where Zechiah Swamp ends and the Wicomico River begins.

I had not been long in the village when a body of cavalry, guided by a man from St. Mary's County named John R. Walton, rode in and dismounted. Some of the soldiers entered Colton's store, where I was sitting, and called for something to drink. Soon afterward Walton came in and exclaimed, "Boys, I have news that they have been seen in St. Mary's," whereupon they all hastily remounted their horses and galloped off across the bridge in the direction of St. Mary's County.

I was confident there were no other soldiers in the neighborhood.

"Now or never," I thought.

It was dark by the time I reached the place. I had never before visited the fugitives at night: I therefore approached with more than usual caution and gave the signal. Herold answered and led the way to Booth. I informed them of what had just occurred at Allen's Fresh.

"The coast seems to be clear," I said, "and the darkness favors us. Let us make the attempt." . . .

With difficulty Booth was raised by Herold and myself and placed upon my horse. Every movement, in spite of his stoicism, wrung a groan of anguish from his lips. His arms were then given to him, the blankets rolled up and tied behind him on the horse, and we began the perilous journey.

The route we had to take was down the cart track . . . to the public road, a distance of about one mile and a half, then down the public road for another mile to the corner of my farm; and then through my place to the river, about one mile further.

. . . After what seemed an interminable age, we reached my place. We stopped under a pear tree near the stable, about forty or fifty yards from my house. It was then between nine and ten o'clock. "Wait here," I said, "while I go in and get you some supper, which you can eat here while I get something for myself." . . .

I entered the house through the kitchen. Henry Woodland was there. He had got in late and was just eating his supper. I asked him how many shad he had caught that evening and he told me. I then said, "Did you bring the boat to Dent's Meadow, and leave it there, Henry?"

"Yes, master."

"We had better get out another net to-morrow," I replied. "The fish are running well."

Some members of my family were in the dining-room when I entered. My supper was on the table waiting for me. I selected what I thought was enough for the two men and carried it out to them. None of the family seemed to notice what I was doing. They knew better than to question me about anything in those days.

After supper we resumed our journey across the open field toward the longed-for river . . . Presently we came to a fence that ran across the path, about three hundred yards from the river. It was difficult to take it down; so we left the horse there and Herold and myself assisted Booth to dismount and supporting him between us, took our way carefully down the tortuous path that led to the shore.

The path was steep and narrow and for three men to walk down it abreast, one of them being a cripple, to whom every step was torture, was not the least difficult part of that night's work.

But the Potomac, that longed-for goal, at last was near.

It was nearly calm now, but the wind had been blowing during the day and there was a swell upon the river, and as we approached, we could hear its sullen roar. It was a mournful sound coming through the darkness . . .

At length we reached the shore and found the boat where Henry had been directed by me to leave it. It was a flat bottomed boat about twelve feet long, of a dark lead color . . .

We placed Booth in the stern with an oar to steer; Herold took the bow-seat to row. Then lighting a candle which I had brought for the purpose—I had no lantern—and carefully shading it with an oilcloth coat belonging to one of the men, I pointed out on the compass Booth had with him the course to steer. "Keep to that," I said, "and it will bring you into Machodoc Creek. Mrs. Quesenberry lives near the mouth of this creek. If you tell her you come from me I think she will take care of you." . . .

I pushed the boat off and it glided out of sight into the darkness.

I stood on the shore and listened till the sound of the oars died away in the distance.

Jones failed or forgot to warn them of the spring flood tide. The boat was carried upstream, along the Maryland shore, and Herold finally put into Avon Creek, a tributary of Nanjemoy. Throughout the day Saturday, he and Booth remained in concealment.

Booth's diary:

> After being hunted like a dog through swamps, woods, and last night being chased by gun-boats till I was forced to return wet cold and starving, with every man's hand against me, I am here in despair. And why? For doing what Brutus was honored for. What made Tell a hero. And yet I for striking down a greater tyrant than ever they knew am looked upon as a common cutthroat. My action was purer than either of theirs . . . I hoped for no gain. I knew no private wrong. I struck for my country and that alone. A country groaned beneath this tyranny and prayed for this end, and yet now behold the cold hand they extend to me . . . So ends all. For my country I have given up all that makes life sweet and Holy, brought misery upon my family, and am sure there is no pardon in the Heaven for me since man condemn me so . . . To night I will once more try the river with the intent to cross.
>
> I have too great a soul to die like a criminal. Oh may he, may he spare me that and let me die bravely.

––––––––––

Saturday night, Booth and Herold crossed the Potomac, landing in Gambo Creek, just above Machadoc. Helped by Mrs. Quesenberry and others, they made their way inland to the Rappahannock, ferried across at Port Royal, and rode three miles further, along the Bowling Green road, to the Garrett farm, where they were taken in, fed, and housed, passing as Confederate veterans.

Booth spent the day—Tuesday, April 25th—reclining on the front porch, with a view of rolling hills and a stretch of the approaching road.

That night, he and Herold, becoming suspicious, moved out of the house to the tobacco barn. The Garrett boys sat up to watch them, thinking they might be horse thieves.

Two o'clock Wednesday morning, the Garrett yard was suddenly filled with Union cavalry. The elder Garrett was awakened and questioned, but would not say where the fugitives were. When the soldiers threatened to hang him, his son, Jack Garrett, directed them to the tobacco barn.

Surrounding the barn, the officers parleyed with Booth, who refused to surrender. Young Garrett was sent in to disarm the men, but quickly emerged, terrorized.

At length, Herold: "Let me out! Let me out!"
     The door opened, and he was passed out to the soldiers, unarmed and shaking.

Igniting loose hay from a candle, the soldiers set fire to the barn; spreading to hay inside, the flames quickly took off, and Booth, armed at both hands and leaning on crutches, appeared in silhouette through the open slats. He dropped one crutch, then the other, and with "a kind of limping, halting jump," moved toward the door. A shot rang out, Booth sprang forward, and fell in a heap.

He was dragged, still living, from the burning barn, and carried to the porch of the farmhouse.
     "Kill me! Kill me!" he whispered . . . One of the Garrett women brought him a pillow, but he could not be made comfortable.

. . . Between five and six—at daybreak—his breathing stopped.

——————

Booth had been shot by Boston Corbett, one of the soldiers.
     "Why in hell did you shoot without orders?" his officer asked.
     Corbett came to attention, and saluted. "Colonel, Providence directed me."

THREE

NINETEEN SIXTIES

ONE

My pedestrian excursions of the last year had given me a relish
for these rambles; I had become convinced that they were both
easy, usefull and full of pleasure, while they afforded me the
means to study every thing at leasure. I never was happier than
when alone in the woods.

                        . . . Constantine Samuel Rafinesque,
naturalist, exploring the Potomac region, 1804-1805. (His real name
was not Constantine Samuel Rafinesque, but Constantine Samuel
Rafinesque Schmaltz.)

I collected many rare and new plants at the falls of Potowmack.
I went to Alexandria to visit the herbal of Hingston, who gave
me several rare plants. The heat becoming oppressive I
returned.

. . . Next to Frederic by the rail road. There I took the Wash-
ington stage to reach the foot of the Sugarloaf, a singular insu-
lated mt. 15 miles around and 500 feet high, (Long says 800), it
is primitive, an avant post of the Cotocton mts. yet omitted in

nearly all the maps. I herborized there and went afterwards to
the Point of rocks or lower water gap of R. Potomak, in the
Cotocton mts.

Crossing the river here into Virginia, I began my pedestrian
rambles; but had to contend against muddy roads and repeated
showers . . . I took Harper's ferry stage for 15 miles to be left in
the mts.; thus surveying them well, and botanizing in the mts.,
the banks of the Potowmak and Shenandoah rivers.

In the South Branch area today, a big-eared bat, first identified by
Rafinesque, may be found.

TWO

The jagged granitic hills, Precambrian, in what is now the Potomac
area, were wind-and rain-swept, relieved only by scattered, primi-
tive algal growths.

Cracks opened in the earth's crust, long fissures, and layer upon
layer of molten lava poured out,

       hardened,

             and metamorphosed into

greenstone . . .

Weighted and eroded, the land sank, and waters from the Atlantic
and Gulf seeped in to form an inland sea—the Paleozoic Sea—the
major surfacing land mass lying to the east.

The sea filled a long, narrow trough from the Canadian Shield
through the Virginia Piedmont and southward, the waters shifting,

ebbing and flowing, land-locked and ocean-connected, fresh and marine, but always shallow, with low, sandy or muddy banks, scattered islands, low capes and peninsulas, straits, lagoons, and inlets. Mud, sand, and gravel washed into the trough from the eastward land masses, at a rate equaling that of subsidence, and the sea remained evenly shallow. Great lenticular layers of sediments were formed—shale, sandstone, and conglomerate, with limy muds, and shell fragments of coral, clam, snail, and crab-like animals— brachiopods, trilobites, and gastropods—to form limestone.

In Devonian time, overgrown ferns and club mosses appeared. There were fish, similar to shark and sturgeon, and, on land, giant salamanders. Later, in Mississippian, the ferns, club mosses, and horsetails grew gigantically, decayed furiously, to form coal.

Toward the end of the Paleozoic era, subsidence of the trough ceased and the Appalachian Revolution began: unknown forces (resulting, perhaps, from continental drift) thrust the earth's crust upward, the Paleozoic Sea fled to the west, and there was great horizontal movement, exerting lateral pressure, southeast to northwest. Earthquakes were common, and the granites, lavas, and sea-floor sediments were wrinkled, folded, shoved, and fractured. Anticline arches broke, elongate blocks were overthrust northwestward, over underlying rocks. Sandstone cliffs stood on end:

The Mother Appalachians grew into being, upwarping, higher and more rugged than the present hills.

Attacked at once by weather and streams, the slopes eroded, spreading muds, sands, and limy silts eastward into down-warped basins, over the Piedmont, and into tidal estuaries . . . until the region was worn to a vast and gently rolling plain, a peneplain in which only truncated mountain roots remain.

The ocean level rose and fell, successively sedimenting Tidewater, the Piedmont-Tidewater border (the fall line) being a shifting shoreline.

Once again, accumulated internal forces came into action: the peneplain uplifted and the broad, sluggish streams, meandering at leisure over the flat terrain, became rejuvenated. Cutting into their beds, flowing faster and more steeply, carrying more sediment, the rivers stripped the softer shales and limestones, leaving the more durable ridges of modern Appalachia.

The east-flowing streams—having a steeper gradient and being closer to their base-level, the ocean—carved back into the head-water divides, pirating the west-flowing stream heads, flowing eastward through Valley and Ridge Province, and—sawing through hard rock and ridge—opening a way to the Atlantic.

At Harper's Ferry, the Potomac once flowed across a plain higher than the tops of the present mountains. As the land rose, the river cut its way down and through, leaving terraces in hard and soft rock alike.

Less powerful streams followed their valleys, seeking a natural outlet, producing on the corrugated landscape a trellis effect.

The Shenandoah, young and sporadic, began at Harper's Ferry and carved its way up the Valley, capturing established streams right and left, converting water gaps into wind gaps, beheading the Rappahannock, the Rapidan, the Rivanna.

The Shenandoah in the Seven Bends and the Potomac at Paw Paw Bends preserve their original peneplain meanders, now incised in the uplifted land.

––––––––––

Dinosaurs, pterosaurs, and other gigantic reptiles thrived during the Mesozoic era. Fossil leaves, lignitized tree trunks, occasional dinosaur bones are found in Potomac formations. The remains of a cypress swamp were uncovered in excavations in Washington.

Modern vegetation came into being during the last 15 to 20 million years.

—————————

Today the upper Potomac harbors relict plants from glacial vegetation. Ice never entered West Virginia, but the region serves as a refuge for northern plants: the paper birch is found here, and the red pine reaches its southernmost points of unassisted growth, on South Branch and North Fork Mountains.

On Spruce Mountain and along the Allegheny Front nesting sites are found for the golden-crowned kinglet, the winter wren, Swainson's thrush, magnolia warbler, and purple finch—species characteristic of the spruce forests of Canada. At lower elevations are the characteristically southern black vulture and loggerhead shrike. During June and July, on shaly grounds, the yellow blossoms of the prickly pear cactus appear, reminiscent of western deserts. In September, the rains of Atlantic hurricanes blow in from the east.

Endemic to the shale barrens are the bindweed, the whitehaired leatherflower, the shale ragwort, shale primrose, shale goldenrod . . . the knotweed . . .

The golden eagle used to nest at Potomac headwaters, was exterminated during the 1930s and '40s, as a varmint. He may occasionally be seen from North Fork Mountain or Hawk Mountain, in migration.

At Reddish Knob, the raven and the red-tailed hawk
   a great horned owl on Thorn Creek
   crossbills, siskins, and grosbeaks
   a grebe at Upper Tract
   a loon from the north, a chat from the south . . .

      the red-headed woodpecker . . .

—————————

In the Smoke Hole, on the South Branch, there is bear sign and shadblow . . .

mosses and lichens, white cedar, Virginia pine

columbine, polypody fern, lovegrass and bent grass, maidenhair and hairy lip fern, the purple cliffbrake

in the depths of the Hole, the crested coralroot, a southern orchid here reaching its northern limit.

Up from the Hole, on the Tuscarora sandstone along the crest of North Fork Mountain, and other sandstone ridges, the silvery whitlow-wort, growing here and nowhere else . . .

To be found in Shenandoah National Park are ninebark, bull thistle, oldfield cinquefoil . . .

fourleaf loosestrife, nodding onion, glorybird

On the ground: the black racer and the blue-tailed skink.

In the water, five cats: channel, yellow, bullhead, Potomac, madtom.

Also, large-mouth black bass, crappie and calico bass, rock bass in Rock Run . . .

On Sugarloaf Mountain there is table mountain pine, and acres of milkvetch on Massanutten

wineleaf cinquefoil on North Fork Mountain

nailworts and quill flameflower at Seneca Rocks . . . at Dolly Sods, red spruce . . .

In 1915, sunfish were abundant in ponds on the rocky headland just below Difficult Run. Other fish taken in Potomac waters were the sea lamprey, the fork-tailed and red-eyed cats, chub sucker and horned chub, black-nosed dace and goggle-eye.

Sunfish, cats, and black bass ran into Dead Run.

In 1876, the Potomac-Side Naturalists' Club compiled a list of 1,083 plant species, also 91 mosses and 28 Hepaticae, growing "in the District of Columbia and its immediate vicinity."

A wartime Washington birdwatcher reported, 1940s, that "a drake American merganser on the Basin was swimming in tight circles about the dead body of a female floating on its side so that only an upturned section of its underparts showed above-water. After two minutes in which the male was obviously invoking the powers of life, he climbed onto the dead body and copulated with it, lifting the limp head in his bill. The mystical act accomplished, the female returned to life and swam off happily with her rescuer."

Fresh and estuarine, fluctuant by reason of tide and rain, wind and season, the Wicomoco River rises in the coarse-stemmed marsh, the weak-stemmed marsh of Zekiah Swamp. Catbird, brown thrasher, and eastern phoebe may be found here, at the northern limit of winter range, and there is a great blue heron rookery.

In the swamp, in the past, a steady fresh-water flow nourished the wild rice, and on Cobb's Island, at the rivermouth, needlerush, saltmeadow grass, and saltmarsh cordgrass grow.

There are teal, shoveler, and sora on the river, and Wilson's snipe in Allen's Fresh. The gadwall winters on Cuckold Creek, and in late summer there are peep on the mudflats, perhaps a great black-backed gull.

On Swan Neck, at Issue, the loblolly pine has been lumbered . . .

THREE

On Christmas Eve 1852, the last spike was driven into the Baltimore
and Ohio Railroad Line, connecting Cumberland with Wheeling.
This marked the beginning of the end for the C & O Canal and for
the adjacent stream, the Potomac River:
The railroad, mills, little industries, mines, municipalities—the very
people themselves—turned their backsides to the river,

> . . . and shat into it.

Fairfax Stone, at Potomac headwaters, stands in a patch of woods
surrounded by—and within sight of—abandoned strip coal mines.
The stream trickles but a few yards before receiving the first
sulphuric acid and yellowy iron hydrate extracted by springs, seeps,
and runoff water from denuded coal strata and spoil heaps. Five to
ten million tons of acid enter the river annually, from abandoned
strips and one-man tunnel mines that pock the hillsides—a rate of
production expected to continue for at least a thousand years.
At George's Creek, solid wastes enter the river in a pickle brine of
acid water . . .

complex wastes from textile industries
suspended materials from food processing plants and liquors
pressed from wet grains at breweries
pickle liquors and piggery wastes
greasy wastes from tanneries
wastes—ligneous, resinous, and carbonaceous—from pulp and
paper plants
penolic, cresolic, ammoniacal, and tarry wastes from gas and
coke plants

greasy, soapy water from laundries, and various complex wastes from chemical and rubber industries

As late as 1946, 75 percent of such wastes were sluiced into the Potomac altogether innocent of treatment.

At a pulp and paper mill in Luke, a portion of the vast, complex wastage is dumped raw, to be added to the effluent of the treatment plant.

Towns and villages along the way dump in raw human sewage: brown lumps, toilet paper, unsanitary napkins, together with the loaded effluent of perfunctory primary plants.
In heavy storms at Cumberland, the combined storm and sanitary sewer systems overflow and it all goes raw to the river.

Opequon Creek is fouled with sewage, Conococheague and Antietam creeks import human manure from Pennsylvania, there are chicken feathers and zinc in the Shenandoah.

In Jefferson's day, the mouth of the Anacostia was one mile wide, and the u.s. Navy, entire, sailed up to Bladensburg.

Today, 2.5 million tons of silt and sediment erode into the Potomac annually, to coat the river bottom, foul municipal filtering operations, cover oyster beds, smother fingerling fish, and rasp the gills of survivors. Lazy farming practices and a shriveled, scrubby timber growth contribute to erosion, but the greatest cause is stripping the soil for construction—roadbuilding, home developments, industrial expansion. More than 25,000 tons per square mile of land thus developed may be washed away, topsoil never to be retrieved.

At public expense, the u.s. Army Corps of Engineers dredges the sludge from the shipping channel and collects construction debris from the water surface.

The Potomac River serves as the principal supply of drinking water for the District of Columbia. In recent drought years, nearly the entire stream flow—which included raw sewage from thirty-one upstream communities—has been sucked into metropolitan water intakes.

Sewage effluent from the District receives less than 100 percent treatment. Solid wastes pass directly into the river, join detritus flowing from upstream, and rock gently back and forth before Washington in the rising and falling tides (a piece of solid matter requires more than a hundred days to clear the river).

In heavy storms, the antiquated sanitary and storm sewers of the District and Alexandria overflow, the entire effluent charges directly into the estuary,

> and seagulls swarm at the storm sewers . . .

The effluents from sewage treament plants, liquid and less toxic, are a rich and oily broth of nitrates and phosphates, stimulating malodorous scums of algal blooms, starving the waters of oxygen . . . The river, in advanced eutrophication, is suddenly old.

On a warm summer day, when conditions are right, the upper estuary may be "one vast inspired pool of fertility—the whole surface of the river . . . covered with a thick bright emerald mat."

———————

New York Times News Service, March 24 1969:

> WASHINGTON—The Potomac River is just about as badly polluted as it was a decade ago, despite an extensive clean-up program, the Federal Water Pollution Control Administration has reported.
>
> In its lower reaches, where the river provides a scenic background for the nation's capital, it is so laden with bacteria as to make swimming or any other recreational contact "hazardous," the agency said.

Much of the raw sewage that used to gush into the river and its immediate tributaries at a rate of billions of gallons a year has been eliminated.

But inadequate sewage treatment facilities, increasing population, and a continuing problem of overflows from sewer lines during storms have left the river's water substantially unimproved.

Black bass in the Shenandoah are slaughtered by zinc . . .
     three million alewives killed in the Anacostia
     rock fish floating by the thousands in the lower estuary
     on the shoreline at Mount Vernon, windrows of dead and stinking carp and perch . . .

J. F. D. Smyth, 1784:

Every advantage, every elegance, every charm, that bountiful nature can bestow, is heaped with liberality and even profusion on the delightful banks of this most noble and superlatively grand river. All the desirable variety of land and water, woods and lawns, hills and dales, tremendous cliffs and lovely vallies, wild romantic precipices and sweet meandering streams adorned with rich and delightful meadows, in short all the elegance, beauty, and grandeur that can be conceived in perfpective, are here united, to feast the fight and foul of those who are capable of enjoying the luxurious and sumptuous banquet.

FOUR

There are seventeen military installations in the metropolitan Washington area, within ten miles of the estuary. Approximately 54 miles of shoreline, and 100,000 acres of land, are included.

FIVE

President Lyndon Johnson, at the White House Conference on Natural Beauty, May 1965:

> The river rich in history and memory which flows by our Nation's Capital should serve as a model of scenic and recreation values for the entire country. To meet this objective I am asking the Secretary of the Interior to review the Potomac River Basin development plan now under review by the Chief of Army Engineers, and to work with the affected States and local governments, the District of Columbia, and interested Federal agencies to prepare a program for my consideration.
>
> A program must be devised which will—
> (a) Clean up the river and keep it clean, so it can be used for boating, swimming, and fishing;
> (b) Protect its natural beauties by the acquisition of scenic easements, zoning, or other measures;
> (c) Provide adequate recreational facilities.

The plan of the Corps of Engineers involved construction of an 85-foot dam at Riverbend above Washington, impounding 36,000 acres of water surface, destroying canal and shoreline back almost to Harper's Ferry. It was planned to draw down the water level ten feet during dry weather, exposing that much raw mud bank, to provide the Washington area with sufficient volume of water to flush the District sludge downstream.

A later plan proposes construction of the Bloomington Reservoir on the North Branch, to impound the mine-acid waters for presumed recreation.

SIX

Construction of the John F. Kennedy Center for the Performing Arts stirred up the soil on the flood plain of the Potomac River.

Nearby, one evening in June, three of us picked lamb's quarters for dinner at the edge of a vacant lot, corner of 24th and G, N.W. One of the locals stopped by and helped us, told us that the lot belonged to a bank (specialists in green stuff) . . .

SEVEN

> The rise in the value of landed property, in this country, has been progressive, ever since my attention has been turned to the subject (now more than 40 years); but for the last three or four of that period, it has increased beyond all calculation . . . I do not hesitate to pronounce that, the Lands on the Waters of Potomack will, in a few years, be in greater demand, and in higher estimation than in any other part of the United States.
>   . . . George Washington, 1796.

The two million inhabitants of metropolitan Washington today are expected, by the year 2100, to increase to six million. By 2166, metropolitan Washington will extend to Harper's Ferry.

From "The Social Aspects of Population Dynamics," J. B. Calhoun:

> Wherever animals live they are constantly altering the environment about them. This occurs through such diverse

phenomena as release of excreta, alteration of surrounding temperature and humidity, construction of trails and burrows, and the development of habits, all of which may alter the behavior of members of their own or later generations.

As soon as animals begin to condition their environment through the elaboration of relatively permanent artifacts such as trails, nests, burrows, and the like, biological conditioning assumes a more definite cultural aspect. To be sure, such artifacts satisfy primary organic requirements: dens are a place of retreat from enemies or inclement weather; nests are places where the young are safe; trails lead to food or harborage, and food caches serve to make food more accessible. However, beyond such primary functions, dens, nests, trails, and the like further serve as a physical mold in which the social matrix takes its form.

From *The Hidden Dimension,* Edward T. Hall:

Western man has set himself apart from nature and, therefore, from the rest of the animal world. He could have continued to ignore the realities of his animal constitution if it had not been for the population explosion . . . This, together with the implosion into our cities of poverty-stricken people from rural areas, has created a condition which has all the earmarks of population buildup and subsequent crash in the animal world . . .

Many ethologists have been reluctant to suggest that their findings apply to man, even though crowded, overstressed animals are known to suffer from circulatory disorders, heart attacks, and lowered resistance to disease. One of the chief differences between man and animals is that man has domesticated himself by developing his extensions and then proceeding to screen his senses so that he could get more people into a smaller space. Screening helps, but the ultimate buildup can still be lethal . . .

If one looks at human beings in the way that the early slave traders did, conceiving of their space requirements simply in terms of the limits of the body, one pays very little attention to the effects of crowding. If, however, one sees man surrounded by

a series of invisible bubbles which have measurable dimensions,
. . . it is then possible to conceive that people can be cramped by
the spaces in which they have to live and work. They may even
find themselves forced into behavior, relationships, or emot-
ional outlets that are overly stressful . . . When stress increases,
sensitivity to crowding rises—people get more on edge—so that
more and more space is required as less and less is available.

Screening is what we get from rooms, apartments, and build-
ings in cities. Such screening works until several individuals are
crowded into one room; then a drastic change occurs. The walls
no longer shield and protect, but instead press inward on the
inhabitants.

By domesticating himself, man has greatly reduced the flight
distance of his aboriginal state, which is an absolute necessity
when population densities are high. The flight reaction . . .
is one of the most basic and successful ways of coping with
danger, but there must be sufficient space if it is to function.
Through a process of taming, most higher organisms, includ-
ing man, can be squeezed into a given area provided that they
feel safe and their aggressions are under control. However,
if men are made fearful of each other, fear resurrects the flight
reaction, creating an explosive need for space. Fear, plus crowd-
ing, then produces panic.

From the *Washington Post*, Saturday, April 6, 1968:

Six thousand armed troops were rushed into Washington's
streets last night and early this morning to combat widespread
burning and looting of the city.

A brigade of paratroopers of the 82nd Airborne Division
from Ft. Bragg, N.C., was to arrive at Andrews Air Force base
shortly after midnight.

At least three are dead from the rioting.

The Mayor imposed a night-long curfew and banned the
sale of liquor and firearms . . . Brazen looting went on just two
blocks from the White House.

The Pentagon spokesman said at 10 P.M. that at least 950 rioters had been arrested here . . .

Firemen said there had been at least 170 fires Friday . . . A thick pall of smoke hung over the inner city . . .

The troops, including both regular army and National Guardsmen, moved into the city with their rifles unloaded but with ammunition in their belts, their bayonets sheathed.

The troops first cleared H Street N.E., then 14th Street N.W., two of the worst trouble spots, then moved to side streets. As they swept along—chanting "March, March, March"—they would drop off a small contingent to keep control of each intersection. By 11 P.M., they were stationed in many sections of the city.

The troops were deployed by means of helicopter . . .

The disturbance caused cancellation or postponement of a number of events. A spokesman for the Cherry Blossom Festival announced that all remaining activities of the Festival, including the annual ball scheduled for last night, have been canceled.

The Washington Senators announced that Monday's opening-day baseball game with the Minnesota Twins had been rescheduled . . .

Despite the greater frequency of vandalism and looting, fire apparently caused the most serious damage.

. . . All evening, police and reporters on the street reported fires burning with no fire fighting equipment in sight.

. . . Black power advocates at Howard University hauled down an American flag and raised in its place a flag of their own design . . .

When they could, policemen took stolen goods from looters or barked at them through bullhorns . . . There was an eerie holiday mood . . .

Washington paid an extra price in its day of rioting and looting yesterday because of a massive traffic jam that tied the city in knots throughout the afternoon.

Police cars, fire trucks and ambulances were among vehicles brought to a virtual standstill as an early exodus of downtown employees clogged all major streets with thousands of autos and buses.

Adding to the problem was the presence of thousands of tourists here for the Cherry Blossom Festival. Their slow-moving cars circulated around the Mall, the Lincoln Memorial and the Tidal Basin area, blocking commuter routes to the suburbs.

In their haste, people drove too fast, slipping traffic lights and using their horns. In the street, pedestrians elbowed each other aside in the dash to quit the city.

"Oh God, I'm scared," said a white girl in an elevator in a downtown office building.

A Negro riding at the rear reached over and touched her arm. "Well, I am too," he said.

EIGHT

The District, Great Falls and Ball's Bluff, Plummer's Island: a zone of floral interdigitation, the species overrunning and intermingling, down and up country, Ridge and Tidewater.

Summersweet clethera, a coastal plant, ascending the Maryland shore, overlapping Appalachian varieties, downstream on the Virginia side.

Potomac and tributary headwaters, scrambling into the Allegheny Front, pirating western springs, became a natural floral highway, importing in flood the seeds of pioneer plants of open or prairie habitat, to become established on expanses of metamorphic granite, schist, and gneiss, and in neutral soils on the benches and flood plains, in the interdigital area.

Scrub pine, above the District, is new since Washington's time, moving in where the land has been clear cut, farmed and abandoned, and surviving one generation only, to be replaced by hardwoods.

Sugar maples survive at the mouth of Difficult Run, with a stronger stand at Riverbend.

At Ball's Bluff, the cliffs have never been cut and farmed, and the display is exceptional: dogtooth violet and shooting star . . .

At the Falls, spangle grass and leather-flower, redbud and shadblow . . .

Notes & Bibliography

IMPRIMIS

The interpretations of Indian place names are from the following:

Davis, Julia. *The Shenandoah*. New York, 1945.

Harrison, Fairfax. *Landmarks of Old Prince William*. Richmond, 1924.

Johnston, C.H.L., ed. *The South Branch of the Potomac*. 1931.

Tooker, W.W. "The Algonquin Terms Patawomeke and Massawomeke." *American Anthropologist*, April 1894.

Facts about the size of the Potomac River basin are from the booklet:

University of Maryland, Bureau of Business and Economic Research. *Potomac River Basin*. College Park, 1957.

Place names found on and near the river are taken largely from a study of u.s. Geological Survey maps.

Berkeley Springs, as an Indian gathering place, is described in:

Writers Project, Work Projects Administration. *West Virginia, A Guide to the Mountain State*. New York, 1941 .

Description of the Indian fishing villages near Little Falls is from:

Holmes, W.H. Stone *Implements of the Potomac–Chesapeake Tidewater Province*. Washington, 1897.

Indian meanings of place names on the estuary may be found in:

Beitzell, Edwin W. *Life on the Potomac River*. Washington, 1968.

DISCOVERY AND INDIANS

Material dealing with early Spanish discovery of Chesapeake Bay and the Potomac is taken from:

Lewis, C.M., and Loomie, A.J. *The Spanish Jesuit Mission in Virginia, 1570-1572*. Chapel Hill, 1953.

Regarding identification of the river, which I take to be the Potomac, the authors offer the following in their notes:

It is difficult to say whether the Rappahannock or the Potomac is meant. The latitude is right for the latter, but Gonzales' latitudes are consistently too high. The depth and description of the southern bank applies to both rivers. The valley could be either Urbanna Creek or Yeocomico River. The land on the north bank of the Rappahannock rises to 80 feet, that on the Potomac to 100 feet. . . . Perhaps the strongest argument for the Potomac is the fact that he speaks of the good condition of the land from the 38th degree north, a natural division to make of the western coast line if the Potomac is taken as the starting point.

Discussion of Potomac Indians is derived from the following sources:

Ferguson, A.L.L., and Ferguson, H.G. *The Piscataway Indians of Southern Maryland.* Accokeek, Maryland, 1960.

Graham, William J. *The Indians of Port Tobacco River. Washington,* 1935.

Holmes, W.H. *Stone Implements of the Potomac–Chesapeake Tidewater Province.* Washington, 1897.

Marye, William S. "Piscataway." *Maryland Historical Magazine,* September 1935.

Mason, O.T., ed. *Aborigines of the District of Columbia and Lower Potomac.* Washington, 1889.

Scharf, J.T. *History of Maryland.* Hatboro, Pennsylvania, 1967.

Stephenson, Robert L. *Prehistoric People of Accokeek Creek.* Accokeek, Maryland, 1959.

Writers Project, Work Projects Administration. *Maryland, A Guide to the Old Line State.* New York, 1940.

Accounts of the voyages of John Smith and of Lord Delaware are from the following:

Smith, Bradford. *Captain John Smith.* Philadelphia, 1953.

Tyler, L.G., ed. *Narratives of Early Virginia, 1606-1625.* New York, 1907.

In exploring Chesapeake Bay, Smith apparently sailed northward, along the eastern shore, to a point opposite the Patapsco River and Baltimore harbor, and then crossed to the western shore and coasted southward, until he entered the Potomac.

Material dealing with early Maryland settlement is from:

Hall, C.C., ed. *Narratives of Early Maryland, 1633–1684.* New York, 1910.

(geography)

Facts on the comparative size of the river are taken from:

Coordinating Committee on the Potomac River Valley. *Potomac Prospect.* Washington, 1961.

EARLY SETTLEMENT

The first part of this chapter is derived from the following sources:

Alsop, George. *A character of the province of Maryland.* Cleveland, 1902.

Force, Peter. *Tracts.* Washington, 1836-46.

Hamor, Ralph. *A True Discourse of the Present Estate of Virginia.* 1615.

Harrison, Fairfax. *Landmarks of Old Prince William.* Richmond, 1924.

McAtee, W.L. *A Sketch of the Natural History of the District of Columbia.* Washington, 1918.

Tyler, L.G., ed. *Narratives of Early Virginia, 1606-1625.* New York, 1907.

The quotations from Henry Fleet's journal are taken from:

Neill, Edward D. *Founders of Maryland.* Albany, 1876.

Instructions for Maryland settlers are found in:

Hall, C.C., ed. *Narratives of Early Maryland, 1633-1684.* New York, 1910.

The final portions of the chapter are derived from the following:

Alsop, George. *A character of the province of Maryland.* Cleveland, 1902.

Durand of Dauphiné. *A Huguenot Exile in Virginia.* New York, 1934.

Harrison, Fairfax. *Landmarks of Old Prince William.* Richmond, 1924.

Hart, A.B., ed. *American History Told by Contemporaries.* New York, 1931 .

Tyler, L.G., ed. *Narratives of Early Virginia, 1606-1625.* New York, 1907.

U.S. Department of the Interior. *The Nation's River.* Washington, 1968.

UPRIVER EXPLORATION

The first two parts of the chapter, on the mountains, are from the following:

Alvord, C., and Bidgood, L. *The First Explorations of the Trans-Allegheny Region by the Virginians, 1650-1674.* Cleveland, 1912.

Durand of Dauphiné. *A Huguenot Exile in Virginia.* New York, 1934.

Force, Peter. *Tracts.* Washington, L836-46.

Harrison, Fairfax. *Landmarks of Old Prince William.* Richmond, 1924.

Maury, Ann, ed. *Memoirs of a Huguenot Family.* Baltimore, 1967.

Tyler, L.G., ed. *Narratives of Early Virginia, 1606-1625.* New York, 1907.

Following are sources for the section dealing with Indians:

Ambler, C.H. *West Virginia, The Mountain State.* New York, 1940.

Bailey, Kenneth P. *Thomas Cresap, Maryland Frontiersman.* Boston, 1944.

Darlington, W.M., ed. *Christopher Gist's Journals.* Pittsburgh, 1893.

Davis Julia. *The Shenandoah.* New York, 1945.

Fowke, Gerard. *Archeologic Investigations in James and Potomac Valleys.* Washington, 1894.

Gilbert, Bill "Exaltation at the Smokehole." *Sports Illustrated,* April 27, 1964.

Harrison, Fairfax. *Landmarks of Old Prince William.* Richmond, 1924.

Johnston, C.H.L., ed. *The South Branch of the Potomac.* 1931.

Marye, W.S. "Patowmeck Above ye Inhabitants." *Maryland Historical Magazine,* March and June, 1935.

Smith, J. Lawrence. *The Potomac Naturalist.* Parsons, West Virginia, 1968.

Material on the two surveys of Potomac headwaters is from the following:

Basset, J.S., ed. *The Writings of Colonel William Byrd.* New York, 1901.

Foster, James W. "Maps of the First Survey of the Potomac River, 1736–1737." *William and Mary Quarterly* 18, nos. 2 and 4.

Kennedy, Philip P. *The Blackwater Chronicle.* New York, 1853.

Lewis, Thomas. *The Fairfax Line; Thomas Lewis's Journal of 1746.* New Market, Virginia, 1925.

Lewis apparently started from Staunton, Virginia; crossed Massanutten Mountain, the Shenandoah Valley, and the South Branch near Petersburg, West Virginia; thence to the North Branch headwaters.

Following are sources for the remainder of this chapter:

Bacon-Foster, Cora. *Early Chapters in the Development of the Potomac Route to the West.* Washington, 1912.

Bailey, Kenneth P. *Thomas Cresap, Maryland Frontiersman.* Boston, 1944.

Browning, Meshach. *Forty-four Years the Life of a Hunter.* Philadelphia, 1859.

Darlington, W.M., ed. *Christopher Gist's Journals.* Pittsburgh, 1893.

Fitzpatrick, John C., ed. *The Diaries of George Washington.* Boston and New York, 1925.

Harrison, Fairfax. *Landmarks of Old Prince William.* Richmond, 1924.

Johnston, C.H.L., ed. *The South Branch of the Potomac.* 1931.

Kemper, C.E. "Documents Relating to Early Projected Swiss Colonies." *Virginia Magazine of History and Biography* 29, no. 1, 1921.

Kercheval, Samuel. *A History of the Valley of Virginia.* Woodstock, Virginia, 1850.

Writers Project, Work Projects Administration. *West Virginia, A Guide to the Mountain State.* New York, 1941.

(estuary)

Facts on the size of the estuary are found in:

Potomac Planning Task Force, u.s. Department of the Interior. *The Potomac.* Washington, 1967.

TIDEWATER COLONIAL

The following sources were used in this chapter:

Beitzell, Edwin W. *Life on the Potomac River.* Washington, 1968.

Beverley, Robert. *The History and Present State of Virginia.* Chapel Hill, 1947.

Burnaby, Andrew. *Travels Through North America.* New York, 1904.

Byrd, William. *William Byrd's Natural History of Virginia.* Richmond, 1940.

Durand of Dauphiné. *A Huguenot Exile in Virginia.* New York, 1934.

Fitzpatrick, J.C., ed. *The Diaries of George Washington.* Boston and New York, 1925.

—*The Writings of George Washington.* Washington, 1931-44.

Freeman, Douglas Southall. *George Washington.* New York, 1948.

Hening, W.W. *Virginia Laws, Statutes, Etc.* New York, 1819-23.

Jefferson, Thomas. *Notes on the State of Virginia.* New York, 1964.

Lear, Tobias. *Observations of the River Potomack.* Baltimore, 1940.

Mereness, N.D., ed. *Travels in the American Colonies.* New York, 1916.

Morrison, A.J., ed. *Travels in Virginia in Revolutionary Times.* Lynchburg, 1922.

Scharf, J.T. *History of Maryland.* Hatboro, Pennsylvania, 1967.

Schoepf, Johann David. *Travels in the Confederation.* Philadelphia, 1911.

Slaughter, Philip. *The History of Truro Parish in Virginia.* Philadelphia, 1908.

Smyth, J.F.D. *Tour in the United States.* London, 1784.

Watkins, C. Malcolm. "The Cultural History of Marlborough, Virginia." *Bulletin* no. 253. Smithsonian Institution, Washington, 1968.

Williams, John R., ed. *Philip Vickers Fithian, Journal and Letters.* Princeton, 1900.

TURNING POINT: 1776

The Revolutionary War on the Potomac was researched from:

Beitzell, Edwin W. *Life on the Potomac River.* Washington, 1968.

Scharf, J. T. *History of Maryland.* Hatboro, Pennsylvania, 1967.

UPRIVER SETTLEMENT

The first two sections of this chapter are taken from the following sources:

Burnaby, Andrew. *Travels Through North America.* New York, 1904.

Fitzpatrick, J.C., ed. *The Diaries of George Washington.* Boston and New York, 1925.

—*The Writings of George Washington.* Washington, 1931-44.

Harrison, Fairfax. *Landmarks of Old Prince William.* Richmond, 1924.

McAtee, W.L. *A Sketch of the Natural History of the District of Columbia.* Washington, 1918.

Smyth, J.F.D. *Tour in the United States.* London, 1784.

The journal of the Moravian brothers is found in:

Mereness, N.D., ed. *Travels in the American Colonies.* New York, 1916.

Meshach Browning's experiences are from:

Browning, Meshach. *Forty-four Years the Life of a Hunter.* Philadelphia, 1859.

The following sources provided material for the balance of the chapter:

Amelung, John F. *Remarks on Manufactures, Principally on the New Established Glass-House.* Frederick-Town, 1787.

Binns, John A. *A Treatise on Practical Farming.* Frederick-Town, 1803.

Cunz, Dieter. *The Maryland Germans.* Princeton, 1948.

Harrison, Fairfax. *Landmarks of Old Prince William.* Richmond, 1924.

Jefferson, Thomas. *Notes on the State of Virginia.* New York, 1964.

Kercheval, Samuel. *A History of the Valley of Virginia.* Woodstock, Virginia, 1850.

Morrison, A.J., ed. *Travels in Virginia in Revolutionary Times.* Lynchburg, 1922.

Quynn, Dorothy. "Johann Friedrich Amelung at New Bremen." *Maryland Historical Magazine* 43: 155-179.

(geology)

The material on Potomac geology is taken from these sources:

Butts, Charles. "Geology of the Appalachian Valley in Virginia. *Bulletin* no. 52. Virginia Geological Survey, Charlottesville, 1936.

Butts, C.; Stose, G.W.; and Jonas, A.I. *Southern Appalachian Region.* U.S. Geological Survey, Washington, 1933.

National Park Service, U.S. Department of the Interior. Brochure, "Shenandoah National Park."

Potomac Planning Task Force, U.S. Department of the Interior. *The Potomac.* Washington, 1967.

Scharf, J.T. *History of Maryland.* Hatboro, Pennsylvania, 1967.

Stose, G.W.; Jonas, A.I.; and Ashley, G.H. *Southern Pennsylvania and Maryland.* Washington, 1932.

U.S. Department of Agriculture. *Potomac River Drainage Basin.* Washington, 1943.

Vokes, H.E. "Geography and Geology of Maryland." *Bulletin* no. 19. Department of Geology, Mines and Water Resources, Baltimore, 1957.

Writers Project, Work Projects Administration. *Virginia, A Guide to the Old Dominion.* New York, 1941.

FEDERAL CITY

Material dealing with establishment of the District of Columbia, and with Pierre L'Enfant, is taken from the following:

Bryan, Wilhelmus B. *A History of the National Capital.* New York, 1914.

Caemmerer, H.P. *A Manual on the Origin and Development of Washington.* Washington, 1939.

Fitzpatrick, J.C., ed. *The Diaries of George Washington.* Boston and New York, 1925.

—*The Writings of George Washington.* Washington, 1931–44.

Kite, Elizabeth S. *L'Enfant and Washington, 1791-1792.* Baltimore, 1929.

L'Enfant's Reports to President Washington . . . Columbia Historical Society Records, Vol. 2.

Nicolay, Helen. *Our Capital on the Potomac.* New York and London, 1924.

Padover, S.K., ed. *Thomas Jefferson and the National Capital.* Washington, 1946.

Material dealing with the War of 1812 and the burning of the capital is taken from:

Scharf, J.T. *History of Maryland.* Hatboro, Pennsylvania, 1967.

These two sources provide the conclusion of the chapter:

Audubon Society of the District of Columbia. *Washington: City in the Woods.* Washington, 1954.

Bryan, George S. *The Great American Myth.* New York, 1940.

(interdigitation)

This paragraph is derived from:

McAtee, W.L. *A Sketch of the Natural History of the District of Columbia.* Washington, 1910.

Writers Project, Work Projects Administration. *Maryland, A Guide to the Old Line State.* New York, 1940.

TRANSPORTATION

Material on the Ohio Company and Nemacolin's Path is from the following:

Bacon-Foster, Cora. *Early Chapters in the Development of the Potomac Route to the West.* Washington, 1912.

Bailey, Kenneth. *The Ohio Company of Virginia and the Westward Movement, 1748-1792.* Glendale, California, 1939.

Bailey, Kenneth. *Thomas Cresap, Maryland Frontiersman.* Boston, 1944.

Hanna, Charles. *The Wilderness Trail.* New York, 1911.

The section dealing with Braddock is from:

Beitzell, Edwin W. *Life on the Potomac River.* Washington, 1968.

Hulbert, A.B. *Braddock's Road.* Cleveland, 1903.

Two sources provided material for the National Road:

Hulbert, A.B. *The Cumberland Road.* Cleveland, 1904.

Searight, Thomas. *The Old Pike.* Uniontown, Pennsylvania, 1894.

Material on the Potomac Company is derived from the following:

Bacon-Foster, Cora. *Early Chapters in the Development of the Potomac Route to the West.* Washington, 1912.

Davis, Julia. *The Shenandoah.* New York, 1945.

Fitzpatrick, J.C., ed. *The Diaries of George Washington.* Boston and New York, 1925.

—*The Writings of George Washington.* Washington, 1931–44.

Hulbert, A.B. *The Great American Canals.* Cleveland, 1904.

McCardell, Lee. "Canal Boat Days." *Baltimore Evening Sun,* August 9-13, 1937.

National Park Service and Fairfax County Park Authority. Brochure, "Great Falls of the Potomac."

Sanderlin, Walter S. *The Great National Project: A History of the Chesapeake & Ohio Canal.* Baltimore, 1946.

Description of the Chesapeake and Ohio Canal is drawn from the following sources:

Bacon-Foster, Cora. *Early Chapters in the Development of the Potomac Route to the West.* Washington, 1912.

Hulbert, A.B. *The Great American Canals.* Cleveland, 1904.

McCardell, Lee. "Canal Boat Days." *Baltimore Evening Sun,* August 9–13, 1937.

National Park Service, u.s. Department of the Interior. *Proposed Potomac National River.* Washington, 1968.

"Regulations for Navigating the Chesapeake and Ohio Canal." u.s. Department of the Interior Archives, no date.

Sanderlin, Walter S. *The Great National Project: A History of the Chesapeake & Ohio Canal.* Baltimore, 1946.

(climate and flow—land use)

Material in this section is from the following:

Federal Interdepartmental Task Force on the Potomac, u.s. Department of the Interior. *Land, People and Recreation in the Potomac River Basin.* Washington, 1968.

u.s. Army Corps of Engineers. *Potomac River and Tributaries, Maryland, Virginia, West Virginia.* Washington, 1946.

u.s. Department of Agriculture. *The Potomac River Drainage Basin.* Washington, 1943.

CIVIL WAR

JOHN BROWN

The John Brown story is derived from:

Brown, John. *Words of John Brown.* Boston, 1897.

Bryan, George S. *The Great American Myth.* New York, 1940.

Forbes, John *Murray. Letters and Recollections.* Boston and New York, 1899.
Frank Leslie's Illustrated Newspaper, December 10, 1859.
Hart, A.B., ed. *American History Told by Contemporaries.* New York, 1931.
Ruchames, Louis, ed. *A John Brown Reader.* New York, 1959.
Villard, Oswald Garrison. *John Brown, 1800–1859.* Boston and New York, 1910.
Warren, Robert Penn. *John Brown.* New York, 1929.

BULL RUN
   Following are the sources for First Bull Run, or First Manassas:
Blackford, W.W. *War Years with Jeb Stuart.* New York, 1945.
Casler, John O. *Four Years in the Stonewall Brigade.* Girard, Kansas, 1906.
Eisenschiml, Otto, and Newman, Ralph, eds. *The American Iliad.* Indianapolis, 1947.
Hanson, J.M. *Bull Run Remembers.* Washington, 1953.
Johnson, R.U., and Buel, C.C., eds. *Battles and Leaders of the Civil War.* New York, 1887-88.
Johnston, David E. *The Story of a Confederate Boy in the Civil War.* Portland, Oregon, 1914.
LaBree, Ben, ed. *The Confederate Soldier in the Civil War.* Louisville, 1895.
War of the Rebellion: *A Compilation of the Official Records of the Union and Confederate Armies.* Washington, 1902.

A SMALL ENGAGEMENT
   The affair at Hanging Rocks is described in:
Johnston, C.H.L., ed. *The South Branch of the Potomac.* 1931.

BALL'S BLUFF
   Following are the sources for the battle of Ball's Bluff—or Leesburg, as the Confederates called it:
Johnson, R.U., and Buel, C.C., eds. *Battles and Leaders of the Civil War.* New York, 1887-88.
Pierson, Charles L. Ball's Bluff, *An Episode and Its Consequences to Some of Us.* Salem, Massachusetts, 1913.
Quint, Alonzo H. *The Potomac and the Rapidan.* Boston, 1864.
Shotwell, R.A. *Papers of . . .* Raleigh, 1929.
War of the Rebellion: *A Compilation of the Official Records of the Union and Confederate Armies.* Washington, 1902.

SPRINGTIME
Quint, Alonzo H. *The Potomac and the Rapidan.* Boston, 1864.

ANTIETAM

Accounts of Antietam—or Sharpsburg—come from the following:

Alexander, E.P. Military *Memoirs of a Confederate*. New York, 1907.

Blackford, W.W. *War Years with Jeb Stuart*. New York, 1945.

Douglas, Henry Kyd. *I Rode with Stonewall*. Chapel Hill, 1940.

Durkin, Joseph T., ed. *John Dooley, Confederate Soldier: His War Journal*. Washington, 1945.

Eisenschiml, Otto, and Newman, Ralph, eds. *The American Iliad*. Indianapolis, 1947.

Freeman, Douglas Southall. *Lee's Lieutenants*. New York, 1942-44.

Hart, A.B., ed. *American History Told by Contemporaries*. New York, 1931.

Heysinger, Isaac W. *Antietam and the Maryland and Virginia Campaigns of 1862*. New York, 1912.

Hood, J.B. *Advance and Retreat*. New Orleans, 1880.

Johnson, R.U., and Buel, C.C., eds. *Battles and Leaders of the Civil War*. New York, 1887-88.

Johnston, David E. *The Story of a Confederate Boy in the Civil War*. Portland, Oregon, 1914.

LaBree, Ben, ed. *The Confederate Soldier in the Civil War*. Louisville, 1895.

Napier, Bartlett. *A Soldier's Story of the War*. New Orleans, 1874.

Noyes, George F. *The Bivouac and the Battlefield*. New York, 1863.

Owen, W.M. *In Camp and Battle with the Washington Artillery of New Orleans*. New Orleans, 1964.

Page, C.D. *History of the 14th Regiment, Connecticut Volunteer Infantry*. Meriden, Connecticut, 1906.

Quint, Alonzo H. *The Potomac and the Rapidan*. Boston, 1864.

Shotwell, R.A. *Papers of . . .* Raleigh, 1929.

Writers Project, Work Projects Administration. *Maryland, A Guide to the Old Line State*. New York, 1940.

GETTYSBURG

The Battle of Gettysburg is derived from the following:

Aldrich, T.M. *History of Battery A, First Regiment, Rhode Island Light Artillery*. Providence, 1904.

Alexander, E.P. *Military Memoirs of a Confederate*. New York, 1907.

Blackford, W.W. *War Years with Jeb Stuart*. New York, 1945.

Casler, John O. *Four Years in the Stonewall Brigade*. Girard, Kansas, 1906.

Durkin, Joseph T., ed. John Dooley, *Confederate Soldier: His War Journal*. Washington, 1945.

Eisenschiml, Otto, and Newman, Ralph, eds. *The American Iliad*. Indianapolis, 1947.

Fremantle, Arthur L. *The Fremantle Diary.* Boston, 1954.

Harrison, Walter. *Pickett's Men.* New York, 1870.

Hart, A.B., ed. *American History Told by Contemporaries.* New York, 1931.

Haskell, Frank, A. *The Battle of Gettysburg.* Boston, 1958.

Johnson, R.U., and Buel, C.C., eds. *Battles and Leaders of the Civil War.* New York, 1887-88.

Johnston, David E. *The Story of a Confederate Boy in the Civil War.* Portland, Oregon, 1914.

Kimble, June. "Tennesseeans at Gettysburg: The Retreat." *Confederate Veteran,* October, 1910.

King, John R. *My Experience in the Confederate Army and in Northern Prisons.* Clarksburg, West Virginia, 1910.

LaBree, Ben, ed. *The Confederate Soldier in the Civil War.* Louisville, 1895

McClure, A.K., ed. *The Annals of the War.* Philadelphia, 1879.

Miers, E.S., and Brown, R.A., eds. *Gettysburg.* New Brunswick, 1948.

Napier, Bartlett. *A Soldier's Story of the War.* New Orleans, 1874.

Page, C.D. *History of the 14th Regiment, Connecticut Volunteer Infantry.* Meriden, Connecticut, 1906.

Pickett, LaSalle Corbell. *Pickett and His Men.* Atlanta, 1899.

Rhodes, John H. *The Gettysburg Gun.* No. 19. Rhode Island Soldiers & Sailors Historical Society.

Shotwell, R.A. *Papers of . . .* Raleigh, 1929.

Stewart, George. *Pickett's Charge.* Boston, 1959.

PRISONERS OF WAR

The account of Point Lookout is from the following:

Keiley, Anthony M. *In Vinculis.* New York, 1866.

King, John R. *My Experience in the Confederate Army and in Northern Prisons.* Clarksburg, West Virginia, 1917.

Pierson, W.W., ed. *Diary of Bartlett Yancey Malone.* Chapel Hill, 1919.

Shotwell, R.A. *Papers of . . .* Raleigh, 1929.

War of the Rebellion: *A Compilation of the Official Records of the Union and Confederate Armies.* Washington, 1902.

APRIL 1865

The Lincoln assassination story is derived from the following:

Bryan, George S. *The Great American Myth.* New York, 1940.

DeWitt, David M. *The Assassination of Abraham Lincoln.* New York, 1909.

Jones, Thomas A. *J. Wilkes Booth.* Chicago, 1893.

Stern, Philip Van Doren. *The Man Who Killed Lincoln.* New York. 1939.

NINETEEN SIXTIES

ONE

The items dealing with Rafinesque (or Schmaltz) are taken from:

Call, R.E. *Life and Writings of Rafinesque.* Louisville, 1895.

Interstate Commission on the Potomac River Basin. *Potomac Playlands.* Washington, 1957.

Rafinesque, C.S. *A Life of Travels and Researches* . . . Philadelphia, 1836.

TWO

The geology and geography of the area were researched from among the following:

Bevan, Arthur. "Origin of Our Scenery." *Bulletin* no. 46-A. Virginia Geological Survey.

Butts, Charles. "Geology of the Appalachian Valley in Virginia. *Bulletin* no. 52. Virginia Geological Survey.

Butts, C.; Stose, G.W.; and Jonas, A.I. *Southern Appalachian Region* U.S. Geological Survey, Washington, 1933.

Davis, Julia. *The Shenandoah.* New York, 1945.

McAtee, W.L. *A Sketch of the Natural History of the District of Columbia.* Washington, 1918.

National Park Service, U.S. Department of the Interior, brochure, "Shenandoah National Park."

Smith, J. Lawrence. *The Potomac Naturalist.* Parsons, West Virginia, 1968.

Vokes, H.E. Geography and Geology of Maryland. *Bulletin* no. 19. Department of Geology, Mines and Water Resources, Baltimore, 1957.

Writers Project, Work Projects Administration. Virginia, *A Guide to the Old Dominion.* New York, 1941.

The material dealing with Potomac flora and fauna is derived from the following:

Gilbert, Bill "Exaltations at the Smokehole." *Sports Illustrated,* April 27, 1964.

Halle, Louis J. *Spring in Washington.* New York, 1963.

McAtee and Weed. "First List of the Fishes in the Vicinity of Plummer's Island, Maryland." *Proceedings of the Biological Society of Washington,* Vol. 28, 1915.

Potomac-side Naturalists' Club. *Flora Columbiana.* Washington, 1876.

Sharpe, G., and Sharpe, W. *101 Wildflowers of Shenandoah National Park.* Seattle, 1958.

Shosteck, Robert. *The Potomac Trail Book.* Washington, 1935.

Smith, J. Lawrence. *The Potomac Naturalist.* Parsons, West Virginia, 1968.

Taylor, John W. "The Wicomico River." *Atlantic Naturalist* 9, no. 3, January-February, 1954.

THREE

Following are sources on Potomac pollution:

Beitzell, Edwin W. *Life on the Potomac River.* Washington, 1968.

Bradley, M. *An Ecological Survey of the Potomac and Anacostia Rivers.* Washington, 1959.

Bureau of Business and Economic Research, University of Maryland. *Potomac River Basin.* College Park, 1957.

Coordinating Committee on the Potomac River Valley. *Potomac Prospect.* Washington, 1961.

Durum, W.H., and Langbein, W.B. *Water Quality of the Potomac River Estuary at Washington, D.C.* Circular no. 529-A. U.S. Geological Survey, Washington, 1966.

Environmental Pollution Panel, President's Science Advisory Committee. *Restoring the Quality of Our Environment.* Washington, 1965.

Federal Water Pollution Control Administration, U.S. Department of the Interior. *Wastewater Inventory, Upper Potomac River Basin.* Washington, 1969.

Interstate Commission on the Potomac River Basin. *Report on Industrial Wastes in the Potomac River Basin.* Washington, 1950.

—*Soils Pollution in the Potomac River Basin.* Washington, 1949.

Lear, Tobias. *Observations on the River Potomack.* Baltimore, 1940.

New York Times News Service.

Potomac Planning Task Force, U.S. Department of the Interior. *The Potomac.* Washington, 1967.

Smyth, J.F.D. *Tour in the United States.* London, 1784.

U.S. Department of the Interior. *Potomac Interim Report to the President.* Washington, 1966.

U.S. Department of the Interior. *The Nation's River.* Washington, 1968.

FOUR

Facts on military land use are taken from:

Project Potomac, U.S. Department of the Interior. *Potomac Valley.* Washington, 1966.

FIVE

President Johnson's message, and the plans of the Corps of Engineers, are taken from:

Federal Water Pollution Control Administration, U.S. Department of the

Interior. *Mine Drainage in the North Branch Potomac River Basin.* Washington, 1969.

Kindleberger, B. "Should the Potomac Be Dammed?" *American Forests,* August, 1957.

U.S. Government Printing Office. "Beauty for America." *Proceeding of the White House Conference on Natural Beauty.* Washington.

SEVEN

Sources for this section are the following:

Calhoun, J.B. "The Social Aspects of Population Dynamics." *Journal of Mammalogy* 33 (1952).

Fitzpatrick, J.C., ed. *The Writings of George Washington.* Washington 1931—44.

Hall, Edward T. *The Hidden Dimension.* Garden City, 1966.

U.S. Department of the Interior. *Potomac Interim Report to the President.* Washington, 1966.

Washington Post, April 6, 1968.

EIGHT

Following are sources for this final section:

Durham, C.J.S. *Washington's Potowmack Canal Project at Great Falls.* The Nature Conservancy, Washington, 1957.

Fairfax County Park Authority and National Park Service. Brochure "Great Falls of the Potomac."

Fosberg, Raymond. Private conversation.

Interstate Commission on the Potomac River Basin. *Potomac Playlands.* Washington, 1957.

McAtee, W.L. *A Sketch of the Natural History of the District of Columbia.* Washington, 1918.